life of Jenna Andersen. We met Jenna in *If The Stars Align*, and learn now that the former star cheerleader's seemingly picture perfect life is not what it appears. Theodore beautifully writes a story about friendship, having faith, the capacity for growth and change and of course, true love. This book is a delightful follow-up to *If the Stars Align*. I can't wait to see where this series goes next!

SARAH IMBERMAN, GOODREADS REVIEWER

relationships. In this book, Theodore effortlessly weaves together relationship trauma, mental health, the power of friendships, and complicated family relations. Jenna and Charlie are loveable characters with powerful and heartwarming stories that will leave you rooting for them to find their happy ending. This book will not disappoint romance fans!

EMILY GIGER, GOODREADS REVIEWER

Nathalie Theodore's latest novel, *If My Wishes Came True*, is a highly anticipated follow-up to her debut, *If The Stars Align*. *If My Wishes Came True* delivers everything I could hope for and more. Once I picked it up, I could not put it down! This is THE ultimate easy-to-read romance novel that I could read over and over again. In this novel, the focus shifts to Jenna, whose quiet charm made a lasting impression in the first book. Her journey is both relatable and aspirational, as she stumbles through her past, uncertainty, hope, and the exhilarating, and (sometimes) messy process of falling in love. I was delighted to reunite with familiar faces from the first novel, and see Jenna step in the spotlight to find the happiness she so deserves. Nathalie Theodore has done it again and written another hit!

PARISSA ANDIDEH, GOODREADS REVIEWER

If My Wishes Came True is a captivating beach read that reinforces the notion that true love exists. Filled with many twists and turns, I couldn't put this book down! Nathalie Theodore's second book from her Dramatic Hearts Club dives into the

all comes out better than imagined once the stars finally align. I can't wait for another book by this author!!

EMILY MATOS, GOODREADS REVIEWER

I just finished reading "If the Stars Align" by Nathalie Theodore and I absolutely loved it. It's such a beautifully-crafted modern love story and the writing is so polished and captivating. The characters feel so real and relatable — I couldn't put it down from the first sentence. Fantastic and highly recommended!

ERIN SLATER, GOODREADS REVIEWER

Nathalie Theodore enters the romance novel genre with quite a splash! I absolutely LOVED *If The Stars Align*! It is so captivating, well-written, emotion provoking and has such well developed characters that it is impossible to put down. Theodore takes us on quite the roller-coaster journey as she brilliantly portrays both Sunny and Dex's inner dialogues. She diligently captures both the flaws and beauty of the characters, and portrays such realistic accounts of the world of law, mental health, family dynamics, complicated friendships and of course, true love. I can't wait for the next book to come out. I have a feeling Nathalie Theodore will be the next big name in romance novel authors!

SARAH IMBERMAN, GOODREADS REVIEWER

NATHALIE THEODORE

TO PARISSA, WHO STAYS UP TOO LATE READING
MY MANUSCRIPTS, AND SENDS THE BEST
MIDNIGHT TEXT MESSAGES. THANK YOU FOR
LOVING MY CHARACTERS AS MUCH AS I DO.

one

I've always been a sucker for a happy ending.

My heart flutters as I watch my newlywed clients in their brand-new home, seated on the loveseat across from me, flipping through my interior design portfolio. They're the picture of happily ever after, fresh off the heels of their fairytale wedding and dreamy honeymoon in Italy. The bride's tucked under the groom's arm, their thighs touching. As she scans each page, her husband's gaze is mostly on her. Whenever she sees a design she likes, she smiles, which makes his face light up. It's the sweetest thing. She's in running shorts and a t-shirt, with her hair in a messy bun, and I can tell from the look in his eyes that he's never seen anyone more beautiful.

It's refreshing to meet a man this devoted. The kind of husband I don't have to worry about. Some husbands I've worked with have wandering eyes. They think I'm dressed to the nines for *them*, which couldn't be further from the truth. I've always loved fashion. Plus, I'm petite, so I wear stilettos for their functionality. I look much younger than thirty as it is, and being the shortest person in the room doesn't help.

But that's not what these husbands are thinking about when their gazes travel from my high heels to the hem of my dress. I can practically read their minds: *She's blonde and bubbly. Sexy. Why not try my luck?* While their wives are busy preparing tea or coffee, they slip me their cell phone numbers, or make passes at me. My blood boils…but I keep smiling as I announce to their wives that I'm on my way to help them in the kitchen.

Thankfully, I don't have to deal with any of that today. And now I know there are at least two honorable men in this world. My new client, Mr. Torres—who just went upstairs to get his wife a sweatshirt because he thought she looked cold (be still my heart)—and Dex Oliver.

Yes, *that* Dex Oliver. The Oscar-winning actor and mental health advocate. I'm good friends with him and his wife, Sunny. And boy, is their love story one for the ages. There's no denying those two were meant to be together. If you saw the way they looked at each other, you'd understand. It's the same with Mr. and Mrs. Torres, here.

After we wrap up our meeting, they walk me to the door, and I can't help but eye the paintings hanging in their foyer. Mr. and Mrs. Torres hired me to design a nursery, so I won't be tinkering with their art collection, unfortunately. Choosing artwork for my clients is the only part of my job that excites me. And there's *a lot* I could do with this wall.

Trust me, I'm the last person you'd ever accuse of being full of herself, but I truly believe I'm a better painter than this particular artist. Never mind that it's been years since I've picked up a paintbrush. A knot forms in my stomach as my gaze sweeps over each painting, imagining the magic I could create with a blank canvas of my own. But before the longing gets too intense, I leave.

The minute I step out of the elevator and into the lobby of their building—a skyscraper in downtown Chicago—I swap my stilettos for the sneakers in my tote bag, so I can walk the mile and a half back home. As usual, I'm in no rush to get back to my empty apartment.

On my leisurely stroll, I admire the city's architecture. I moved here from LA two months ago and still can't get over how beautiful Chicago is. I decide to walk out of my way a bit, toward the lake. And I can't resist stopping at Olive Park, which has the most breathtaking view of the skyline.

It's a perfect summer day. The sky is clear blue. The sun is glinting on the lake's subtle waves. The trees all around me are lush and bright green. I let myself get lost in all the different colors I see.

I do this a lot—imagine what paint colors I'd mix on a palette to replicate each shade. I'd have to start with a deep—

A wolf-whistle interrupts my daydream.

When I turn around, there are three frat boys in Kappa Sigma gear stopped dead in their tracks, staring at me. Their eyes are practically bugging out of their heads.

"Damn, she's hot as fuck!" the one on the left exclaims, elbowing his friend in the middle, whose jaw drops.

"We're on our way to the beach," says the guy on the right. "Wanna join us?" The way he and his buddies are ogling me makes my skin crawl.

This happens to me so often, I figured at some point I'd get desensitized—but no. I'm *screaming* on the inside. Regardless, I playfully roll my eyes and smile at them. "Sorry, guys…I have a boyfriend," I lie. Then I turn around and pray they'll keep walking.

They do, but not without one last comment from the bro on the left. "That dress would look great on my bedroom floor!" he yells as his friends laugh.

I bite my tongue to keep from cursing at him. But I'm not the cursing type, anyway. I'm Jenna Andersen. Head cheerleader. Homecoming queen. That's what people want from me, so that's what I give them. If stifling feelings were an Olympic sport, I'd be a gold medalist.

I make it to my high-rise building without further incident. There's a moving truck parked out front, and I see a man pulling boxes from it, but he's turned away from me. Still, there's a pang of dread in my gut. I happen to know the apartment next to me is vacant because I looked at it too, before I settled on mine. Now all I can think is, *Please don't tell me this guy with his toned, tanned arms and backward baseball cap is moving in next door to me.* Odds are, he's no better than the frat boys who catcalled me at the park.

Ugh. I wish I could curl up on my couch and watch romantic comedies for the rest of the night. But I have a first date to get ready for. I'm in a great headspace for it, I know.

It doesn't matter—I'm not looking for anything serious, anyway. I gave up on love a long time ago. Not for others, of course. Like I said before, I've always been a sucker for a happy ending. And when it comes to romantic movies, the sappier the better.

I just don't think that kind of love is in the cards for me.

There was a time in my life I was sure I'd found *the one*. But I was wrong. And while I didn't give up on love right away, every major relationship I've had since then has blown up in my face. So I'm trying to keep my relationships casual. But it's a lot easier said than done, especially now that I'm thirty. Suddenly every man in my age bracket is looking to settle down.

Which is why, tonight, I'm going out with a guy who's forty-five and recently divorced. He's the brother of one of my interior design clients. Since neither of us is looking for anything serious, she offered to set us up.

Back in my apartment, I pick a rom-com to half-watch as I get ready for my date. Some people need a playlist of their favorite songs to hype them up, but I prefer stolen glances from across a crowded room and first kisses in the rain.

I choose *Four Weddings and a Funeral*. I was a freshman in high school when I first saw it with Jake Brenner, a junior. The young male attendant almost turned us away because the movie was rated R, and I was only fourteen. But when I batted my eyelashes at him, he let us in. I've kept that weapon in my arsenal ever since.

I know I'm lucky to look the way I do. I only wish more people cared to see what's beneath the exterior. Jake definitely didn't. Inside the theater, he sat with his arm around me, and I had to keep swatting his hand away from my breast. I was stupid to think he wanted to get to know me—everyone knew he had a thing for blonde cheerleaders. As soon as his gropey fingers made his intentions clear, I lost interest in him.

But damn if I didn't fall in love with romantic comedies that day. I was totally smitten with the idea of love at first sight. Of true love announcing itself with a flash of lightning and thunder. I couldn't wait for it to happen to me.

I was naïve then.

I have zero expectations of experiencing a thunderbolt tonight. But after I've changed my outfit, had a snack, and made it to the part of *Four Weddings* where the music swells and everyone's happy, I'm feeling much more chipper, and I walk into the restaurant where I'm meeting this guy with renewed energy.

Who knows? Maybe my client's brother will be exactly what I'm looking for. Someone to explore the city with. Try out new restaurants with. To sleep with, if the chemistry's right. But with *no* strings attached. Is that too much to ask?

I don't know. But right off the bat, this date is off to a rocky start. He's late. And he hasn't called or texted.

I sit at the bar and ask for a glass of the house red. Before I know it, twenty minutes pass. *Did I just get stood up?* The bartender asks if I want more wine, and I nod. He winks as he turns to grab the bottle, and I smile out of habit. At least he's not as obnoxious as the guys at the park.

After he refills my glass, I let myself get lost in the velvety red color of the wine. I take a slow sip, and catch a hint of bright magenta at the rim. Just the *idea* of painting a bright swirl of pink on a background of burgundy makes me a little bit giddy.

When I look back up, the bartender's watching me. "Whoever you're waiting for must not know what they're missing," he says as his gaze travels from my eyes to my chest.

I giggle. Again, out of habit. But as I'm about to quip back, someone starts frantically tapping my shoulder. I turn around and recognize my date from a picture his sister showed me. He's panting and wiping sweat off his brow.

"Jenna?" he asks with no hint of a smile.

"That's me," I say brightly, ignoring his scowl, when I'd love nothing more than to match it. "And you must be Greg?"

He nods with a furrowed brow. "I would have texted, but my goddamn phone died," he says, pulling his cell out of his pocket and staring at the unresponsive screen. He shakes his head, and now I'm wondering if he's more upset about his phone than the fact that he's twenty-five minutes late.

"Then my cab got stuck in traffic because the idiot driver took Lake Shore during *rush hour*, and I had no way of contacting you, so I ran all the way here from Michigan Avenue," he goes on.

My chest tightens. I haven't known this guy more than two minutes, but he seems like a colossal jerk. He's got plenty of excuses, but he didn't even apologize for being late. I *hate* that he called the cab driver an idiot. He's acting like a toddler in the middle of a tantrum.

And now he's repeatedly tapping his dead phone screen.

"You look like you could use a drink," I tell him—not because I want him to join me, but because I'm a little concerned about his stress level.

Finally, he puts his cell away and looks me in the eyes. That's when his expression softens. "Christ," he says, his gaze moving down the length of my body. "My sister sent me your picture, but you're even hotter in person."

I want to cry. "You're not so bad yourself," I say instead, flipping my hair.

But it's true, he's very handsome. The first thing I notice when I meet someone new is their eyes. And Greg's eye color is rare and captivating—a dark, steely gray around the edges, with a lighter silver in the middle. He looks a little older than in the picture his sister showed me, but his laugh lines and salt-and-pepper hair suit him.

Greg grabs a cocktail napkin from the bar and wipes the remaining sweat off his brow. "Are you hungry?" he asks, pointing toward the crowd enjoying their meals behind us. "I know we were meeting for a drink, but I made you wait so long, the least I can do is buy you dinner."

Honestly, I'm tempted to call it a night as soon as I finish my glass of wine. Maybe the universe sent this abrasive man my way as a sign that I should throw in the towel and give up on dating altogether. If I leave now, I could be home in time to watch *The Bachelorette*. Ranking another woman's suitors from the comfort of my sofa seems much more appealing than dealing with the real-life bachelor waiting for my answer.

But on the other hand, I don't want to spend yet another night in my empty apartment. I'll admit it—I'm lonely.

So what if Greg was rude at first? He was stressed about his broken phone. We've all been there. And he's offering to make it up to me now. I should give him a chance.

"I could eat," I say with an enthusiastic grin to camouflage my ambivalence.

Once we're seated at a table by the window and Greg has his

own glass of wine, he leans in toward me. "So you're new to Chicago, right? Where did you move from?"

"LA, most recently."

"Most recently," he repeats with raised eyebrows. "So you move around a lot?"

"You could say that. I'm from Columbus, Ohio. When I was eleven, we moved to Beachwood, which is near Cleveland. After that, I lived in Ann Arbor, then New York, then Pittsburgh—"

"Geez. Are you on the run, or something?" he jokes.

I laugh, even though his comment hits a nerve. My sister, Christy, calls me "Runaway Jenna." It's true, I *have* packed up my life several times and picked a new city for a new beginning.

If only it helped. I guess you can't run away from a broken heart.

"Life's too short to stay in one place for very long," I say, batting my eyelashes to distract him.

"I guess you have a point," he agrees, smiling at me. "Well, hopefully you'll stay here awhile. My sister's recommending you to all her friends. She says you're a fantastic interior decorator."

"Interior *designer*," I correct him.

"Basically the same thing, right?" he says as he takes a piece of sourdough from the bread basket.

"No, actually. Interior decorators focus on aesthetics. Designers focus more on the functionality of the space."

"It's like you're speaking a foreign language," he says while chewing. "I'm a finance guy, so this artsy stuff goes over my head. What kind of degree do you need for this interior decorating—sorry, *designing* thing?"

"I have a master's in architecture," I tell him. "From the University of Michigan."

Greg looks at me with wide eyes. "Architecture? Wow. And from Michigan? A buddy of mine went there—that's a highly ranked program."

"You're surprised," I say before I finish what's left of my second glass of wine. I'm used to this reaction, but it still irritates the heck out of me.

He gives me a sheepish grin. "Don't get me wrong, I'm just impressed. I mean, we exchanged a few text messages back and forth, but, um, you're very different in person, that's all."

My face turns beet red. Greg and I only texted about when and where to meet, but now I understand what he's getting at.

"I'm dyslexic," I explain. "I try to proofread my texts before I send them, but even then, I still misspell words sometimes. Or I'll let my phone autocorrect, and it picks the wrong word, and—"

"Shit," he says. "Jenna, I had no idea."

"You must have thought I was an idiot," I go on with a laugh, even though I feel like I got punched in the gut.

"It's not a big deal," he says. "I shouldn't have brought it up. I feel like an ass."

And *I* feel like I'm sitting across from my dad. Dean of the most selective private school in Beachwood—the one my little sister, Christy, went to—that I couldn't get into. For a moment, Greg's striking gray eyes are full of the same mix of pity and disappointment I see when my father looks at me.

"I can't imagine it was easy getting through architecture school with dyslexia," Greg says, his attention back on the bread basket.

I watch him consider his options, squeezing the ciabatta and poking at the focaccia. "It was hard as hell," I tell him. "But I did it anyway."

"Good for you," he says, deciding on a breadstick. "Want one?" He tilts the basket toward me.

Not after you touched every piece of bread in there, I think, feeling slightly queasy. Less than ten minutes ago, he was wiping sweat off his face. "I'm fine, thanks," I tell him.

"I'm not surprised you don't eat carbs," he says as he angles his head to peer at my waistline.

I fantasize about dumping the remaining contents of the bread basket on Greg's head and leaving. Of course I would never do such a thing. Although I do enjoy the look on his face when the waitress comes back to take our order, and I tell her I want the linguine.

For the rest of our date, I nod, and smile, and ask him questions about his life. I go through the motions, flipping my hair and laughing at his terrible jokes.

But in the back of my mind, scenes from my childhood are replaying—grainy and choppy, like old home movies.

I'm seven years old, standing at the front of my second-grade classroom with shaky hands. Staring at letters on a page and praying that, somehow, this time, they'll make sense. But they don't. And when I get mixed up, the whole class starts laughing at me.

They started teasing me that day, and they never stopped— even though my dyslexia was relatively mild, and I worked with a tutor to manage it. "You're lucky you're pretty, 'cause you're dumb as rocks," my first crush, Gavin Smith, told me.

That's why we moved from Columbus to Beachwood. And that time, at least, running away actually worked. I started sixth grade as "the new girl." Within a week, I was known as "the cute girl." By the end of the month, I was "the most popular girl in school." And I leaned into it. Why not, right? I'd never stand out for my intelligence, but at least I could use my looks to my advantage.

Greg has certainly proven that he doesn't care what's on my mind. He's been talking about himself nonstop for the past hour, and the only reason I'm smiling is because I've nearly made it to the end of this unbearable date. Of course, he thinks I'm grinning because I'm into him. He just walked me to the front door of my building, and now his arms are around my waist.

"Want me to come upstairs?" he whispers in my ear.

His hot breath makes me shudder, and I'm tempted to knee him where I know it'll hurt. But his sister's well-connected in Chicago, and I'm not looking to make enemies here.

So I kiss him on the cheek. "Not on the first date," I say with a tilt of my head. I let him down easy and give him hope, while making a mental list of excuses I can give when he asks to get together again. I could say that my sister broke up with her boyfriend and moved in with me, so I won't be able to meet up for a while. After a week or two, he'll lose interest.

"I'll call you," he says.

"You do that," I reply with a wink. Then I turn around and hurry into the lobby before he tries to put his hands on me again. The doorman, who's probably the same age as my father but actually has a sense of humor, greets me with a smile and a dad joke, and I give a genuine laugh for the first time all day—

which is sad.

That's why my eyes start welling up in the elevator. By the time I make it to the twentieth floor, I'm crying. I'm unsuccessfully searching my purse for a tissue as I walk through the open elevator doors and, as luck would have it, I crash right into someone waiting to get in.

"Oh my gosh, I'm sorry!" I tell him.

And when I look into his eyes—*something* happens.

I don't know how to explain it. I've never experienced anything like it before. I feel like I already know him, but that's impossible. If I did, there's no way I could forget him.

He's the most beautiful person I've ever seen. His eyes are the deepest, richest shade of brown, and his dark eyelashes are even longer than mine. His hair is chestnut-colored and cut short, but you can tell if he kept it longer, there'd be some curl to it. He has the loveliest bronze tone to his skin, with a rosy glow in his cheeks. He looks like he spent the summer on a boat in the Mediterranean.

He isn't wearing a baseball cap, and his arms are covered by his sweatshirt, but I can still tell they're toned. He's the man I saw earlier today, unloading the moving truck. I never saw his face, but there's no doubt in my mind.

I'm still staring at him when the hallway light above us flickers like lightning and, at the exact same moment, there's a loud crack of…thunder?

"Did you hear that?" I ask him, wondering if I'm losing my mind. I must have watched *Four Weddings and a Funeral* one too many times, and now I'm imagining thunderbolts, when they're impossible. I was outside a minute ago, and it wasn't raining. And even if it were storming outside, I doubt we'd be able to hear it this clearly from the elevator bank on the twentieth floor of our building.

The man standing in front of me blinks a few times before he takes his gaze off mine, then reaches into his pocket. "Sorry, that was my phone," he says, sheepishly. "I should probably change my ringtone—it's a little jarring." He frowns at the screen, then puts his cell back in his jeans. When our eyes lock again, he squints at me. "Have we…have we met?"

The elevator doors squeak shut behind me. "I don't know," I say. "I don't think so…"

"Hmm." His gaze shifts from curious to concerned. "Are you okay? You look like you've been crying."

I lift my fingers to my tear-streaked cheeks, embarrassed. I'm sure I have mascara running down my face. Of course I'd run into the most gorgeous man I've ever laid eyes on when I look like a complete and utter disaster.

"I'll be fine," I say, wiping my tears with the backs of my hands. "It's nothing."

He looks down and pats his pockets. "I don't have a tissue. But…may I?" He pulls the sleeve of his sweatshirt over his hand and offers to wipe my tears with it.

I nearly start crying again at the kindness of his gesture. "You'll get makeup on your sleeve," I tell him.

He smiles, his gaze fixed on me. "I don't mind."

So I nod, and he gently presses the ribbed fabric of his gray hoodie to my face.

A split second later, I hear *music*. The upbeat orchestral kind that swells when lovers kiss in the movies.

"Where is that coming from?" he asks, confused.

Down the hall, one of my elderly neighbors opens her door, and the symphony gets louder. It's coming from her apartment. She ambles down the hallway with a small trash bag, puts it in the garbage chute, then walks back into her home and shuts the door.

The interruption brings me back to earth. I don't know what movie moment I thought I was having, but my life isn't a romantic comedy.

Yes, this man is impossibly handsome—and whatever I felt when I looked at him, he seemed to feel it too—but I'm sure it was just lust. There's no point in sticking around and indulging in a silly fantasy.

"I'd better go," I tell him, pointing to my apartment.

"Of course," he says, making room for me to maneuver past him.

"I'm sorry, again, for running into you," I say as I begin to walk toward my door.

"It was my fault," he says, even though we both know that's not true.

As I fumble to put my key in the lock, I glance at him one more time. "Have a good night," I say with a nervous laugh that's pretty uncharacteristic of me.

I don't think any man I've ever met has made me feel this flustered.

"You too," he says with an easy grin. "I'm Charlie, by the way. Your new neighbor."

"Jenna," I tell him as I finally manage to open my door.

"Nice to meet you, Jenna," he says as the elevator arrives again to whisk him away.

There's something about the way he says my name that makes my heart skip a beat. I watch him smile one last time before he disappears.

I'll have to avoid him like the plague. The last thing I need is to get involved with my neighbor. There's no way to keep things casual when you live that close to someone.

I've been there before—I know.

As I get ready for bed, I put on another rom-com for background noise. I opt for a classic—*She's All That*. But it's like pouring salt on a wound. Not only does Laney Boggs get her happy ending, she's also an artist. My eyes fill with tears as I watch her paint.

I gave up on love years ago, because I couldn't take any more heartbreak. But why did I give up on art?

As a girl, all I ever wanted to do was paint. My mom always encouraged me. When I was in preschool, she set up a little easel in the corner of our kitchen, and while she'd cook dinner in the evenings, I'd experiment with different brushes and colors.

But when I was diagnosed with dyslexia, my dad put my easel in the attic, along with all my other art supplies. I cried for weeks, even though I knew he'd never budge. He had no appreciation for the visual arts at all. And he didn't care that my mom thought I had a gift. She wasn't an artist herself, so why should he listen to her? In his eyes, being a painter wasn't good enough. He wanted me to be an *intellectual*, like him. He insisted I work on assignments from my reading tutor every night, instead of painting. My mother didn't feel like it was her place to intervene. Because she was a stay-at-home mom, and my dad was the academic, she left the important decisions up to him.

Now my tears are dried up, and my anger is raging. But the person I'm most livid with is *me*. Yes, my dad made me feel like my dreams were worthless, so I never painted for pleasure again—only when it was required for my art classes in school, and even then, I felt like I was committing some cardinal sin. But I'm a grown woman now. What's stopping me? I may not be able to control my love life, or lack thereof. But I can control whether or not I paint.

Maybe I don't get the happy ending that comes with thunderbolts and music swelling. But maybe I can give seven-year-old Jenna the happy ending she always wanted—an easel that no one can take away.

I grab my laptop and look up the art studio I always pass on my way to the grocery store. I don't even give it a second thought when I click the button to register for class. When I'm done, a small weight lifts from my chest.

I go to bed expecting to sleep as soon as my head hits the pillow. I'm exhausted from that godawful date. Relieved that I'm finally going to make my way back to painting.

But I don't drift off. I *can't*.

Instead, I'm wide awake, thinking about my new neighbor, Charlie...and the way my heart skipped a beat when he said my name.

I don't know what's come over me.

I've barely slept all week. I keep tossing, and turning, and dreaming about…

Charlie.

It's absurd. We barely spoke. The whole interaction probably lasted two minutes, if that.

But I can't get him out of my head. His flushed cheeks. His warm smile. His eyes, and the curious way he looked at me.

And his body, when we collided, was so solid and strong. I walked right into his chest, which felt like the perfect place to rest my head. And his arms looked like they would feel so good around my waist…

What the heck is the matter with me? It *has* been a while since I've slept with someone. That must be what this is about.

Luckily, I haven't seen my new neighbor since I ran into him the other night. And it *is* lucky, considering how many times I've lingered by the elevator over the past few days.

But there's no time to worry about Charlie now anyway, because I'm taking my very first painting class today. I'm so excited that I arrive at the studio about fifteen minutes early. The classroom door is open, and when I peek inside, I see two women mixing paint on a palette.

"Come on in!" the younger of the two says with a giant smile as she waves me over. She looks to be about my age. "We don't bite."

I smile and step into the studio. Everything everywhere is covered in paint splotches. Turquoise. Violet. Fuchsia. Saffron. All the colors of the rainbow, and then some. My sister, Christy, would be horrified. She's a neat-freak, like our dad. But I don't see splatter as mess. I see it as freedom.

This is a place where I can be myself.

I take a deep breath, and the unmistakable aroma of oil paints, turpentine, tin cans, and charcoal pencils envelops me like a hug from an old friend. I haven't smelled anything like this since high school art class. My teacher, Mrs. Swanson, told me I was the most talented student she'd ever had. She begged me to consider entering a competition, but I lied and said I wasn't interested. It would have required extra work outside of school, and my dad never would have allowed it.

But he doesn't get to decide for me anymore, I think with a flutter of excitement as I reach the women at the front of the classroom. "Hi, I'm Jenna," I say, beaming.

"Vanessa," says the younger one, holding out her hand. "And this is my Tati Marie."

"*Tati?*" I ask.

"It means aunt, in Haitian Creole. I was born in Port-au-

Prince," Marie says with a grin as bright as her niece's. "Welcome to class. I'm so happy you're here," she continues, then hugs me as tightly as if I were family.

It nearly brings tears to my eyes. My own parents don't hug me like this. Marie's warmth is rare and genuine, and I feel like I could melt in her arms. I make sure to pull away before I do.

"How long have you been teaching?" I ask her.

She looks at me with glimmering eyes. "I've been painting all my life. But today is my first day teaching."

"Tati just retired from a long and boring career at the bank," Vanessa chimes in with a laugh. "This is an exciting day for her."

"Congratulations, Marie!" I turn back to Vanessa. "And are you her assistant?"

She shakes her head, smiling. "Not me—I can barely draw a stick figure. I moved here from New York recently, and I thought it'd be fun to take Tati Marie's class so we could spend more time together."

"She works too much," Marie says with a frown. "Never comes over for dinner."

"I'm sorry, Tati…but it won't always be this bad," Vanessa says to her aunt before turning to me. "I'm the new director at a refugee resettlement agency, and our assistant director is on maternity leave, so there's a lot on my plate right now."

"Vanessa's been in Chicago for six months and doesn't have a single friend," Marie tells me, her brow creased with concern. "Not to mention a man."

I look at Vanessa and can't imagine she isn't single by choice. She's absolutely stunning. Tall and statuesque—she has to be 5'9" or 5'10". She towers over my barely 5'4" frame. Her eyes are light brown, with flecks of gold that match her honey-colored skin. Her hair is in long braids, which she's wearing half-up. She has on faded jeans and a t-shirt, and looks like a supermodel.

"I *do* have friends, Tati!" Vanessa tells her aunt. "There's you…"

"See what I mean?" Marie says to me with one eyebrow raised.

"And Denise—that's my sister," Vanessa explains to me. "Oh, wait—and then there's Sam!"

Marie's eyes widen. "What? Who's Sam? Are you dating someone? A boyfriend?"

Vanessa giggles. "No, Tati, Sam's a woman. She's a friend from New York, but she moved here over the summer. She's a philosophy professor now, at Northwestern. But I haven't seen her yet, since we've both been busy settling into our new jobs."

"I just moved here too, from LA. And I'll be honest, I haven't made a ton of friends in Chicago either," I admit.

"Then it's settled," Marie says to her niece. "You're going to bring Jenna and Sam to my birthday party tomorrow night."

Vanessa's eyes light up. "Perfect! We're celebrating at my sister's restaurant. Have you tried Haitian food before, Jenna?"

I shake my head, smiling. "I haven't. But are you sure you want me to come? It's a family party, and I don't want to intrude—"

"Nonsense," Marie says sternly, but there's still warmth in her words. "The more the merrier."

"That's very generous, thank you," I say as a few more students start trickling into the room.

"Let's grab easels next to each other," Vanessa says, linking her arm to mine like we've been best friends forever. I've known her for ten minutes, but somehow it already feels that way.

Once everyone in the class has gotten settled, Marie begins. "As you may have guessed, we're going to work on self-portraits today—which is why I asked everyone to bring a photograph."

Just hearing her words wakes up something inside me I thought I'd never feel again. I'm three-year-old Jenna standing at my brand-new easel for the very first time.

I have to bite my lip to contain my excitement.

After a brief tutorial from Marie on mixing colors to match our unique skin tones, we gather our supplies, and she unleashes us. The moment I sweep my paint-dipped brush over the smooth, stretched canvas, a sense of calm takes over me—like *finally* something in my life feels right.

I want my eyes to be the focus of my self-portrait, so I paint them larger than life. I spend a lot of time getting the olive-green color just right, and the specks of white from the light reflected in them. Above my eyes are a hint of my eyebrows, and below are my pink cheeks, my sun-kissed nose, and my lips turned up in a smile. I'm in my zone and don't realize how much time has passed, until I hear Vanessa say something beside me.

"Holy shit," she exclaims.

When I turn, her jaw is dropped. "Jenna…" she continues after a minute. "This is incredible!"

Overhearing her niece, Marie joins us. "I agree," she tells me. "I've been watching you paint from the back of the classroom, because I didn't want to interrupt your process—but your work is truly remarkable."

"You're much too kind," I tell them with a dismissive wave of my hand. I don't have a hard time accepting compliments from my interior design clients, but this feels different. As Vanessa and Marie stand to examine my work, it's like they're peering into my soul. It's a little unnerving, to be honest.

"Your eyes are so expressive," Vanessa says, still staring at my painting. "And see the juxtaposition with her mouth, Tati? She's smiling, but there's a wistful look in her eyes. It's amazing, Jenna. I don't know how you captured that!"

I grin, but my stomach clenches. I'm used to hiding under a bubbly exterior, but my portrait gives me away. I feel so vulnerable, so exposed…I may as well be standing here naked.

"You don't see talent like this every day," Marie agrees. "Are either of your parents artists?"

I shake my head. "Neither of them. I have no idea where this passion of mine came from."

"Well, you should be very proud, Jenna," Marie says, turning to me. "You *do* know this is a beginner's class, right?"

I exhale a laugh. "It's been so long since I've painted, I wasn't sure what to expect from myself." The last time I picked up a paintbrush was for a required art class my senior year of high school. That was twelve years ago.

Marie gently squeezes my shoulder. "Expect greatness, Jenna," she says before walking away.

I'm so touched, it takes everything I have not to burst into tears. I don't think anyone I've known in my entire life has ever expected greatness from me.

I lift my hand to my heart and feel it crack open just a bit.

After class, Vanessa suggests we get a drink, so we walk to a nearby pub. I'm immediately at ease with her, which is rare for me. Yes, I was one of the most popular kids at Beachwood High, but I honestly always wondered why every girl there wanted to be my friend. Was it because I was head cheerleader and homecoming queen? They were always by my side for the good times—sneaking beers out of my parents' basement refrigerator and partying with the varsity football players—but when I was laid up after an emergency appendectomy the weekend of our Valentine's dance junior year, not a single soul came to visit me. I'd always suspected my friendships were superficial, but that confirmed it. It hurt worse than the actual recovery from my surgery.

Which is why sitting at the bar with Vanessa tonight feels so special. She seems like the type of person who, if she likes you, cuts past the small talk because she's eager to connect on a deeper level. Half a beer in, we're already chatting about our exes.

"Boy, do I have war stories," she says with a shake of her head before taking a swig of her drink. "Tati Marie's worried because I'm thirty-two, and she wants grandnieces and nephews," she continues with a laugh. "She doesn't have kids of her own, so she's invested in this."

"Is that what *you* want?" I ask her.

She nods. "I do. And I was about to have it all, but…" She sighs deeply, her gaze fixed on mine. "I left my fiancé at the altar."

I can see the pain in her eyes. The glint of gold is gone, replaced with a deeper amber. "I'm so sorry, Vanessa. Did this happen recently?"

Her cheeks flush. "It's been a little over three months," she says.

"Are you okay?" I ask as her eyes start to glisten.

She bites her lip. "I will be. I just feel terrible for the way I left things with him."

A tear rolls down her cheek, so I reach for a cocktail napkin and hand it to her. "Do you want to talk about it? I know we just met, so if you don't feel comfortable—"

"No, I do—feel comfortable," Vanessa tells me. "It's strange. I don't normally click like this with other women right away."

"Neither do I," I confess.

I'm not even very close to my sister. Christy's only two years younger than I am, but we have absolutely nothing in common. She's the smart one in the family. Loves to read, just like our dad. She got her degree in English literature at Columbia, and now she's a literary agent in Manhattan. It's like Dad won the lottery with his second daughter, after discovering the first one was defective.

Vanessa smiles and takes another sip of beer before she begins. "Nico and I had this adorable meet-cute. I was sitting under a tree in Central Park, and he asked if he could share the shade with me. We got to talking, realized we had a lot in common, and became friends right away. I'd gone through the most brutal breakup, and I wasn't interested in a relationship at the time. But Nico was single, too. And fine as hell. Eventually, our boundaries got blurred. One night we ended up sleeping together. And when you sleep with a friend, things can get...."

"Complicated," I offer as she nods. "I know what you mean. I've been there, too."

With Dex.

We were friends with benefits for about a year, while he and Sunny were broken up and she was engaged to someone else. But I don't tell anyone I've slept with megastar Dex Oliver. I'm pretty private about my relationships as it is, and I don't want to have to dodge uncomfortable questions about what he's like in bed.

"We got lucky though," I go on after taking a swig of my drink. "We ended things without any drama, but I think it's because we both knew we didn't belong together."

Sunny and Dex's connection is so electric, you can feel it in the atmosphere. He and I never had anything remotely like that.

Wait a second…is that what I felt with Charlie?

Jenna, stop it. You know nothing about this man.

"I wish I could say it was like that for me and Nico," Vanessa tells me. "Once we crossed that line, it felt like there was no going back. It was either stay together as a couple, or lose him as a friend. And at that point, he was the best friend I'd ever had. I thought the choice was clear. But then we got engaged, and that's when I started to worry that something was missing. I knew I loved him—and I still do—but it's not the earth-shattering love I've always wanted." She shakes her head. "I don't know. Maybe I read too many romance novels, and have unrealistic expectations. I mean, he's a stand-up guy. And easy on the eyes, too. I'd show you a picture, but I deleted them all a few weeks ago. I kept going back through them and wondering what woman in her right mind would give up a man that good-looking."

"I'm really sorry you went through that, Vanessa. I know how hard it must have been. But I think you did the right thing," I tell her.

My mind flashes back to that night with Hunter in my college apartment, when I gave back my engagement ring. I see the look in his eyes as clearly as if he were sitting next to me, and it tears my heart apart all over again.

Hunter Reed. With his dirty-blond hair and ocean-blue eyes, we looked like Barbie and Ken together. Like the wedding cake toppers you always see. I thought we were made for each other. I thought we'd be together forever. But it didn't work out that way.

Don't go there, Jenna, I beg myself, then take a swig of beer before Vanessa sees my lip quiver.

"Thank you," she goes on with an appreciative smile. "I just hope Nico can forgive me."

"One day, he'll understand," I tell her. "You let him go so he can find the happiness he deserves, too."

Vanessa tilts her head. "You sound like you're speaking from experience."

For a split second, I consider telling her about my relationship with Hunter...

But I can't.

I'd be opening Pandora's box. And the last time I did that, I completely fell apart.

I don't think I have it in me to go through that again.

So I tell Vanessa about Scott instead. A much less devastating disaster.

"I've known for a while now that I don't want children," I

begin to explain, in between sips of beer. "I just never realized how hard it would be to find a partner who's okay with that. I *thought* I'd found that with Scott. I met him years ago, after I moved to Pittsburgh. We flipped houses together."

"You're a house flipper?" Vanessa asks with an excited glint in her eye. "Those are my favorite shows to watch on HGTV."

I smile. "I used to be. I went to school for architecture, but didn't want to use my degree in a traditional job, so I decided to try my luck flipping houses. I started out on my own and did really well. Scott was a real estate agent, and I was his biggest competition."

Vanessa smirks. "I bet he didn't like that."

I laugh. "No, he didn't. So he convinced me to join forces. He was incredibly irritating at first. He always thought he knew better than me. But when I threatened to kick him to the curb, he started taking me seriously. Once we found our groove, we made a great team. And one night, after our biggest sale, I kissed him. It was impulsive—we'd had some champagne to celebrate—but we'd been spending so much time together, I guess he started to grow on me."

"Classic enemies-to-lovers," Vanessa says, beaming. "That's my favorite romance novel trope."

I giggle and take a sip of beer before I go on. "It was definitely unexpected. Scott was even more stunned than I was. I mean, he's a cute guy, but the type who has no idea he's attractive. I think he thought I was way out of his league. After I kissed him, he confessed he'd had a massive crush on me since we started working together. So we began dating. I told him right off the bat that I didn't want kids, and he said he didn't either…" I trail off with a sigh.

"Something tells me he changed his mind," Vanessa says with a wince.

I nod. "He was twenty-four, and I think he would have said anything to keep sleeping with the girl of his dreams. The first time we broke up was his twenty-fifth birthday. He had one of those quarter-life crises, and started wondering if he did want to be a dad one day. So he left, and that should've been the end of it."

"It's never that simple," Vanessa says, shaking her head.

"After a month apart, he said he was absolutely miserable without me, and begged me for another chance. He promised he'd taken enough time to think about things, and he said he was sure he didn't want children. So we got back together. Six months later, he started having doubts again. That time, I was the one who broke things off. For good."

"Jenna, I'm so sorry," Vanessa says, reaching for my hand. "That's brutal."

"I should have seen it coming," I say with a wry laugh. "Live and learn, I guess. Scott's married with a baby on the way now. We don't talk, but we're still Facebook friends."

"Have you had any relationships since then?"

"Nothing serious. Scott isn't the first guy who felt conflicted about me not wanting kids. So for the past three years, I've decided to keep my relationships casual. But you know what? Casual dating *sucks*, and I'm about ready to give up on that, too." I finish the last of my drink.

When my new friend frowns, I continue.

"I'm not saying that because I want anyone to feel sorry for me," I go on. "I don't need a relationship to be happy—especially now that I'm painting again. I'm starting to see a life that could be fulfilling, traveling the world and making art."

Vanessa nods, and smiles sympathetically. But I'm not sure she believes what I'm saying.

I'm not sure I believe it myself.

three

When I wake up the next morning, before I even open my eyes, I'm smiling. I stretch out luxuriously in my bed and revel in this happiness that feels much too foreign.

I painted yesterday. And on top of that, I made a new friend. Maybe it's no coincidence. Maybe this city is where I stop running. Where things finally start falling into—

Okay, let's not get carried away.

I should know better than to believe things happen for a reason. Best to enjoy the moment and not expect too much from it.

I have a leisurely Saturday ahead of me before Tati Marie's birthday party tonight, and I know exactly what I want to do with it. I throw on shorts and a t-shirt, make myself a smoothie to drink on the go, and get in my car. Twenty minutes later, I'm walking into the largest art supply store in Chicago.

My first thought is that I want to buy everything I see. But it turns out, I nearly have to. I'm starting from scratch, so I need paints, brushes, a palette, a palette knife, canvases, and Gesso, among many other things. And an easel, of course. I buy so much stuff that the shop owner offers to help me carry it to my car. I politely decline with a bright smile, even though I could use the help. But he's already hit on me twice, and I'm not interested. Besides that, I'm pretty stubborn about doing things myself. I have been since high school.

When I was a junior, I qualified for an individual cheerleading competition in Columbus. As I was packing up my mom's car, I noticed she had a flat tire. I asked my dad to help me put on the spare, but he said he had to get Christy to school on time, so she wouldn't miss her English Lit class.

My mom was no help at all. She was sick with the flu, and didn't know a thing about tires. So I called Vic McCabe, a classmate I'd been on a few dates with. He said he'd be happy to change the tire…*if* I had sex with him. I was a virgin, then, and all we'd ever done was kiss. I broke up with him on the spot, but he still tried to negotiate for a blow job.

Devastated, I sat on the hood of the car and cried. Then our next-door neighbor, Mrs. Rosen, walked up to ask what was wrong. I'd never spoken to her before. She told me she'd learned how to do all sorts of things since her husband had died. But instead of changing the tire for me, she instructed me and supervised as I did it myself.

It was a lesson I never forgot.

It takes me two trips to load everything into my trunk. But it's such a long walk to get from where I park in my building's garage to the elevator, I decide to see if I can carry everything at once. I've got multiple bags hanging from the crook of each elbow, canvases under my arms, and a portable easel strapped over my shoulder. It's not easy, but it's not impossible. Kind of like getting through grad school with dyslexia.

On the twentieth floor, I prop the elevator door open with my foot as I transfer my purchases into the hallway. I'm loading myself up like a pack mule again, when I hear my name.

"*Jenna*," he says softly.

It's not a question, even though we only met once, and briefly. I'm facing away from him with my unwashed hair pulled back, but he knows it's me—just like there's no doubt in my mind that the man standing behind me is tall, and handsome, and sun-kissed, with a curious gleam in his eyes. The buttery sound of his voice gives me goosebumps.

"Hi, Charlie," I say when I turn around to meet his gaze.

Yikes. He's even more handsome than I remember.

I lose myself in his coffee-colored eyes, and the familiar way they're smiling at me. In the way his quiet presence eases the tension in my body, and makes my heart beat slow and steady. It's like the world's moving at half-speed until—

The bottom of one of my bags rips open, and tubes of oil paint tumble down to the floor. There are paintbrushes everywhere. Startled, I look down, and another bag slides off my wrist, its contents rolling in various directions as the easel starts slipping off my shoulder.

I'm mortified. Why do I have to keep making a fool out of myself in front of this ridiculously handsome man?

But Charlie seems unfazed. "Let me help," he says with an

easy grin. Out of habit, I open my mouth to tell him I'm fine, but clearly that's not the case. As he's kneeling to collect my runaway supplies, I almost lose my grip on one of the canvases.

"I think I've got everything," Charlie tells me as he stands up. He's got paintbrushes in the pockets of his jeans, a palette tucked under one arm, and a very full bag he's hugging close to his chest.

"Thank you so much," I say, both embarrassed and relieved. "I'm sorry to keep you from wherever you were going."

Charlie lets out a sheepish laugh as we walk down the hall to my apartment. "I actually wasn't going anywhere. I went to get coffee this morning, and I locked myself out. I'm waiting for someone with the master key, but since it's Saturday, they might be a while."

"Oh," I say after setting down my things and putting my key in the door. "Did you want to come in? While you're waiting?"

As soon as the words are out of my mouth, I regret them. It's a *terrible* idea. He's my neighbor. If we get involved and things go south, I'll have to relocate again.

And I'm so sick and tired of moving.

"Are you sure?" he asks, his dark eyebrows knitted together. "I don't want to impose."

Normally, when a man tells me he doesn't want to impose, he's simultaneously undressing me with his eyes. But not Charlie. All it takes is the earnest look on his face to strip away any doubt I had. I'm calm now, my heartbeat steadying. "Of course," I say. "It's the least I can do."

He's the first guest I've had since I moved in two months

ago. The first person to see where I live. And his reaction is—priceless.

"Wow," he exclaims, his eyes wide. "It's like an art museum in here."

We put my supplies down in the foyer, and he gravitates toward the gallery wall I'm so proud of. I smile as he peruses his way from left to right. "These are great," he says, his eyes on my two favorites: Picasso-style cubist portraits I picked up at a flea market in Pittsburgh. "Are any of them yours?"

"You mean…did I *paint* them?" When he nods, I giggle. "Oh gosh, no. These are pieces I've collected over the years. I'm not much of a painter."

It's such a *Jenna* thing to say—bubbly and self-deprecating. Normally, I wouldn't think twice about it. But the way Charlie's looking at me, it's like he can see right through the act.

"I think you're being modest," he says, confirming my suspicions.

The look in his eyes makes my knees weak, and my first instinct is to flip my hair—but I can't, because it's pulled back. It unnerves me.

"Either that, or I just aided and abetted an art supply heist," he continues, nodding toward the foyer where my painting materials are lined up.

His joke disarms me, and I relax again. "You're probably better off not knowing," I say with a wink. His face flushes ever-so-slightly.

Oh no. I'm flirting with him.

"Well, you certainly have an artistic eye," he goes on, stepping back to take in my gallery wall in its entirety. "What do you do for a living?"

"Interior design," I say, biting my lip sheepishly when he turns back toward me. "And you're right…maybe I was selling myself short before. I *do* paint. It's been a while, but I'm starting to get back into it."

When Charlie smiles, his entire face lights up and—

I think I just swooned a little. I lean on a side table for balance.

"I'm getting back into photography, myself," he goes on to tell me.

And he's an artist, too?! God help me, the room is spinning. I need to sit down.

It's strange, because I'm usually so graceful. I never lose my balance. There's a reason I was always at the top of the pyramid—single-leg stunts were my specialty. It's how I qualified for that individual cheer competition during my junior year of high school. And *won*.

"It's just a hobby right now," he continues with a sigh as I make my way to the couch. "I have a business degree, but it's not my passion."

"I know how you feel," I tell him with a growing smile. "I have an architecture degree, and it's not my passion either."

"Is that right?" Charlie sits on the opposite end of the sofa from me. And this time, when he grins, I feel something I haven't felt since the first time Hunter Reed's lips brushed mine.

Butterflies.

Oh lord. If Charlie can make me feel like this sitting six feet away, what would it be like to kiss him? What would it be like to—

"Where did you study architecture?" he asks, stealing me away from my fantasy.

And what a crash landing back to reality it is to hear *that* particular question come from Charlie's kissable lips. My heart sinks. *This is it.*

This is where everything comes to a screeching halt. Where Charlie shows me he's no better than Greg—a guy who looks at me and only sees a blonde airhead. Thank goodness I haven't heard from him since our disastrous date. Sure, Greg had already decided I was an idiot when he read my misspelled messages. But regardless of whether I've texted someone first, the typical response I get when I say I went to such a highly-ranked program is wide-eyed, open-mouthed shock.

I brace myself for Charlie's reaction. "I went to the University of Michigan," I tell him.

But if he's surprised, he doesn't show it. He only grins. "My college roommate was from Michigan. He always used his hand to show people where he grew up. Do you do that?"

I nod, laughing. A *real* laugh—not a fake giggle. "The Michigan hand map. You kinda have to do it when you Go Blue."

"Show me," he says, holding up his right hand. "Where's Ann Arbor?"

I have to shift closer to him on the couch so I can reach. Is it possible that's why he asked? Now I notice how good he smells, like fresh laundry. How attractive his broad shoulders are. I definitely have a thing for broad shoulders. It's probably a remnant from my days doing cheer stunts. Those were the guys I wanted to spot me—strong and supportive. I always felt safe with them.

Being close to Charlie also feels safe. It feels natural, and I'm baffled by it. But instead of questioning it, I lean in. "Ann Arbor's right here," I say, sending my fingertips to the bottom of his hand, below his thumb. And when our hands meet, it's—

Electric.

I think he feels it, too. Because when I look at him, the pink hue in his cheeks is a few shades deeper than it was before we touched.

If the guy with the master key doesn't get here soon, I'm afraid I'll forget all about why I gave up on love in the first place. It's so easy to get lost in his gaze. Time slows, and there's nothing else but me and Charlie and the magnetic pull between us.

Until a sudden boom of thunder disconnects us.

Charlie's phone. He pulls it out of his pocket and frowns at the screen.

"Is everything okay?" I ask him. I wonder if the key guy is delayed. My head and my heart are at odds about whether that would be a good thing.

"It's my boss," Charlie explains with a wry smile. "I don't use that ringtone for everyone. Just him."

"He seems pretty intense," I say. "Does he always text late at night and on weekends?"

Charlie nods, running a hand over his hair. "Yeah. His boundaries could use some work."

Even though I can see he isn't happy receiving his boss's messages, it doesn't ruffle his feathers. He has this even-keeled vibe about him that feels rare, to me at least—considering the family I grew up in. My dad and Christy are wound super tight. I guess it's hard not to be, when you won't accept anything less than excellence from yourself. Or others.

My mom is on the opposite end of the spectrum. She's a beautiful woman. Everyone says I'm the spitting image of her. But she's never expected much out of herself. Of course my dad didn't, either. It was assumed she would stay home and take care of me and Christy. I don't think it made her happy, though. She often seemed like she was going through the motions—bored, and listless. The only time her eyes lit up was when she watched me paint all those years ago. Before my dad took that away from both of us.

Charlie's phone chimes, but it's a normal ding this time. He frowns again. "That's the guy with the master key."

"Oh." My heart plummets twenty stories, to the ground floor. I guess I wanted the key guy to be delayed after all. But seeing the weight of disappointment on Charlie's face lightens my heart a bit. I don't think he wants to leave either.

"Thanks so much for taking me in, Jenna," he tells me.

"It was my pleasure," I say. But not in the bouncy, bubbly way I usually do. This time, I mean it.

When Charlie steps into the hallway, I fight the urge to offer him my phone number. It would be a friendly gesture, in case he ever got locked out again. If only my feelings for him were merely friendly.

But…this can't be where it ends, can it? Will I ever speak to him again, other than a quick hi, here and there, by the elevator?

I stand in the doorframe as Charlie and the key guy exchange hellos. Then Charlie turns back to me. "Hey, let me take you to coffee," he says with an unassuming grin. "To thank you for your hospitality."

I have to work to keep from smiling as big as I want to. "I can't say no to coffee."

His eyes gleam. "You free tomorrow morning?"

"Sure am."

"I'll pick you up at ten," he says, before the key guy lets him in.

I close the door and lean against it, afraid I'll lose my balance again. Then I shut my eyes and breathe deep, trying to reconcile every emotion that's hitting me at once. I honestly don't know whether to laugh or cry.

What I do know is…I'm in trouble.

This feeling that Charlie stirs up in me? It isn't just lust. It's far worse than that.

It's *hope*.

And hope is a dangerous thing.

I can't pick a romantic comedy to watch while I'm getting ready for Tati Marie's party. I sit on the couch, sorting through my entire collection of DVDs, but the pictures on the boxes alone are far too triggering. These dashing leading men with their glimmering eyes, their easy grins, their perfectly broad shoulders—they all remind me of Charlie.

So instead of watching a movie, I take a cold shower. It doesn't help.

Vanessa saves me from myself when she calls to let me know she's downstairs. As soon as I see her brilliant smile, I relax and decide to live in the moment. I can worry about Charlie tomorrow, when we meet. But tonight is about Tati Marie, Vanessa, and their family—and I'm incredibly grateful they invited me to be a part of their celebration.

The restaurant is on the north side of the city, about a fifteen-minute drive from where I live. Vanessa parks down the block, and I can already hear the vibrant Caribbean beats when I get out of her car.

"It's called *kompa*," she tells me when she catches me moving to the rhythm. "It's a type of merengue music. Makes you want to dance, right?" She takes my hand and twirls me on the sidewalk. I'm wearing the perfect dress for it. Emerald green with a skirt that flares as I spin.

"I'd twirl you back, but I'm not tall enough," I joke, and Vanessa bursts into laughter. It's true, though. She's tall to begin with, but tonight she's towering over me in gold heels that pair beautifully with her coral minidress.

"Come on, shorty," she says, linking her arm with mine.

I'm practically giddy inside. This is exactly what I need to get my mind off of droolworthy Charlie, and that electric *zing* that happened when we touched.

A girls' night.

I haven't had one since college—unless you count the times I nursed a glass of wine at a bar in Manhattan, while my uptight sister sat next to me skimming manuscripts for work. *I* certainly don't.

When Vanessa opens the door to Denise's restaurant, the first thing I notice is color. Everywhere. The walls are painted in tropical hues—mango yellow, lime green, and sea blue—giving lush island vibes. There are potted palm trees in clay pots in every corner, and vases with bright orange and pink hibiscus flowers on every table. And the artwork is so mesmerizing, I stop to soak it all in. On the wall beside the host stand are canvases featuring what I assume are Haitian landscapes. My gaze travels across them, admiring the vivid tones of the ocean, the sky, and the hillsides peppered with rainbow-colored houses.

"Aren't these beautiful?" Vanessa says, next to me. "Tati Marie painted them."

"They're spectacular. Her impasto technique is to die for."

"Her *what* now?" Vanessa asks me with raised eyebrows.

"Impasto," Marie chimes in, appearing behind us. "It's the way I layer the paint to create texture. And thank you, Jenna. That's an honor, coming from such a talented artist."

I nearly shake my head to object, but decide only to smile as she pulls me in for a hug. "Happy birthday, Marie."

"Bòn fèt, Tati," Vanessa says in Creole.

"Thank you, my dears. And Jenna, I hope you're hungry, because Denise made enough food for an army."

"Where is my sister, by the way?" Vanessa asks, surveying the crowd.

"Over by the buffet. Go—enjoy! I'm going to get myself a birthday mojito," Marie says with a wink before she dances her way to the bar. I watch her, and my heart swells. I still feel her joy even though she's halfway across the room. And it's not only her. Everywhere I look, people are smiling, laughing, dancing. I think of the soirees my parents hosted when I was growing up. They were nothing like this. Just a roomful of my dad's colleagues making pretentious literary references. I would rather have watched paint dry. Literally.

When I turn back to Vanessa, she's reading a message on her phone. "My friend Sam's on her way, but she's running late, so let me introduce you to everyone. This is my entire family, except my parents, who live in Miami. They're allergic to cold weather," she jokes.

Every aunt, uncle, and cousin greets me with open arms and beaming smiles. Finally, we make it to the buffet table, where a lovely young woman as tall and statuesque as Vanessa smiles at me. "You must be Jenna," she says, pulling me in for a hug.

I could get used to this.

"Vanessa tells me you've never tried Haitian food before, so I'm going to give you a quick tour of the buffet table," Denise continues. My mouth waters as I eye the spread, which looks almost too beautiful to eat.

"We'll start with the *pâté*. It's a savory pastry filled with ground beef and spices," she begins. "Next we have *banan peze*, which are crispy fried plantains. Then there's *diri*—that's rice—with black beans. And finally the entrees: red snapper, stewed chicken…and it wouldn't be a party without *griot*."

"That's fried pork," Vanessa explains.

"Oh, and this is *pikliz*," Denise adds, pointing to something that looks like coleslaw. "It's spicy—so consider yourself warned."

"It all looks delicious. I can't wait to try it," I tell her.

Vanessa and I pile our plates high with food, then find an empty table. A minute later, she waves at someone across the room. "Sam's here! Now, I'm sure you'll get along great, but a word of warning—she has absolutely *no* filter," my friend says all in one breath, a split-second before Sam reaches our table.

"V!" Sam squeals when we stand to greet her.

"Long time no see! You look fantastic!" Vanessa says, hugging Sam. "I love your dress."

It *is* an amazing dress. Very bohemian chic. It's white linen and hits right above the knees, with a deep V-neck and ruffled sleeves. It looks stunning with the contrast of her dark eyes and hair.

"Thanks! It's vintage, from the seventies. The only downside is, I can barely keep my tits in it! I had to use tape." Sam looks down at her breasts, then squeezes them a few times. When she's satisfied everything's in place, she reaches out her hand to me. "Hi! I'm Sam."

I barely contain a laugh. "Jenna. Nice to meet you."

"*Wow*," she says looking me up and down. "You're a total smoke show."

"Oh! Um…thank you." My cheeks burn.

"I told you Sam has no filter," Vanessa says with an amused grin.

Sam laughs. "It's my fatal flaw. I'm sorry. But if it makes you feel any less uncomfortable, I promise I wasn't hitting on you. I'm into dudes, unfortunately. Although I *have* been told I have masculine energy. But I think it's just because I'm a thirty-year-old woman who doesn't want to be tied down."

Vanessa chuckles, then turns to me. "She's still sowing her wild oats."

"If only it were that easy. The guys I meet are all so needy." Sam rolls her eyes. "Give me an orgasm and be on your way, okay? We don't need to cuddle all night and have breakfast in the morning." She shudders.

"Okay, then!" Vanessa exclaims with a clap of her hands. "On that note, I'm going to make you a plate, Sam. I know how much you love Haitian food, so I'll be sure to give you a little bit of everything."

"Thanks, V," Sam says, taking the empty seat next to mine as Vanessa heads to the buffet.

"So, you and Vanessa met in New York?" I ask Sam.

She nods. "We used to frequent the same coffee shop when I was in grad school. I wrote most of my dissertation there, and whenever I needed a break, I'd strike up a conversation with the poor sap at the table next to me. Young, old, male, female—I didn't care. Most people want nothing to do with you, but occasionally someone'll stick, like Vanessa. I started doing it in the study lounge in undergrad. It's a fun way to make friends."

"Where'd you go to college?" I ask.

"Northwestern. You?"

"I went to Michigan. But a friend of mine from high school went to Northwestern. I'm sure you've heard of her. She's kinda famous now, since she married a celebrity. Sunny Dexter?"

Sam blinks at me for several seconds. Then her eyes go wide. "Holy fucking shit! Are you Jenna *Andersen*?"

"Um…yes," I say with a tentative smile, but my gut clenches. Here I was thinking I might get lucky and make two new friends this week, but with the way Sam's looking at me right now—somewhere between shock and horror—that doesn't seem likely. Why would she know my name?

Oh god. Is it possible someone leaked salacious photos of me and Dex to the press sometime in the thirty minutes since I last checked my phone?

Surely not. It's been three years since we slept together, and why would anyone care? Plus, I'm sure my phone would be blowing up like crazy, and I haven't felt it vibrate once.

I wish that fear weren't always in the back of my head. But the thing is…it wouldn't be the first time something like that happened.

In grad school, this guy I dated during our last semester texted a picture of me half-naked and asleep in his bed to a third of our class. Alex was the first guy I dated after Hunter, and I truly believed he had feelings for me. Turned out he'd made a bet with his friends that he could get me to have sex with him before graduation.

"So you're *the* Jenna Andersen, from Beachwood, Ohio? Head cheerleader? Homecoming queen? Most popular girl in school?" Sam says, pulling me back to the present. "And you're telling me you and Sunny are *friends*?"

Well, that settles it…I guess Sam does know Sunny. At least I can breathe easier knowing there aren't leaked photos of me and Dex floating around online. But something tells me I'm about to get an earful from Sam about my history with him. She probably sees me as a threat to Sunny, and now I'll be stuck having to defend myself. I glance at the buffet table to see if Vanessa's heading back, but she's busy talking to her uncle.

Dammit.

"Sunny and I *are* friends," I tell her.

Sam eyes me skeptically. "I don't buy it. Last I heard, you two were rivals, vying for the same man."

My jaw drops. "Did Sunny really say that?"

"Granted, this was a while ago…right after she and Dex got back together. And she was a little more diplomatic, of course," Sam admits. "But I'm not known for sugarcoating things."

"Yeah, no kidding," I say after a heaving sigh. "Well, Sunny and I have cleared the air since then. She knows that Dex and I were friends with benefits, and nothing more. I was never in love with him."

Sam crosses her arms. "You hooked up with him in high school, and then again, a few years ago. Call it what you want, but you seem pretty interested in him to me."

I shake my head. "First of all, Sunny and Dex never dated in high school—so, as far as I knew, he was fair game. I only asked him out after my friends convinced me we belonged together, because we were Homecoming King and Queen. It was silly. Our relationship was purely physical. He never said as much, but I could tell his heart belonged to someone else."

Sam nods, but doesn't respond.

"Second of all, the only reason he and I became involved in LA was because Sunny got engaged to Jeremy," I continue. "Dex was miserable, and I was heartbroken over a past relationship, too. We were both looking for a meaningless distraction."

Sam purses her lips as she contemplates my answer. Before she replies, she squints at me. "I guess that tracks. And I know Sunny isn't one to hold a grudge…but she's one of my closest friends, and I feel very protective over her, that's all."

"Like I said, Sunny's my friend now, too," I tell Sam. "I mean, it's not like we sit around comparing notes about Dex. There are certain things we don't talk about, obviously. But it's all in the past. If she's okay with it, shouldn't *you* be?"

Sam exhales deeply. "Of course Sunny's okay with it. She doesn't have a mean bone in her body—never has." She smirks.

"Unless you count Jeremy."

A laugh escapes me before I frown. "He really was a jerk. Poor Sunny."

Sam nods solemnly. "Yeah, she's been through a lot. That's why I want to make sure you're not some scorned ex-lover who's plotting to steal back her husband. I mean, this is *Dex Oliver* we're talking about. No one could blame you if you weren't over him."

"Sam, when Dex told me he and Sunny got back together, I was over the moon. They were made for each other. Sunny has no reason to feel threatened by me," I insist.

"Well, she definitely felt threatened by you in high school," Sam says pointedly.

I look down at my lap. "Which is ironic, because I was always in awe of Sunny. Not only is she beautiful, she was a star student, too. Especially when it came to English class. Meanwhile, I was a dyslexic cheerleader. It was impossible for me not to compare myself to her."

To be honest, I still do. Sunny quit her law career to pursue her passion. I don't think I'd ever have the guts to quit interior design.

Sam bites her lip. "I had no idea. I guess the history between you, Sunny, and Dex is more nuanced than I thought."

"If there's one thing I know about Dex, it's that his heart belongs to Sunny," I go on. "Plus, they're having a baby. Nothing and no one could tear them apart now. And believe me, I'm the last person you need to worry about. I don't even want a relationship. I prefer to keep things casual, same as you."

But…Charlie.

My mind cuts back to the moment our hands met on the couch. The glimmer in his eyes. The flush on his cheeks. How can I know his face so well, when we only just met? It's as if I could reach out and touch him, my memory of his features is so crystal clear.

I shake my head to shatter it.

"Okay," Sam concedes. "You've convinced me. I'm sorry I was an asshole." She elbows me playfully. "Maybe we can be friends."

I laugh.

"By the way," Sam adds, "did you ever tell Sunny how much you admired her in high school? I bet she'd like to know."

"I did. We had a conversation about it after I read her book, and it brought us a lot closer."

Sam gasps and reaches for my arm. "You've already read her novel? How?! It isn't coming out until next month!"

I chuckle, even though she's gripping me so hard I'm pretty sure it'll leave a mark. "Sunny gave me an advance copy. The book's loosely based on her romance with Dex, and there's a character modeled after me. Head cheerleader, homecoming queen, etcetera. She wanted to make sure I approved."

Sam lets go of me, then squeals excitedly. "Sweet baby Jesus, I need details! Was it amazing?"

I nod. "Sunny's so talented. I don't usually fly through books, but I couldn't put hers down. This was my first time reading romance, and I loved it."

"You know why it's my favorite genre? Romance is rebellious. Well, the romances *I* read are, at least. They subvert stereotypes, and smash gender norms. And the sex positivity is delicious."

Her eyes go wide. "Speaking of which, is Sunny's book super steamy? Please tell me the love scenes are open-door."

"Open-door?" I ask.

"It's when sex happens on-page, versus off-page. Closed-door romance novels are pointless, if you ask me. Why would I suffer through three hundred and fifty pages of sexual tension if I don't even get to be there for the release?"

I laugh so hard a tear rolls down my cheek. Sam is hilarious. "Don't worry," I say after I regain composure. "Her book is open-door. Like, wide open."

Sam pumps her fist in the air. "That's my girl. I knew Sunny wouldn't let me down."

"What did I miss?" Vanessa asks, finally returning with Sam's plate.

"Jenna and I were just bonding. Turns out we have another mutual friend," Sam says with a little wink at me.

I smile back, relieved she didn't mention anything about Dex. My friendship with Vanessa is new, but she doesn't seem the least bit intimidated or threatened by me, which is refreshing. That might change if she knew I used to sleep with a movie star.

"How have *you* been?" Sam brings her focus to Vanessa. "Since the breakup with Nico?"

Vanessa sighs. "Well, a guy asked for my number this morning, when I was waiting in line to get coffee." She shakes her head. "He was attractive, too…but I couldn't do it. I ended up giving him a fake one."

Sam nods knowingly. "Did he look like he'd be bad in bed? Sometimes you can tell right away. It's something about their posture, I think. The way they slouch, you *know* their hips are tight."

Vanessa laughs. "It most definitely wasn't because of that. I guess…I'm just not ready to date yet."

She bites her lip, her brow crinkled, and I know what's on her mind. The angst in her eyes looks familiar to me, because it's something I've seen in my own many times.

When will I be ready to move on? What if I never am?

I sigh. "You know what we need? We need to finish this incredible meal and get out on that dance floor."

And that's what we do. Sam and I get mojitos and rum punches from the bar, since we're not driving; Vanessa gets virgin daiquiris; and the three of us dance our broken hearts out.

Well, I'm not sure Sam's heart is broken. I don't know her story yet, but she seems pretty free-spirited and carefree. Although, finding non-clingy men with loose hips does appear to be a thorn in her side.

After we close down the restaurant, Vanessa drives us home. First she drops off Sam, who gives me a big squeeze when she gets out of the car. Maybe it's because she's had one too many rum punches, but I do think she likes me now. I guess it's safe to say I have two friends in Chicago.

Or three. Does Charlie count?

I can't stop thinking about him the closer we get to my building. It doesn't help that I'm tipsy. I want to run into him again by the elevator. I want to bring him into my apartment. I want to feel his kissable lips on mine, and his muscular arms around my waist, his hands traveling up my back, unhooking my bra and—

"I really have to pee," Vanessa tells me when she pulls up to the curb. "Too many virgin daiquiris. Mind if I come upstairs?"

"Oh my gosh, of course! Follow me."

Two visitors in one day! I'm on a roll. Damn, those drinks were strong.

I take Vanessa to my apartment, and I'm disappointed we don't run into Charlie in the elevator or the hallway. I show her to the bathroom. But while she's in there, I have a thought. *What if Charlie's in the hallway right now?* It's silly, but I'm tipsy. Maybe even drunk. I open my front door and peek out, but he isn't there. Bummer.

"Hey lady," Vanessa says behind me.

Startled, I slam the door shut.

"What was that all about?" she asks with an amused look on her face.

I shake my head and laugh. "I have a new neighbor, and he's incredibly hot. I was hoping to catch him in the hallway, but he's probably asleep. We're having coffee tomorrow morning."

"That's so exciting, Jenna!" she says with a beaming smile. "I'm happy for you."

I shrug. "I don't actually know if it's a date. Maybe he only wants to be friends."

Vanessa raises an eyebrow. "You're kidding, right? Have you *seen* yourself? It's probably safe to assume he's interested in you. And the way your eyes light up at the thought of him?" Her playful grin turns hopeful. "Do you think this could be more than just 'casual'?"

The mojitos I drank tonight certainly seem to think so. But as usual, my broken heart is more convincing. "I'm not looking for more than casual."

Vanessa sighs. "If you say so. Well, let me know how your coffee date goes, regardless. I'm going to head home and let you get some sleep."

I give her a hug. "Do you have everything?"

"I tossed my purse on your couch. I'll go grab it." Vanessa leans over the sofa, but immediately turns back to look at me. "Wait just a minute—what have we here?"

I walk toward her to see what she's talking about.

Oh no. My DVDs. My *rom-coms*.

When I meet her gaze, she has her arms crossed and one eyebrow raised. "You've given up on love, huh?"

I cross my arms back at her and tilt my head. "What? I can't give up on love, but still appreciate good cinema?"

Vanessa chuckles into her fist. "*Good cinema*? Okay, I am definitely not buying what you're selling. I know a hopeless romantic when I see one, and this is irrefutable evidence—like the romance novels stacked on my nightstand."

I shrug. "Maybe I was a hopeless romantic, once upon a time. But I'm not anymore."

Hunter.

He's holding the ring between trembling fingers. The floorboards of my college apartment creak when he takes a step toward me. "Jenna, no. Please...I'm begging you. Don't do this." Tears stream down his face.

"Can't you see I'm doing this for you?" I plead with him.

"Because I love you more than anything?"

He shakes his head. The light fades from his beautiful ocean-blue eyes. Now they're dark. Grim. Full of disappointment. Maybe even disgust. And when he speaks, I don't recognize the voice coming out of his mouth. "You're not the person I thought you were."

They're the last words he says before he leaves. And I know they'll haunt me for the rest of my life.

"Moving on from heartbreak is easier said than done," Vanessa continues with a sigh. "Trust me, I know. But you deserve your happy ending."

The best I can do without bursting into tears is smile and wrap my arms around my new, sweet friend.

But as I'm hugging her, all I can think is—*she's wrong*.

The jarring sound of my cell phone startles me out of a hazy dream of bright pink hibiscus flowers and lush green palm trees. I must have forgotten to turn off my ringer last night. After Vanessa left, I made myself a grilled cheese sandwich, drank some Gatorade, and went straight to bed. I know this because there's a plate of crumbs and a half-full glass on my nightstand. My dress is at the foot of my bed, and all I have on is my underwear.

I glance at the art deco clock on my wall. There's only one person who would call me at eight o'clock on a Sunday morning. I don't even have to look at the caller ID.

"Hi, Christy," I mutter into the phone, still groggy.

"Are you okay?" she asks immediately, sounding less like a little sister and more like a mom. Not *our* mom. Our mom has always been a bit too emotionally checked out to notice what's going on with us. And even if she did, she's never been one to dish out maternal advice. But I stopped wishing for that kind of relationship with her a long time ago. I hardly ever call her anymore. And I rarely hear from her, unless it's a special occasion. I guess that's why Christy's taken it upon herself to check in on me.

"I'm fine. I was out late last night, that's all." I sigh. "I wish you wouldn't worry about me so much."

"Were you on a date?" she asks me after a beat, her tone more hopeful.

I roll my eyes. "No…I was out with friends." At least I can say that much. Hopefully it's enough to satisfy my sister. She doesn't like the idea of me being alone in a new city.

"Oh, good! I'm glad you're meeting people," she says, the relief in her voice making me feel totally pathetic.

It's ironic how the tables have turned since we were teenagers. Christy always wished she were as popular as I was back then. No, she didn't have a constant entourage like I did—but the handful of friends she had were *really* good ones. They're all still in touch, and Christy's been a bridesmaid in two of their weddings so far. I can't say the same about the girls who worshipped me in high school. Maybe now my sister finally understands how superficial my friendships were.

"And how's work?" she asks, going down her mental list of weekly questions for me.

"Work's been good. I got two more referrals this week. I don't think I'm gonna have any trouble keeping busy."

It's the one area of my life I've always had success with—if only I enjoyed it.

"How are things with you?" I ask Christy, to take the heat

off me.

"The usual," she says. "I just signed a new client. I'm up to my eyeballs in manuscripts."

"I guess that's to be expected when you're the star agent at Hanover Literary."

She scoffs. "Hardly the star. I'm just trying to keep my head above water. My entire life is basically work, and training for the marathon. Kyle and I are about to go for a run in Central Park."

I smile wistfully. "It's sweet that you always run together."

My sister met her boyfriend, Kyle, junior year of college, and they've been inseparable ever since. Right after graduation, they moved into a tiny apartment in the East Village, where they've been living for the last six years. The only reason they aren't already married is because they can't yet afford Christy's dream wedding at the New York Public Library.

She's quiet for several seconds before she responds. "Wouldn't it be nice if you had someone to go for runs with in the morning?"

"I prefer yoga," I say casually, because I know it'll annoy her.

My sister sighs, already exasperated with me (it doesn't take much). "You know what I mean, Jenna."

"And *you* know that I don't like talking about this stuff with you, Christy."

"All I want is for my big sister to be happy. Why does that offend you so much?"

"Because you don't think I can be happy unless I'm in a serious relationship. But you're wrong. Being single isn't the end of the world. You only think it is because you've been with the same person for eight years. That's practically your entire adulthood so far. Would you even know how to navigate life on your own?"

"This isn't about me. I'm happy. You're not."

"Who says I'm not happy?" I snap back, more defensively than I wanted to.

"You're my sister. I *know* you. You've always dreamed of being in love. You're the girl who picked Mom's roses and made me scatter the petals on our driveway, so you could walk down it in that incredible dress you designed out of toilet paper. And that was only the beginning."

I scoff. "I was a kid playing make-believe, Christy."

"But every game you played starred you as the blushing bride. And it wasn't only when you were little…" She pauses to clear her throat, a nervous habit she inherited from our dad. "I found the diary you kept in high school."

"I never had a diary," I tell her, matter-of-factly. The only writing I ever did was for school, and that was bad enough. I never would have chosen to write for fun.

"Well, maybe *diary* isn't the right word. It was a journal. With drawings in it."

My eyes go wide.

I look in the mirror, and my face is turning bright pink.

"Oh my god! You went through my things?!"

"What else was I supposed to do while my gorgeous big sister was out on dates? Your life was so much more exciting than mine."

It breaks my heart that Christy grew up feeling insecure because of me. While I got our mom's features, she got our dad's. But even though his personality leaves a lot to be desired, there's no denying he's a handsome man. And Christy—who's taller than I am, with long auburn hair and brown eyes—is absolutely beautiful. She just was never a blonde cheerleader. I've tried telling my sister a million times that looking like Barbie isn't all it's cracked up to be, but I still think she'd trade looks with me in a heartbeat.

That doesn't justify her rummaging through my stuff, though.

"You had no right to look at my journal, no matter how bored you were," I tell her. "But I guess it doesn't matter now, anyway. I don't even remember what was in it."

The truth is, I know precisely what the notebook contains, because it's right here, in my nightstand. I just don't want Christy to know how special it is to me.

My sister clears her throat. "It was sort of like a…graphic novel. But without any words. Just drawings. *Beautiful* drawings, of a man and a woman meeting and falling in love. Going for walks with coffee, and cooking dinner together, and traveling around the world. You put so much time into it, Jenna—there's no way you could have forgotten."

I attempt a giggle, but it sounds forced. "They were doodles. Something to pass the time when I was bored, because I couldn't paint. Drawing was the next best thing."

Christy sighs again. "They weren't just doodles. They were *wishes.* Those drawings were everything you used to wish for—"

"Who cares what I used to wish for?" I blurt out, tears welling in my eyes. "My wishes never came true."

"*I* care. Because you're miserable. I can hear it in your voice. And it's only a matter of time before—"

"Before *what*?" I sob. "Before I fall apart again, like I did after grad school? Before you and Kyle have to drive down here, and pull me out of bed, and take me back to New York with you, so you can watch me like a hawk for six months? Make sure I shower and eat? Well, you don't have to worry about me ever inconveniencing you like that again. Once was enough."

My sister gasps. "You could never be an inconvenience to me! I *love* you. So much. That's why I worry about you. Because you scare me sometimes. Because…"

She pauses and sniffles.

"When I brought you to New York, all you did for weeks was stare at the TV and sleep. There was no light in your eyes, no joy in your smile…and do you know who you reminded me of?" She clears her throat again. "Mom."

"What's that supposed to mean?" I ask, my voice thin and shaky.

Christy exhales deeply before she answers. "Kyle thinks Mom has depressive tendencies."

I scoff. "Kyle's a radiologist, not a psychiatrist."

"Well, he did a psych rotation in med school. But come on, you don't have to be a doctor to see it. Mom's never been truly happy."

"I'm *not* like her," I try to argue, but it sounds more like a plea.

"You didn't used to be. But ever since Hunter—"

"Christy, stop. Please. I really can't talk about Hunter right now—"

"You *never* want to talk about him! That's your problem. It's been eight years, and you're still not over—"

I hang up on her.

By the time Charlie knocks on my door two hours later, I've recovered from the phone call with my sister. I get over it the same way I always do, which is to blast whichever Lola Piper album best fits my mood. I've been a diehard Pipette since her debut, and I can always count on her music to lift me up. Today, I listen to *Limitless (Lola's Edition)* while I eat breakfast and pretend the conversation with Christy never happened.

I pause for a beat before I turn the knob, though. I can already feel the electricity between Charlie and me buzzing through the door, and I just don't understand it. It's thrilling, of course—but upsetting at the same time. I decided years ago that I would never feel this way again. Now my heart's betraying me by manifesting an inexplicable connection to a man I don't even know.

I was hoping our coffee date today would help break the spell. That I'd come back free of any lingering hope that Charlie could be the love I used to wish for.

But so far, we're off to a bad start. I haven't even seen his face yet, and there's pure, unadulterated joy coursing through me. It's the same way I felt when I painted the other day.

And that terrifies me.

He knocks again.

I shake my head to reset myself so he doesn't see the hearts in my eyes. As soon as I open the door, though, Charlie's face lights up like a kid on Christmas morning, and I'm so giddy, I have to bite my lip to keep my smile an acceptable size.

"Hey, Jenna," Charlie says brightly.

"Hi, Charlie," I reply.

Then, without even thinking, I wrap my arms around him.

My body's betraying me again, but I don't care. Being this close to him feels even better than I imagined. He's much taller and bigger than I am, but the way our bodies mold together, it's like there's a Jenna-sized space between his arms where we fit like puzzle pieces. It settles my mind, and I feel present in a way I'm not used to.

I never felt like this with Scott. When we were in bed and he'd start kissing me, and unbuttoning my jeans, my thoughts would be everywhere *except* on him. I'd be making grocery lists in my mind, or thinking about backsplashes for the house we were flipping. But I never pressed my head against his chest and listened for his heartbeat the way I'm doing now with Charlie.

Even with Dex, I was always preoccupied, wondering how my body compared to the gorgeous models and actresses he'd been with. He gave me absolutely no reason to feel insecure, but I couldn't help worrying about the stretchmarks on my hips and the cellulite on my thighs. I mean, he dated Ava Elwood, the supermodel—quite possibly the most beautiful woman in the world. Even if her photos are airbrushed, she's still 5'11" with legs for days. I don't know her, of course, but from what I've seen in interviews, she seems really sweet, and down-to-earth, too.

And when Hunter and I—

Dammit. I should probably end this hug with Charlie before it gets weird.

But there's no sign that he's uncomfortable when I pull away. He just gives me his gorgeous, easy grin and says, "You look nice."

"Thanks," I say, returning his smile. I'm wearing high-waisted black shorts with a simple white crewneck. But Charlie isn't even looking at my outfit—or my body—when he compliments me. He's looking into my eyes.

"You ready to go?"

"Sure am," I say, slipping on my sandals.

"I was at the beach earlier this morning; the weather's great. I was thinking we could take our coffees to the lake, if you're up for a walk," he says with a sweet shrug.

I wonder if my eyes are lighting up. They feel like they are. "Walking and coffee are two of my favorite things," I tell him.

Charlie's already-rosy cheeks flush. "Then let's do it. I'm up for anything that makes you smile like that."

If only Christy could see me now. I *am* happy. For the time being, at least.

It's such a relief to be out of my head. I don't want to waste time worrying about my vow to keep things casual—and why this man I hardly know makes me want to break it. For once,

I'm too focused on being in the moment to question it.

We walk to a nearby Belgian bakery, where Charlie buys us two chocolate croissants to eat as we sip our iced lattes. "I have a sweet tooth," he admits as we start heading toward the lake. "It's why I had no choice but to become a runner."

I laugh. "Is that what you were doing at the beach this morning? Going for a run?"

"I was taking my cousin's yoga class. She became certified to teach a couple of weeks ago, and I wanted to support her."

"That's sweet," I say. "I love yoga. Was this your first time?"

He nods as he swallows a bite of croissant. "I enjoyed it a lot more than I thought I would. I'll definitely go again. You can join me sometime, if you like."

"I just might take you up on that," I tell him. Then my mind flies back to my phone call with Christy. I may not want to join Charlie for runs by the lake, but I would love someone to go to yoga with. Why not a *hot* someone with excellent taste in coffee and croissants?

Charlie slows his pace and turns to me, smiling. We've made it to the Lakefront Trail, where dozens of runners and bikers whiz past us, soaking up the last days of summer in Chicago.

But as the world moves around us, Charlie and I stand still in the golden glow of the morning sun. He lifts his hand to my face and places his thumb at the corner of my mouth. "You have a little chocolate…right here," he says, gently wiping it away.

"Thanks," I say. And this time, I'm not even embarrassed that I'm a mess. I'm full from breakfast, plus the croissant I inhaled, but I'd eat a second one without thinking twice if it meant he'd touch me like that again.

"Want to find somewhere to sit?" he asks.

I nod, so we cross the paved path and choose a spot at the water's edge that's furthest away from the crowd at Oak Street Beach. It's quiet and peaceful, with only the sound of the waves and the soothing warmth of Charlie's arm against mine.

"This coffee is delicious," I say after a sip. "And I'm a pretty tough critic. I started young."

He grins. "How young are we talking?"

"I had my first cup when I was fourteen," I tell him. "It was a big day for me, and not just because of the coffee. I kind of… ran away from home." But when Charlie's brow furrows with concern, I add, "For a few hours."

"I'm guessing everything turned out okay, since you're sitting next to me, smiling," he says, his beautiful long lashes framing his earnest eyes.

Normally when I go to the lake, I get lost in the colors of the sky and water. But not today. Today all I see is Charlie, and the way he looks at me.

"It ended up being one of the best days of my life. But it didn't start out that way. My parents were supposed to take me to the art museum in Cleveland. It's barely a twenty-minute drive from our house in Beachwood. My art teacher had mentioned a Picasso exhibit there, but I knew my parents wouldn't take me unless I told them it was mandatory for class." I pause and sigh. "My dad didn't support my dream of being an artist. That's putting it mildly."

Charlie nods, but there's something more than pity in his gaze.

"My dad feels the same way about my interest in photography."

I let out a wry laugh. "No wonder we're both dissatisfied with our careers."

He shakes his head with a deep inhale, as if to say, *Don't get me started.* Instead he settles his eyes on mine and asks, "So, did your dad back out?"

I nod. "I had a friend over the night before, and my dad brought up the 'mandatory' museum trip because he was so irritated by it, and my friend spilled the beans. I should have talked to her beforehand. My dad was so mad, he refused to take me. He insisted on us all going to the country club instead, so he could play golf with his pretentious colleagues."

"But you had other plans," Charlie guesses, an amused gleam in his eye.

"I looked like hell the next morning, because I'd been up crying half the night. My mom figured I was coming down with something…so I let her believe it. My family left me at home, took off for the country club, and within twenty minutes, I was in a cab on my way to the museum. I felt like Ferris Bueller," I say, grinning.

"I think I see where this is going," Charlie says with a knowing smile that almost moves me to tears. He's interested in my story. Interested in *me.* Sadly, this isn't a typical experience I have with men. If they're interested in anything at all, it's getting in my shorts. They certainly don't want to hear about my high school shenanigans.

But Charlie does. "You're at the art museum, and you run into your art teacher. Am I right?"

I nod, relishing in the look of satisfaction on his face. "Mrs. Swanson."

"Did you tell her why you were there alone?" he asks, his brow furrowed with belated concern for fourteen-year-old me. And it occurs to me, again, how safe I feel with Charlie. And how rare that is.

I sigh. "I was too embarrassed to admit that my parents chose a country club over me. So I told her they were home sick, and she took me under her wing. We walked through the entire museum together, discussing the different emotions each painting evoked. I felt so grown-up. She was my parents' age, but treated me like an equal, which is something that didn't happen at my house. And before we left, she took me to the café and bought me my first cup of coffee. Maybe it was because I'd had such a wonderful day, but it was love at first sip." I laugh. "I haven't been able to stop thinking about coffee ever since."

"I know the feeling," he replies, his dark eyes sending heat to my cheeks. Suddenly, I'm not sure if we're talking about coffee anymore.

"Want to tell me about your first time? Um—drinking coffee, that is," I add, fidgeting with the hem of my shirt.

Charlie smiles. "It was pretty memorable, too, although I was a little older. Coffee never interested me much in high school. Don't laugh—but I was really into chocolate milk."

"Your sweet tooth," I say matter-of-factly, like I've known him for years. The more time we spend together, the more it feels like I have.

"Exactly," he says, his cheeks now the rosiest I've seen them.

His skin is the most beautiful bronze color, mixed with the pink hue that deepens when he looks at me—and I have the sudden urge to paint him. His coffee-colored eyes make me feel as warm inside as my all-time favorite drink.

Charlie's so gorgeous, he takes my breath away.

"Maybe it's fitting that I had my first cup of coffee on the day I got into college. I really did feel like I became a man, that day." He chuckles. "I'd just found out I was going to follow in my father's footsteps and go to Dartmouth…and I knew he'd be proud."

This time, I nod with a knowing smile.

"So, I get my acceptance letter, and of course he's the first person I want to tell. But he was on a business trip and wouldn't be home until later that night. That's when I decided to pick him up from the airport. Which was basically pointless… because he had his own driver."

"A driver? That's fancy," I say before taking another sip of my iced latte.

Charlie laughs. "Yeah, I guess you could say that. My dad runs his own business, and he's pretty successful."

"Oh yeah?" I ask, intrigued. "What kind of business?"

"Have you heard of Sutton's? The—"

"Grocery store?"

Charlie nods. "That's the one."

"It's my favorite place to shop. Your dad *owns* Sutton's?" I ask, my eyes wide.

"Yep." He lets out a wry laugh, then puts his iced latte down on the pavement beside him. "I guess I didn't properly introduce myself," he says, extending his hand. "Charles Sutton."

"Jenna Andersen," I say. And when I put my hand in his, he holds it for several seconds, smoothing his thumb over my skin before he lets go, leaving the spot he touched warm and tingly.

"Thank you for your patronage, Jenna Andersen," he says with a wink that gives me butterflies.

Now blazing hot, I take another sip of my cool drink. "So, you decide to pick your dad up at the airport," I say, trying to steer my mind away from thoughts of bringing Charlie back to my apartment.

"Right. I couldn't wait to see the look on his face when he found out, so I called his driver and told him I'd pick Dad up myself," he continues. "Well, it turned out his flight got majorly delayed. I was waiting for him at the airport for three hours, and I'd been up late the night before studying for an exam. I didn't want to make my dad drive us home, because—"

"You were a man now," I finish for him.

"Exactly." He laughs. "So I bought myself a large cup of airport coffee. It was *awful*. Basically brown water. But when my dad finally arrived, and I told him the news..." Charlie sighs. "I'd never seen him so happy. He had tears in his eyes, and he's not an emotional guy. When we got in the car, I took another sip of that coffee and, let me tell you—it tasted pretty damn good."

I'm fighting the urge to reach for Charlie's hand when thunder cracks between us.

"Speak of the devil," he says, pulling his phone out of his pocket and frowning at the screen.

"Your dad?" I ask, perplexed. "I thought you only used that

ringtone for your boss."

He sighs. "My dad and my boss are one and the same. Unfortunately."

"Ah," I say, putting the pieces together. "Sounds complicated."

Charlie runs a hand over his short hair. "It is," he says, then pockets his phone.

I nod, sensing that he doesn't want to get into the details. "Want to keep walking?"

Charlie gets up and offers his hand to help me. I take it, and when we're both standing and facing each other, I keep my palm connected to his, waiting to see if he'll let go. He doesn't.

He steps closer to me, and I know he's searching my face for a sign.

He wants to kiss me. But he's not sure if I'm ready.

Neither am I.

I want him more than I've ever wanted anyone—that's not the problem.

The problem is, I think I could fall in love with this man. He sees me in a way no one else ever has. And when our eyes meet, we connect on a different plane. There's something so familiar and safe about him.

But when I moved to Chicago for another fresh start, falling in love wasn't part of the plan.

Neither was painting. I guess plans change.

I wasn't prepared for Charlie Sutton to come into my life, but here he is. And now I have a decision to make. Can I put my past behind me and finally move on?

I'm frozen, staring into his sexy, deep brown eyes, when

something—or someone—pushes me forward into his waiting arms.

"Oops! Sorry!" a runner yells as she continues past us down the trail. She's staring at her phone, and I suspect she accidentally elbowed me because she was distracted. If she'd pushed me any harder, Charlie could have fallen backward into the lake.

But he's standing steady, with his arms around my waist, just like I've craved. Maybe this runner gave me the nudge I needed.

I should thank her.

I tilt my head up, ready for my lips to meet Charlie's, when I feel something fall down the side of my neck.

"Oh no, my earring," I say with a frown when I check my lobes and notice one's missing. The clasp on the hoop must have opened when the runner bumped into me.

I glance down at the pavement, but don't immediately see it. I'd be so upset if I lost it. These earrings are the most expensive purchase I've made for something nonessential. They're two-carat diamond drop earrings I bought after I broke up with Scott. I figured they'd be the only diamonds I'd ever own.

I turn around to look behind me, but don't see anything there either. When I spin back to face Charlie, he's on one knee, carefully examining the ground. Then he looks up with a smile.

"Got it," he says.

But the sight of him kneeling with a sparkling diamond between his fingers sends shockwaves through me.

Hunter.

I'm in my college apartment. It's the night after we graduated. From outside the window, I hear a song…

"Can't Help Falling in Love."

My boyfriend of four years and his frat brothers are serenading me.

I run downstairs, and Hunter gives me the biggest bouquet of red roses I've ever seen. "A rose for every month I've known and loved you," he tells me, his ocean-blue eyes sparkling.

And then he gets down on his knee.

"Jenna? Are you okay?" Charlie stands, and I look at the earring in my hand.

I shake my head. "I'm sorry. I um—I just realized I have to go. I'm meeting with a client a few blocks west of here, and if I don't leave now, I'll be late."

It's a total lie of course.

But seeing Charlie on one knee, with a diamond in his hand, reminded me why I vowed never to love again.

It's not only to protect my heart. It's to protect his.

I had a wonderful man like Charlie once. And I'll never forgive myself for letting him down. Hunter Reed deserved so much better than me.

And so does Charlie Sutton.

"Oh," he says, nodding. "Yeah, of course. I don't want you to be late for your meeting."

He's so sweet, so polite, I almost can't tell he's disappointed. Almost.

"I had so much fun with you, I lost track of time," I say, because seeing him sad breaks my already-broken heart. And also because it's true.

"Me, too," he says with a nod.

"Thanks for the coffee and croissant." I give him a quick hug, because if I let him hold me longer, I'll change my mind.

And then I run away.

Just like I always do.

seven

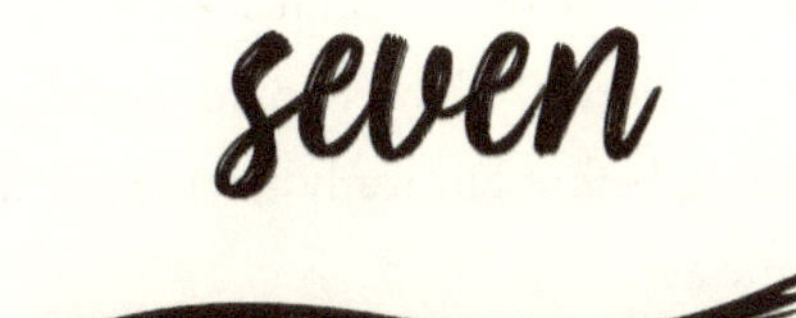

The next morning, I wake up early for a *real* client meeting. Not the fake one I made up to keep myself from kissing Charlie.

After I left him by the lake, I took a long walk and ended up in the River North Gallery District, which has the second-largest concentration of art galleries in the country, after Manhattan. As a designer, I bring my clients to these galleries all the time to help them choose pieces. But until yesterday, I'd never been on my own, just to browse. I thought it would feed my soul—but instead it left me feeling hungrier. Hungry to quit my design job. Hungry to make my own art and see it hanging on these walls. And let's face it…

Hungry for Charlie.

But I made my decision, and I'm sure he'll be much better off without me in his life. So instead of feeding my desire for Charlie Sutton, I stopped by his family's grocery store and tried to satisfy my hunger with a hundred dollars' worth of sweet and salty snacks. Not surprisingly, it only made me feel worse. I woke up this morning with a pounding head and heartburn on top of my heartache.

Which is why, as I stand outside the front door of the Gold Coast home my client inherited from her wealthy grandparents after they moved to Florida, I have to take several deep breaths and practice smiling before I'm ready to ring the doorbell. As soon as I do, Katie appears.

"Jenna, ohmygod, hi!" she squeals, hugging me and hopping up and down.

I'll give it my best shot, but I doubt I'll come close to matching her energy this morning. She's bouncy and bubbly, like I try to be most days. But, lately, it's getting harder for me to pretend.

Katie's twenty-two, recently graduated from college with a degree in filmmaking, and lives in one of the country's most affluent neighborhoods—in a converted building big enough to house two large families. Her style couldn't differ more from her grandmother's, who decorated mostly with florals and lace, so Katie hired me to help modernize her new home. We've been working together since I moved to Chicago two months ago, and today I'll be putting the finishing touches on the place with a shipment of art pieces that arrived over the weekend.

"Come on in," Katie says, grabbing my hand and pulling me into the first of two living rooms on the main floor. "Doesn't the house look amazing? I know we still have artwork to hang, but I'm already so happy with how everything came together."

I have to admit, the place looks stunning. I undoubtedly fulfilled Katie's wishes, with brighter colors, modern furniture that's stylish yet functional, and a remodeled kitchen with an extra-long island that will be perfect for entertaining. She wanted a home she could enjoy now, but also grow into—and she got it.

"So it turns out my family won't be able to visit me until Thanksgiving," she says with a frown. "But I was thinking of posting a video on my YouTube channel so they can see what a phenomenal job you did. I hate to ask…but do you think I could film you explaining your design process? I mean, no one watches my videos besides my family, so it doesn't have to be perfect or anything."

There's a look in Katie's eyes that I know all too well.

She's lonely.

Of course she's lonely, living by herself in this enormous house. In this big city, without her family. Square footage aside, I know how she feels.

I would have said yes to letting her film me regardless, but now I'm determined to stop feeling sorry for myself and help put the bounce back in Katie's step, by making a video both she and her family will love.

After we arrange her new artwork, Katie starts filming. She starts with some B-roll footage of the outside of the house, as well as every individual room, to establish the setting. When she's finished, we go to the kitchen, and she puts the camera on a tripod so she can film us chatting about her vision for the space.

Then, as we walk through each room, I talk about my creative process—which mostly entails learning about my clients' favorite things. They tell me about the music they listen to, their hobbies, their most beloved clothes and accessories, and I look for emerging themes. Then I start curating pieces that have a similar feel. In Katie's case, since she grew up near the ocean and gravitates toward blues and sea-greens, we chose accents in those colors. Her clothing style is minimalist—nothing too bold or busy—so I picked furniture to match that aesthetic. Finally, she loves yoga, so I designed the bathrooms to have a tranquil, spa-like feel, with orchids, wood accents, and a centerpiece bathtub surrounded by river rocks and greenery.

"Now tell everyone at home about the artwork we chose for the primary bedroom," Katie directs me from behind the camera.

"Well, since you shared with me that you're a big fan of Lola Piper, and your favorite album is *Nightfall*, we decided to go with a starry sky theme," I explain.

As I make my way around the room, Katie films me discussing the paintings—and now I don't have to work so hard to radiate joy. The smile on my face is real. "These watercolors in various shades of blue fit perfectly with your color scheme, and the muted tones provide the perfect calming atmosphere for a good night's sleep."

"Eek, that was perfect!" Katie exclaims when she turns off the camera. "Thanks so much, Jenna! My family is going to love this."

"It was my pleasure. And be sure to share the link to your video with me. I'd love to see the finished product," I tell her.

"That's sweet. I will," she replies with a thoughtful nod, before she hugs me.

The following evening, Katie shares her video with me over text, but I don't watch it right away, because I'm too busy deep-cleaning my apartment in an effort to keep myself from knocking on Charlie's door.

Every time my phone rings or chimes, I think it's him—which is unlikely, considering we never exchanged numbers.

Also, because I abandoned him by the lake.

If he were to Google me, he'd find my interior design website, and he could send me a message via my web form…but why would he want to do that? Even if he *had* been interested in me, I'm sure he moved on the second I rounded the Lakefront Trail and scurried out of sight.

Yet, I still find myself wondering what I'd say if he knocked on my door. The more I think about his sultry eyes, and the pillowy lips I almost kissed, the more I keep trying to convince myself that what I feel for Charlie is only lust. At least then, I could spend more time with him.

If I'm being honest, that's what I want more than anything. More time. Because our coffee date on Sunday was the most perfect date of my life. And here I am, two days later, missing him. *So much.*

It's totally normal to deeply miss someone you only have lustful feelings for, right?

After I finish scrubbing my kitchen tiles, I put myself to bed early and hope I'll wake up in a better state of mind. Luckily, all that grunt work exhausted me, and I sleep like a baby. But I'm still not prepared for what I wake up to the next morning.

When I check my cell phone, which I'd silenced before bed, I have eighteen missed calls…and thirty-seven text messages.

My first instinct is to worry that there's been a family emergency, but the missed calls aren't only from my parents and Christy. They're from Sunny, Vanessa, *Greg* (the guy I had that terrible date with), a dozen people I haven't spoken to since college or grad school—and my client, Katie. Why the heck are so many people from so many different chapters of my life calling me?

I chew on my bottom lip as I open my text messages. What I see makes me queasy.

You're internet famous! one of the messages says.

Holy shit, u went viral, reads another.

Omg you're a star!

And so on and so forth. Until:

I just watched your video!!!

My eyebrows draw together, wondering what video my friends and family could be talking about. I barely have a few seconds to wrack my brain before I receive another text—from Dex this time.

Call me.

My heart stops. Is this the moment I've feared? All these years I've worried about photos of me and Dex getting leaked…

Is it possible someone posted a video of us?

I mean, he did have security cameras all over his house. Not in his bedroom, of course. But there were certainly times when we—

Oh god.

Panic courses through me as I go back to the screen displaying my missed calls.

Sunny tried to reach me an hour ago. I can only imagine how she must be feeling, and the thought makes me ill.

Do I call her back first? Or should I talk to Dex?

I'm in the middle of an existential crisis when my phone rings again.

It's Christy.

"Hello?" I ask with a sinking feeling in my gut. If this *is* all about me and Dex—and what else could it be?—I have no idea how my sister will react. We *never* discuss our sex lives. As far as I know, she's only ever been with her boyfriend, Kyle. And while she knows that Dex and I hung out in high school, she has no idea we became involved again when I moved to LA. Well, not until today, anyway.

"Jenna! Finally! Where have you been? I've been calling you all morning!" she says, the urgency in her voice clear as day. "I'm so incredibly proud of you!"

She's *proud?* That I slept with a movie star and it's all over the Internet?

Hmm. I guess Christy's more progressive than I thought.

"You looked gorgeous," she goes on. "I mean, of course you did—you always do. Everyone's so excited!"

"Everyone's…what?" I stammer.

"Excited! Yeah, Mom already sent the video to her entire book club."

"Her…her…book club?" I ask, breaking into a sweat.

"And that says a lot, considering Mom's not easily enthused," Christy goes on, her tone gleeful.

My racing mind comes to a screeching halt. "Wait a minute— Mom *called* you?" A pang of jealousy hits my gut. Our mom never calls me.

"No, I called her," my sister corrects me, barely skipping a beat. "Oh, and Kyle enjoyed the video, too. He thought you had some great techniques and could teach me a thing or two."

My jaw drops. "Christy…you showed the video to your *boyfriend*?!"

She laughs. "Well, of course I did, silly! I'm going to show it to everyone I know! It's not every day your big sister goes viral for her design work."

Design work… Design work!

Oh my gosh, did Katie's video go viral?

As I'm putting the pieces of this puzzle together, my phone starts chiming again.

"Is that your cell?" Christy asks. "You must be getting so many messages."

"I really am. Can I call you back? I have a ton of voicemails to listen to."

"Of course!" Christy says brightly. "And congrats! I bet business is going to be booming for you after this!"

My gut clenches, and my first thought is, *God, I hope not.*

On the bright side, though, at least I'm not a porn star.

After I hang up with Christy, I open another new text from Dex:

We're so happy for you. Congrats! Getting on a flight, but I wanted to ask where you got the paintings for your client's bedroom. Sunny loves the starry sky theme for the nursery—thought I'd surprise her with them.

I breathe a giant sigh of relief, my heartrate slowing. A hint of a smile creeping onto my lips as I silently scold myself for being so paranoid.

Then I find Katie's message and click on the link to her video, to see what all this fuss is about.

It has one million views. And counting.

How did this happen?

Baffled, I start reading through the comments:

@gymtanlaundryxxx

Hey sis, you didn't tell me your interior designer was smokin' hot. Can I get her number?

@katiekins88

no

@gymtanlaundryxxx

Dude, I'm forwarding your video to my entire frat

@katiekins88

you're stupid

@robocox69

Wtf man, this is the girl of my wet dreams

@gymtanlaundryxxx

Told you

@chestercheetayayay

Yum. That's a playboy bunny right there

@tonymackeroni

Fuckkkkkk. Sending this to everyone I know

@brianfinch0043

Think those tits are real? They're so damn perfect

@katiekins88

would you buttholes get off my channel?

@robocox69

Oh, don't worry. I'm definitely gonna get off

I bury my head in my hands. Ugh—gross.

But once I get past the frat boys, the comments start to change. There are other designers admiring my work. Women saying they'd love to hire me. Old friends from high school, who brag about knowing me, and remember that I was a talented artist, even back then.

As I'm scrolling down the page, it occurs to me that I haven't watched the video yet, so I hit play. There I am, bouncy and bubbly, with my beige bodycon dress that leaves little to the imagination. I wore it to cheer myself up, because I was feeling so down about Charlie. I thought if I put on a killer dress, blew out my hair for more volume, and went for a little extra makeup (including the sexy, smoky eye I usually only wear on dates) it would improve my mood.

I never in a million years imagined I would go viral.

The moment I'm done watching the video, my phone rings

again.

It's Katie. When I answer the call, she's crying.

"Oh my gosh, Katie, are you okay?" I wonder if she's upset because it's her video, yet I'm the one getting all the attention. I wouldn't blame her. It would be like middle school birthday parties all over again, where the guys hovered around me, instead of the girl blowing out the candles.

"Ohmygod, ohmygod, ohmygod, Jenna," she says in between sobs. "Lola…Piper…tweeted…the link…to…my…video!"

Then she screams.

"Wait, are you kidding?" I ask, although I have a distinct feeling she's not.

Katie sniffles. "No, it's true! Lola said, and I quote, 'Love the *Nightfall* theme, Katie and Jenna! Xoxo.' Can you believe it? This is the best day of my entire life!"

Oh. My. God.

The rest of the week is chaos. My phone's ringing off the hook, I'm getting text messages from guys I haven't seen or spoken to in years, wanting to "meet up for coffee." I have dozens and dozens of requests from potential clients who want to book me. The designer of the bodycon dress I wore wants me to model for them at New York Fashion Week. And BuzzFeed calls me to get quotes for an article they're writing: "Bombshell Interior Designer is More Than Just Her Looks."

I should be happy. I'm being applauded for my talent for once (although it never would have happened if Katie's younger brother hadn't forwarded the video to every horny nineteen-year-old guy he knew). But instead, I feel more confused than ever. I have enough interest in my business to book myself through the end of the year and beyond, but the thought makes my stomach churn.

As a designer, I'm bound by my clients' preferences. I can be creative, but only within the confines of what *they* want. That's why painting feels so freeing to me. I guess it's no wonder I crave that freedom so much, since my dad took it away from me when I was little.

Thank goodness I have painting class today. I'm sure a few hours with a brush in my hand will help take my mind off this madness. While I do have all the art supplies I need at home now, I haven't started painting there yet, because I've been so distracted by my pinging phone—and thoughts of Charlie Sutton. I guess I shouldn't be surprised that he's the one person I haven't heard from this week.

"Hey, superstar!" Vanessa says with a beaming smile when she walks into class fifteen minutes late, after a busy day at work. We've talked and texted plenty since I blew up the Internet on Wednesday, but the last time I saw her was nearly a week ago, at Tati Marie's party.

I chuckle but roll my eyes. "I still can't believe this is happening."

"You know what?" Vanessa says as she pulls back her long braids and twists them into a bun. "I was so distracted by your sudden celebrity that I forgot to ask how your coffee date went last weekend."

I sigh—heavily.

Vanessa cringes. "That bad, huh?"

"Not bad at all." I shake my head. "It was amazing, actually."

"So, why the sad face?"

"Because...I freaked out." I put down my paintbrush and turn toward her. "Charlie's the type of guy I could see myself in a serious relationship with. But, that's not what I'm looking for." When Vanessa gives me a disbelieving look, I add, "Right now," to appease her.

"Even *if* that were true, I think you're getting ahead of yourself, Jenna. I mean, you just met this man, and you've only been on one date. Is it possible you're projecting?"

I laugh as I pick up my paintbrush again. "Spoken like a true therapist." Vanessa has a master's in social work, and provided therapy at a counseling center in New York before she took on her role at the refugee resettlement agency.

Vanessa chuckles. "It's hard to turn off, sometimes. All I'm saying is, maybe you've built this guy up in your head, without getting to really know him first. You said he's hot, right?"

If I hadn't already finished my self-portrait, I'd need a lot of pink for my cheeks right now. "He's the most gorgeous man I've ever seen."

She nods. "Well, that explains it. You're blinded by his looks. You see this guy who's perfect on the outside, and you assume he must be perfect on the inside, too."

I perk up and have to fight off a giddy grin. "So you think I should go out with him again? Get to know him better?"

Maybe my friend is right. If Charlie isn't as perfect as I imagine, I might be able to keep things casual with him after all.

Vanessa shrugs. "Couldn't hurt, could it?"

eight

The following morning, I jump out of bed as soon as my eyes blink open. I shower, get dressed, and make myself some eggs with multigrain toast. And coffee, of course.

I wait until ten on the dot, then toss my phone and keys into my purse so I can go out into the hall and knock on Charlie's door.

He doesn't know I'm coming, and I have no idea if he'll be there.

He may even have a woman over, for all I know. It's a Saturday morning, after all. What if he met someone last night and brought her home? It's entirely possible.

But now that Vanessa's helped me put my longing for Charlie in perspective, I'm so eager to spend more time with him that I'm apparently willing to risk total humiliation. It's been six agonizing days since I saw him last Sunday, and I can't wait another minute.

When I swing open my door, though, it's like a scene from one of my favorite movies. Because guess who's standing there?

That's right. Charlie.

He's a foot away from me, his arm raised, about to knock.

"Oh," I say with a giant smile. "Charlie…hi."

"Hey, Jenna," he says, giving a relieved grin as he slides his hands into his pockets.

I laugh. "Would you believe it if I told you I was on my way to knock on your door?"

"Really?" His eyes crinkle at the corners, and he does nothing to hide the joy on his face.

It melts me. Charlie Sutton wears his heart on his sleeve, and I love that about him.

No—I *lust* that about him.

That's all this is. Lust.

"I wanted to apologize for having to rush off last Sunday," I say. "I was going to stop by your place earlier in the week, but then—"

"You became famous?" he says with a chuckle.

"You saw the video?" I wonder if he read the frat boys' comments too.

"I follow Lola Piper on Twitter." He runs a thumb over his chin. "And yes, I'm secure enough in my masculinity to admit I'm a fan."

God help me. I'm trying to see Charlie as less than perfect, but he isn't making this easy.

"That's why I stopped by," he continues. "To make sure you're okay with all the attention. I'm not sure I would be. I mean, I don't even have a Facebook account, because it feels invasive to me."

"So, that explains why I couldn't find you. I was going to send you a friend request," I admit with a coy smile.

"Well, consider it accepted." Charlie's cheeks get rosier. "Yeah, I prefer to keep my life offline…but I'm a pretty private person, so maybe I'm in the minority. Still, I imagine it's not easy knowing the entire Internet is talking about you, no matter what they're saying."

I guess he did read the comments. The good, the cringey, and everything in between.

I nod. "Thanks. It's been overwhelming, to say the least." And then I take a step closer to him, wrap my arms around his neck, and hug him. He pulls his hands out of his pockets and holds me, his palms warming my skin through the thin fabric of my t-shirt. I take a deep breath and let myself relax into the space over his heart that feels like it was made just for me.

To lust over.

When we pull apart, Charlie looks down at his shoes before his gaze lands on mine. "There's a photography exhibit at the Museum of Contemporary Art that's been getting a lot of buzz. I was on my way to see it. Would you, um, like to join me—?"

"Yes," I say, the happiest I've been all week. "I would love that."

Charlie and I walk around the museum for hours. We stroll through the photography exhibit, stopping for minutes at a time to admire the artwork, and he tells me everything he knows about light, and color balance, and composition. He learned some basics from a class he took as an elective at Dartmouth years ago, but most of it he picked up on his own, from books, or blogs, or experimenting with his camera. I hang on his every word—not only because there are parallels to painting I find really interesting, but because the passionate way he talks about art is so unbelievably sexy, I can hardly take my eyes off him.

After we've seen every photo on display, we tour the other exhibits, and I tell him what I know about painting. We talk about how the artwork makes us feel, and it reminds me of the day I spent at the Cleveland Museum of Art with Mrs. Swanson. A day that solidified my love of art, and quite possibly changed the course of my life.

Will today be a day like that, too?

Every time Charlie and I find a piece that's so abstract we have no idea what we're looking at, we take turns making up wild theories about it. It's the most fun I've had in as long as I can remember. There's one painting in particular that has us laughing so hard, one of the guards shushes us. Twice.

Careful not to get us kicked out of the museum, Charlie whispers his final interpretation in my ear. "Maybe it's a man locked out of his apartment…and the incredible woman who rescues him."

When I turn to him and smile, he winks at me, then moves on to the next wall full of artwork. I hang back for a few seconds to take one last look at the minimalist painting. A few minutes ago, all I saw were two circles—one dark brown, one olive green—and a scribble of what looks like black permanent marker between them. But now I can see us there, too. Brown-eyed Charlie, green-eyed Jenna, and the spark between us drawn in with a Sharpie.

Finally, after hours on our feet, Charlie and I sit in the Commons, a beautiful community space on the second floor, and we continue our conversation. There's never a lull, never an awkward silence.

Until his dad texts him.

Charlie still hasn't changed his ringtone, but I've heard the thunderclap enough times that it doesn't startle me anymore. As he reads the message, his forehead creases, and when he's done, he pinches the bridge of his nose, squeezing his eyes shut.

"Everything okay?"

"Not really…to be honest." He runs a hand over his hair, then looks at me like he's debating whether or not to pour his heart out. It doesn't take him long to decide.

"You know the reason I wanted to work for Sutton's?" he says. "It's because my dad was always so busy when I was a kid, I figured the only way I'd ever spend time with the man was if I worked for him. So after getting my MBA, I moved back to Denver, where Sutton's is headquartered, and my dad made me the regional VP. I rented an apartment about a mile away from where my parents live, and I figured I'd buy my own home there, eventually."

He lets out a wry laugh. "But I did so well that, the next year, my dad moved me to Atlanta to train *their* regional VP. Then he sent me to Houston, and—I guess you see where this is going. Working for Sutton's was never my dream, but I thought the sacrifice would be worth it if it brought me and my dad closer. But I haven't lived in Denver in nine years, and I hardly ever see him. All I get are these damn texts every hour. And I'm so tired of him moving me around the country on a whim, like I'm a pawn on his chessboard."

I feel awful for Charlie. From the way his eyes are glistening, it's clear how much he's hurting.

"I'm so sorry," I say with a frown. "Are you thinking of quitting?"

He lets out a deep sigh. "A buddy of mine from college is a travel journalist, and he's writing a guide for Italy. He remembered my dream of being a travel photographer, so he called me up last week and asked if there was any chance I'd take the job. It won't be until next summer, so I have some time to think about it…but I have to admit, I'm tempted. I mean, who wouldn't want to spend an entire summer touring Italy and taking pictures?"

"Sounds like a dream," I say. "I've always wanted to go to Italy. The art museums alone put it at the top of my list—and it's a long list."

"Is that right?"

"I've never been anywhere outside the country," I explain. "My dad is a high school dean, but the way he spends his salary, you'd think he's a neurosurgeon, or something. All so he doesn't have to feel self-conscious when he's playing golf with the Beachwood elite. That's why we never traveled much—there wasn't enough left in the budget for it. I know I could always go now, but…"

"What?" Charlie asks when I hesitate.

I bite my lip. "It's embarrassing."

Charlie smiles and looks down at his shoes, then back at me. "I just told you about my daddy issues. If anyone should feel embarrassed, it's me."

I laugh. "You have nothing to be embarrassed about—and I guess I shouldn't either. It's just that, Europe seems like such a magical place…I'd rather experience it with someone special than go alone."

Charlie takes my hand in his, and pauses for a moment. Then he says, "It is magical. And I hope I get to experience it with someone special someday, too."

I watch as he rubs his thumb in circles over my skin, and I wonder if he notices when I inch closer to him on the bench.

I guess he does, because he puts his arm around me. And before I know it, my head has gravitated toward his shoulder, and I feel nothing but calm and happy resting there. It's like we're a couple who's been together forever. Sitting on our favorite bench at the art museum, like we do every Saturday morning.

"How would your dad take it if you quit?" I ask after a minute of comfortable silence. "Not well, I'm guessing?"

I'm still leaning on Charlie, but I feel him sigh beneath me. "I don't know if he'd ever speak to me again."

Now I turn to look up at him. "Are you serious?"

He shrugs a shoulder. "My sisters think he'll come around, eventually. They're not close with him either, but all three of them are married with kids, and have their own families to worry about. Plus, I don't think they ever cared about my dad's approval the way I did. The way I do—I should say."

When Charlie mentions his sisters, I find myself wondering if he wants kids. Now's not the time to ask, of course. If we keep hanging out, though, I'll have to tell him that I don't. And after what happened with Hunter, I dread that conversation more than anything.

But that's not important right now. "You're his only son," I say to Charlie. "It makes sense that you crave that closeness with your dad."

He gives me a wistful smile and, for the first time in my life, I consider myself lucky that I gave up on my dad's approval long ago. Like Charlie's sisters did.

"Well, enough about my dad—for now, anyway," he says with a chuckle. "How's your painting going? Are you putting those art supplies to good use?"

I wince. "I haven't started yet."

"Well, it's been a busy week for you."

I smirk. "You can say that again. I want to paint, but I've been too distracted."

"Maybe you'll feel inspired today," he says.

I know he's referring to the perfect morning we spent admiring art—but it's the way he looks at me like I'm the most interesting person in the room that inspires me.

"I already do."

We stroll back home hand-in-hand. When the elevator opens to the twentieth floor, he walks me to my front door and turns to me.

Whichever part of my brain is responsible for racing thoughts has gone radio silent. There's no pleading voice begging me to run away this time.

Charlie puts his hands on my waist. His eyes are asking me the same question they asked by the lake last Sunday. *Can I kiss you?*

I don't think—I just nod.

He cups my cheek with one warm palm as the other travels to the small of my back, pressing me closer to him. I place my hands on his broad shoulders, and he lowers his forehead to mine. A simple gesture that might go unnoticed by some—but not me.

It's been forever since a man has touched me like this. So tenderly and sweetly.

I close my eyes, smiling, and when Charlie finally kisses me, I levitate off the ground. That's what it feels like, at least. My body is light as a feather, and I float away from my heartbreak, to a place where my wishes come true. Where the sketches in my journal become real.

His pillowy lips are even softer than I imagined. I sigh a little into his mouth, and our tongues touch the slightest bit. He tastes like coffee and mint. It's the best kiss I've ever had. Something tells me I'll never be the same.

Something tells me I'm in love with him.

But how can I be in love with someone I've known for a week, and have only been out with twice? Even with Hunter, it didn't happen this fast.

And I was sure Hunter Reed was the love of my life.

The thought breaks whatever spell I was under, and my fairytale is over before it starts. The urge to run overtakes me again, like Cinderella fleeing the ball at midnight so Prince Charming can't discover who she really is.

When I step back from Charlie, I'm so lightheaded, I have to brace myself against the doorframe. "Oh my gosh," I say, lifting my fingers to my lips.

"I know," Charlie says, sounding equally stunned.

Vanessa was wrong—I wasn't projecting. I knew Charlie was special the moment I laid eyes on him. And I never should have agreed to another date. Now I'm in over my head.

"Charlie," I begin. "I…I'm not, um…"

I'm not looking for anything serious.

I've said the words so many times, this should be second nature. But it's like I've forgotten how to speak. So I stand there, trying not to cry.

Charlie steps toward me and takes my hand, looking at our intertwined fingers before his gaze meets mine again.

"Jenna, this can be whatever you need it to be," he says, softly. "No pressure. I've jumped into relationships before I was ready, and I don't want to make that same mistake again."

It's like he's reading my mind. He can see right through me, as though I were made of glass—like Cinderella's slipper. He knows I'm a flight risk.

I choke back a sob. "Really? Are you sure?"

He nods, his lips curved into an earnest smile. "I will take whatever you're able to give, if it means I get to spend more time with you."

I'm so relieved, I let out a little laugh through my tears.

Then, like a true prince, he kisses my hand and wishes me goodnight.

nine

When I walk into my apartment, I can still feel the warmth of Charlie's lips on the skin right above my knuckles. I ignore my plans to catch up on the hundreds of email inquiries sitting unread in my inbox—something that's been hanging over my head since I went viral. I'll never be able to focus on work after that incredible second date with Charlie. There's only one thing in the entire world I want to do right now. And that's paint.

I run into my guest room, now a makeshift art studio, and throw on a smock. My fingers are trembling with excitement as I mix colors on my palette. As soon as I'm finished, I start painting. My hand flies across the canvas with a mind of its own, vibrating from the spark of Charlie's kiss. Before I know it, an image begins to take shape. Rosy cheeks, tanned skin. Chestnut-colored hair, with a bit of lighter hazelnut mixed in. Dark brown eyes, framed by gorgeous long lashes.

Charlie.

When I step back to look at the finished product, hours after the sun has set, my heart flutters. It's like I'm back in the hallway with him again. He knew exactly what to say to put a smile on my face: "This can be anything you need it to be."

If it were any other guy saying those words, I'd feel relieved. I could keep things uncommitted and uncomplicated. But the problem is, for the first time in years, I don't want a casual relationship.

I want this to be what my gut tells me it is. The love story I've waited for my entire life. The one I drew in my high school journal. The one I gave up on because I didn't think I deserved it anymore.

Because I felt guilty. I still do.

I think back to the day I left Christy and Kyle's Manhattan apartment, after recuperating from something I'm sure Kyle has since deemed a "depressive episode." Finally, after six long months under their watchful eyes, I felt well enough to go through with the plan I'd made before I graduated from my architecture program. I was going to move to Pittsburgh and start flipping houses there. But I could tell from Christy's frown when I said goodbye that she was still worried about me.

"Jenna, I'm so glad you're doing better, but…" She paused to clear her throat. "I'm afraid what happened with Hunter will keep coming back to haunt you, if you don't go to therapy. I mean, it's been three years, and look how it's affecting you."

I rolled my eyes. "Christy, I spent the last three years earning a master's degree—which I imagine is still pretty damn hard, even when you don't have dyslexia. Of course I fell apart after graduation! I couldn't afford to break down before, without worrying about falling behind in my classes. And this wasn't only about Hunter. It was about Alex, too. If a guy you were dating sent a picture of you naked in bed to all his friends, wouldn't you be upset?"

My sister nodded, her forehead still creased.

"Yes, I was a mess, but I got it out of my system," I told her. "That's what counts. And I guarantee you, I am fine now."

But I wasn't fine. I was convinced I'd ruined Hunter's life. Every morning, when I woke up, the first thing on my mind was that look of utter disappointment in his ocean-blue eyes. I believed *I* was the bad guy. I couldn't tell Christy that, though.

Maybe she was right about me needing therapy. It's been five years since we had that conversation, and I can't say I'm any better off.

Especially now that I've met Charlie. As much as I want to believe we're meant for each other, I've seen enough romantic comedies and read enough fairytales to know that the bad guy doesn't get a happily-ever-after.

By the time I clean my paintbrushes and lay them flat to dry, it's nearly 10:00 p.m. I'm ravenous, so I whip up a late-night dinner of blueberry pancakes, using my favorite boxed mix from Sutton's. I crack a smile, thinking that it's almost like Charlie made them for me himself. Then I frown, wondering if I even deserve that.

My ambivalence is killing me. But at least the pancakes are delicious. I'm finishing the last fluffy bites, dipped in Sutton's golden maple syrup, when I hear a rustling sound coming from the foyer. Sometimes the building's maintenance staff slips notes under residents' doors to advise us of water shut-offs or repairs that need to be made, so I don't think much of it. I rinse my plate, put it in the dishwasher along with my utensils, then head to the front door.

But there's no note from maintenance on white letter paper. Instead, I see what looks like a postcard. I bend down to pick it up, and my heart skips a beat. It's a photograph of the abstract painting that Charlie and I spent nearly thirty minutes trying to interpret this afternoon. A painting titled simply, *Abstract No. 3*—but which I will forever think of as *Brown-Eyed Charlie and Green-Eyed Jenna.*

A huge grin blooms on my face. As I examine the photograph more closely, I notice the handful of museum-goers standing in front of the painting. An elderly gentleman with a cane. A woman carrying a sleeping toddler. A couple holding hands.

And me.

Charlie must have snapped this before I joined him over at the next wall. All that's visible is my profile, but I'm smiling so wide in the picture, you'd think I was seeing my own painting on display at the Museum of Contemporary Art.

I flip over the photo and see a note from Charlie on the back:

Jenna,

I took this picture so I'll always remember laughing with you over this painting. It was a great moment, and I feel lucky to have shared it with you. I got even luckier when I captured this expression of sheer joy on your face. Your passion for art inspires me.

I was going to text this to you, then realized we haven't exchanged numbers. So here's mine, for the next time you want to hang out—or if you ever get locked out of your apartment, and need me to return the favor.

He signed it *Charlie* in beautiful cursive, followed by his phone number underneath.

I turn the photo over again to examine my happy face. I may not have realized it then, but I know now that it wasn't only the art that made me so ecstatic. It was Charlie's sweet interpretation of the painting—and the fact that, of all our interactions, he chose to reference the one time I helped him, instead of the other way around.

I was starting to feel like a damsel in distress, the way Charlie wiped my tears with his sleeve when we first met and picked up my scattered art supplies after I'd dropped them. Not to mention, the time he got on his hands and knees to find my diamond earring on the Lakefront Trail.

But Charlie Sutton doesn't see me as a hapless victim.

He sees me as a heroine.

And as I sit here, staring at Charlie's number on the back of this perfect photo that he printed for me, I'm more conflicted than ever.

For one thing, I was kinda happy *not* to have his phone

number, because that meant not having to worry about texting him misspelled words. Something tells me, though, that, unlike Greg, Charlie wouldn't jump to the conclusion that I'm an idiot. And while I typically don't talk about my dyslexia with the men I date—for fear of reinforcing the "dumb blonde" stereotype— the idea of telling Charlie doesn't bother me at all. I'm already so comfortable with him.

But if I were to call or text him right now, what would I say? He put the ball in my court, and I have a decision to make.

It's late. I guess I'll sleep on it and decide tomorrow.

When I wake up the next morning, however, I'm distracted by another wave of design inquiry messages sent via the contact form on my website.

I let out a giant exhale. *Great.*

Since I went viral earlier this week, I've only booked one new client. I told the others I'd be happy to put their names on a waitlist, which I hoped would buy me some time to decide if I want to go full steam ahead with this design business. I have a considerable amount of money saved from both my house- flipping sales and design work. I learned from my dad's reckless spending habits what *not* to do with my earnings and, instead, I invested wisely. If I wanted to quit my design job and try my hand at being a painter for a year or two, I could easily do it.

But still, there's this nagging voice in my head. No, not my dad's. Like I said, I gave up on his approval a long time ago. It's my own voice, telling me that the only way I'll ever be taken seriously is if I'm a successful businesswoman.

Now that I've gone viral for my work, what will people think if

I throw it all away just to paint? Will they say I'm too dyslexic and dumb to do anything else? Will I become the laughingstock of the Internet, like I was the laughingstock of my elementary school?

With a pit of dread in my stomach, I open one of the messages that came through only a few minutes ago, the subject line of which reads, *Time-sensitive Request*:

Hello, Jenna. This is Genevieve Grant, reaching out on behalf of my client, R.J. Miller. Mr. Miller re-located to Chicago recently and would like to hire you to assist with the interior design of his penthouse. Due to his busy schedule, he would prefer to meet today at noon. Please let me know if that works. You can reach me via email or on my cell phone.

It's an unusual inquiry, considering it's ten o'clock on a Sunday morning, and whoever this R.J. Miller is wants to meet almost immediately. I do a quick Google search on him, but come up empty. I have to admit, I'm intrigued. And it's not like I have anything better to do. If I stayed home, I'd probably spend the entire day stressing about my feelings for Charlie.

So I call Genevieve Grant and let her know I'm available. She gives me an address that's only two blocks away from me. Then I shower, get dressed and, at ten to noon, I walk over to R.J. Miller's place.

But as the elevator opens to the penthouse, my jaw drops in stunned silence when I see the all-too-familiar face of the man waiting on the other side of the sliding doors.

He looks just like he did when I last saw him. Except, this time, his ocean-blue eyes are smiling at me.

ten

"You're not R.J. Miller," I stammer.

I'm stating the obvious. But I'm so shocked, they're the only words that come to mind.

He laughs. It's the same throaty laugh I remember from years ago. "I'm sorry for catching you off guard with the fake name. I just figured if you knew it was me, well—you probably wouldn't have come."

"What are you doing in Chicago?" I ask, bewildered.

"I'm here for work," he says. "Indefinitely."

Part of me is tempted to turn around and take the elevator back downstairs.

But it's the other part of me—the curious part—that wins.

"Let me get you something to drink," he says. "Coffee? Tea? Juice? You name it, I've probably got it."

"Coffee's fine," I say, a bit curtly. Well, curtly for me, anyway. So I follow it up with a softer, "Thanks," because I don't want to seem ungrateful. What happened between us is ancient history. I need to stop dwelling on the past and focus on the present instead.

I follow him as he makes his way to the kitchen. It's only the two of us in an expansive urban palace, with floor to ceiling windows and a panoramic view of the city. It takes my breath away.

"Cream and sugar?" he asks.

"Just a splash of almond milk, if you have it."

He nods. As he tinkers with his state-of-the-art coffee maker, I stand at one of the many windows and admire the lake, which is speckled with sailboats on this warm summer day.

When he's done making my coffee, he hands me a steaming hot cup and stands beside me at the windows. I thank him, still in complete shock that I'm in the presence of this man I thought I'd never see again. At least not in person, anyway.

He's a movie star, after all. His face is everywhere. Even up close, he's picture perfect, with that chiseled jaw and jet-black hair—and the ocean-blue eyes that remind me so much of Hunter Reed's.

His name is Grady Brooks. He's a megastar on par with Dex—although neither actor would appreciate the comparison. According to the media, they have a longstanding rivalry that started early in their careers. They rose to fame around the same time; they were both young and incredibly hot; and they went up against each other for a lot of the same roles. Eventually, Dex was branded as Hollywood's hero, while Grady took the title of quintessential bad boy. You'd think the tension between the two would have ended there, since they weren't vying for the same parts anymore. But as far as I know, Dex and Grady are still more frenemies than friends.

"You look good, Jenna," Grady says, eyeing me up and down. "Haven't changed a bit since the last time I saw you."

"The *only* time you saw me," I remind him. Grady and I met just once, about three years ago, at a small gathering Dex offered to bring me to, because we'd been hanging out when he got the invitation. There were only ten or eleven people there—all A-list celebrities, except for me. I felt like I was dreaming, especially when Grady Brooks started hitting on me.

"You made quite an impression," he says, fixing me with his smoldering eyes. The ocean-blue eyes that are so similar to Hunter's, I have to work hard not to succumb to the shame and guilt that are always bubbling beneath the surface, threatening to drown me. Especially these days, since I met Charlie, and wish more than anything that I could wipe the slate clean to let myself love him.

But thinking about the mess I'm in will do me no good now. I need to keep my wits about me. I'm not sure what Grady wants from me, but I'd be shocked if it were interior design.

"You made quite the first impression, too," I tell him with a wry smile. "I guess you already know that, considering you used a pseudonym to lure me here."

He laughs in the lighthearted way that only an obscenely rich, gorgeous Hollywood bad boy would deem appropriate under the circumstances. "Touché," he says.

When I roll my eyes and take a sip of coffee, though, his movie star grin fades. "Look, I'm sorry if I was out of line that night. You told me you and Dex weren't a couple, so I figured you were giving me the green light to ask you out."

"You did *not* ask me out, Grady. You told me you wanted to…um…" My cheeks burn as I look down at the floor.

"Fuck you," he says without any hint of embarrassment in his voice. "Yes, I remember. You ignored me the rest of the evening. I was heartbroken."

"Yeah, I could tell from the way you kept looking at me with those sad puppy dog eyes. I guess that usually works for you, huh," I say, turning back to see an amused look on his face.

"Hey, let's not forget, you're the one who gave me your number," he says, playfully. "Can you blame me for thinking you were interested?"

I scoff. "I gave you my number *before* you propositioned me… and only because you said you might need an interior designer. Had I known you were going to use it to send me dirty texts about all the things you wanted to do to me—"

"I was drunk." For the first time, I see an expression that resembles sheepishness on his face. "I'm sorry."

"Grady, it wasn't only one time. You texted me for months. I had to block you."

He lets out a breathy exhale. "Look, I'm not being glib. I actually was drunk most of that time. I had a drinking problem, Jenna."

I'm quiet for several seconds. "Oh," I finally say.

"I try to laugh it off, but it almost killed my career," he goes on. "It ruined most of my personal relationships. I had a lot of amends to make while I was in rehab. I should've reached out to you, too." He sighs. "I'm really sorry."

There's something different about his face now. A pretense

that's melted away. In his eyes, I see genuine pain.

"Okay. I accept your apology," I say, quietly. "So, um…you're doing better now?"

He smiles, then pulls a bronze medallion out of his pocket. "One year sober."

"Congratulations," I reply with a sincere grin that matches his.

I have another sip of coffee, then take my gaze around his penthouse—or as much as I can see of it from where I'm standing. It looks like something you'd find in the city issue of *House & Garden* magazine. Open and spacious. Simple, yet stunning in its contrast of textures. The combination of supple leather sofas with natural wood tables and glass pendant lighting is undeniably alluring. There's even an impressive collection of modern art pieces that experiment with color and form. I guess that's not surprising. Like Grady Brooks himself, the paintings on his walls don't play by the rules.

"So, why am I really here?" I ask him. "This place is gorgeous. I have a hard time believing you need an interior designer."

After a deep sigh, he explains. "I fired the last designer because she was trying to gouge me. I know tons of celebrities who sign off on their bills without even looking at them—but I grew up poor, so that shit won't work on me." He shakes his head. "Anyway, she was nearly done with everything, but one of the guest rooms never got finished. I saw that tweet from Lola about your design work—"

"Ah yes, Lola," I say casually, as though the popstar were also a good friend of mine.

"And when I looked you up online and saw that you were

in Chicago, I thought to myself—here's someone I can trust," Grady continues. "I mean, you've been friends with Dex for a long time, so you don't seem like the type to take advantage of someone's fame."

"Of course not," I say.

I bite my lip, tempted to ask about his relationship with my famous friend. I never told Dex about my conversation with Grady at the party, but I guess I didn't need to. When we were on our way back to his place that night, I remember Dex saying something along the lines of, "I know we're not committed, and it's none of my business who you date, but trust me—you can do a lot better than Grady Brooks."

At least I think that's what he said. I was pretty tipsy. Regardless, I didn't ask Dex to elaborate, because it was obvious to me, even from our limited interaction, that Grady was no gentleman.

But now I know Grady had a drinking problem. I wonder if that also explains the bad blood between him and Dex. Although I'm curious, I decide against bringing up the rivalry between them. It probably makes more sense for me to call Dex later and ask him. At least I know he'll be honest, because he isn't trying to get in my pants.

I'm not sure I can say the same about Grady.

It's no secret he's attracted to me. I'm sure many women would kill to be in my shoes right now. To have *the* Grady Brooks standing less than a foot away, gazing at them longingly.

But it only makes me long for Charlie, and the warmth and safety of his arms around me. I miss him.

"So, whaddya say?" Grady asks. "Want to check out that guest room, and tell me what you think?"

"I can take a look." No harm in that, I guess.

He leads me down two very long hallways, and I admire the beautiful artwork on the walls as we walk. Whoever the last designer was, I have to admit she did an amazing job. Too bad she wasn't trustworthy.

The room is pretty bare, with only a bed, nightstand, and dresser. I ask Grady to show me the four other guest rooms for comparison, and he does.

"I'm guessing you want to maintain a similar aesthetic for the final room?" I ask him afterward, as we walk back into the living space.

He stops and turns to me. "I want you to do what you do. You know—that process you talked about in the video. I want you to get to know me."

I laugh, raising my eyebrows. "I see."

"Come back for dinner tonight," he says. "We'll have a nice meal, you can ask me your questions, and we'll call it a day. Like I told you, Jenna, I've changed. I'm not trying to sleep with you, I promise. Unless *you* wanted to, of course—"

"I don't," I say decisively.

"Understood," he replies with the kind of amused grin that tells me it's no skin off his back if I don't have sex with him. He's Grady Brooks, he's obviously not short on options.

"So, why dinner? We could sit and chat now, and I could have a proposal for you by the end of the day."

He shrugs. "Everyone's gotta eat, right? Besides, I'm a good cook. Before I made it big, I was a sous-chef in Manhattan, at Le Bernardin."

"Impressive," I say, despite myself.

"See, there's a lot you don't know about me, Jenna. I'm aware that the media makes me out to be this complete asshole, but that's just branding. It's the image my publicists decided on a decade ago, to differentiate me from your friend, Dex. It's all Hollywood bullshit."

I raise a skeptical eyebrow again.

"Give me one chance to make a better first impression than I did in LA," he says. "Consider this my way of making amends. I'll make your favorite dinner. And hey, who knows, maybe we'll end up being friends."

"You want to be friends with me?" I cross my arms, unconvinced.

He shrugs. "I mean, you're friends with Dex...so, why not me? I'll be here awhile, filming a new HBO series, and I barely know anyone in Chicago."

I nod. "I can sorta relate."

"Alright, then it's settled," Grady says, running a hand through his jet-black hair. "What do you want me to cook for you?"

I bite my lip. Grady's already a step ahead, while I'm still deciding if I want to take him up on his offer. He assumes he'll get his way...and I'm sure he does, most of the time. He's so damn good-looking, and boy does he know it. Ugh.

There's no such thing as quiet confidence where Grady Brooks is concerned.

But if I judge him by his appearance, I'm no better than the strangers I meet who automatically peg me as an airhead. Just because he oozes charm and swagger from every pore on his perfect, built-like-a-linebacker body doesn't mean I shouldn't give him a second chance.

Besides, it doesn't make a huge difference whether I stay here to work with him now, or come back to ask my questions over dinner later. Either way, it's work—not a date. Plus, I do believe he's changed. Grady was definitely drunk the night I met him at that party. But he's been sober a year, and I don't want to brush off the progress he's made.

And a gourmet meal prepared by a former sous-chef at one of the best restaurants in the world? That's pretty hard to say no to. I went to Le Bernardin once, to celebrate Christy and Kyle's college graduation. It was one of the best meals of my life.

"I love seafood," I tell him. "I'll have whatever your specialty is. Surprise me."

"Done," he says with a wink.

I'm feeling pretty good about my decision until I walk through the door to my apartment, and see the photo and note from Charlie sitting on my front hall table.

I'd much rather be having dinner with him tonight. Talk about quiet confidence. The fact that Charlie is as gorgeous as any movie star, but doesn't flaunt it, makes him infinitely sexier than Grady Brooks.

Maybe I should call Grady and tell him I'll meet him in the morning.

Damnit. Here I go again.

It's so incredibly hard for me to trust men. After Alex taking that nude picture of me in grad school, and Scott going back and forth about wanting kids, and nearly every guy I meet only wanting me for one damn thing, I can't help but question most men's intentions.

But I need to get out of my own way. Doing design work for Grady could change my entire career. The buzz I've gotten from Lola Piper's tweet has been great—but I'm squandering a lot of opportunities if I don't pick up new clients from it. Especially A-list celebrity clients. I planned to offer my design services to Sunny and Dex as a wedding gift, until I found out Dex's cousin's wife is also an interior designer, and she beat me to it. Now she's the most sought-after designer in Ohio.

No designer in their right mind would waste an opportunity like this. If I give up this chance with Grady, I might as well give up my design business. And as much as I'm questioning my career path these days, I'm still not convinced I want to jump ship just to paint. It would be a terrible waste of my master's degree.

Wouldn't it?

At the very least, I should follow through with this dinner before I make any life-altering career decisions.

It probably wouldn't hurt to call Dex first and ask what he thinks of Grady, though. Just in case.

Unfortunately, my call goes straight to voicemail, so I leave Dex a message saying I have a question for him. Then I call Sunny, but I get her voicemail, too. They must be traveling. I know Dex has some speaking engagements scheduled these next few months, before the baby's born.

I go about the rest of my day, running errands around the city. But the hours pass, and I'm back home and getting ready to leave for Grady's, and I still haven't heard from either Sunny or Dex. I try Dex's cell one more time before I go, but no luck.

It's not until the elevator doors open to Grady's penthouse, and I'm standing face-to-face with him, that my phone vibrates in my hand.

I glance down at the screen and see Dex's name, of course.

But I can't very well answer it now. So I toss the phone into my purse instead.

I tell myself that I can always duck into the bathroom and call Dex for advice if I'm feeling unsure about his frenemy's intentions. But from the moment I step out of the elevator, Grady Brooks—Hollywood's notorious "bad boy"—is all business, and I immediately feel at ease.

Before we sit for dinner, I ask him to show me some of his favorite things around the penthouse, and he does so eagerly. I have to admit, I was expecting him to boast about his Bang & Olufsen plasma TV, which, I happen to know from working with other wealthy clients, costs over a hundred grand. In fact, his entire living space is peppered with B&O electronics, as if he'd walked into the high-end store on a whim one day and said, "I'll take one of everything."

But Grady doesn't mention any of his expensive tech gadgets. He shows me old photographs instead. Drawers full of faded pictures of his grandparents, who raised him in their tiny Bronx apartment. His mom, who was barely eighteen when she gave birth, had gotten pregnant by a married man who wanted nothing to do with their baby. "Apparently she didn't either," Grady adds. "When I was two months old, she ran off with some Wall Street banker, and never looked back."

"That's awful," I say with a frown. "Has she reached out at all? Since you…"

"Since I became rich and famous?" He shakes his head. "I changed my name a long time ago. I doubt she knows that Grady Brooks is her son. If she does, I guess she doesn't care."

"I'm so sorry," I say, my forehead crinkling.

He shrugs. "What can you do, right? My grandparents more than made up for it. My grandma's the one who taught me how to cook, and my grandpa loved watching his favorite old movies with me. It's the reason I wanted to become an actor. They made me who I am."

"Where are they now?" I ask.

"I set them up in the Outer Banks. When I started making a little money as a sous-chef, I took them there on vacation—you know, to thank them for everything. I'd never been, obviously, but a girl I was dating at the time told me about it. Said it was the most perfect place she'd ever visited. My grandparents fell in love with it. So, as soon as I was able to afford it, I bought them a house there. And they still keep a bedroom for me, after all these years. I love it. It feels like home, even though it's not the room I grew up in." He smiles wistfully.

"Tell me about it," I say with a grin to match his.

"It's…beachy," he replies. "Everything's wicker and white linen."

I nod. "Well, it sounds like we have some inspiration for your guest room. Of course we'll keep it modern and tie in elements from the rest of your apartment, so the room won't look out of place. And we should make a gallery wall with your family photos. We'll put them in vintage frames."

Grady beams at me. "You really are good at your job. You should be doing this on HGTV. I've got friends there; I can hook you up, if you're interested."

My gut clenches.

If I were to take him up on his offer, I'd have to be damn sure that I want to commit to being a designer for the foreseeable future. And lately, I feel less and less certain by the day. "That's so nice of you, Grady. I'm just—I'm still trying to figure out what I want my career to look like long-term."

"I get it," he says with a knowing grin. "Once Lola Piper tweets about you, the world's your oyster. Just keep me posted."

"I will. Thanks," I say casually. But I'm relieved he doesn't press it further. What would Grady Brooks think if I told him I'm considering giving up my booming business so I can paint? He'd probably raise an eyebrow and say something like, "You'd rather be a starving artist than a star? I guess you really are a dumb blonde."

Hmph. The Grady in my head sure knows what to say to make me question my own judgment. And he sounds an awful lot like me. I've been living with this chip on my shoulder since I was seven, after all.

Who would I be if I didn't constantly feel like I had to prove myself? Will I ever be brave enough to find out?

"I think we've done enough work for tonight," Grady says

before I get too lost in my thoughts. He straightens his family photos into a neat pile on the coffee table. "Are you hungry?"

"I am," I say, eager to start dinner. If I make it home early enough, maybe I can call Charlie to thank him for the photograph. The fact that I haven't responded yet has been weighing on my mind since I got here. I meant to reach out earlier, but this unexpected meeting with Grady distracted me.

At least now I know he really did seek me out for my design skills. He's been a complete gentleman all evening—the polar opposite of the man who came on to me at that party three years ago. Grady's changed. I could see myself being friends with him.

I follow him to the kitchen and sit at the island while he pulls a bowl out of the fridge. "I made a seafood salad," he says. "Not the kind you'd buy at a deli…this is the real deal. Fresh lobster, calamari, scallops, and mussels." I watch him plate the fish with lettuce, frisée, a perfectly ripe avocado, and various herbs he sprinkles over the entire dish.

"This looks delicious, Grady. Thank you," I say as he hands me my plate.

"I hope you don't mind it's low-carb. I'm on a diet, as always," he says, rubbing his hand over the ripples of abs I can practically see through his t-shirt.

"I'll survive," I say with a chuckle.

"You know what? I do have a nice bottle of wine, though. A sauvignon blanc that would pair well with this. Can I get you a glass?"

"Oh," I say, a bit surprised. "I wasn't expecting—"

"A recovering alcoholic to have wine in the house?" He grins as my cheeks warm. "Normally I wouldn't. But this was a housewarming gift from one of my neighbors. Honestly, you'd be doing me a favor. I'd feel bad throwing it out. Once a poor kid, always a poor kid, I guess."

"You're *sure*? I don't want to be disrespectful—"

Grady shakes his head. "I don't mind if people drink around me—it happens all the time. Not many Hollywood events are dry," he goes on with a laugh. "And my grandpa has a glass of whiskey every night before bed. Doesn't bother me one bit. I promise."

I tilt my head. "Alright then. I'll take a small pour, for now."

"You got it," he says, uncorking the bottle.

The meal is delicious, and we chat about his movies, mostly. Grady did a couple of rom-coms in the early days of his career—before he was branded as a "bad boy"—and I tell him about my favorite scenes, and ask him questions about his co-stars.

But something strange happens midway through dinner. Grady's ocean-blue eyes begin to remind me more and more of Hunter's. Maybe it's because we're seated so close to each other, eating and laughing like old friends.

Hunter wasn't only my college boyfriend. He was my best friend. We used to stay up for hours each night talking—which, I guess, is what happens when you're not having sex. He'd been raised in a religious household, and wanted to wait until we were married. I didn't mind. I wanted to sleep with him, of course. He was so handsome. But it was nice knowing that a guy was interested in me for more than sex.

Hunter and I did eventually sleep together, but not until—

"More salad?" Grady asks.

"Um, sure," I say. "Thanks." I gulp down what's left of my sauvignon blanc, hoping it'll take the edge off. And when Grady grabs the bottle and pours a little more for me, I don't object.

I suppose it's no wonder I've been thinking about Hunter Reed a lot lately. My intense feelings for Charlie have thrown me for a loop.

And now, here I am, reunited with a man who has the exact same eyes as the former love of my life. Is it a sign that I should stay away from Charlie? A reminder that I don't deserve him?

What kind of twisted game is the universe playing with me?

I drink more wine and refill my glass when I'm done. Rinse, repeat. Before I know it, the bottle's empty.

And I'm *drunk*.

But at least I'm not thinking about Hunter.

"Play me some music on those fancy speakers of yours," I tell Grady, hopping off my chair. The room spins a little. I pick up my plate to carry it to the sink, but he takes it from me with a quiet chuckle.

"I've got it," he says, because I guess he doesn't trust me with his gazillion-dollar fine china.

Whatever, Grady.

"You want some water?" he offers. "Or coffee?"

"No, thanks!" I say, shaking my head vehemently. My brain is just the right amount of fizzy to forget all about my man troubles. "Music, please!" I remind him. "I wanna dance."

"Your wish is my command," he says as I follow him to the living space. I plop down on the couch while he fiddles with electronic thingies.

"I take it you're a fan of Lola?" he asks, playing her newest album.

"I mean, who isn't, right? She's a freaking genius." I kick off my heels and twirl around the room.

Grady stifles a laugh, but I don't care. He's just mad because he can't dance like me.

Whoa. I'm dizzy.

"Have a seat," he says, leading me to the couch. "I'm going to get you some water."

"Grady Brooks…I'm tooootally fine," I slur through a hiccup.

"I think you had a little too much wine," he says with a sympathetic frown. "I feel bad. I probably should have said something when you kept pouring. You're so petite, after all—"

"Well, I wouldn't be so petite if you weren't so freakishly tall," I tell him, which makes us both laugh. "And besides… the only reason I'm drunkity-drunk is because you fed me two tablespoons of fish with some leaves, and no carbs."

Grady chuckles into his fist. "That's a fair point," he finally says.

"Do you have any cookies?" I ask through another hiccup.

He sighs. "Nope. But I do have another avocado. I could make you a vegan chocolate mousse?"

I pout. "I don't want avocado anything…I want cookies. Charlie would have cookies."

"Who's Charlie?" Grady asks, amused.

"The man I'm in love with," I reply, leaning back on the couch.

"Lucky guy," Grady says, seeming sincere.

"He doesn't know I love him yet," I say, twirling my hair.

"Well, don't waste too much time before you tell him," Grady advises me. "I did that once, and I'm still kicking myself for it. She was the love of my life, and now…she's the one who got away."

"*Who?*" I ask, my eyes wide. I've always loved celebrity gossip. "Is she famous, too?"

Grady nods. He rolls up his left shirt sleeve and shows me a tattoo on the underside of his bicep.

"La vita è Bella," I read slowly. "Life is beautiful?"

"That's the literal translation, yeah," he says. "But in this case, it means: Bella is life."

"Bella," I say with a crinkled brow, the wheels in my head turning. "As in, Bella Landry?"

"The one and only," he says with a frown.

"I love her!" I exclaim. "She's America's sweetheart! I didn't even know you two dated."

What I do know is that Dex and Bella dated briefly, before he and I reconnected in LA. But of course I don't mention that.

"It didn't last long," he admits, running a hand through his dark hair. "Want another piece of unsolicited advice? Never get a tattoo for someone who may not be in the picture forever."

A wry laugh escapes me. "Too late."

I stand on wobbly feet and pull the waistband of my skirt down to uncover the rose tattoo on my right hipbone.

I look from the tattoo, back up into Hunter's ocean-blue eyes, and I can hear his voice clear as day in my head. "A rose for every month I've known and loved you."

Grady reaches out to touch the ink on my skin, but I pull my waistband up before he can. "I'm weird about people touching it," I say before I stumble backward onto the couch.

"How about I get you that water now?" he offers again.

This time, I accept. I don't know how long he's gone, but when he comes back, I realize I'd fallen asleep. I look up at Grady, and he's changed out of his t-shirt and jeans, into sweats.

"Have I been sleeping awhile?" I ask, confused and groggy.

"Maybe an hour."

"Oh my gosh, Grady. I'm such a mess. I'm sorry."

"You have nothing to apologize for," he says. "It's my fault, for not feeding you enough. Why don't you stay here tonight? You can have my bed. It's the most comfortable."

I shake my head. "No, I couldn't do that." But when I stand up from the couch, I'm so lightheaded, Grady has to reach for my arm to steady me.

"Follow me. And drink this," he adds, handing me a glass of water.

"You're a good guy, Grady Brooks," I tell him as he leads me to his bedroom.

I wake up the next morning with a raging headache.

God, I'm such an idiot.

I can't believe I put myself in this position. I drank an entire bottle of wine and spent the night in Grady's bed. I'm *so* lucky he didn't try to take advantage of the situation.

When I stand and look in the mirror, I see that I'm wearing one of Grady's t-shirts, and it takes me a few seconds to remember why. He gave it to me so my own clothes wouldn't get wrinkled.

I find my skirt and tank top in his bathroom, where I changed last night, put them back on, then look for Grady. He's in the kitchen, drinking a green smoothie.

"How are you feeling?" he asks, his forehead creased with concern.

My cheeks are flaming hot. "I have a headache, but I'm fine otherwise. Just embarrassed. I'm so sorry I got wasted and took your bed."

"I've done far worse, Jenna," he says. "Believe me. It's no big deal. You want a smoothie?"

I shake my head. "Thanks, but I need to head home and get ready for a client meeting this afternoon."

He nods, and walks me to the elevator. "I'm flying out to New York tomorrow, but I'll call you so we can make a plan for the guest room."

"Sounds good," I say, turning to him. "And, thank you…for everything. For dinner, and for taking care of me last night. I really appreciate it."

"The pleasure was all mine," he says with a nod.

The elevator door opens, and I give him a hug. "Bye, Grady."

When I pull away, he winks at me and smiles.

On the walk home, I begin to think that maybe the universe sent me to Grady's for a reason. A corrective experience, to make up for the times I couldn't trust men in the past. And not only that…

Is it possible that seeing Grady's ocean-blue eyes smiling at me was precisely what I needed to heal? Maybe their resemblance to my ex-boyfriend's wasn't a warning to stay away from Charlie— but a reminder that Hunter loved me once. A sign that I can be that loveable girl again. The one who believed in her own happy ending. I know that Hunter will never forgive me. But maybe it's time I forgave myself and moved on. With Charlie Sutton.

Grinning, I take my phone out of my purse the minute I get home and scroll to his number, which I put in my contacts before I went to sleep on Saturday night. It's Monday morning now, and I'm sure he's anxious to hear from me. I can't wait to finally thank him for the beautiful photograph.

But as I'm about to call him, my phone rings.

It's Dex.

"Hey!" I say brightly. "How are you guys?"

"Um…good," he says, his voice low and gravelly. He doesn't sound like himself. He sounds *angry*, which is rare for Dex. It makes my stomach flip.

"Are you sure?" I ask, my heart beating faster. "Wait—is everything okay with the baby?"

"The baby's great," he says, his voice softening a bit. "Sunny had an ultrasound just the other day. But—where are you right now?" he asks, that unfamiliar edge creeping back into his tone.

"I'm home. Why? What's going on, Dex?"

He lets out a deep sigh. "I just got a text from Grady."

"Oh," I say, my brow furrowed. "Yeah…that's why I called you yesterday. He hired me to design one of the rooms in his penthouse."

"Look, Jenna. I don't want to overstep here, but you're my friend, and…I think you should know that Grady Brooks is *not* a good guy."

I nod. "I understand why you think that. But he's changed.

He's been sober for a year, and he was a perfect gentleman when I met with him yesterday. You have nothing to worry about."

Dex clicks his tongue. "I know it's none of my business who you sleep with—"

"I'm not sleeping with him. And I don't plan to. I could see us becoming friends, though. He took care of me last night. I had dinner at his place, but I drank too much wine, and he let me sleep it off in his bed. But he didn't make a move on me, or anything. He slept in one of the guest rooms."

Dex is quiet.

"What?" I ask, my palms sweating.

"That fucker," he finally mutters under his breath.

"What do you mean?" I ask, losing patience. "Just tell me what's going on."

"Grady's had it out for me for years," he begins to explain. "He thinks I stole Bella Landry from him."

"Oh," I say, remembering Grady's tattoo. "Yeah…he told me she was the love of his life."

Dex scoffs. "I guess he didn't mention that he cheated on her with a stripper. She found out while we were filming, and—"

"You were there for her," I say.

"Ever since then, Grady's made this game out of sleeping with as many of my exes as he can," he goes on. "It's sick. He asked me about you after that party, and I told him to stay away. Obviously, that backfired. I'm so sorry, Jenna. I would've warned you, but I hadn't heard he was filming in Chicago."

"But I didn't sleep with him. Like I said, he didn't even try."

"That's the thing…" Dex pauses, and my stomach churns.

"He sent me a picture of you."

My heart lurches. *This can't be happening again.* "He did what?"

"He texted me a picture of you, asleep in his bed. Wearing his shirt. But he didn't stop there. I don't want to repeat what he wrote. But he described your rose tattoo, in detail."

"Oh my god," I say, lifting my hand to my mouth. "I did show him my tattoo, but that was it…we didn't kiss, or anything."

"You don't need to convince me, Jenna, I believe you. Grady's a total piece of shit," Dex says, his voice infused with anger again. "I guess this was his backup plan, when he realized you weren't going to sleep with him. I'm really sorry. I hate having to tell you this—I just figured you should know."

I nod, wiping my eyes. "No, I'm glad you told me. I just can't believe what a liar he is. Now, I don't know if a single word he said to me last night was true. I mean, he showed me these beautiful old photographs of his grandparents, and told me this sob story about his mother leaving him…but was any of it real? Or was he just trying to manipulate me?"

A chill runs down my spine. I already had trust issues with men before Grady. What is this going to do to me?

"Well, he brought his grandparents to the Oscars last year, so I guess that much is true. And…come to think of it, I do remember him mentioning his mom to me once. This was a long time ago, in the early days of our careers, before the Bella ordeal. We were at a party, and he was drunk, and said his mom was a heartless bitch—something like that. So, I guess that tracks. But it's no excuse for how he treats women. I mean, Sunny's dad abandoned her, but it didn't make her cruel."

"Exactly," I say, sniffling.

"Are you gonna be okay?" he asks me. "What can I do to help?"

I try my best to hold it together. Dex doesn't know that something similar happened to me in grad school. He has no idea how triggering this is for me.

"I'll be fine," I say after a deep breath. "Really. But thanks for telling me. I'm gonna go now—I have to pull myself together for a work meeting. Give my love to Sunny and the baby, okay?"

I hang up before he can answer.

My eyelids flutter open when harsh sunlight fills my bedroom again. I keep forgetting to close the damn blinds. It's Wednesday, now. I think. It's hard to keep track of time when you're barely getting out of bed.

I felt this coming on as soon as Dex told me what Grady did. So, before I went down, I emailed my clients and told them I was sick, and that I'd be in touch to reschedule our meetings. I already knew what to expect. I've been through this before.

When Christy drove to Ann Arbor and dragged me out of bed, I felt just like this.

Not sick. But numb.

Lifeless.

I wonder how often my mom feels this way.

I think about calling her…but I haven't asked her for emotional support once in my life, so why start now? I doubt she has any to give. If anything, she'll call my sister, and make her come to my rescue.

But I promised Christy I wouldn't burden her like that ever again. Which is why I responded to her phone call yesterday morning with a text message that took me an hour to write. I had to make it sound like bubbly and bright Jenna—which seemed impossible, given the storm cloud in my head. Finally, I came up with: **Hey! Doing well! Super busy with work since I went viral. Promise to call soon!!**

I think the exclamation marks helped sell it. Made it seem like I'm not back in that dark place again. I hope so, at least.

I sent the same message to Dex when he called on Monday night to check on me.

And I cut and pasted those words in a text to Vanessa, when she called last night to ask how my weekend was, and if I'd had another date with Charlie.

My god, that feels like a lifetime ago. It's been four days since he slipped that sweet note under my door, and he hasn't heard a thing from me. I'm sure he's given up and moved on.

I hope he doesn't think I'm some cold-hearted bitch who ghosted him.

Tears stream down my face at the thought.

Heartbroken, I close my eyes and fall back to sleep, because it's the only way I get a break from feeling this low. This rotten. Empty.

And even though I know the goddamn blinds are still open, I can't muster the energy to do anything about it.

I wake up on Thursday morning with the worst headache of my

life. My mouth is dry, and I can't remember the last time I had anything to drink.

A wave of anxiety rushes through me, and for the first time since Monday, I want to get out of bed. I amble to the kitchen, my muscles stiff and achy, fill a glass with tap water, and down it all in a few large gulps.

Suddenly overwhelmed by hunger, I scarf down whatever I can get my hands on, which isn't much, since I haven't been grocery shopping this week. I find a banana in a bowl on the counter, and one last cup of yogurt in the fridge. After I eat, I stand in front of the mirror in the foyer and begin to cry.

I look like hell. I haven't showered since before I left for dinner at Grady's. I still have the same makeup on that I fell asleep in at his place. It's been four whole days.

I wipe my tears and walk to the bathroom, strip off the sweaty pajamas I've been sleeping in since Monday, and wash my hair and body.

The fact that I'm doing basic things like eating and showering gives me the slightest bit of hope that this won't be as bad as last time. It can't be. I don't have Christy here to take care of me.

"I'm getting better," I repeat as many times as it takes for me to believe it.

I step out of the shower feeling a little less sad than when I entered. And clean, at least.

After I'm dressed, I pause in the doorway of my art studio, grateful that I covered Charlie's painting with a sheet yesterday. I kept bursting into tears every time I laid eyes on it.

I wonder if I can paint today.

Slowly, as if drawn by some magnetic force, I walk to my palette on the other side of the room and start mixing colors.

An hour later, I'm looking at a pair of bright blue eyes.

But I'm not sure if they're Hunter's or Grady's.

On Friday morning, I get a text from Vanessa: **Hey lady, I miss you! You're coming to class this afternoon, right?**

Damnit. I forgot all about my painting class. Am I in any shape to go?

I'm certainly feeling better than I was a few days ago. The hours I spent in my little art studio helped ground me, for sure. But the ground I'm standing on is still shaky. I was hoping to spend another couple of days in this bubble, alone, before I ventured out into the world again.

I text Vanessa back: **I miss you too! Not feeling well today, so I'm going to stay home. Next week for sure.**

She doesn't reply.

Three hours later, I'm in my art studio when I get a call from the doorman.

"Vanessa's here to see you," he practically sings. "She's on her way upstairs. I hope you don't mind I let her in—I remember her from last week. Real nice gal."

"Oh! Um…that's great!" I say, panic flooding me.

I don't want her to see me this way.

I don't have the energy to be bright and bubbly. How the hell will I get through this visit?

The sound of her knocking startles me. I comb my fingers through my hair, then open the door. Here goes nothing.

"Hey! Shouldn't you be at work?" I ask, a smile blooming on my face the moment I see her. It's only now that I realize how lonely I've been this week. Tears sting my eyes, but I blink them away.

"I'm taking a long lunch break," she says with a shrug as she bends down to pick up a brown paper bag. "And I brought my Haitian remedies."

She walks past me to my kitchen island, where she sets down the bag and starts pulling things out of it: fresh herbs, jars of spices, lots of fruits and vegetables, and raw honey.

I tear up again. "What's all this?"

She grins. "I'm going to make you Tati Marie's tea recipe. And a smoothie that has enough Vitamin C for an army. You'll feel better in no time."

"This is so nice of you, Vanessa. You didn't have to…" I begin to say before I get choked up. I've never had a female friend take care of me like this. Only my sister.

"Oh, hush," she says, playfully. "Do you like ginger?"

I nod. "I love it."

"Good, because you're about to get a heavy dose of it," she says with a wink.

Vanessa fills a pot with water, adds grated ginger, cinnamon sticks, star anise, and mint, then brings it to a boil. Afterward, she turns down the heat and, while the tea simmers, she makes my smoothie. I sit at the kitchen island watching her slice mangoes as we catch up. I take the lead in asking her questions because I'm so terrified that, the more I talk, the more she'll see right through me. She's a trained therapist—and here I am at what I'm hoping is the tail end of a brief depressive episode.

Please let it be brief. Please don't let this be like last time.

"Hey, you okay?" Vanessa asks, her forehead creased.

Now I see that she put my smoothie on the island in front of me. I must have spaced out for a minute.

I swallow a sob, which strains my throat. I fight my tears, but I don't know how much longer I can keep up this act.

I am not okay.

I am not okay.

I am not okay.

I am not okay.

I haven't been for a long time. Not since November 9, 2002, when Hunter called and told me—

"Jenna?"

I look into Vanessa's concerned eyes. She's sitting next to me now, at the island. I take my gaze down to my lap, where I see my hand in hers. A tear falls onto our intertwined fingers.

My shoulders slump from the tension I'm holding in my body. I'm so damn tired of fighting, I want to crumple into a heap on the floor.

"I can't do this anymore," I say out loud, although I'm not sure I meant to.

"Do what?" Vanessa asks, tenderly squeezing my hand.

I look up at her again. "I can't keep pretending I'm fine."

✦

Eventually, I tell her my story.

It's all out of order, though. I start with what Grady did to me—but for that to make sense, I have to tell her about my relationship with Dex. And for her to understand why Grady taking a picture of me sleeping was especially triggering, I have to go back and tell her that my ex, Alex, did the same thing to me in grad school. Except that I was naked in that picture, with only a bedsheet covering me from the waist down.

She already knows what happened with Scott, so I don't have to revisit that mess. But as I watch her process my past, I can tell she knows there are pieces missing from the puzzle.

Finally, after two cups of tea and a lot of prodding, I tell Vanessa about Hunter.

I cry, and cry, and cry. And while I'm crying, she holds me.

Could this be the reason she came into my life? A therapist with a heart of gold who cares about me? Who listens without judgment and wipes away my tears?

All I know is, I feel a huge weight lift after being honest with Vanessa. But when I tell her that, she makes it clear that this is only the beginning of my path to healing.

"I'm going to print out a depression assessment, so I can help you figure out where to go from here."

After I answer each question, I give her the assessment to score. When she's satisfied that I'm not a danger to myself, her shoulders relax, and relief washes over her face.

But she insists I see a therapist.

"You need a professional to help you process what happened with Hunter," she says, gently.

It's the same advice my sister gave me years ago. I wish I had listened. This is only the first time since then that I've been so depressed I couldn't get out of bed—but what if it's not the last?

And even though I've been functional in between these episodes, that doesn't mean I've been happy.

Let's face it: what Christy said to me on the phone the other week is true. I'm miserable living without love in my life. I *do* want a relationship.

I want a relationship with Charlie.

But for that to happen, I have to stop punishing myself. I guess I learned the hard way that my sister was right. If I don't process my trauma, it will keep coming back to haunt me.

I don't doubt that a therapist can guide me through this. I've seen the benefits of therapy with my own eyes. The way Dex's life changed after he finally reached out for help isn't lost on me. But he's such a good person. He deserved to feel better.

I wasn't sure I did—until today.

When I opened up to Vanessa, I told her more about my relationship with Hunter than I've ever told anyone, including my own sister. And she didn't judge me.

That's why, when Vanessa mentions therapy, I don't object this time.

"As much as I wish I could help you myself," she continues, "there's only so much I can do from a professional standpoint, because we're friends. But I'm going to be here for you, as a friend, every step of the way."

I reach for a tissue and dab my eyes. "That's so sweet of you to say. But I don't want to burden you. I mean, we only met a couple of weeks ago."

Vanessa shakes her head with a tender smile. "But it doesn't feel that way."

I grin through tears. "No, it doesn't."

"It's not often you meet someone and feel like you've known them forever, right? That's special," she says. "You have to lean into it."

I nod, thinking of Charlie.

Before she leaves, Vanessa taps all her resources to find me a therapist, and even books my first appointment for Monday.

"I would offer to stay, or bring you back to my place for the weekend, but I'm leaving early tomorrow morning to visit my parents in Miami," she says before biting her lip nervously. "I'll check in while I'm there, but please promise you'll call or text if you need anything."

"I'll be fine," I say with a genuine smile.

Because this time, I truly believe it.

The next morning, I get out of bed as soon as my eyes open. I shower, get dressed, and eat breakfast. And then I leave my apartment for the first time in six days, which is a huge feat, even though I'm not going very far.

I stand outside Charlie's apartment for several seconds, thinking about what I want to say to him. But right as I lift my hand to knock on the door, he opens it.

When his gaze meets mine, his dark brown eyes widen with

a mixture of joy and relief. "Would you believe it if I told you I was on my way to knock on your door?"

They're the same words I said to him a week ago, when he invited me to the art museum.

I tear up instantly. "Really?"

He nods, looking down at his shoes, then up at me again. "After we kissed, I could tell you were wrestling with something, so I wanted to give you space. But, it's been a while, so…I wanted to make sure you were okay."

I wipe my eyes. "I'm sorry I didn't stop by sooner. Or call after you left that sweet note under my door. I wanted to. I meant to. I meant to thank you a lot earlier, but…"

Normally I would lie. I'd fight my tears, put on a bright, bubbly smile, and say something came up at work. And, even though I'm sick and tired of burying my feelings, I have to admit it's tempting. Being vulnerable is scary. But I'll never get to where I want to be if I don't try.

"Something happened this week that, um, triggered me. It opened an old wound from my past and…that's just the tip of the iceberg, Charlie," I say with a wry laugh. "The truth is…I'm a bit of a mess. When it comes to love, especially. For years, I've been telling myself that I didn't want a relationship. And I believed it… until I met you," I confess to the man who's had an inexplicable hold on my heart since I ran into him by the elevator.

The pink in Charlie's cheeks deepens, his gaze steady on mine as he listens.

"But I can't move forward with you until I face my issues. So I'm starting therapy on Monday. I don't know how long this will take. And I certainly wouldn't ask you to wait for me—"

"No…of course not," he agrees.

I nod, my lip quivering. Even though I know I'm doing the right thing, I'm devastated. It's all I can do not to sob.

"But the thing is, Jenna…you don't have to ask," Charlie continues, his eyes gleaming.

"What?" I stammer, confused.

"I don't care how long it takes," he says as he pulls me close. "I'm in."

thirteen

I'm sitting in Dr. Esther Adelman's waiting room with sweaty palms and a stomachache, wondering if I'm anxious, or actually sick. I've never felt so nervous that I thought I might faint—but here we are. I guess this is what happens when you finally go to therapy after avoiding it for eight years. My heart is racing, and I can barely catch my breath. I wonder if this is how poor Dex felt for so many years of his life. It's awful. My heart breaks at the thought of him suffering like this when he was a kid.

But he got help. And that's why I'm here. That's why I need to resist the urge to run out of this small, windowless room that feels like it's suffocating me, and back to the comfort of my couch, where I can watch a rom-com marathon and ignore my problems, like I usually do.

Although I wouldn't be able to get away with that, even if I tried. Vanessa drove me here, and she's parked outside, waiting for me. She scheduled my appointment early on purpose, so she could bring me before work. She knew this would be my first time going to therapy, and wanted to support me.

I still don't know what I did to deserve a friend like her. But I've stopped questioning it. I'm just going to lean into it, like Vanessa said, and be the best friend to her that I can be.

When the door to Dr. Adelman's office creaks open, I practically jump out of my seat. If she noticed how startled I was, she doesn't let on. Instead, she greets me with a nod and a warm smile that makes me breathe a little easier.

I'm still a nervous wreck, though. I spent the last ten minutes in her waiting room going over what I need to tell her, but now it's all jumbled in my head.

"You must be Jenna," she says, her voice gentle and kind. She's petite, like me. Her sleek silver hair is in a loose chignon, and she's wearing a pair of tortoiseshell frames that make me wish I needed glasses. I'm guessing she's in her sixties, but her bohemian style gives her a youthful, artsy vibe that I'm instantly drawn to. She's in a bright coral kimono draped over a cream-colored shell and matching pants, and has colorful mala beads around her wrists.

"Hi, Dr. Adelman," I say as I walk toward her. "It's nice to meet you."

"Please, call me Esther," she replies, still smiling as she invites me into her office.

I sit on the couch and look at the paintings on the wall opposite me. They're abstracts that remind me of the day I spent at the museum with Charlie. My heart swells, and a wave of calm washes over me as I remember why I'm here.

It's been years since I've wanted someone the way I want

Charlie. And I need to see where this goes. Best of all, he feels the same way. He's willing to wait for me to be in a better place emotionally, and I'm going to do the work to get there.

"So, Jenna," Esther says softly, once she's seated across from me. "Tell me what brings you here today."

This is it. Do I dip a toe in and test the waters? Start by telling her about Grady and work my way backward? Or do I dive in head-first and talk about Hunter?

"I'm not sure where to begin," I admit with a sheepish laugh.

She nods sympathetically. "Beginning is the hardest part. Why don't you tell me a little bit about yourself?"

"Sure. I can do that." I lean back on the couch, relieved that I can start with something relatively easy.

I talk about my family, and the early years we spent in Columbus. About my dyslexia, and moving to Beachwood because the kids at my elementary school never stopped making fun of me. I explain what it was like when I started developing in middle school, and grown men twice my age would leer at me. I share stories about the boys who dated me just to see how far they could get with me. I tell her that it made me not want to give them any part of me at all. And maybe that's what drew me to Dex. He was practically the only guy in our grade who wasn't trying to get me in bed.

"I'm talking about Dex Oliver, by the way…the movie star. We went to school together in Beachwood," I explain.

Esther nods, calmly. She doesn't look at me wide-eyed or slack-jawed, which I take to mean that she either isn't interested in celebrity gossip or, if she is, she hides it well. Either way, I feel even more relaxed when I continue.

"Before Dex, I hadn't gone farther with a boy than kissing. I mean, I'd been grabbed and felt up plenty of times. But Dex was the first guy I *wanted* to touch me. And I think it was because everything that happened between us was initiated by me. I never had to push him off me, or slap his hands away. Because the truth is…I wasn't the one he wanted to be with. He was in love with someone else, and somehow that made him less threatening to me." I pause for a beat, my eyes stinging. "I guess that's pretty messed up, huh."

Esther shakes her head. "It's not messed up at all. You had every reason to feel threatened by other guys. Dex was different. Not because he didn't want you—but because he respected you. You knew you could trust him."

"You're right, I did. I always have. That's why I wanted to sleep with him before college. Because I was afraid I'd never trust a man like that again. The only part I regret is telling him I loved him afterward. It wasn't love in the romantic sense…I just loved how safe I felt with him."

Esther moves a box of tissues toward me, and I pick it up from the coffee table and keep it next to me on the couch. I wipe my eyes. "And then I went to college and, um…"

My stomach clenches.

I close my eyes for a breath, and I see Charlie's encouraging smile. I feel Vanessa's arms around me. I hear Dex's Oscar speech in my head.

Then I continue.

"I met a guy during orientation week. Hunter Reed. I was at

a frat party, talking to a group of girls from my dorm, and when I looked up, my eyes met Hunter's from across the room, and… he took my breath away. He was about a foot taller than me, and looked like he'd stepped out of an Abercrombie catalogue. He smiled, and walked over to introduce himself…and the rest was history, as they say.

"He was the sweetest guy I'd ever met, Esther. And the best part about our relationship was that he wanted to wait for marriage to have sex. Maybe that would've been a dealbreaker for other girls, but not me. I was thrilled, because I knew he liked me for *me*. And it wasn't long before I fell head over heels in love with him.

"And Hunter loved me, too." Tears stream down my face. "Within a few months, he started talking about marriage. I got so swept up by how romantic he was, I never paused to think that maybe things were moving too fast. I was eighteen, and he was my first love. So we started making plans to get engaged after we graduated. We talked about what kind of ring I wanted. Where we'd go on our honeymoon. We talked about the incredible sex we'd have," I say with a little laugh through my tears.

"But as we got closer to graduation, our conversations started to change. We were seniors, and suddenly Hunter was talking about starting a family as soon as we got married. I hadn't even turned twenty-two yet. I knew he was getting ready to propose, but I never imagined he'd want to try for a baby right after the wedding. I figured, since we were so young, we could enjoy just being married for a few years. At least while I was in grad school."

I pause to look at Esther, hoping she understands. The deeper I get into this story, the more I begin to worry that she'll judge me.

But when she responds, there's nothing other than compassion in her eyes. "Did you tell Hunter you were concerned about starting a family while you were in grad school?"

I sigh. "Yes. And all he said was that we would figure it out. But that answer was too abstract for me. With my dyslexia, I had to work ten times harder in college than anyone I knew, and getting into that architecture program was no small feat. I was proud of how far I'd come, and getting my master's was important to me. It felt like Hunter was a lot more concerned with me taking care of our home and kids, though. I could see my future with him unfolding, and it didn't look anything like the life I wanted. Hunter would be at work all day, doing finance with the skills he'd learned in school—and I'd be stuck at home, barefoot and pregnant, and wasting my degree. And the thing is…I wasn't totally sure I wanted children."

"Did Hunter know that?" she asks.

My lip quivers. "Not before it was too late. I figured I was still so young, and that maybe I'd change my mind about not wanting kids. But after Hunter proposed, I panicked. He wanted to be a father more than anything, and what if the urge to become a mother never kicked in for me? I'm not sure it ever did for my mom—I could tell she didn't enjoy staying at home. She always seemed so bored, and I didn't want to end up like her. So I gave him back the ring. And the way he looked at me…"

I pause to grab another tissue. "He had the most beautiful blue eyes I'd ever seen. And he'd always gazed at me with so much love. But now, he looked at me like I was a monster. He said he never imagined I'd turn out to be the type of girl to put career before family. He told me—he told me—"

I heave a sob, my heart aching.

"Take your time, honey," Esther says, sounding like the mom I've always dreamed of having.

"Thank you." I force myself to breathe deeply. After a minute, I'm able to get the words out. "He told me I wasted four years of his life."

"I'm sure that was hard to hear," Esther says, tilting her head. "You were Hunter's first love, and he was heartbroken. But ultimately, you spared him a lot more pain by ending the relationship before you got married."

I shake my head, tears spilling onto my lap. "No, Hunter was right...I wasted his time...and if I could do it all over again, I never would have given back the ring...if I'd known that I would ruin his life..."

I can hardly see Esther through my tears. I can barely hear her over my cries.

When I told Vanessa about Hunter, I gave her an abbreviated version. I didn't revisit every moment in my head, didn't relive every word we spoke, the way I'm doing now. It's unbearable. I bury my face in my hands.

Several seconds later, I feel the couch cushions move as Esther sits beside me. She rests a hand on my shoulder. "Why do you think you ruined his life, honey? Are you still in touch with him?"

I take a ragged breath. "I wish I were."

"Did you ever try reaching out?"

My gaze lifts to meet hers. "I can't," I say, simply.

I think she understands why I'll never speak to Hunter again. Something shifts on her face—from sympathy to heartache. I can tell by her frown that she hopes she's wrong, and I find myself feeling sorry for her, and wishing I had a different answer to the question in her eyes.

But I don't, so I tell her the truth. "I can't reach out to Hunter…because he died."

Esther lets me cry on her couch for a good ten minutes. She hands me a glass of water, and even offers me tea. I ask her if we're running out of time, and she only smiles and tells me not to worry. I say I have a friend waiting for me downstairs, and she encourages me to check in with her. Vanessa insists I stay as long as I need. She's keeping busy, writing emails in her car.

So I tell Esther I'd love a cup of chamomile. She prepares it, then takes her seat across from me again.

After a few sips, I'm calm enough to continue our session.

"Did you ever see Hunter again after that night?" she asks, her brows knitted together.

"Not for a while. We'd just graduated, so I packed up my things and drove home to Beachwood for the summer. And I assumed he was at his parents' house, not far from Ann Arbor. Then I went back to Michigan and started grad school, and I was sufficiently distracted—until he called me. It was November 9, 2002. I'll never forget the date.

"When I saw his name come up on my phone, I was afraid he

was going to ask me to get back together. I didn't want to have to break his heart all over again. The more time that passed, the more I felt sure I didn't want kids.

"But that's not why he was calling, Esther. And I feel guilty, to this day, for the dread in my gut when I picked up the phone, worrying that he wanted me back. If only that were the reason he reached out."

"You couldn't have known, dear."

"No…I guess I couldn't have." I take a sip of tea. "It came as a total shock when he told me he'd been to the doctor earlier that week, and that he'd just gotten back his test results. He said he was sick…but he didn't elaborate. And I was too terrified to ask him what was wrong. I just wanted to know if he was going to be okay. When I asked, he said he hoped so.

"I know it wasn't much, but I held on to that hope. I told him to come see me, and he did. I gave him my address, and he was at my apartment an hour later.

"And he looked good, Esther. A bit thinner maybe, but he didn't look sick. I was so relieved, I threw my arms around him and kissed him the moment he walked through my door. And the way his eyes lit up…I knew that he still loved me."

I take a breath before I go on.

"He asked me if we could pretend we never broke up. Just for a weekend. He wanted to go back to how things were before. I said I'd been thinking the same. And I told him I loved him— because it was true. That's why I let him go. I wanted all of his dreams to come true, and I knew his biggest dream was to become a father.

"But we didn't talk about any of that. We held hands and kissed. We slow danced to our song in my kitchen. And that night, when I took him to my room, we…"

I wipe my eyes. "We made love. We were kissing in bed, and our clothes came off slowly, one piece at a time, and it just happened. It felt so natural…so right. And I knew how meaningful it was for him. It was special for me, too. I'd had sex once before, with Dex, but this was different. Hunter and I loved each other. And, Esther?"

"Yes, honey?"

"I've never felt loved like that since. It's been eight years."

Esther nods, frowning. "I'm so sorry, dear."

"After that weekend, I asked him to stay with me. I told him I wanted to take care of him. And I meant it. But he said he couldn't do that to me. He wanted me to focus on school. He'd had a lot of time to think after I gave back the ring, and he felt awful for not taking my career plans more seriously. Before he left, I begged him to reconsider…but he said he loved me too much."

"That's why he had to let you go," Esther says. "I imagine his illness put a lot in perspective for him."

I nod, biting my lip. "I tried keeping in touch. But after a while, he wouldn't return my calls. Or he'd send short text messages saying he was fine. And then, four months later, his mom called…and told me he'd died. I've been a mess ever since."

Esther leans forward in her chair. "You said earlier that you'd ruined Hunter's life, but, honey—I don't see it that way at all."

"When I look back on our relationship, I don't think about the beautiful weekend we spent together before he passed away.

I remember the look in his eyes when I gave back the ring. I remember him saying that I wasted four years of his life. Those were the *last* four years of his life, Esther," I say with a sob.

"They weren't a waste, dear. He loved you. He came back to you. He wanted to be with *you* before he died."

"I loved him, too. So much. And if I hadn't broken up with him when I did, we would have been together that summer. And maybe I would have noticed something was wrong. Maybe I would have sent him to the doctor sooner, and he could have started treatment earlier, and—"

"Oh, Jenna," Esther sighs. I look up, and her eyes are teary, too. "Honey…it's not your fault that Hunter died."

I'm crying so hard that she comes back to sit near me on the couch. This is the first time I've ever admitted to anyone how guilty I've felt all these years. And it's the first time anyone's said the words I've been desperate to hear.

It's not your fault.

"Sometimes I feel like I'm stuck there," I tell her. "I'm thirty now, but a part of me is still twenty-two years old, and grieving the love of my life."

"That's a common response to unprocessed trauma," she says, resting her hand on mine. "But we're processing it now, together. And you will get through this."

Just hearing her say that feels like the weight of the world lifts from my shoulders. My head aches from crying, and every muscle in my body is exhausted, but I'm grateful.

"Thanks, Esther. Can I come back again soon?" I sniffle. "Like, tomorrow, maybe?"

She smiles. "Absolutely."

I text Vanessa to let her know I'll be downstairs in a few minutes. And when the elevator door opens, she's standing in the lobby, waiting for me.

As soon as she sees my tear-streaked face, she pulls me into a hug.

Over the next two weeks, I see Esther four times. I still have a long road ahead of me, and a lot more to work on with her (my self-esteem and career woes topping the list), but as far as my relationship with Hunter, for the first time in nearly a decade, I don't feel wracked with guilt.

My perspective started to change when Esther asked me to imagine what would've happened if Hunter had lived. He would've gone on to meet the mother of his children. He would have become a dad. And I would have peace of mind, knowing that breaking up with him was the right decision. His death robbed us both of seeing his life unfold the way it was meant to.

Rather than defining our relationship by Hunter's death at the expense of everything else we shared, Esther encourages me to reframe our story: We were madly in love. But ultimately, we weren't right for each other, because we wanted different things. So we let each other go. It's still a sad ending, even if he'd lived. But it's also a beautiful tale of love and sacrifice.

Eventually, I start talking to Esther about Charlie. Even though I'm in a better place, emotionally, than I was two weeks ago, I know my trust issues with men aren't going to disappear overnight. And I don't want to bring that baggage into my new romance.

"Do you think I'm ready to be in a relationship?" I ask Esther, anxious to hear her opinion. "I know Charlie said he'd wait for me—and it's only been two weeks—but I miss him like crazy, and I'm dying to see him."

Esther tilts her head for a beat before she answers me. "How about this: you spend the next month hanging out with Charlie, and getting to know each other as friends. Take sex out of the equation. You said you were grateful for that aspect of your relationship with Hunter, right? You didn't have to worry about him wanting you for superficial reasons. What if your relationship with Charlie began the same way?"

I like the idea, and I'm smiling all the way home from Esther's office, because I'm so excited to make plans with him. I honestly don't care what we do—or don't do. I just want to be near him. When the elevator doors open to the twentieth floor, I almost expect to see Charlie standing there, but there's no one in sight. As I pass his apartment, I consider knocking, but it's nine on a Saturday morning, and he might still be sleeping, so I decide to wait another hour.

But right as I'm putting on my smock and getting ready to paint, I hear someone at my door. My heart skips a beat.

Charlie.

I can only imagine how silly I must look with my paint-splotched smock over my tank top and shorts, and my hair up in a messy bun, but I don't care. And I know he won't either.

I open the door with a huge smile on my face—that instantly falls flat. My mouth gapes. My stomach churns. "What the hell are you doing here?"

Grady Brooks has the audacity to smile at me. "I owe you an apology."

I stand there in stunned silence.

He gestures toward the inside of my apartment. "May I come in?"

I fold my arms over my chest. "Absolutely not. And how did you even get up here, anyway? The doorman's supposed to call me first."

Grady grins. "I got lucky. The door*man* was a woman. I told her I was surprising you, let her take a selfie with me, and here I am. The perks of celebrity."

"You're the worst," I tell him, wondering if there's actual steam coming out of my ears, because it sure as hell feels that way.

If there is, though, Grady doesn't notice. He's too busy looking me up and down. "Are you wearing clothes under that thing?" he asks, referring to my smock.

"Please leave," I say, beginning to close the door, but he braces his hand against it to stop me.

"Jenna, wait," he says, taking a step back. "Look, I know you hate me. And for what it's worth, I'm sorry."

My hands are on my hips. "It's worth nothing, Grady. Nothing at all."

"I shouldn't have involved you in my beef with Dex," he continues. "And I definitely should have known that he would snitch," he adds under his breath.

I shake my head. "Are you kidding me? *That's* your apology? You betrayed my trust. You manipulated me. You got me drunk, and—"

He raises a finger. "Technically speaking, *you* got yourself drunk."

I stifle a scream. "Was any of it true? Did your neighbor really drop off that bottle of wine? Or did you buy it, hoping I'd get wasted, succumb to terrible decision-making, and have sex with you?"

The angrier I get, the more amused Grady seems to be. "If there's one thing you can trust about me, Jenna, it's that I want to sleep with you. I've been honest about that from the day we met. You're the only woman I know who's impervious to my charm, and it drives me insane."

"You are such an entitled prick," I say, my voice shaking. "You play women like pawns in this sick, misogynistic game of yours—get them in bed, then send pictures to Dex—and you think that's *charming?*"

He smirks. "Oh, please, let's not be naïve. Most women would kill to spend the night with me. Don't you keep up with celebrity news? My exes love to talk about how I'm the best sex of their life—and needless to say, my reputation precedes me. I'm as much of a conquest to the women I sleep with as they are to me. More often than not, the selfies in bed are their idea—so they can brag about me to their friends the next day. So, believe me, no one's a victim here."

My eyes tear up. "No one's a victim, huh? Do you want to

know how I reacted when Dex told me about the picture you sent? *I fell apart!* I didn't get out of bed for four days. I didn't leave my building for a week. I was so depressed, I started therapy."

Grady's eyes go wide.

"And if that twisted brain of yours thinks you're special for having such a powerful effect on me, think again," I continue. "You're only one in a very long line of men who've betrayed my trust. That's why I was so triggered by what you did. But don't tell me your stupid games don't have victims, because you're wrong."

Grady sighs and runs a hand through his hair. When he looks at me again, I see something resembling remorse in his eyes. But I'd be willing to bet my life that he's acting.

"Jenna, I'm really sorry." He shakes his head. "That fucking sucks. If I had known this would upset you so much, I never would have done it. Everyone's so jaded in Hollywood, I forget there are real people out there with real feelings."

"That's no excuse," I say, rolling my eyes.

He scowls and looks down at his shoes. "Tell me what I can do to make it up to you, and I'll do it. You already rejected my first apology gift—"

"Apology gift? What apology gift?"

Grady raises an eyebrow at me. "Did you not get a call last week? From HGTV?"

I did. Someone left a message saying they'd seen Lola Piper's tweet, and wanted to set up a meeting with me. I'd just come back from my third therapy session with Esther, and I was feeling happier than I had in years. But as soon as I heard the message, my heart sank.

I knew what I had to do. I called them back and thanked them profusely, but said I'd just committed to a long-term art project.

It's not even a lie, really. I have six paintings in my makeshift studio so far. At my last class with Tati Marie, I told her about my progress, and she said she'd be happy to connect me with a friend who owns an art gallery, when I'm ready to show my work. My reaction was the polar opposite of when I listened to the voicemail from HGTV. I was giddy.

"The guy I spoke to at HGTV never mentioned you. I had no idea you set it up," I tell Grady.

He shrugs. "Yeah, they're supposed to use production companies for casting, but I had him bend a few rules. He's an old buddy of mine, and owed me a favor. Anyway, I was shocked when he said you declined. So, tell me, Jenna…what will it take for you to forgive me?"

He looks at me with a smoldering gaze, thinking it will soften me, I bet—but I'm so enraged I start shaking. "Can't you see that I want nothing to do with you?" I cry out. "Just leave, okay? All I want is for you to leave me alone."

We both turn our heads when another door creaks open. My heart jumps for joy the moment Charlie steps into the hallway.

He looks from me to Grady and back again, assessing the situation. I hope he doesn't get the wrong idea. I hope he can tell, from the expression on my face, that I *really* don't want Grady anywhere near me.

He must know—because, within seconds, Charlie's by my side.

"Hey, babe," he says, kissing the top of my head and putting his arm around my shoulder. I watch as he eyes Grady, then holds out his hand. "I don't believe we've met. I'm Charlie Sutton. Jenna's boyfriend."

I do nothing to hide the giddy grin on my face. Charlie to the rescue again—but this time I don't worry about him seeing me as a damsel in distress. He knows I'm more than that.

I lean into him, sighing with relief.

Grady shakes Charlie's hand with a stern look on his face, and only says, "Hey."

Charlie's brows knit together. "And you are…"

Grady narrows his eyes. "You're joking—right?"

He looks agitated, and I don't want this turning into a fistfight. "Well, Charlie and I are running late for brunch," I interject, "so we'd better—"

"Yeah," Grady says, abruptly. "I was just leaving, anyway."

As he turns toward the elevator, I pull Charlie into my apartment and lock the door behind us. Then I hug him, my heart racing against his.

"Are you okay?" he says, his voice laced with concern.

I nod into his chest. "I'm fine—thanks to you."

"I heard you yelling at him to leave." Charlie steps back, so he can take a better look at me. "He didn't…put his hands on you, did he?"

I shake my head, my heart swelling at the worry in his eyes. "No, it was nothing like that. He's just a jerk I met years ago, and can't seem to shake."

Charlie breathes a sigh of relief. "Good. Because, to be honest, I'm not entirely sure I could take Grady Brooks in a fight. But I sure as hell would've tried."

I laugh. "So you *did* recognize him."

Charlie smiles. "I thought it would be fun to mess with him. He seems pretty damn full of himself."

"Well, you had me fooled," I say. "You're a good actor. I think you could give Grady a run for his money."

"You're not so bad yourself. I liked that line about us running late for brunch."

My cheeks heat as I take a step closer to him, reveling in his gorgeous smile. "And *I* liked the part where you said you were my boyfriend. It was very believable."

Charlie looks down at his shoes before his eyes meet mine again. "Thanks. But I'm not so sure I was acting."

"No?" My stomach flutters.

He shakes his head. "Grady looked pretty jealous. I thought he might try to punch me."

"I honestly think you could take him," I say with a wink.

My fingers skate up Charlie's muscular arms and around his neck. It's only been two weeks since I last saw him, but he's somehow even more handsome than I remember. His hair's grown out a bit since we first met, and there's a little curl to it now that looks sexy on him. And the way his gaze is locked on mine, I can tell he's missed me as much as I've missed him. I take another step forward, into his arms, and before I know it, my lips are gravitating toward his.

"Shoot," I say, just milliseconds before impact. "I didn't ask Esther if I'm allowed to kiss you."

Charlie steps back, a curious look on his face. "Um…Esther?"

I chuckle. "She's my therapist. She suggested we spend the

next month hanging out and getting to know each other…without having sex. Are you okay with that?"

"Of course," he says right away. "I told you I'd wait as long as you need, and I mean it, Jenna." The pink in his cheeks deepens. "I'm just happy I get to spend time with you."

"Me too," I say, taking him in my arms again. "So…what do you think? Should we kiss?"

"You're in the driver's seat." Charlie tucks a strand of hair behind my ear. "Or I guess you could let Esther decide."

I bite the smile on my lips, very aware of the pull I feel toward his body. There's barely a few inches of space between us, but I'm desperate to close the gap.

I think back to my session with Esther again. She'd suggested starting my relationship with Charlie the same way mine started with Hunter.

Well, Hunter and I kissed plenty…so, I guess I have my answer.

I press my body and my lips against Charlie's, and his hands move to my waist. But he lets me take the lead. I slip my tongue into his mouth, rake my fingers through his hair, and he does the same to me. It feels so good, I arch into him, baring my neck for him to kiss. He does it eagerly, his mouth traveling down to my collarbone, and up to my ear, then back to my lips.

"Charlie, oh my god…wait," I say, breathless.

He steps back to give me space.

I place a hand over my racing heart. I've never been this turned on, just making out with someone. "I'm sorry, you're such an amazing kisser…if we keep going, I don't think I'll be able to stop."

"Like I said, you're in the driver's seat," he tells me with an amused grin.

I'm so warm, I have to fan my face with my hand. "We probably shouldn't kiss. I mean…that was intense, right? And I don't want to…you know, get you all hot and bothered and not be able to, um—"

Charlie laughs. "You don't have to worry about that. I mean, I'm extremely attracted to you, don't get me wrong. And I foresee a lot of cold showers in my future. But, um…" He looks at me earnestly. "I want to wait before we have sex, too."

I raise my eyebrows. "You do?"

He steps toward me and takes my hand. "I think this could be really special, Jenna—you and me. I've never felt this way about someone I just met, and if I'm being honest, it's a little scary. Not because I don't want this, but because of how much I do. And I know you've been burned in the past, and I have too, so…I just want to make sure we do this right."

It occurs to me that I've been so focused on my own relationship history that I haven't thought much about Charlie's. But I guess I'll find out in due time. From what I can tell, he learned enough from his past relationships to know what he wants now—and the fact that it's me has me feeling over the moon.

Charlie moves his hands to my waist. "When we sleep together, I want it to mean something," he whispers.

I wipe a tear that rolls down my cheek. "I don't know how… but you always say the right thing." Smiling, I circle my arms around him, and the magnetic pull between us moves my lips toward his again, but he stops me.

"I thought you said no kissing," he teases.

"Hmm. How about no tongue?" I counter.

"Deal," he says, and presses his lips to mine. The kiss is short and sweet this time. "Are you hungry?"

I nod. "Starving."

"Good," he says. "Because word on the street is, we're running late for brunch."

I grin. "I'll go get changed." But when I glance down expecting to see my shorts and tank top, all I see are paint splotches. "Oh my gosh, I completely forgot I was wearing my smock!" I throw my head back, laughing. "How the heck were you able to kiss me that passionately, when I look this ridiculous?"

Charlie shakes his head. "Are you kidding me? You could wear a tent and still be beautiful."

My laughter fades, and I gaze up at him, my heart melting.

Men don't typically say I'm beautiful. Hot, or sexy, yes. But being called beautiful feels different. Like it's not only about my physical appearance, but about me as a person.

"You okay?" he asks me.

I smile. "I'm just happy."

He pulls me into him. "Yeah? Is therapy going well?"

"It really is. And I want to tell you all about it. But there's a lot to catch you up on…and some of it is pretty heavy." I sigh, feeling overwhelmed at the thought.

He lifts his hand to the side of my face. "There's no rush. We have time."

We have time.

My mind travels back to my last kiss with Hunter, before he

left my apartment that weekend. I remember wishing for more time together. But that wish never came true.

I guess you never know how much time you're going to get. Which is why, when you find someone worth your time, you don't waste it. You lean in.

And I'm ready to do that with Charlie.

fifteen

When I meet Vanessa and Sam for drinks that night, I have to work hard to keep the lovestruck grin off my face.

I just had the most perfect day with Charlie.

After brunch, we took a leisurely stroll to Olive Park, since he'd never been before. We stopped at his apartment to pick up his camera on the way, because I guaranteed him he'd want to take pictures of the skyline. It's early September, but it still feels like peak summer, and Chicago's beauty is on full display. But even though Charlie was impressed with the view, he ended up taking more photos of me than anything else.

It started with a kiss that got a little carried away. It was my fault, of course—apparently my tongue has a mind of its own. But when we pulled apart, Charlie said I looked so beautiful, he wanted to take my photograph. I agreed, and it turned into a mini photoshoot. I sat on the grass, with the Navy Pier Ferris wheel in the distance behind me, and Charlie knelt in front of me. He looked through his camera lens, doing his photographer thing, and he was so sexy, it took all I had not to beg him to break our rules and sleep with me.

I don't know how I'll make it through an entire month of only chaste kisses. It's not that I can't go four weeks without sex. I've had much longer dry spells than that, and been fine. It's just that this is the first time in years that I have feelings for someone.

And sex with feelings is something I haven't had enough of in my life.

Not to mention, the connection I have with Charlie is like nothing I've ever felt before. If this were a romantic comedy, I'd be dancing in the streets right now, my heart feels so light and free.

"What's with the smile, Jenna?" Sam asks as soon as I'm settled into the seat next to Vanessa. We're in the back corner of a new wine bar on the north side of the city. It's cozy and intimate, and the perfect place for girl talk. Which, I guess, is why Sam follows up her question with another, more direct one: "Wait…did you just have sex?"

A laugh escapes me, and I turn to Vanessa, who gives her friend a heavy dose of side-eye. "Sam, you didn't even say hello, and you're just going to launch into questions about Jenna's sex life?"

Sam shrugs, a mischievous glint in her eyes. "Well, look at her, V! She's glowing." She turns back to me. "And hello, by the way."

"Good to see you again, Sam," I say through a giggle.

Vanessa fixes her gaze on me. "You are kinda glowing," she concedes.

"I didn't have sex," I say, shaking my head, but still grinning.

"New vibrator, then?" Sam asks.

I chuckle. "Nope." *But that's probably not a bad idea, given how difficult it is for me to keep my hands off Charlie.* "Just a really great date," I continue.

"Looks like Charlie's still giving you butterflies," Vanessa says with her bright smile. "That's her new neighbor," she explains to Sam.

"How convenient! And judging by the hearts in your eyes, I'm guessing you want this to be more than casual?" Sam says, recalling our conversation at Tati Marie's birthday party, when I'd told her I wasn't looking for a serious relationship.

I answer with a vigorous nod.

"Well if it's going so well, why is he only giving you butterflies, and not orgasms?" Sam asks with a furrowed brow.

"We can always count on Sam to cut to the chase," Vanessa teases.

Sam crosses her arms. "I don't get why people are so uptight when it comes to talking about sex. I mean, everyone does it, right? With the right person, it's a natural, healthy, beautiful thing. Now tell us, Jenna—why aren't you getting laid?"

"Do we have a waiter yet?" I ask, fanning my face. "I could use a glass of wine for this conversation."

"We ordered a bottle of red before you got here. Should be coming any minute now," Vanessa assures me.

"Thank god," I say on a deep exhale. Then I turn back to Sam. "I'm sure Charlie and I will have sex soon enough…but for now, we're taking it slow."

"I've never understood that concept," Sam says with a pensive gaze.

"That's because you don't want a long-term relationship," Vanessa chimes in.

"Yup. I defy gender norms, much to the dismay of my mom," Sam says, rolling her eyes.

"Is she still calling you an old maid?" Vanessa asks with a sympathetic frown.

Sam chuckles. "That's my grandma—and the term she likes to throw around is 'spinster.' But every time the Lebanese side of my family gets together, my mom ends up crying on her sisters' shoulders, wondering where she went wrong with me. Who knew that getting a PhD and a faculty position at an elite university could be so disappointing? If she found out I'm having casual sex with a twenty-three-year-old barista with a penis piercing, I bet she'd spontaneously combust."

"Well, I will always have a soft spot for your mom," Vanessa says at the tail end of a chuckle. "Remember that time she showed up at your apartment in Manhattan, without telling you she'd booked a flight?"

"You mean ambushed me?" Sam raises an eyebrow.

"And since we were hanging out, she invited me to go with you guys to that Middle Eastern grocery store? She was so sweet. She bought me tabbouleh, and pita bread, and, like, four tubs of hummus. That's when I fell in love with her," Vanessa jokes. "Food is the key to my heart."

Sam laughs. "She's a lovely woman, don't get me wrong. And I know she means well. She just wants me to be happy—but she can't understand that my definition of happiness is different than hers."

"And includes penis piercings," I chime in.

"Precisely."

We're all laughing when the waiter arrives with our bottle of wine. As he's pouring, Vanessa's phone rings. But when she looks at the name on the screen, her smile fades.

"Is everything okay?" I ask.

Vanessa sighs, bringing her forehead to her palm. Her eyes are glistening. "That was Nico. He's been calling me."

"Oh no." I scoot my chair closer to Vanessa, so I can put my arm around her. "Do you know what he wants?"

She shakes her head. "I haven't picked up, and he isn't leaving messages. I feel awful not calling him back, but we agreed not to talk for a while, and I think that's for the best."

A tear rolls down her cheek.

My heart aches for her. She broke up with Nico to find the love of her life, but she hasn't gone on a single date, four months later. She must be wracked with guilt. Either that, or she regrets leaving him. Maybe it wouldn't be the worst thing in the world for them to talk.

"You're not over him, V," Sam says, as though reading my mind. "I think it's pretty clear. I mean, I tried setting you up with that hot psychology grad student I met on campus, but you wouldn't even consider it. What if you met up with Nico for coffee, or something? Because if he's calling you, my guess is, he's not over you either."

Vanessa sighs. "Nico doesn't live in Chicago anymore. When we broke up, I told him I'd move out of our apartment and live with my sister, but he insisted I stay. He said he'd figure something out. A few days later, he made arrangements to pick up his things and said he'd decided to go back to New York."

"So what?" Sam says. "One of you will move again. No big deal. Just call him."

Vanessa wipes her eyes and forces a smile. "No, I'm just having a rough week, that's all. Work's been crazy, and I'm exhausted. I'll be okay. I know I will. It's just taking a little longer than I expected."

Sam leans back in her chair. "Well, if you change your mind about the hot grad student, let me know. And if you don't change your mind…well, let me know that, too, because I might go after him when I'm done with the barista." She winks at Vanessa, like she's joking, but I'd be willing to bet she's not.

"Will do," Vanessa says with a laugh. "And thank you both for listening. I appreciate it."

"That's what friends are for," Sam replies with a sincere tilt of her head.

"It's true. Whatever you need, we're here to help," I say, squeezing Vanessa's hand. "I mean that."

After what she did—taking care of me when I broke down, and finding Esther for me—I wouldn't think twice about giving her one of my kidneys, if she needed it. I love her like a sister.

Which reminds me. I have an actual sister in New York whose calls I've been avoiding for two weeks…

And she deserves an apology.

After Sam, Vanessa, and I polish off this bottle of wine, I'm going home, and straight to bed. Christy usually calls me at 8:00 a.m. on Sundays, but I want to be the one to reach out

first this time.

I owe her so much more than that. But it's a start, at least.

When Christy answers the phone the following morning, her voice is riddled with anxiety. "Jenna? Are you okay?"

Normally, this type of greeting would trigger me, and I'd respond sounding annoyed or defensive. But today, all it does is make my heart ache for worrying my little sister so much over the last several years.

"As a matter of fact, I'm feeling better than I have in a very long time," I tell her. "And I have you to thank for that."

"What? Really? Um…why?" she says, sounding as confused as I expected her to. Our conversations tend to be a lot more tense than this, even right off the bat.

"I finally took your advice and started seeing a therapist. You were right that I needed help processing my grief over Hunter's death." A wave of relief hits me as soon as I get the words off my chest. "Do you remember the new friend I mentioned? Vanessa?"

"The social worker?" my sister asks.

"Yup. She found me an amazing therapist, and I've been going twice a week.

"Oh, Jenna."

That's all she gets out before she starts sniffling and crying into the phone. I don't have to see her face to know her tears come from joy.

"Christy, I'm so sorry for—"

"You have nothing to apologize for. You were twenty-two, and lost your first love. Of course you were devastated. I only wanted you to know that you didn't have to deal with your pain all alone." A sob escapes her before she continues. "I just hope you didn't think I was trying to offload you onto a therapist because I thought you were a burden. I promise that was never my intention."

My eyes well up. "Of course not. And I'm sorry I made you feel that way. I think I was just embarrassed because you had to take care of me for months. I'm sure you didn't mind—but *I* did. You're my little sister, and you're always the one looking out for me. You're the one who has it all together, with the dream job and the serious relationship. I know I shouldn't compare our lives…but I did, and I felt like such a mess."

Christy's quiet for several seconds before she starts crying again.

"What's wrong?" I ask. This time, her sobs don't sound happy.

"I'm the real mess," she nearly whispers through tears.

My brow furrows. "Huh?"

My sister takes a ragged breath. "I may have a dream job—but the serious relationship? Not so much. I, um…broke up with Kyle."

"Oh, no!" I gasp. "I'm so sorry. And shocked…honestly." Christy and Kyle have been practically glued to each other for eight years. They did everything together. Exercising, and cooking, and shopping for groceries. They were like an old married couple. I always imagined they would be, one day. "When did this happen?"

Christy sighs. "About a month ago."

"Wait…what?"

"It might be closer to five weeks now, actually."

I shake my head, perplexed. "But wasn't he with you the other week, when my video went viral? You said you'd just shown it to him, and he liked it. And every Sunday, when we talk, you tell me you and Kyle are about to go running in Central Park. I don't get it. Are you broken up, but still living together?"

Christy sniffles. "Not exactly."

"I'm so confused right now."

She sighs. "I've been lying to you. Kyle moved out after I ended things. We haven't spoken since."

My jaw drops.

It was one thing for Christy to sneak peeks at my journal when we were in high school. That kind of behavior is to be expected among teenage sisters. But to lie to me about her breakup, at this stage in her life, doesn't make sense. Why would she keep it a secret?

She starts sobbing again. "The truth is…"

When she doesn't finish her sentence right away, my heart sinks. Did Kyle cheat on her? Did he gamble away their savings? What if he's not the man he says he is? My mind races, thinking of every episode of *Dateline* I've ever watched, while Christy remains quiet (except for all the sniffling). What is this truth my sister's so reluctant to tell me?

"What is it, Christy?"

I brace myself to hear something shocking.

"The truth is," she continues, "I…*really*…hate running."

"You hate…running?"

"Yes. More than hate. I despise it. And it's all Kyle ever wanted to do. He had every day of our lives mapped out, and it was all running, and marathons, and the same lackluster protein shake every morning, and it was just so…so…*boring*, Jenna!"

I stifle a chuckle. I always found Kyle a little boring, too—but I never told Christy that, of course. I always figured his predictability was part of the appeal for my sister. I mean, it's not like she's a wild child. For as long as I've known her, she's been a planner. In high school, she inventoried her entire closet, made a list of outfits, and wore them on rotation, so she never had to think about what to wear.

But maybe she's changed. Or maybe I don't know her as well as I thought.

"I couldn't take it anymore," she continues. "My life was flashing before me, and I knew exactly what it looked like. There were no surprises. Saturdays were for groceries and meal prep, and Sundays were for long runs, and on Mondays we folded laundry, and on Tuesdays we ate turkey meatloaf, even when I wanted tacos—and he even scheduled *sex*, Jenna!"

"Oh," I say, my cheeks warming. I don't think I've ever heard Christy say the word "sex" before.

"He'd only sleep with me on Fridays, because he didn't have to be at the hospital early on Saturdays. And, quite frankly… it wasn't enough for me. But god forbid I try to get in his pants any other day of the week! I mean, would it have killed him to be a little more spontaneous? It's not unreasonable to want to have sex on a Wednesday, every now and then, is it?"

"Not at all," I assure her. I catch a glimpse of my face in the mirror over my dresser, and I'm beet red. It's not that I mind Christy opening up to me—I want her to. I'm just not used to hearing her talk this way.

"I had no idea you were unhappy," I continue. "Why didn't you tell me sooner? You and Kyle were together for so long…I can't imagine it's been easy keeping these feelings bottled up."

"I wanted to talk to you about it," Christy admits. "But my issues with Kyle seemed trivial compared to what you went through with Hunter. I guess I didn't feel right venting to you, because you were still in so much pain. When you told me you started therapy, though, I figured it would be okay. You already sound so much better."

Now I'm the one sniffling. "Your breakup isn't trivial. It's your life, and you're my sister. I want to be here for you whenever you need me—no matter what I'm going through. That's what family's for. And…I love you, Christy."

When the words come out of my mouth, I realize how infrequently I say them to her. My heart stings with regret, and I vow to do better from now on.

"I love you, too, Jenna," she whispers.

For a minute or two, it's just blubbering and sniffling and nose-blowing, before either of us can speak again.

"So, how *are* you doing with the breakup?" I ask.

"I was relieved to begin with. I mean, no more protein powder and twenty-mile runs—what could be better than that? I've already gained five pounds, and I couldn't be happier," she says with a chuckle. "But now…I think I'm beginning to freak out a little."

"You're lonely." It's a feeling that's practically defined me—until recently.

"Exactly," she says. "And dating in New York City feels impossible. There are too many people. Too many options."

"Then come here," I tell her. "Chicago needs literary agents, too."

She laughs. "Yeah, but how long will you actually be living there…"

She's not asking, so much as telling me she wouldn't uproot her life and follow me to Chicago, when there's no guarantee I'll be here long-term. I get it—I'm "Runaway Jenna," after all.

Or, I *was*.

"Something feels different here, in Chicago," I say. "For the first time in my life, I'm starting to put down roots. I have a great therapist, and I'm painting again, and making new friends, and I'm even—"

My heart flutters thinking about Charlie, and our plans to hang out again today.

"What?" my sister asks. The excitement in her voice is unmistakable, and it fills me with pure joy. She knows where I'm going with this.

I smile. "I'm dating someone. His name is Charlie. He's my new neighbor, actually. I literally crashed right into him when I was walking out of the elevator."

"Sounds like the perfect meet-cute," Christy says.

"It definitely felt like a scene from a movie," I tell her. "When our eyes met, something sparked between us. I know it sounds crazy. Maybe it was just lust, but…sometimes I wonder if it was love at first sight."

"Oh my god." She sounds choked up. "You have no idea how long I've been waiting to hear you say something like this."

"Thanks," I tell her, on the verge of tears again, myself. "But don't get your hopes up too high, yet. Charlie and I have only been out a few times."

"Just knowing that you're open to loving someone again…it's the best news I could wish for," she says.

I wipe my eyes. "You're the sweetest sister in the world. And I know you're going to find someone special. So, don't worry, okay? If things don't work out in New York, just come here, and I'll be your matchmaker."

"You'd really want me to move to Chicago?" she asks after a beat.

I nod. "We haven't lived in the same place since I went away to college. It'd be nice, wouldn't it?"

"I've always wanted us to be closer," Christy says. "Not just geographically, but…"

"I know you have," I tell her when she trails off. "And I feel terrible that I spent the last eight years pushing you away. It's only because you could see right through my act. You knew that I wasn't okay, but I didn't have the strength to face it yet. But all that's changed now. And I promise to do everything I can to fix what I broke between us."

"You didn't break anything," my sister says. "Maybe just a small dent, but nothing's broken. Our relationship is stronger than that. I need it to be, Jenna. Because Mom and Dad…"

"What about Mom and Dad?" I ask, my curiosity piqued. As far as I know, Christy gets along great with both our parents. Or as well as one can, given their personalities.

"They kinda suck," she says.

I throw my head back, laughing. "I had no idea you felt that way, too! I mean, Mom is Mom…she's not super involved in either of our lives. But I always thought you and Dad got along."

Christy sighs. "He's less of a jerk to me, I guess…but I've never been a fan of the way he treats you. He never supported you in anything you wanted to do, whether it was art, or cheer. He snubbed his nose at it, because he didn't think it was impressive enough to brag about to his friends at the country club. Meanwhile, he boasted about my academic achievements like they were his own, even though *I* was the one who did all the hard work. Well…fuck him."

I lift my hand to my mouth, overcome with an unfamiliar sense of validation. Also, I'm stunned, because I've never heard Christy say "fuck." We Andersen girls don't swear much.

"I'm sorry I never spoke up to Dad about it," she continues. "I should have told him he was being unfair to you. It's selfish, but I was afraid he would turn on me, too. And then I'd have no one. Because you'd go away to college, and Mom would keep being Mom. Dad was actually engaged in my life, since he was Dean of my school. It wasn't the father-daughter relationship I dreamed of having…but it was something."

"I understand," I tell her. "And it doesn't matter. You were a kid, for one thing. You shouldn't have to teach your dad how to parent. Besides, he never would've listened to you, anyway. He's far too stubborn."

Christy lets out a little laugh. "That's true."

I pause for a beat. "Do you think Mom would consider therapy if I told her how much I'm benefiting from it?"

Maybe all my mom needs is someone who cares enough to find her help—the way Vanessa did for me.

"It's worth a shot," my sister says. "I don't think Mom is beyond hope, the way Dad is."

"I'll talk to her about it. I'd rather do it in person, though... so maybe over Thanksgiving. Are you going to come home?"

"Absolutely, if you're there. I'll help you talk to Mom. After Dad *retires* to his study," she adds, and I can practically see her eyes rolling back in her head.

I chuckle. "Okay, great. And after they go to bed, we can stay up watching movies, and drinking wine, and eating leftover pie. Whaddya say?"

Typically, after Thanksgiving dinner, I'd meet up with old friends from high school who are in town. But, this year, I'd much rather hang out with my sister.

"Count me in," Christy says. "Sounds perfect."

"It really does."

I brush a happy tear from my cheek. If I'd known that going to therapy would have the added bonus of helping me get closer to my sister, I may have gone sooner. But better late than never. I've always longed for us to have a relationship like this. I just thought we were too different. Now I think we may be more alike than I thought.

"I love you, Christy," I say again.

"I love you, too, Jenna."

As soon as we hang up, I walk straight into my art studio

and set a blank canvas on my easel. Before I pick up my brush and palette, my gaze travels across the six paintings I've done so far, all in a row, leaning against the wall. Like the self-portrait I painted in Tati Marie's class, which is first in line, the pieces that follow all focus on the subject's eyes—like a zoomed-in photograph that starts just below the hairline, and ends right above the chin.

Staring back at me are my mom's olive-green eyes, which are identical to mine, except for the faraway look she always has.

My dad's stern, disapproving gaze is next to her.

Then Hunter's ocean-blue eyes—no longer dark and stormy, like the image that haunted me, but placid and peaceful, like I want to remember them.

After him is Charlie, and the wonder in his gaze when we first met.

And finally, Esther, my most recent portrait—her kind, thoughtful gaze inviting me to heal.

It hurts my heart that I never thought to paint my sister until now. They say that eyes are the windows to the soul, and maybe that's why I couldn't do it before. Because I hardly knew her. My buttoned-up, perfectionist sister, who seemed to have it all together, has always been a bit of a mystery to me.

But the wall between us is crumbling now, and I'm starting to see Christy for who she really is. Someone who's followed the rules all her life, and is yearning to break free. To experience the joy, and pleasure, and adventure she's denied herself for years.

Whose eyes are full of hope…and maybe a hint of mischief.

I pick up my paintbrush, and that's where I begin.

An hour and a half later, Charlie and I are on our way to his cousin Maya's beach yoga class. As soon as she catches sight of us walking toward her, her eyes light up, and she reaches out to give me a hug.

"It's so great to meet you, Jenna," she says in a lovely English accent that I wasn't expecting. Charlie and I were busy engaging in flirtatious banter on the way to the beach, so I didn't get a chance to ask him about his cousin. But now that I see her, I'm even more curious about Charlie's background. While there's a hint of family resemblance in the shapes of their eyes and noses, their coloring couldn't be more different. Where Charlie looks like a bronze statue, all golden and sun-kissed, with chestnut hair and rich brown eyes, Maya is fair-skinned and freckly, with strawberry-blonde hair and blue eyes. She's beautiful—good looks obviously run in the family. But she looks like she'd sunburn easily, so I'm relieved she's wearing a white linen shirt over her tank top and leggings.

"I'm so happy to meet you, too," I tell her. "And I'm excited for class. I haven't done yoga on the beach in ages."

Maya grins. "When my cousin said he was bringing you, I was thrilled. And, just between us," she stage-whispers, "I don't think I've ever seen him quite so smitten."

My heart flutters, and even more so when Charlie wraps his arm around my waist. I glance up at him, and there's no hint of embarrassment in his eyes. Only that same sparkle I see every time he looks at me. He *is* smitten.

"Well, the feeling's mutual," I tell Maya as I'm smiling at Charlie. In response, he kisses the top of my head.

Maya's freckled hands float to her heart, and she lets out a happy sigh. "Alright, lovebirds, feel free to grab a spot anywhere, and we'll get started in just a few."

Charlie and I stay up front, as a small crowd behind us begins to get settled. The beginning of class is delightful, with a heavenly breeze coming off the lake. It's a perfect seventy-five degrees and sunny.

But halfway through the hour, it starts getting steamy. I'm used to practicing yoga in a heated studio, so it doesn't bother me at all. What I'm not used to, however, is seeing Charlie without a shirt on. We're standing in the Warrior II position, front knees bent and arms outstretched, when he hits his limit and lifts off his white tee. He's facing away from me, but the view is still spectacular. Broad, muscular shoulders and arms, and—

Oh god, he's turning around.

We're supposed to face the opposite direction now, but I'm moving in slow motion, unable to tear my eyes away from what I see. Charlie's chest is a literal masterpiece. The man is so impressively sculpted, I have to resist the urge to cry. I'm not sure if it's because I'm moved by his beauty—the way I'm moved when I see a stunning piece of art—or if I'm just sad, because I want to touch him so badly, and I can't.

Probably the latter.

I feel a little better when my eyes work their way up to Charlie's face, and he's checking me out, too. When our gazes meet, I smile, and he winks at me.

Begrudgingly, I turn to face the other way in Warrior II, but my heartrate has picked up, and my skin is glistening—and it's not because of the heat index. Somehow, I make it through class, but I'd be lying if I said I didn't spend the entire time in Savasana, our final resting pose, fantasizing about Charlie's hard body pressed against my soft curves.

"What'd you think of class?" Maya asks us afterward. "Hot, wasn't it?"

"Very," I say, trying not to watch Charlie wipe down his muscles with a towel. "But it was such a great flow. You're a fantastic teacher! I can't believe you just got certified."

"Agreed, you're incredible, Maya. Congrats," Charlie says, looking proud.

"We're planning to get breakfast in the neighborhood," I tell her. "Would you like to join us?"

Maya smiles. "I'd love to, but I have a coffee date of my own this morning."

Charlie's face lights up. "No way! Maya, that's awesome."

Her freckled cheeks turn red. "Thanks, cousin." Then she

faces me. "I just came out at the ripe old age of twenty-five, and your beau is the first person I felt comfortable telling in our family," she continues, beaming at Charlie.

He smiles, but waves his hand dismissively. "I'm your only family in Chicago. Who else were you going to tell?"

Maya laughs. "No, really, Jenna. This guy, here, has a heart of gold. The best of the best. He sat right next to me when I Facetimed my mum last week to share the news. It was a shit conversation…but having him by my side made me feel so supported. And safe."

Now Maya's eyes are shiny, and mine are stinging as well. I've been wondering how I can feel so comfortable with someone I haven't known very long—but I guess that's just the kind of guy Charlie is. A guy with a heart of gold, like his cousin said.

The guy I've been waiting for my whole life.

I glance at Charlie, whose cheeks are a deeper shade of pink now, too. Could he really be this perfect? What's the catch?

Just as I'm asking myself that question, Charlie pulls his cousin into a hug and says, "I'm here for you. Whatever you need," and my heart melts.

Well, if there is a catch, I guess I'll have to deal with it—because I'm completely head over heels for this man.

"I'm sorry the talk with your mom didn't go well," I tell Maya, when she and Charlie pull apart.

She gives me an appreciative nod. "Being a Sutton isn't always easy."

I take my gaze from Maya to Charlie. He's looking down at the sand, his jaw clenched in silent agreement.

"Sorry, Jenna, I didn't mean to unload my life story on you after a relaxing yoga class," Maya continues with a laugh. "You just have one of those faces I feel like I can trust. And if my cousin likes you, that means you're a good egg."

"You can talk to me anytime, Maya," I tell her, which puts a smile on her face and Charlie's. "So, who is this lucky lady you're meeting for coffee?" I ask, giving her a playful nudge.

"She's a med student called Elle. She's lovely, and smart, and—god, I hope she likes me," she goes on with a worried sigh.

"She will, if she's as smart as you say," I reply with a grin. "Well, we don't want to make you late for your date, so—"

"Right, I'd better dash," Maya says, blowing kisses at me and Charlie as she starts to trek through the sand. "Enjoy your brekkie!"

"Brekkie," I echo, turning to Charlie. "I love that."

"My dad and his sister were born and raised in London. Maya grew up there, too, hence the accent," he explains with a smile.

"I had no idea that Sutton's had an English owner," I say as we start walking south to a nearby strip of eateries. "But now that you mention it, you guys do have an amazing tea selection."

"My dad does pride himself on that." Although he says it with a chuckle, there's a hint of longing in his eyes—I imagine for the relationship he wishes he had with his father. I don't mention it, of course. Instead, I use the opportunity to ask Charlie about his family tree.

"So that makes you half English," I begin, hoping he'll fill in the blanks for me. I'm dying to know what combination of genes resulted in this beautiful man.

Luckily, he takes the bait. "I'm a mix of a handful of things. Sometimes I make people guess, because it's fun to hear their answers. But I'm not going to put you on the spot like that."

"I wouldn't even know where to begin," I say, relieved that I don't have to.

He laughs again. "Well, my dad is English on his father's side, and Moroccan on his mom's. I know you've noticed Sutton's tea selection, but have you ever tried our tagine?"

My eyes go wide. "Charlie, are you kidding? I love it! I have at least four boxes in my freezer at all times."

"That's my grandmother's recipe," he says with a wistful smile. "She lived with us for several years when I was young, before she passed away. And she taught me how to cook. So I can make you the real thing sometime, from scratch."

"I would love that," I say, adding cooking to my mental list of Charlie's perfect qualities.

"Great," he replies with an easy grin. "So, that's my dad's side of the family. And on my mom's side, I'm a quarter Black and a quarter Danish."

As we approach Michigan Avenue, busy with tourists and shoppers, I grab his arm to turn him toward me. "Charlie, you will never, ever guess what I'm about to tell you," I deadpan.

"You're Danish, too," he says with a knowing smile.

"Dammit," I joke. "Was it the blonde hair that tipped you off, or the name Andersen?"

"Any relation to Hans Christian?" he quips back as we cross the street.

I giggle. "No. But, when I was in grade school, I used to tell kids he was my uncle."

Charlie throws his head back, laughing. "A nineteenth-century author of fairy tales? You didn't."

I nod. "I thought it would win them over."

Now his smile fades. "Why did you need to win them over?"

"I was diagnosed with dyslexia in second grade. And, you know how kids can be. I got teased," I say matter-of-factly.

Charlie frowns and takes my hand as we continue to stroll. "I'm sorry you went through that."

"I'm okay now," I say.

And it's true. Maybe it's the comfort level I feel with Charlie, or the confidence I'm gaining from my therapy sessions with Esther—or both—but my cheeks don't flush when I talk about my dyslexia this time.

As we wait to cross the street again, Charlie plants a kiss on the top of my head. "How do you feel about the Pancake House? I've never been."

I smile. "It's my favorite place for breakfast."

"Well, then we're definitely going."

Thirty minutes later, we're seated on their patio with chilled glasses of orange juice, giant mugs of coffee, and Swedish pancakes so thin and buttery, they melt in your mouth.

"These are incredible," Charlie says, spooning a heap of lingonberry jam onto his plate.

"Is your sweet tooth satisfied?" I ask as I watch him savor a bite.

He nods, grinning. "For now. It'll probably reactivate around dinnertime." After a sip of coffee, his gaze turns pensive. "Maybe this is too much too soon—we did spend most of the day together yesterday—but I'd love to make you that tagine tonight. I don't know if you're free, or—"

"Yes," I reply right away.

Relief washes over his face. "You sure? You're not getting tired of me?"

"Charlie…I don't even think that's possible."

He reaches across the table for my hand, his thumb moving in slow circles over my skin, which sends shivers up my spine. The littlest touch from him makes me feel so alive.

"I can't believe this is only our fourth date," he says, his gaze landing on mine. "I feel like I've known you forever."

"I know," I reply, wondering how it was only yesterday morning that I told him about Esther's suggestion to take things slowly for a month. "Has it been thirty days yet?" I half-joke, every cell in my body yearning to be closer to this man.

He laughs. "I don't even think it's been thirty hours."

I let out a playful groan. Every minute I spend with Charlie only confirms how right this feels. Do I really need to wait a whole month to know that he isn't just in this to sleep with me? I think it's pretty clear his motives are more sincere than that.

"My cousin was right earlier, Jenna. I am smitten with you," he says—as though reading my mind, once again. *Is that a soulmate thing?* the hopeless romantic inside me asks.

"Likewise," I reply, squeezing his hand.

"I have a few hours of work to get done this afternoon, so want to come by around seven for dinner?"

"That's perfect," I say. "As long as you let me bring dessert— for your sweet tooth."

"Deal," he says with a glimmer in his eyes.

"Speaking of your job," I continue, "I haven't heard any thunderstrikes coming from your phone lately. Is your dad getting better with boundaries?"

Charlie chuckles. "I guess you could say that. My mom convinced him to go on a trip for their fortieth wedding anniversary. And because she knows my dad so well, she booked a spa hotel in France that locks up your electronic devices while you're there."

"Sounds like heaven."

"Not if you're my dad," he replies with a wry smile. "My guess is, he's spent the better part of the week trying to sweettalk the staff into getting him his phone back. Or paying them off, more likely."

As I'm laughing, an adorable little girl in pigtails walks up to us from a neighboring table. She can't be more than three or four years old. "Hi," she says. "I'm Lucy."

"Hey, Lucy! I'm Jenna, and this is Charlie," I say, smiling.

"Come on back, Luce," her mom calls out from their table. "I'm sorry, she's in a very chatty phase right now," she explains with a sheepish grin.

"Oh, it's no trouble at all," I tell Lucy's mom. "She's adorable."

"Alright, time to go, honey bunny." Lucy's mom stands from her chair, gathers their things, then takes her daughter's hand.

"But I don't wanna go!" She stomps her feet.

Her mom heaves a deep sigh.

"We're about to leave, too," I tell Lucy. "Can I get a high-five before you go?"

Lucy beams and slaps my palm.

"Oh, you're so strong!" I tell her, pretending my hand hurts.

Lucy giggles. "Bye bye!" she calls out as she lets her mom lead her to the patio door.

When I turn back to face Charlie, he's smiling ear to ear. "You were so sweet with her."

The late summer sky is still perfectly blue and clear, but it's like a storm cloud rolls in over my head. My heart sinks, and my grin fades.

How could I forget? I haven't told Charlie that I don't want kids.

This is where it ends. This is where the other shoe drops.

This is where my wishes don't come true.

"Jenna…are you okay?" he asks, concern written on every crinkle of his forehead.

But there's no point in delaying the inevitable. I am who I am—and if Charlie and I aren't compatible, it's better to know now than later.

My heart will break, yes. But now I know that, if I work hard enough, the pieces will come back together.

"I don't want to be a mom," I tell him, my pulse racing. "I don't want children. Is that…a dealbreaker?"

When Charlie's brow unfurrows, I wonder if I'm imagining things. But then, he says, "No, Jenna. It's not."

"It isn't?" I have to be sure I heard him right.

He smiles. "It's not a dealbreaker. I always thought I could go either way. If my partner wanted children, I wouldn't have ruled it out. But lately, since I've become more serious about pursuing travel photography, I can't imagine how young kids would fit into that lifestyle. Plus, I never dreamed of becoming a father. Maybe it's the strained relationship I have with my dad, I don't know. But I have four nieces and three nephews I adore, and that's enough for me."

Yet again, he says all the right things.

I'm so relieved, I begin to cry. Charlie gives me a questioning look.

"When I fill you in on what I've been working on in therapy, this reaction will make sense," I say with a little laugh through my tears. "Suffice it to say, dating is sometimes tricky for a woman who doesn't want kids."

Charlie moves around the table to sit next to me, then puts his arm around my shoulder. "Jenna, nothing could be a dealbreaker for me when it comes to you. Nothing."

The intensity in his gaze leaves no room in my mind for doubt. I believe him.

This isn't the end. This isn't where the other shoe drops.

This very well might be where my wishes come true.

seventeen

Before I leave for dinner at Charlie's place, I spritz perfume on all my pulse points. And over my cleavage—just in case.

My freshly washed hair has the perfect amount of volume in its signature long bob. I'm wearing my favorite smoky gray eyeliner that makes my green eyes pop. And my lips are a kissable, velvety pink.

I'm in the beige bodycon dress that I was wearing in my client's viral video. The one that perfectly hugs my curves.

I guess you could say I'm trying to tempt fate. Or, at the very least, I'm trying to tempt Charlie. After all, he was the one who took his shirt off during yoga this morning, and I haven't been able to think straight ever since.

This dress is payback.

I grab the plate of brownies I made from scratch for dessert, and head down the hall. A smile blooms on my lips as I envision the look on Charlie's face when he sees me dressed up for the first time.

And the reaction I get when he opens the door is every bit as satisfying as I imagined. His eyes widen, his lips part, and he takes in a quick, ragged breath.

What I did *not* anticipate was the way my heart would stop the moment my gaze landed on him.

He looks like a supermodel. He's in perfectly tailored charcoal dress pants, and a light gray button-down shirt that fits like a glove over the ripples of muscles I've been thinking about all day. His chestnut hair is styled to bring out the little bit of curl I love so much. And he smells so damn good, I want to rip his shirt open and—

"Wow," he sighs out, running a hand over his hair. "You look amazing, Jenna."

Judging by the flush in his cheeks, I'd say my dress did its job. He's definitely tempted.

And the feeling is mutual.

"Thanks," I say, standing on my tiptoes and wrapping the hand that's not holding brownies around his neck. I steal a glance into his apartment behind him, which is immaculately clean. His aesthetic is modern and minimalist, with neutral colors and framed black-and-white photographs on the wall, highlighting his passion. The vibe is sexy—just like him.

When we stopped by yesterday so he could grab his camera on our way to the park, it didn't look like this. He hadn't anticipated company, and he apologized profusely for the disarray, even though I've seen bachelor pads in way worse shape. Charlie's mess just made him more interesting, because I got a glimpse into his real life. There were stacks of photography books on the couch I could tell he'd been flipping through. Travel magazines strewn on the coffee table. Weights on the floor near the windows, where he'd been working out. A Dartmouth sweatshirt thrown over a chair, and an empty cup of takeout coffee here and there. It was a relief to see this more human side of Charlie, beneath the picture-perfect exterior.

But tonight, his place is as spruced up and sparkling as he is, and I don't mind that either. It's sweet that he put so much effort into impressing me.

Although he didn't need to. If there's one thing I know for certain, it's that Charlie Sutton is the best thing that's happened to me in a very long time.

Maybe ever.

He takes his palm to the small of my back and presses me into him as our lips meet.

I let him lead, and the kiss is soft, sweet, and gentle.

No tongue. He's playing by the rules, which is both incredibly sexy and unbearably frustrating. His impressive restraint and unwavering respect for me only make me want him to throw me over his shoulder, toss me onto his bed, and have his way with me.

One thing's for sure. The ball will be in my court tonight.

"Come in," he says, closing the door behind me. Then he eyes the plate in my hand. "Did you make brownies?" he asks with an adorable grin that reminds me of a kid on Christmas morning.

I nod. "Now, I don't want you to feel threatened, because the Sutton's brownie mix is respectable…"

He chuckles, giving me a look out of the corner of his eye that turns my legs into putty.

"But these are the chocolatiest brownies you'll ever have," I continue. "I used to make them for cheer meets in high school. I'm kinda famous for them."

Charlie just looks at me for a moment with that smitten gaze of his. Then he shakes his head. "God, I love—"

My breath hitches.

"Brownies," he says after the slightest pause. "I love brownies. You know, with my sweet tooth, and all."

"I had a feeling," I say with a smile, although my pulse is racing. Did Charlie almost tell me he *loves* me?

As he takes the plate from my hand and puts it on the kitchen island, I shake the thought from my mind. It's still so early in our relationship. That thunderbolt that struck the instant we crashed into each other was just lust, right? He couldn't possibly love me yet.

Although the look in his eyes sure seems to say otherwise.

"So this is the famous dress you were wearing in the viral video," he says before turning his attention to the stove. The tagine is simmering in a pot, and the mix of spices in the air is intoxicating, making me hungry for more than just Charlie. "Did you ever get back to the designer about modeling for them during Fashion Week?"

My cheeks warm. "I'm surprised you remember that." I'd only mentioned it to him once, a couple of weeks ago, when we were walking home from the Museum of Contemporary Art. He'd asked what I was planning to do with the rest of my day, and I told him I'd be replying to all the inquiries I'd received since going viral. I guess I can add "good listener" to his list of swoonworthy qualities.

"I decided against it," I continue. "I mean, I'm flattered, of course. But I think my fifteen minutes of fame is finally coming to an end, and I'd like to keep it that way."

Charlie looks at me over his shoulder as he stirs our dinner, and smiles. "Not a fan of the spotlight, I take it?"

I tilt my head. "It's not that, really. I'm just afraid walking in their runway show will put me back in the news as the 'Bombshell Interior Designer,' and I'll get slammed with design inquiries again—when, deep down, my heart's not in it."

He turns from the stove and steps toward me, his arms settling around my waist. "You just want to paint," he says, matter-of-factly.

I nod, enjoying the way Charlie understands me. And the way his hands feel on my body. "I do. And life's too short not to follow your heart, right?"

He tucks my hair behind my ear, then grazes his fingers down my jawline and under my chin. "Ain't that the truth," he says with a glimmer in his eyes as he lifts my head to kiss me.

His lips are so pillowy soft that I can't help but wonder what they'd feel like on other parts of my body.

It's not like me to want someone this much. It's not that I don't crave sex. But more often than not, the reality doesn't live up to the fantasy in my head—and instead of passionate kisses, frenzied touches, and mind-blowing orgasms, it's just me trying to keep my mind from wandering to my to-do list.

Something tells me I won't have that problem with Charlie.

My body has never reacted this way to anyone before. Just his lips on mine makes me pulse, everywhere, with desire. I feel the rush of blood flow to my breasts, and deep inside my core, and between my thighs. I sigh into his mouth, letting our tongues touch, pulling him so close that I can feel my heart hammer against his rock-hard chest.

I don't just want him. I *need* him. There's a fire burning inside me that only Charlie Sutton can put out. As he threads his fingers through my hair, the heat between us rises so high, I can practically hear a sizzle in the air—

"Dammit, the tagine," Charlie says breaking away to check on the food. He lifts the lid of the pot and breathes out a sigh of relief. "We're good. Wanna eat before I burn down the building?"

I giggle. "Absolutely. It smells amazing."

"I hope you like it. I made a chicken tagine with apricots and almonds. And I have a few bottles of wine for you to choose from."

He pulls the selection from his wine fridge, and I pick an Italian pinot grigio, trying not to get too lost in a daydream of me and Charlie on vacation there together. Ever since he mentioned that his friend, the travel journalist, invited him to Italy next summer to take photographs for his book, I haven't been able to get my mind off the idea that maybe—if the stars align, and we're still dating—I might join him.

I've been dreaming of a trip to Italy since I was a teenager. There's even a drawing in my journal to prove it. Christy was right that I put all my wishes in it for safekeeping. It's like the inside of my heart, transferred to paper. And on the very last page is a sketch of me and the man of my dreams, kissing in front of the Colosseum in Rome.

"Great choice," Charlie says as I hand him the wine bottle. "You'll feel like you're in a vineyard in Tuscany." He winks at me and I have to lean against the kitchen island for support.

"Speaking of Tuscany…have you given any more thought to that photography gig in Italy this summer?"

Charlie heaves a sigh as he pours a glass for me. "Well, I've certainly given it more thought while my dad's been on vacation the past week. It's a lot easier to consider the offer when he's not texting me fifty times a day," he goes on with a wry laugh. "He won't handle the news well, though. So if I'm going to tell him that I want to quit the family business to be a travel photographer, I have to mean it. And I have to be prepared for it to blow up my life—maybe more than just a little."

I frown, my heart aching for the tough decision he has to make. "Your dad'll be that upset, huh?"

Charlie tilts his head. "Let's just say, my father's not known for his easy disposition."

He shrugs the statement off with a grin that feels practiced, and I wonder if I'm as good at seeing through Charlie as he is at seeing through me. But I don't press the issue. I know firsthand how hard it is to be torn between the life you want and the career you think you should have. And I don't have the added complication of being heir to a grocery empire.

"Well, you can pretend for now," I say, clinking my wine glass to his. "This would be more effective if I knew how to say 'cheers' in Italian," I go on with a laugh.

Charlie smiles. "*Salute.* Or you can also say, *cin cin.* It's less formal."

"Well then, *cin cin*," I repeat after him. "Wait a minute…do you speak Italian?"

He nods. "It's a beautiful language. I studied it in college."

I bring my palm to my forehead.

"What?" he asks with a chuckle.

"Charlie," I say with a stone-cold serious look on my face. "You're killing me, here."

"Is that right?" he quips back with a playful grin.

"I saw your abs at the beach this morning," I say with my hands on my hips. "You have, like, an eight-pack. But you love dessert."

He laughs, the pink in his cheeks deepening. "I told you, I run."

I shake my head. "Lots of people run. But they don't also get to eat brownies and still look like an underwear model."

"Okay, I might have a freakishly fast metabolism," he admits with a sheepish shrug. "Runs on the Sutton side of the family. I know it's unfair, so I don't like to brag about it."

"Fine," I concede. "I'll give you the fast metabolism. But you're also devastatingly handsome, you went to an Ivy League school, you cook gourmet Moroccan meals—"

"You have to at least taste it before you call it gourmet," he jokes.

"You're a talented photographer," I continue with a laugh, "*and* you speak the sexiest language on the planet?"

He's cracking up, and it's adorable.

"You literally couldn't be more perfect," I tell him.

"Well," he says, before kissing the top of my head, "now you know how I feel about you. You're smart, and funny, and creative—"

I love that he listed "smart" first.

"Not to mention…" He pauses for a beat and his cheeks get rosier still. "*Sei più bella di tutte le stelle del cielo.*"

"Hmm…I picked up the word pretty, but that's about it."

"You're prettier than all the stars in the sky," he tells me.

My heart swells to about ten times its size, and I have to fight the urge to cry. "That's really sweet," I rasp before I plant a kiss on him. "Now, let's eat, before I swoon."

Dinner is incredible, and easily earns the right to be called "gourmet." We sit next to each other at his kitchen island, our knees brushing as we talk, and laugh, and flirt, and kiss between bites of perfectly spiced chicken with sweet apricots. The meal's so delicious, I forget to leave room for dessert, so we save the brownies for later.

Afterward, we have a second glass of wine on his couch and, because I'm feeling so calm and comfortable with him, I take the opportunity to tell Charlie about my therapy sessions. About Hunter.

I explain everything, and he listens quietly, his eyes full of compassion and even heartbreak. "I'm so sorry, Jenna," he says with a furrowed brow before he takes my hand and kisses it.

And then, because I expect he'll see my tattoo sometime in the near future, I tell him the story behind it. It's something I've never admitted to anyone, not even Esther.

"After Hunter's funeral, I felt guiltier than ever. I'd convinced myself that if I hadn't broken up with him, I'd have noticed he was sick, and he wouldn't have died. I saw the pain in his parents' eyes, and I blamed myself. So I stopped at a tattoo shop on my way home. And I told the owner I wanted a rose, right on my hipbone."

A rose for every month I've known and loved you.

"I'd lost a lot of weight, since I was depressed and hardly eating. And the tattoo artist told me it would hurt like hell because I was so thin. I had to beg him to do it. He asked me to consider putting it on the softer flesh next to the bone instead, but I convinced him I had a high pain tolerance, which wasn't true at all. The truth is, I *wanted* the pain. I wanted to punish myself.

"I've never told anyone the meaning behind it. But when I'm with a guy, and he tells me how sexy it is, I feel like I'm hiding something. And I don't want to feel that way with you. That's why I'm telling you the truth. I know we're taking things slow, but when you eventually see me…I want you to see *all* of me."

If I'm not mistaken, Charlie's blinking back a tear. "Come here," he says after a long exhale.

He pulls me into a hug, and I settle my head on his solid, supportive shoulder. "I'm sorry for dampening the mood."

I feel him shake his head. "Are you kidding? I want to know everything about you, Jenna. It doesn't have to be all sunshine and rainbows."

He's telling me that I don't have to be bright, bubbly Jenna with him. Only if it feels genuine. And god help me, if I wasn't already convinced that what I'm feeling is love, not lust—Charlie Sutton just sealed the deal.

But as much as I want to go all the way with him, I have to keep in mind that he told me he wanted to wait to have sex, too.

I tilt my head up to look into his eyes and thread my fingers into his hair, bringing his mouth to mine. After a sweet kiss, I pull back. "I'm going to go now. Even though I really want to stay."

He nods and presses another kiss to the top of my head. "Let me walk you home."

I giggle. "You sure you're up for it?"

He just gazes at me and smiles.

A few minutes later, after he walks me to my door and gives me another chaste kiss, I'm home, on my bed, flipping through my high school journal—which I haven't cracked open in a while. Not since before I met my boyfriend. I guess I've been distracted.

But now that I have met him…I see my drawings through different eyes.

And my heart stops the moment I realize what I'm looking at.

The sketches are of me and Charlie.

I mean, they're doodles—but the man I drew has the same, gorgeous, dark eyes as Charlie, the same impossibly long lashes, and the same slight curl in his hair. He's tall and muscular like Charlie. He even has his rosy cheeks.

In the first drawing, we're crashing into each other—just like our meet-cute by the elevator. I even drew the sparks between us as jagged lightning bolts.

In another sketch, we're walking on the beach with iced coffee. Check.

Admiring paintings at an art museum? You better believe it.

Now, we're eating pancakes at an outdoor restaurant. Been there, done that.

He's making me dinner. That tracks.

And here's the one in Rome that I remember so clearly. This wish hasn't come true yet…but is it only a matter of time?

Maybe it's a coincidence. I mean, these are all fairly typical things to do on a date. Right?

Or maybe it's fate.

Honestly, I don't care.

Charlie Sutton is the man of my dreams, and I don't want to waste another second taking things slow with him.

But—dammit. What if *he* still wants to wait?

Oh, to hell with it. I'm going over there. If he isn't ready to take our relationship to the next level, he'll let me know.

With tears in my eyes and a smile on my face, I slam the journal shut and leave my apartment again.

I knock on Charlie's door.

"Hey," Charlie says, licking a little chocolate off his thumb. "I was just about to text you. Did you come back for brownies? I swear I only had one small bite—maybe two."

I laugh. "No, I didn't come back for brownies, Charlie. I came back for you."

I grab him by the shirt collar and plant my lips on his. Within seconds, his hands are on my waist, pressing me into his hard body, where I belong.

He pulls me into his apartment and slams the door shut behind us. I lean against it, and he takes his kisses up my neck as I work to unbutton his shirt. "You're still in the driver's seat," he whispers in my ear.

I strip him down to his undershirt and slide my fingertips under the hem and over every ripple of his abs. "I need this to come off, too," I direct him.

"Yes, ma'am." He pulls off the white tee, and that chest I've been dreaming about all day practically gleams with the golden glow of his skin. I move my hands over his perfect pecs, across his broad shoulders, and down his muscular arms.

"If you still want to wait to have sex, that's okay," I tell him. "We can just make out. But I'm ready to go all the way, when you are."

Charlie laces his fingers with mine. "What made you change your mind?"

"Besides your beach body?" I joke.

He chuckles.

"I've been waiting my whole life to feel this way about someone," I tell him.

He exhales deeply. "Me too."

I sigh with relief. But before we take this to the bedroom, I want to make sure Charlie and I are on the same page. As desperate as I am for us to fully explore our physical attraction to each other—without silly rules, like "no tongue"—I also don't want him to feel rushed.

"Are you still afraid of jumping into this too fast?" I ask.

Charlie scrapes a hand over his jaw. "Feels like it's been a lifetime since I said that."

I giggle. "I'm pretty sure it was yesterday."

He heaves out a breath. "Well, then I guess I changed my mind, too. You opened your whole heart to me tonight when you told me about your past. You showed me who you are, and…I love what I saw," he tells me with an unwavering gaze.

I blink back a tear.

He looks down at me and half-smiles. "I'm not going to say no to you, Jenna. I don't think I have it in me. So, if you want me, I'm yours."

This is really happening. The man of my dreams wants me. Charlie Sutton is mine.

"I want you more than anything," I say before I kiss him.

Just after our lips meet, thunder roars in the distance. It's not Charlie's phone this time, but a late summer storm. The rain starts pelting down, tapping against the windows as we kiss.

While his fingers are traveling up the nape of my neck and into my hair, my hands go to his belt, which I yank off without tearing my mouth from his.

He grips my waist and lifts me effortlessly to wrap my legs around him. Then shirtless Charlie carries me to his bed, where I've longed to be since the moment I met him.

"Do you have to work tomorrow morning?" he asks when I'm on my back and he's hovering over me.

I shake my head no, biting back a smile.

"Good," he says. "Because I want to take my time with you."

Another crack of thunder booms, closer this time, dialing up the adrenaline that's already coursing through my veins as I anticipate what Charlie Sutton wants to do with the hours that lie ahead of us.

With past lovers, I was typically the one to take control. I'd be the one on top, choreographing our every move. But with Charlie, I feel so at ease that my body softens in a way I've never experienced before. I'm completely surrendering myself to him. Because I trust him.

"You can take the lead," I say.

He starts by peeling off my little beige dress. Then he agonizes me by gently sucking the skin on my neck while slowly grinding into me. Even through the layers of his pants and my underwear, it's immediately obvious to me how big he is.

I arch into him, longing for more, responding to every thrust of his hips with a soft moan. By the time he slides down my undies, I'm sure they're soaked through.

With one hand, he unhooks my bra with expert ease. I can't help but wonder how much experience he's had, because his confidence in the bedroom is sky-high. It's a side of him I haven't seen before. Where he's typically sweet and mild-mannered, when it comes to sex, Charlie Sutton likes to take charge.

I don't mind it a single bit.

He pauses to look at me now that I'm completely undressed. After several seconds, he sighs and shakes his head. "You are…a work of art. All of these beautiful lines, and curves." He takes a finger and traces down my collarbone, over my breast, and in a circle around my nipple. Then he sweeps along the arc of my waist, and stops just before he gets to my rose tattoo.

"Can I kiss you here?" he asks.

I nod, and he shifts down the bed and meets my inked skin with the softest kiss.

In that moment, the last small piece of my broken heart mends. And I'm whole again.

"I'm so sorry for the pain you suffered," he says when his gaze meets mine.

"You helped me heal, Charlie," I whisper through the pattering of the summer storm.

I reach out my arms, and he slides into my embrace. I help

him out of his pants and boxers, and then we're skin to skin, warm against each other as the rain keeps pouring.

Charlie's hand moves up my thigh and between my legs. I've never been this wet in my entire life, and I wonder if it's even normal. But the groan that comes from his throat when his thumb glides over me in circles, tells me he likes it. A lot. With his thumb still busy, he slips a finger inside me while he takes my nipple in his mouth. After a few minutes, the pleasure is so intense, I already feel the first wave of an impending orgasm, which is insane—it usually takes me forever to come.

Before I do, Charlie moves his hands to part my knees, and kisses his way from my breasts, to my navel, and further down, where his tongue takes over for his fingers. And where the touch of his hand was gentle and soft, now he licks me hungrily, working absolute magic on me with his mouth.

I can't take it. It's too good. *He's* too good. "I'm gonna come," I tell him as my legs are already shaking, and the muscles deep inside me shudder in successive waves of ecstasy. His tongue doesn't stop until my body stills.

"Oh my god," I sigh out afterward, trying to catch my breath. "I've never come that fast in my life."

Charlie looks very pleased with himself—as he should be. I giggle as he shifts to lie down next to me. "Don't worry, there's more where that came from," he says.

I raise an eyebrow at him. "You mean…more orgasms?"

He nods.

"After *that?*" I shake my head. "Um, I don't know if I can. I've never had multiple orgasms before."

Charlie tilts his head. "You've also never come that quickly. So, I guess there's a first time for everything."

The seductive glint in his eyes sends a new rush of blood between my legs.

"I suppose it doesn't hurt to try," I say with a coy smile.

Charlie reaches into his nightstand for a condom, and puts it on. Then he shifts back on top of me.

As we kiss, he presses into me just a little—and it's still a lot. I sigh, yearning for more, arching my back to bring him deeper inside me.

"Not yet," he teases.

I reach for him, wrapping my hand around his impressive length, and he groans as I stroke him.

"Two can play at this game," I quip back, which Charlie responds to with a sexy grin.

I have to beg him for another inch. The incredible orgasm I just had is already a distant memory, and I'm chasing the next high.

I can feel him throbbing inside me. "Give me more, Charlie. I know you want to."

He lets out a breathy laugh. "Think you can handle all of me, Jenna?"

When I nod, he pushes in all the way, hitting the deepest part of me. I've never felt anything like it before. Every time he thrusts into me, it sends a ripple of pleasure right through my core.

"I'm going to give you the best orgasm of your life," he whispers in my ear, and I have absolutely no doubt he'll deliver.

But this time, as my ecstasy builds, I have the added turn-on of seeing the bliss in his eyes, hearing his moans and sighs, and feeling how rock-hard he is inside me.

"You feel like heaven," he says, which makes me deliriously happy.

We last longer than I expect to, considering how amazing the sex is. While the storm hits its crescendo, then starts to die down, we keep kissing, and touching, and pleasuring each other, experimenting with different positions. Every time I'm on the brink of unraveling, Charlie slows down, then builds back up again, over and over until the need for relief is so dire, we hit a point of no return.

When I start to shake again, he lets go of all restraint, and our climaxes become one.

And he's right. It's the best orgasm of my life.

Afterward, Charlie goes into the kitchen to get us water and comes back with my plate of brownies, which we eat together, naked in bed.

"These are leaps and bounds better than Sutton's," he says after his second one.

I giggle. "Best you ever had, right?"

Charlie chuckles before his smoldering gaze lands on me. "You're the best I ever had, Jenna Andersen."

And then he starts kissing me again.

When we finally go to sleep, it's nearly dawn. As I fade into a dream, the last image in my head is of one of the sketches in my journal. I'm curled up in bed with my eyes closed, a smile on my face. And my rosy-cheeked lover's arms are wrapped tightly around my waist—exactly the way Charlie is holding me.

nineteen

Charlie Sutton had better be the one. Because he's officially ruined me for all other men.

I wake up at 10:00 a.m. to the smell of coffee, as he sets a steaming hot cup on the nightstand beside me. I sit up, smiling, and stretch, feeling cozy in the worn college t-shirt I picked from his drawer to sleep in. Then I notice a tray on the bed with breakfast—two perfectly plated omelets that look like photographs torn from the pages of *Bon Appetit*, served with chicken sausage, fresh berries, and buttered multigrain toast.

I stare at the feast for several seconds before I give my boyfriend a sideways glance. "Did you go to culinary school somewhere in between graduating from Dartmouth at the top of your class and running the family business?" I ask, not entirely joking. "These omelets look like they were made by a French chef." There are even fresh chives sprinkled on top.

Charlie shakes his head, grinning. "I watched a YouTube video this morning."

"Of course you did," I say with a smile back at him. As soon as he's settled in bed beside me, I circle my arms around his neck and kiss him.

If it weren't for the breakfast tray in our way, I know things would start getting hot and heavy between us. Immediately turned on, I take Charlie's bottom lip between my teeth and pull ever-so-gently, which elicits a sexy groan.

"As tempted as I am to see where this is going," he says, "we should probably eat first. If we're going to spend the rest of the morning in bed, we'll need the energy."

"You don't have to work?" I ask, my cheeks warming as I remember all the ways he pleasured me until sunrise.

"I told my assistant I was taking a personal day," he says with a wink before taking a sip of his coffee.

"Lucky me," I reply, now chomping at the bit to finish breakfast. There's nothing I'd rather do than spend the morning in bed with Charlie, further exploring our undeniable chemistry.

This must be what it's like for Dex and Sunny—and why he never gave up on getting her back. I'm so grateful he didn't let me settle for a relationship without passion. Now I have everything I could ever hope for. Not only do I feel at ease with Charlie, but we have passion in spades.

After the gourmet breakfast courtesy of my drop-dead gorgeous boyfriend, we get back to kissing. Charlie takes no time lifting his shirt over my head so I'm naked again. We're both so eager that we don't spend nearly as long on foreplay as we did last night—although Charlie makes it clear that he will do anything I need to get me ready.

"I woke up ready," I tell him as I reach for the box of condoms on the nightstand. I put one on him, then straddle his lap, my heart racing as I guide every glorious inch of him inside me.

Charlie sits up so we're pressed against each other, his soft lips traveling from my collarbone to my breasts. He takes one in his mouth while he massages the other with his hand, sending waves of pleasure down my body. Then he kisses me, his fingers moving to grip my ass as he works my hips to meet his thrusts. A ray of morning light peeks through his window shades, and between every kiss, I catch him looking at me like I'm the most beautiful woman who ever walked the earth. There's something reverent in his gaze that makes me feel more adored than I ever have in my life.

When I'm on the brink of coming, Charlie moves his hands up my back and shifts us, so I'm lying down. Then he hooks my knees over his broad shoulders and, in this position, I feel him reach the very depth of me.

"Holy fucking shit," I cry out in ecstasy.

Charlie lets out a breathy laugh. "You never say 'fuck,'" he says on a deliciously deep thrust. "I like it."

I moan as he brings me closer and closer to peak pleasure. "No one's ever made me feel this fucking good, Charlie."

He brings his lips to my neck, which makes me tingle everywhere, my nerve endings sparking in response to his touch. "We were made for each other. That's why this feels so right."

Not five seconds later, I'm completely undone—fireworks exploding in my core, where Charlie's simultaneously climaxing.

Afterward, I rest my head on his shoulder, and his fingers

massage my scalp and play with my hair as we recover. It's bliss.

"Have you ever been to the Chicago Botanic Garden?" he asks me after a beat.

An amused smile forms on my lips. It's not the sort of thing I'm used to hearing after sex. Typically I get a recap of how good it was, or how hot I am, or questions about when we can do it again. But that's not where Charlie's mind is. He wants to make plans with me—outside the bedroom. It makes what we just shared so much more meaningful, knowing our connection isn't purely physical.

When I look up at him, my heart flutters. "No, but I heard it's beautiful."

"Me too. Want to go check it out this afternoon?"

"That sounds perfect," I reply, wondering if life gets any better than this. Good food, great sex, and someone special to explore the city with? I'm in heaven.

"I was thinking of bringing my camera," Charlie goes on. "You inspired me yesterday, you know."

"Oh yeah?" I say, smiling up at him.

He nods. "I admire how dedicated you are to painting. And I know that if I want to transition careers, I'm going to have to put more time into my photography, too. So, I've decided to do that—starting today."

"Charlie, that's so exciting!" I squeal, hugging him. "I'm happy for you."

Italy, here we come.

We shower and get dressed in our respective apartments, then Charlie drives us to the botanic garden in his black Range

Rover, looking incredibly sexy behind the wheel. Although, I also thought he looked sexy brushing his teeth this morning. After the last twelve hours, I can hardly look at him without thinking about how damn good he is in bed. This sexual side of Charlie is such a pleasant surprise. Turns out, underneath the golden boy exterior, there's a naughty guy who's just the right amount of assertive and dominant. Since I'm so petite, compared to his tall, muscular frame, he can easily pick me up and throw me around the bedroom—and it is such a turn-on.

Another major turn-on is how happy he looks behind his camera. The botanic garden is stunning. Located in a suburb of Chicago, it boasts twenty-seven gardens on 385 acres of land. It's like walking through a living, breathing Monet painting, complete with arched wooden bridges and waterlilies. But even amid the vivid natural beauty of flowers, and ponds, and trees, I can't take my eyes off Charlie, and the way he comes to life when he looks through his lens.

"I know you're still working on putting together a collection of paintings," he says to me as we stroll in the late summer sunshine, "but I'd love to see some of your work, when you're ready to show me. No rush, of course."

We're journeying across the Malott Japanese Garden bridge, which is so magical in its beauty, it makes me feel like we're walking through a fairytale. We pause at the top of the bridge to take in the lush greenery that surrounds us in every direction, and although the view is serene, my stomach flutters with anxiety.

Of course I want to show Charlie my work. But my favorite piece is the one I did of him, and it's obvious, to me at least, that I have very strong feelings for my subject. The golden glow of his skin, the rosy stain on his cheeks, those full, kissable lips…and let's not forget that gleam in his eyes. It's the lust—or love—or whatever I saw when he looked at me for the first time. How will he react if I work up the nerve to tell him that? Will he confirm it was love at first sight when we crashed into each other? Or will my not-so-subtle interpretation of our meet-cute leave him feeling flustered? Maybe he's not ready to admit the depth of his feelings for me. Even worse, will he tell me I have it all wrong? He's smitten with me, yes, but maybe his version of smitten has less to do with love, and more with physical attraction.

"Soon," I say with a coy smile. It's the best I can do for now. After another week or two, maybe I'll feel secure enough about Charlie's feelings for me to reveal my innermost desire. I *want* this to be love at first sight. I want Charlie Sutton to be my last first kiss. I want him to be my soulmate.

By the time we get back to the city, it's early evening, and I offer to make him dinner at my place. As soon as I lock the door behind us, he puts his arms around me and leads me several steps in reverse, so my back is pressed against the wall of my entryway.

The look in his eyes when he peels his lips from mine tells me that his intentions are anything but innocent. Right before he kisses me again, though, he pauses. "Is this too much? I don't want to hurt you."

I giggle and shake my head. "It's not too much, Charlie. I've been wanting you all day."

He smiles before his gaze turns serious again. "You promise you'll let me know if you need a break?"

I nod and bring his mouth toward mine, and we kiss feverishly as he unbuttons my shorts and they fall to the floor. I step out of them, then Charlie sweeps my lace underwear to the side and hooks a finger in me.

"I love how wet you are for me," he says, his lips grazing the soft skin below my ear.

When I start moaning, he pulls a condom out of his wallet. A minute later, my panties are off and he's fucking me against the wall, which is unbelievably hot. If there's anyone in the hallway, I have no doubt they can hear how much I'm enjoying it. Normally I'd feel self-conscious, but when I'm having sex with Charlie, my focus is only on him, and the expert way he handles my body.

I wasn't sure I'd be able to come in this position, but he has me lifted with one arm, as though I were light as a feather, and his other hand is between my legs, his fingers rubbing me in all the right places. Before long, he's giving me my fifth orgasm in less than twenty-four hours.

"You're amazing," he tells me afterward, with that smitten look on his face.

"You're a sex god," I reply, completely serious, but he laughs anyway. "I'm not kidding, Charlie. You bring out a side of me I never knew was there."

"I aim to please," he says, letting me down gently and holding me until my feet are steady on the ground.

I kiss him, then look to the floor for my clothes. He bends

down to pick up my underwear and shorts, then hands them to me. "Thanks," I say, smiling. "I'm going to go freshen up…I'll be right back. Make yourself at home."

He kisses me and smacks my bare ass as I turn to walk toward my bedroom.

After putting my clothes back on and brushing out my sex hair, I walk down the hallway, to the living room, but stop when I hear Charlie's voice. He's on the phone.

"It was one day," he says with a frustration in his tone I haven't heard before. "When was the last time I took a day off, much less a vacation?" After a pause, he continues. "Of course I was checking messages." He sighs heavily. "I told you, Dad. I was with my girlfriend."

Oh no—his dad. He wasn't supposed to be back from his trip until the end of the week, and now he's laying into Charlie, all because he was playing hooky with me. I feel awful. At the same time, I'm fighting a grin because my boyfriend didn't hesitate to acknowledge me as his girlfriend, even to his curmudgeon of a father.

I'm about to head back toward my room to give Charlie some privacy, but he turns at the same time, and sees me standing in the hallway. I point my thumb over my shoulder, indicating that I'll leave him to his conversation, but his face softens and he motions for me to come to him.

"She's an artist," he tells his dad with a smile that gets bigger as I walk toward him. "She does interior design, but her real passion is painting. We have a lot in common."

There's another brief pause, in which Charlie brings his free palm to his forehead.

"I'm talking about photography," he says to his father. "Right. No, of course you forgot."

Charlie reaches for my hand and pulls me in for a hug. But as I'm resting my head against his chest, his heart starts thumping louder and faster. I step back, and his face is crimson, his nostrils flaring.

"No, it's not like that at all," he argues. "Dad—don't start." Charlie exhales. "I'm not going to talk to you about this right now, I have to go." Another pause. "Yes, I'll have the report to you by morning."

When he hangs up the phone, he takes my hand again and leads me to the couch. He sits in silence for a moment, his jaw clenched, his face still crimson.

"So…your dad's back from France, I take it?" I say with a wince.

Charlie half-smiles in my direction. "He cut the trip short. Told my mom never to book a hotel without Wi-Fi again."

"He sounds fun."

A laugh escapes Charlie, and he puts his arm around me. "Thanks for the comic relief. I could use it right now. I don't know how much you picked up from my end of the conversation, but he's pissed I took a day off."

I frown. "It's my fault. You were playing hooky with me."

Charlie shakes his head. "Are you kidding? It's not your fault… or mine. My dad's completely unreasonable. But I guess you don't become a grocery store tycoon by taking personal days."

"You really don't want this. To follow in his footsteps," I say. I don't need to ask, because the answer's written all over his face.

Charlie blows out a breath. "No, I don't. But admitting that to you is one thing. Moving on from Sutton's feels a lot more complicated. It doesn't help that my dad thinks of photography as a meaningless diversion…not an actual career."

My stomach clenches. Charlie's dad sounds a heck of a lot like mine. And I can't help but wonder what this could mean for our budding relationship. If the senior Mr. Sutton doesn't respect his son's choice to be an artist, he certainly won't respect mine. He might even say I'm a bad influence. On the other hand, if Charlie can't stand up to his dad, and continues to live at his mercy, will he resent me for pursuing my passion?

"We don't need to figure this out now," Charlie says, probably picking up on the fact that my wheels are spinning. "Want me to help you with dinner? I'm sorry I have to eat and run, but my dad wants this damn report from me first thing tomorrow."

"Why don't you go back to your place and get started on it now," I suggest, placing a gentle hand on his knee. "I'll bring you dinner when it's ready."

He shakes his head. "No way. I already committed to dinner with you. And I *want* to have dinner with you. I won't let work get in the way."

"Charlie, it's one thing to be up all night having mind-blowing sex," I begin. "I'll allow that…"

He grins.

"But losing sleep because of work is nowhere near as satisfying. It sounds like you're in for a busy week now that your dad's back, and you'll need some rest if you're gonna stay focused. I promise I'm fine," I tell him.

"You sure?" From the worried look on his face, I'd be willing to bet that Charlie's job has interfered with his past relationships.

"Yes," I assure him. "I'll come over with pasta in a little bit."

"Thank you, Jenna. Seriously. You're the best," he says before kissing me.

I walk him to the door and say goodbye with a smile.

But I can't ignore the sinking feeling in my gut as soon as he turns to leave.

twenty

"I failed my assignment," I tell Esther two days later.

Her brow crinkles. "What assignment, dear?"

I bite my lip. "I had sex with Charlie." *So much sex with Charlie.* "The best sex of my life, actually."

To my surprise, Esther grins. "Good for you, honey."

I raise my eyebrows. "Really? But what about the thirty days to get to know each other?"

My therapist's lips quirk up with the hint of a smile. "It was only a suggestion. You wanted to make sure you were ready for a relationship. Sounds to me like you didn't need a month to make your decision."

"I told him everything there is to know about me. I showed him who I am, and he said he loved what he saw." I let out a swoony sigh. "I'm head over heels for him, Esther. And I think he feels the same way. He says he's smitten."

"I'm happy for you," Esther says. "You deserve this. It's been a long time coming."

"Thank you," I reply, looking down at my lap. "There's just one thing that concerns me."

My gaze meets Esther's again. She's nodding, encouraging me to continue.

"Charlie's a regional vice president for his family's business… and his dad works him like a dog," I explain. "His parents just got back from a week's vacation, and his father's been making up for lost time by slamming Charlie with assignments over the past three days. He's still made every effort to see me, but…I can tell how stressed he is. He's like a different person, compared to the man I spent the weekend with while his dad was away. Charlie was so happy and carefree then. And you should have seen the way his eyes lit up when he was taking pictures. His real passion is photography. But his dad doesn't approve, of course."

When Esther's neutral expression turns into a frown that matches mine, I can tell she understands. "Sounds like someone else you know."

"Yup…my father." I blow out a breath. "I feel like Charlie's stuck in the same place I was years ago, when I still cared about my dad's approval. When I let him convince me that painting was a waste of my time. But now I'm in a place where I finally feel confident enough in who I am to do what makes me happy…"

"And you're worried Charlie will never get there," Esther finishes for me when I pause.

I nod. "Charlie's so perfect in every way. He's intelligent, sweet, and talented. He's gorgeous…and an amazing lover." My cheeks warm. "It's hard to believe some lucky lady didn't snatch him up a long time ago. Maybe this is the red flag I've been afraid of. If his job is ruining his relationships, and he can't stand up to his dad, it doesn't bode well for us."

Esther sits forward in her chair. "Let's focus on what *you* can control in this situation."

I tilt my head, considering her question. "Well…I'll stay committed to pursuing my passion, for one."

"That might inspire him to do the same," Esther adds. "You never know."

"He already said as much," I tell her. "I guess that's a good sign. He also said he'd love to see my paintings, whenever I'm ready. I know I'll muster up the courage to show him eventually…but the idea of displaying my work at a gallery still terrifies me, for some reason. Which is frustrating, because that's my ultimate goal."

Esther's gaze is sympathetic as I continue.

"I figured the confidence I've gained in therapy would carry over into sharing my art with the world…but I don't think it has yet. I mean, it's one thing to show my pieces to the people who know and care about me. But baring my heart and soul to strangers, who may not connect with my paintings or understand them? It makes me feel so vulnerable."

Esther nods. "Artists do make themselves vulnerable. It's a risk to open yourself up to the opinions of others. Ultimately, you'll have to decide if it's a risk you're willing to take."

"I want to make a career out of painting, I really do. And I think I'm getting closer to taking the leap. It sure would be nice if the universe sent me a sign that the timing's right…you know, gave me a little nudge, or something," I joke.

My therapist smiles.

"A girl can dream, I guess. And as for my dilemma with Charlie's job…I guess the only other thing I can do is talk to him about how I feel. But I think I'll wait a bit, and see if his dad mellows out after a few days."

"That's a good plan," Esther agrees.

I leave the session feeling a little bit lighter, and looking forward to spending more time with Charlie. Later that night, he comes over to my place for dinner. We're eating carryout pizza and watching baseball on TV. It's Charlie's favorite sport. He played Little League as a kid in Denver, and is a diehard fan of their MLB team. Tonight they're in the Windy City, playing the Starlings at Wrigley Field. Unlike Christy, who played softball on a coed recreational team with Kyle, then became a baseball enthusiast, I don't know a ton about the sport, so Charlie's teaching me. He's in the middle of explaining what a 6-4-3 double play is, when thunder strikes his phone.

He ignores it, but his dad is relentless, sending text after text, until Charlie finally caves and reads the messages.

He pinches the bridge of his nose, squinting his eyes shut.

"Everything okay?" I ask, rubbing his arm.

"I have to be in Denver for a lunch meeting tomorrow. That I'm leading—apparently." His jaw clenches.

My eyes go wide. "And you're not prepared, I take it?"

He shrugs. "I'll get it done. I'll prep a little after we're done watching the game, and I can take care of the rest on the plane in the morning. I was looking forward to spending the night with you, though."

"Me too," I say, threading my fingers through his. When I

look back up at him, he cups my face with his free hand and kisses the hell out of me. I pull him on top of me as I lie down on the couch.

"My workload should ease up soon," he says, his gaze apologetic, and maybe the slightest bit anxious. "Dad's looking to make a few new hires, which should take quite a bit off my plate."

"Don't worry about me, Charlie. I just want you to be happy."

If he's happy, *we'll* be happy. Isn't that what I learned from Dex and Sunny? They had to choose to be true to themselves before they could be together.

"You make me happy," he says before kissing me softly.

"We should go on another adventure this weekend," I suggest after his lips part from mine. "The arboretum, maybe—someplace scenic. I know you want to make more time for your photography."

Charlie frowns. "I won't be back until Sunday evening, most likely. My mom asked if I could stay the weekend. It's been a while since I went home."

"Of course." I weave my hands into his hair as he lies on top of me. "We'll have an adventure some other time."

"Thank you for being so understanding," he says before planting a kiss on my forehead that gives me butterflies.

I bite my lip. "I guess this is the last time we'll see each other for a few days, huh."

He nods with a furrowed brow, then reaches for the remote on the coffee table and switches off the TV. "We should probably make the most of it," he says, his free hand cupping my breast.

"What about the game?" I ask him with a teasing smile. "And

that 6-2-1 play, or whatever it was?"

He laughs into my neck as his hand travels up my thigh. "It can wait. But this can't."

My plan is to spend the entire weekend painting. Charlie's in Denver. Vanessa just left for Europe with her sister, Denise. They'll be gone for two weeks—on the tour that was supposed to be Vanessa's honeymoon with Nico. They'd scheduled it four months after the wedding to accommodate Vanessa's new job.

I haven't told her yet that I'm sleeping with Charlie. This seems like a tough time for her, and I don't want to gush about my new relationship. I can't imagine taking this vacation with her sister will be easy, but I'm hoping, somehow, it'll provide the closure she needs to move on. Who knows, maybe she'll meet someone on the tour that will sweep her off her feet. It doesn't even have to be love—a fling might do her some good.

Or it could leave her yearning for more, which is how I feel with Charlie out of town. I really miss him—and not just the sex. I miss his company. The way I can tell him anything, and never feel like he's judging me. I miss the adorable way he laughs at my jokes, and the way he holds me while we sleep. I miss the look in his eyes right before he kisses me.

I miss him so much that I contemplate texting Sam to see if she wants to hang out and help me get my mind off him, but she'll take one look at me and know that I'm having mind-blowing sex, then grill me about it. And I don't like to kiss and tell.

But when I call Christy and mention that I have the weekend free, she books a flight to Chicago on a whim. It's the first time I've seen her since we were home for Christmas, over eight months ago.

I pick her up from the airport on Friday afternoon, and I almost don't recognize her. My tightly wound little sister, who typically sports a sleek, high ponytail, along with a sensible outfit from her carefully-curated capsule wardrobe, looks happier and more relaxed than I've ever seen her. She has on a breezy floral sundress that shows off those new curves she acquired when she stopped marathon-training, and she's wearing her beautiful auburn hair down, in loose waves.

"Christy, you look amazing!" I squeal when I see her. "Where did this gorgeous wavy hair come from?"

She laughs. "Apparently this is what happens when I stop flat-ironing."

"Lucky you," I say, threading my fingers through my stick-straight mane. "And the dress?"

"Post-breakup shopping spree," she explains. "My entire closet was black and beige. I was so sick of it."

"I like this side of you," I say before I pull away from the curb.

We head back downtown, where I park in my building's garage, then we walk to a nearby restaurant for happy hour. Christy orders a dirty martini—a far cry from her usual glass of pinot noir—and we have the best time catching up, just the two of us. Although we do get a lot of male attention. Typically I'd be annoyed, but not tonight…because my sister has been approached by three hot guys so far, and she's grinning from ear to ear.

"Isn't it great, Jenna? All I had to do was change my hair and wardrobe, and boom—men are finally noticing me," she says before taking a sip of her martini.

I shake my head. "You've always been beautiful, Christy. You didn't have to change a thing about the way you look. You're just happier and lighter now. That's what these guys are picking up on."

She heaves a sigh. "I probably should have broken up with Kyle a long time ago. I'd been unhappy with our relationship for years."

"But look at you now," I say, reaching across the table for her hand. "You're glowing. I have no doubt that you're going to find an amazing guy who's spontaneous, and fun…and will want to have sex with you *any* day of the week."

She giggles. "I hope you're right. My chances seem decent based on tonight, at least. Maybe I *should* move to Chicago."

My eyes go wide. "Would you really?"

She tilts her head, smiling. "Let's see how the rest of the weekend goes."

I can barely contain my excitement, but I try to play it cool. "Deal," I say, clinking my glass to hers.

After taking Christy to my favorite neighborhood Italian place for dinner, we start heading back to my apartment. As we're walking, I pull my phone out of my purse, and see a couple of sweet text messages from Charlie—and a voicemail from Tati Marie.

I'd left her a message earlier, letting her know I wouldn't make it to class, because my sister's in town. But why would she call me back? Curious, I listen.

"Jenna, dear…it's Marie. I'm calling with good news. My friend who owns an art gallery reached out to me today. She's hosting a show for local artists, and wanted to see if I had any talented students who would be willing to contribute a painting. I told her I'd speak with you."

"Oh my gosh," I say, my heart pounding and my head spinning. *Is this really happening?*

"Take the week to think about it, and let me know what you decide," she goes on. "I know it's sooner than you planned, but I think you're ready."

"What's going on?" my sister asks when I hang up.

I let out a breathy laugh. "Christy…I think I just got the little nudge from the universe I was hoping for."

As I walk Christy into my art studio, I have major butterflies—a mix of excitement and nerves. Well, mostly nerves. But if I'm going to take the leap and make a career out of painting, I'm going to have to show my collection at some point, and I'm grateful that the first person to see it will be my sister. As a literary agent, she has a gift for spotting talent, and I wouldn't be surprised if it carried over to different art forms. When it comes to food, wine, and fashion, Christy's always had discerning taste. But, even more than that, I'm over the moon that we're getting closer, and showing her my paintings will only strengthen our growing bond.

Unless she hates them, of course.

Thankfully, the smile on her face says otherwise. "Jenna…oh my gosh!" she exclaims, wide-eyed.

The seven paintings that make up my collection are leaning against the wall, and I watch her gaze travel slowly across each of them. When she gets to the last portrait—the one of her—

her hands fly to her mouth, and her eyes fill with tears. I follow as she takes several steps forward and kneels to examine it more closely. My heart picks up speed, wondering what she's thinking. With her fingers still covering her lips, I can't tell.

Does she like it? Is she moved by it? It is possible she's offended?

Oh god. Maybe she thinks I have zero talent, but doesn't know how to tell me.

What was I thinking? I'll never make it as a professional painter. Thank goodness I haven't quit my design job yet—

"Jenna." My sister stands and faces me. Finally, she drops her hands to her sides, and I'm no longer second-guessing what I want to do with the rest of my life, because she's beaming. "These are amazing. *You're* amazing."

Before I can thank her, I burst into tears, and she hugs me. "That's the best thing I've ever heard."

"It's true. You are so incredibly talented…I mean, you captured something in each piece that I'd only expect to see on a living, breathing person. You painted real emotion on their faces. Just one look, and I can tell what they're thinking." She turns to look at each portrait again. "Mom's sad. And Dad's an ass—"

I chuckle.

"And I absolutely adore the hint of mischief in my eyes," she continues with a playful smile. "It's the new me. Single and ready to grab life by the balls. Or grab a hot guy by the balls, at least. Consensually, of course."

I throw my head back, laughing. "I should introduce you to my new friend, Sam—that's short for Samira," I add, to avoid confusion. "I met her through Vanessa, but she and Sunny Dexter go way back, since college. I think you two would have fun taking the Windy City by storm. She definitely enjoys grabbing life by the balls. And she'd make an excellent wingwoman."

"You're making Chicago look pretty darn attractive," Christy admits with a smile. "I could use some help in the dating department. I've been out with a few guys since Kyle, but there's never any chemistry. Maybe I'm too picky."

"Promise me you won't settle," I tell her. "Because you *will* find what you're looking for, and once you do—there's no going back."

My sister grins at me. "Speaking of Charlie…this has to be him," she says, pointing to his portrait.

I nod.

"Wow," she says on a deep exhale. "First of all, he's insanely gorgeous. But second of all, does he really look at you like that?"

My cheeks warm. "Yeah, he does."

Christy shakes her head, still smiling. "He adores you."

"It feels that way," I say, my heart fluttering.

"*This* is the portrait you have to show at the gallery. Charlie's. It's perfect."

"I was afraid you'd say that," I reply before biting my lip.

"Why?" she asks, her brow furrowed.

"Because if I choose it for the gallery, I'll have to show it to him soon, to make sure he approves. And when I do, I want to tell him the truth…that this painting was inspired by the look in his eyes when we first met. You said it yourself, it looks like he adores me. I do think it was love at first sight, Christy. Or something even more inexplicable than that," I say, picturing my sketchbook full of wishes. I haven't told anyone—not Christy or even Esther—about my journal's connection to Charlie. I'm still trying to process it, myself.

"I feel like I've always loved Charlie Sutton," I go on, "even before I knew him. Which makes no sense."

"It does if you're soulmates," Christy says, matter-of-factly.

I smile, relieved she doesn't think I'm crazy. My sister's a romantic at heart, like me. It's a little surprising, given our parents aren't the picture of a loving marriage. I don't think I've ever seen them kiss—or even hug, for that matter. Maybe the lack of romance in their relationship is what makes me and my sister crave it so much in our own lives.

I take in Charlie's portrait again, and almost get lost in his dark brown eyes. "He says we were made for each other," I tell my sister.

"Then he feels the same way," she replies. "Show him the painting—you have nothing to worry about."

"Hopefully," I say. "I just…I can't shake the feeling that this is all too good to be true."

Christy puts her hand on my shoulder. "I'm sure that's normal, given what happened to Hunter. You're finally getting everything you've always wanted, and you're afraid you're going to lose it."

I nod. "That makes sense. I'll keep working on it with Esther, in therapy."

"You'll get there," my sister tells me. "It might just take some time."

I hope to god she's right.

The rest of the weekend with Christy is everything I hoped it would be. Since I turned the guest room into my art studio, her options were to either crash on my living room couch, or sleep in my bed. She chose the latter. We never shared a room growing up, so it's a new experience for us, and even better than I could've imagined. We stay up late, drinking wine and watching rom-coms and giggling about guys, and I tell her things I've never told anyone—things you're only supposed to tell your sister, if you're lucky enough to have one you're close to. And Christy makes jokes at Kyle's expense, and tells me all about her dream man. During the day, I take her all around the city, and she marvels at how beautiful it is. When we hug goodbye at the airport, I'm almost convinced she'll move here.

Afterward, I drive back home. I'd originally planned to pick up Charlie, because his plane from Denver was supposed to arrive soon after I dropped off Christy, but his flight got delayed. So I go back to my place and catch up on the design projects I've been putting off. I haven't missed any deadlines, and I know I'll get everything done before it's due, but typically I'm way ahead of schedule. More and more, though, I have to resist the urge to close my laptop, put on a smock, and paint instead. Tonight, I find it so hard to stay out of my art studio that I decide to call the one person I know will understand— because she's been there.

"Hey, Jenna," Sunny says when she picks up the phone. She

sounds pleasantly surprised.

"I'm not calling too late, am I?" It's 10:30 p.m. in Beachwood, an hour later than Chicago. Normally Sunny's a night owl, but it just occurred to me that her sleeping habits may have changed, now that she's pregnant.

"Not at all," she assures me. "Well, Dex is fast asleep, but the baby's always really active at night, and she's kicking up a storm right now. I wouldn't be able to sleep if I tried."

"You're about halfway there, right?"

"Yup. Nineteen weeks. She's not even here yet, but she's still found a way to keep me up all night," Sunny jokes.

I giggle. "Already a troublemaker, huh. Will you text me a picture of your baby bump? I bet you look adorable."

"Sure. Dex took a picture of me just this morning."

Several seconds later, I get the photo on my phone. Sunny's standing at the window of their beautiful new home, looking radiant in a cream-colored dress. Her olive skin is tanned from the summer sun, and her hair is half-up, half-down, falling in pretty ringlets down her back. She's got one hand below her belly, which isn't big yet, but visibly rounder than the last picture she sent me. She's smiling and looks so, so happy.

"You're glowing," I tell her. "A stunning mom-to-be."

"Thank you. That's sweet."

"I'm sorry about the lack of sleep, though," I go on. "That sounds rough."

"It's okay," she replies. "I've been using the extra time to work on my next novel."

"Wow, good for you. And the first one's coming out in a couple of weeks! You must be so excited. I just pre-ordered mine."

"That's really thoughtful, thank you," she says in a heartfelt tone. "But you didn't have to do that—you know I would have sent you a signed copy."

I shake my head. "No way. I want to help drive up your sales. Get you on the bestseller lists, where you deserve to be. I will take you up on that signature though, the next time I'm in Beachwood."

"Absolutely."

"I'm so happy for you, Sunny. That's why I'm calling. I'm thinking about making a career change, like you did. Close up shop on my design business, and focus on painting. It's something I've always dreamed of doing, but I never thought I'd get the chance, until recently."

"Jenna, that's incredible! I had no idea you loved to paint."

"It's kind of a long story," I begin with a wry laugh, and then I tell her all about my passion for art, my thwarted dreams, and my journey back to them. "I want to take the leap, but I'm scared I won't be successful. Did you ever feel that way? When you quit law to become a writer?"

She lets out a heaving sigh. "Definitely. And I'm still scared… maybe even more so now. People are going to read and review my novel and, who knows, they might rip me to shreds. Tell me I never should have quit my day job—"

"That'll never happen, Sunny. You're so talented."

"Thanks. I appreciate it. Either way, I'll never regret my decision to leave law. I hated being a lawyer. It just didn't feel like *me*. And I'd much rather pursue my passion and fail miserably, than never even try."

A smile lights up my face—and my heart. "You're right."

"I mean, what's the worst that can happen?" Sunny continues. "You've already built two successful businesses. If painting doesn't work out the way you hope, I have no doubt you'll still land on your feet. And if you *are* able to turn art into a career…"

"Then I've made my dreams come true."

"Exactly."

"Thanks, Sunny. I'm so glad I called you for advice."

"Me too. How are things in Chicago, otherwise? I hear you've been hanging out with Sam," she says, sounding excited.

I chuckle. "Yeah. I think we're friends now…but she definitely vetted me first."

Sunny sighs. "I'm sorry about that. Sam doesn't mince words, that's for sure."

"I honestly find her a little intimidating," I admit. "She's just so…confident. So self-assured. And she's beautiful, with these delicate, feminine features, but the things that come out of her mouth…"

Sunny laughs. "She talks like a guy, I know. Sam's one-in-a-million. But underneath the unfiltered banter, she's got a heart of gold. You'll see."

"That's good to hear. Because my sister might move to Chicago, and I'm thinking of setting them up as friends. They're both single, and I think they'd have a lot of fun playing wingwoman for each other."

"Wait," Sunny says. "So, if you want Sam and your sister to hang out because they're both single…does that mean what I think it means? Are you dating someone?"

Her voice is full of hope, which makes my heart swell. I haven't told Sunny or Dex about Hunter yet, but they know I have a complicated history when it comes to love. It's so sweet they've both been rooting for me to find it.

"As a matter of fact, I am," I say with a beaming smile. "His name is Charlie, and he's my next-door neighbor. He's amazing, and we have the best chemistry. It's still early, but…I think he might be the one, Sunny."

All I hear on the other line are sniffles.

"Sunny? Are you crying?"

"It's the pregnancy hormones," she tells me before blowing her nose. "I'm just so happy for you, Jenna. You deserve this."

"You know what?" I say. "I finally feel like I do."

The next morning, after I roll out of bed, I'm on my way to the kitchen to make coffee when something catches my eye: another photograph slipped underneath my front door.

Charlie.

I pick it up, smiling. This one's of Denver, and it's breathtaking—an urban landscape that's a striking contrast to the magnificent mountains behind it. Overhead, a sunset paints the sky in pretty purple, pink, and orange hues.

I flip over the picture.

Missed you so much this weekend.
Can't wait to see you later.

And below his signature, the postscript reads: *Open your door.*

Beaming, I follow his instructions and find the most beautiful bouquet of wildflowers, in colors that match the sunset in Charlie's photograph. Right away, I text him to say thank you.

I can't wait to see him tonight. But first, I have an important day of work ahead of me.

I eat breakfast, get dressed, and drive north on Lake Shore Drive to my client Nadine's high-rise condo. Since I moved to Chicago, we've been working together on small projects throughout her home. She recently split with her partner of ten years, but got to keep the apartment in the settlement, and wants it to look more like her. Nadine's style is quirky and eclectic, and she loves bright colors, which makes her a lot of fun to work with.

"Jenna, sweetheart, come in," she says in her heavy New York accent. "Do you like matcha? I have matcha, and I have coffee—but it's not the good coffee I like from Sutton's. They were out this morning. Can you believe it?"

"Shame on them," I say, suppressing a giggle. "Matcha's great, thanks."

"Alright, follow me," she says, hurrying into the kitchen. After she pours my tea, she turns to face me. "So how do I look?"

I smile. "Fabulous, as always." Nadine is petite, like me. Her hair is cut short and dyed jet black, and she has on bright red lipstick to match her eyeglass frames. She's wearing kelly green pants with a royal blue sweater, and a canary yellow scarf draped over her shoulders. It's a vibrant ensemble, yet somehow, it works on her.

"But do I look any different?" she presses.

I examine her more carefully as she stands, posing with her hands on her hips. I don't notice anything out of the ordinary. My eyes land on her face. Botox maybe? But surely she doesn't want me to ask her about that…

When I shake my head, Nadine laughs. "I'm another year older. Just turned fifty."

"Oh my gosh, happy birthday! You look amazing."

"New decade, new chapter," she says, handing me the cup of matcha. "Come. Let's take a look at the guest bathroom and see how we can spruce it up."

We decide on a beautiful blue Spanish tile and potted plants to bring the space to life, along with updated fixtures and some art on the walls. After we've made a plan, Nadine walks me back out to the living room.

"You know, Jenna, I have a neighbor who's looking for a good designer, and I'd love to recommend you. But you must be up to your eyeballs in requests after Lola Piper tweeted about you."

I laugh. "Yeah, it's been an interesting few weeks, that's for sure. But going viral forced me to think about what I want my career to look like, long-term. And…I made a decision."

Last night, after talking to Sunny.

"Tell me," Nadine says with an encouraging nod.

"I'm not taking on new design clients. I'm going to wrap up with the amazing people I'm currently working with," I say with a wink, "and once we're done, I'm going to hang up my hat and try my hand at being a working artist. A painter, specifically."

It is such a relief saying the words out loud. I kept going

over them in my head on the drive over, because I knew I'd be making this announcement today. Every time I visit Nadine, she wants to refer a friend to me. I hate saying no, but I've finally made the choice to move forward as an artist—and I need to act accordingly.

Nadine claps her hands. "Perfect. I need paintings."

"Oh," I exclaim, taken by surprise. "Well, I thought we'd pick those out from the gallery district."

My client shrugs. "What for? I'd much rather commission something from an artist I know."

My heart flutters. "Really? But…you haven't even seen my work."

"So, show me," she says, matter-of-factly. "You're so creative, I'm sure it's fantastic."

I put down my cup of tea, pull my phone out of my bag, and navigate to my photo albums. When I show her my paintings, her eyes go wide.

"Holy smokes," she utters, grabbing my cell to get a closer look.

"You like them?"

"How did you do this?" she asks, stunned. "Did you paint from photographs, or did you have people sit for you?"

"Neither," I say. "I just painted them from memory."

Nadine squints at me. "Do you know how incredible that is?"

"I guess I never really thought about it. But thank you." I pick up my cup of matcha, which I'd set down on an end table, and take a sip while Nadine keeps perusing the photos.

"And who is this hottie?" she asks, pointing to the portrait of Charlie. "Your boyfriend?"

I nod, beaming.

"What I wouldn't give for someone to look at me like that," she says with a sideways glance at me. "He's in love with you."

"I hope so," I answer, my cheeks on fire.

"Well, I'm calling it: you're going to be the next big name in the art world. Do you only do portraits?" she says, handing my phone back to me.

I slip it into the back pocket of my linen pants. "That's my focus for this particular collection, but I don't want to limit myself. I'd like to build a portfolio of landscapes, too."

With Charlie's interest in travel photography, I was thinking it would be fun to turn some of his photos into paintings someday. And I'd start with the one I found under my door this morning. The mountains against the backdrop of that gorgeous sunset sky would be so much fun to recreate.

"Then it's settled," Nadine says. "I'll take three paintings. Two landscapes, and a portrait of my mother. I have this beautiful picture of her when she was young—she was a beauty queen, you know. That's where I get my looks."

"Wow…my very first sale. I don't know how to thank you. This is amazing." I want so badly to give her a hug, but Nadine's not one for big emotional displays. So I take another sip of matcha instead.

"Alright, now let's talk money," Nadine continues, getting down to business. "I'll give you the fifteen grand I was going to spend at the gallery district—is that enough for three paintings?"

I almost choke on my drink. "Is that *enough*? Nadine, I couldn't possibly…it's too much. I'm just starting out."

"You may just be starting out, but these are not amateur paintings, sweetheart. I'm considering this an investment. Your work will probably be worth a fortune one day."

"Oh, Nadine," I blubber, tears rolling down my cheeks, and—I can't help it—I give her a hug.

She pats my back awkwardly before stepping out of my embrace. "Alright, enough with the mushy stuff. I've got a pedicure appointment downtown I have to get to. I'll email you a copy of my mom's picture. You can start there, and we'll talk about the landscapes after you're done."

I nod and follow her to the front door, barely maintaining my composure.

"Thanks again, Nadine," I say after I step out into the hall. "You have no idea what this means to me."

She just winks at me, and I try my best not to start crying again until the elevator doors close.

When Charlie knocks on my door that night, I'm giddy—and not only because I get to see my sweet, smart, hot-as-hell boyfriend.

I can't wait to tell him about my day. I did it. I took the leap. All I had to do was say the words out loud—*I'm going to be a painter*—and within minutes, I made my first sale.

I swing open the door and jump right into Charlie's arms, and he holds me tight as ever, my feet off the floor and my heart against his, where it should be. He takes a few steps to cross the threshold with me, and kicks the door shut behind us.

"I missed you so damn much," he whispers.

"Me too."

Eventually, he puts me down, and we kiss as if it's been a hundred days since we last saw each other—not only four.

"So what did I miss while I was away?" he asks when we finally take a break. "Besides the fun time you had bonding with your sister."

Charlie texted me often while he was in Denver, just to shoot the breeze, which warmed my heart. So I sent him live updates throughout the weekend—including all the naughty thoughts I was having about him after a few glasses of wine. Needless to say, Charlie enjoyed those messages immensely.

I smile. "Funny you should ask. I have big news…I did something brave today."

Charlie's grin lights up his entire face. "What'd you do?"

"I decided not to take on new design projects. And when I'm done with the ones I'm working on now, I'm going to pivot and focus exclusively on my art."

"Wow, congrats! What motivated you to take the plunge? Tell me, please—I could use the inspiration," he goes on with a chuckle.

"Well, it was a few different things," I admit. "I finally worked up the nerve to show my paintings to my sister, for one thing. And she loved them. She was really encouraging. I also called a friend from home who quit law to become a writer, and asked for her advice. And she reminded me how important it is to trust yourself enough to follow your dreams."

Charlie nods, looking thoughtful.

"And then there's you," I tell him, my cheeks warming.

His eyebrows fly up. "Me?"

I step closer to him, and he takes me in his arms again. "I've shown you who I am, Charlie. Not just the bubbly cheerleader on the surface, but the parts of me I used to be ashamed of. My dyslexia, my grief…my history of depression. And you've embraced all of me. You've made me feel so comfortable being myself that I want to lean into that. I want to be unapologetically me. And in my heart, I truly believe I'm an artist."

"I'm so proud of you," he says, his eyes gleaming. "I know you're going to do great."

"Thank you," I say with a huge grin. "Oh, and I forgot to mention the best part! When I told my design client today that I was switching gears, she commissioned *three* paintings from me. Can you believe it?"

"Of course I can," he says, holding me tighter. "So does this mean you'll show me your work soon?"

I nod. "Tonight. After dinner."

I'm not even nervous anymore. Everything in my life is finally falling into place, and my relationship with Charlie is no exception. It feels so right. Why should I waste my time worrying about it?

"Sounds good. And again, I'm so sorry I had to cancel our plans last night," he says, his eyes losing their glimmer.

"It's not your fault that your flight was delayed."

"I know." He sighs. "I just hate disappointing you."

The angst in his gaze breaks my heart.

"Charlie…can I ask you something?"

"Of course. Anything."

I lead him over to the couch, and he sits next to me. "Has your work interfered with your relationships before? Because you seem really worried about that happening to us."

"It has," he says without hesitation.

My gut clenches, although I do appreciate the fact that he's being so open and honest.

"I mean, ultimately, those relationships weren't right for me," he goes on, "and I'm more sure of that than ever—now that I've met you."

His words give me butterflies.

"But being at the mercy of my demanding boss, who also happens to be my father, is a pretty big buzzkill when it comes to dating," he continues. "And I do want to move on from Sutton's—eventually. It's just such a bad time. When my dad makes these new hires, it should be easier. I won't be leaving him in the lurch. But in the meantime, the idea of losing you because of this damn job wrecks me. The thing is, Jenna, I love…"

My eyes widen as I wait for him to finish his sentence.

"Um…I love what we have."

I'm pretty sure he wanted to say something else.

"We're so good together," he goes on. "And I'd never forgive myself if I let my career and family issues come between us."

I take his hand in mine. "You're not going to lose me over this job, Charlie. I think we're both too damn smitten to let that happen."

My words elicit the most adorable grin on his face. "I don't know what I did to deserve you."

Then he kisses me with such intensity that we almost skip dinner, and end up in bed. We surely would have, if not for the tempting smell of the takeout Thai food I ordered. So we put our make-out session on pause, and eat at my kitchen island while sharing a bottle of Riesling.

Afterward, I take Charlie's hand and lead him into my art studio. Maybe it's the wine, but I'm totally calm when we walk into the room. Even more so when my boyfriend's eyes widen with wonder.

I watch as his gaze moves over each portrait. First me, then my family, then Hunter, and Esther. I rearranged the canvases this morning, saving Charlie's for last. I covered it with a sheet and separated it from the rest of the paintings, so I could surprise him.

"Wow," he says on a heavy exhale. "These are *stunning*. I mean, I already knew you were talented, but…you have a real gift. The way you convey emotion in each piece, with these subtle lines around the eyes and lips…it's so realistic, I feel like I'm looking at a photograph."

"Thank you," I say, leaning into him.

Charlie can't take his eyes off my artwork, which thrills me. He points at the paintings at the top of the line. "So there's you, then your mom, dad, and sister, I'm guessing? I can see the family resemblance."

"Yup. And Hunter and Esther on the end," I explain. "And… there's one more I want to show you."

I unclasp my hands from Charlie's waist and walk to the other side of the room. When he joins me, I unveil the portrait I painted of him.

I watch as he takes it in.

First he sighs. Then he chews on his perfect bottom lip, which I've never seen him do before. Then his forehead crinkles. Next thing I know, he's blinking back tears.

"When did you do this?" he asks, turning to me. His voice is barely a whisper.

I don't know what to make of his reaction. Regardless, I tell him the truth. "I painted this after our first kiss. But the look in your eyes…that's what I saw the first time we met. When we crashed into each other by the elevator."

Charlie nods, then swallows. After a beat, he stares down at his shoes, his hands on his hips.

Whatever sedative effect that Riesling had on me is gone now. My palms are sweating.

"Jenna, there's something you should know," he says. "I probably should have told you this before…but I'm still trying to wrap my head around it, myself."

My heart is hammering as I wait for him to explain.

"I was painfully shy as a kid. And it only got worse in high school. I didn't look anything like I do now. I had acne, for one thing. I wore braces for years. I was tall and gangly—my fast metabolism wasn't doing me any favors back then," he says with a wry smile. "All of that to say, I graduated without ever having kissed a girl.

"But that summer before I started college, I had this unforgettable dream about the most beautiful woman. We kissed, and it felt so real, I was convinced it was a premonition." He lets out an uneasy laugh. "And if you think *that* sounds crazy, wait until you hear the rest."

I nod, still nervous, unsure where he's going with this.

"When I got to Dartmouth, I looked for her everywhere. I thought for sure she'd be in one of my classes, or living in the same dorm. I thought we'd run into each other, and sparks would fly—and instantly I'd know it was her. I waited an entire year. I lifted weights a lot, to pass the time. That's where these muscles came from. Then my acne cleared up, and I started getting attention from girls…and finally I caved and took Amanda Meyer out on a date. She was my first girlfriend.

"I've had several more since then. But I never forgot the woman I kissed in that dream. I couldn't forget her, because I kept dreaming of her, year after year. Bright blonde hair. Gorgeous olive-green eyes—"

My breath hitches.

"Velvety pink lips. Petite."

I bring my hand to my mouth.

"That's why I looked at you the way I did when we first met," Charlie continues, his lip quivering. "It's because I already knew you, Jenna. You are literally the woman of my dreams."

As tears start streaming down my face, Charlie takes my hands in his. "I can't explain it, but now I know it's true. The look in my eyes that you painted? That's love. I must have fallen in love with you in my dreams. And it's taken all I have not to tell you how I feel. I almost slipped a few times—"

I knew it.

"But I'm not holding back anymore. I love you, Jenna Andersen."

I throw my arms around him and sob into his neck. His warm tears fall on my shoulder, too.

I want nothing more than to tell him what he's longing to hear in return—but there's something he needs to see first.

I unwind myself from Charlie and wipe the tears from his cheeks. "Come with me," I say, grinning.

I race to my bedroom, plop down on the bed, and motion for my boyfriend to sit next to me. When he does, my heart swells.

He's the same sweet, smart, hot-as-hell Charlie he's always been—but now I can add *in love with me* to the list.

Then I open the drawer of my nightstand and hand him my journal.

"This is the diary I kept in high school," I explain while the notebook's still closed on his lap. "Writing felt like a chore because of my dyslexia, so I drew instead. Take a look."

Charlie examines the first page and smiles. But while looking at the next two, his forehead crinkles. And halfway through, he's stunned. Finally, he turns to me wide-eyed and says, "This is us."

"I can't explain it either," I say with a shrug. "But this can't be a coincidence, right? Do you really think we're…"

I don't know how to finish my thought without sounding like I've watched one too many romantic comedies.

"Meant to be?" Charlie offers.

I nod.

He moves my journal to the nightstand, then leans me back onto the bed and shifts on top of me. "Fuck yeah, I do."

Beaming, I take him in my arms and, for the briefest moment, reflect on the three little words I'm about to say—and how very long it's been since I've uttered them to a man. And how much more significant they feel, now that I'm saying them to my soulmate.

"I love you, Charlie," I whisper, my heart beating wildly against his.

"I love you so much, Jenna." His lips brush mine over and over again, and I can't stop smiling.

"How much?" I tease, wrapping my legs around him.

His lip quirks. "You want me to show you…don't you."

I nod, desire flushing my skin as Charlie takes off every stitch of my clothing and makes his way down to kiss between my thighs. He works his tongue expertly, switching up the pressure and intensity and driving me absolutely batshit crazy, in the best possible way.

"Don't come yet," he tells me when my breaths start getting shorter and faster.

"Why not?" I ask, barely able to stop myself from unraveling.

"Because I love the way you taste," he says.

He slows his tongue and savors me, keeping me on the verge of orgasm for so long that by the time he lets me climax, it's so goddamn intense, I'm seeing stars.

"So that's how much you love me, huh," I say afterward, when he's lying beside me.

He shakes his head. "No…I'm only getting started."

What happens between us next is *otherworldly*. Knowing how we feel about each other—believing wholeheartedly that we belong together—takes the sex to a level I didn't realize existed.

Because it's not just pleasure we're experiencing. It's pure, unadulterated joy.

In between sighs and moans, we whisper *I love you*, and smile, and kiss, and interlace our fingers, and marvel at how perfectly we fit together. Nothing has ever felt this right, and my body relaxes to let Charlie deeper inside me than ever before.

And when I come, it isn't only in my core—it's everywhere. A full-body orgasm that I thought was only a myth until now.

My climax is so intense that, when it's done, I collapse onto the bed next to my boyfriend and start giggling uncontrollably. Before I know it, there are tears streaming down my cheeks, but I feel absolutely euphoric.

Charlie brushes the hair off my face and kisses my tears. "If you weren't smiling so wide, I'd be worried."

"I have no idea what just happened," I say, trying to catch my breath. "I've never had an orgasm like that in my life. It was so powerful—like my entire body was coming."

My soulmate grins. "I was aiming for your G-spot. I guess it's safe to say I found it."

"Oh my god," I gasp. "Is *that* what that was?"

Charlie, being the highly skilled sex god he is, laughs at me. "You're adorable."

I giggle again and pull him close. "I love you."

"I love you more."

We're up early the next morning because Charlie has to go into the office. While we're sipping coffee in bed and he's checking work messages on his phone, I get a new notification on mine. It's an email from Vanessa, who's in Barcelona, on the Spanish leg of her European tour.

Having the best time, but I miss you. Keep thinking of you whenever I walk into an art museum. I bet your work will be on display one day! And Tati Marie can say she discovered you, lol. Wish you were here!

Can't wait to catch up when I get back. How's it going with Charlie?

Smiling, I hit reply:

I'm so glad you're having a great trip! I wish I were there, too. Although I did just have the best night of my life with Charlie. I can't wait to fill you in soon. XOXO

The fact that Vanessa's been thinking of me during her vacation makes my heart swell. Our friendship already feels closer than any other I've had, and I'm so grateful.

My phone chimes again, this time with a photo of Vanessa sitting on the serpentine bench at Park Guell. I recognize the famous monument, with its bright, multicolored mosaics, from studying the architect, Gaudi, in grad school. The view from the park is stunning, and I can't help but fantasize about Charlie and I going there together one day. I let out a dreamy sigh.

"What's up?" Charlie asks, turning to smile at me.

"My friend just emailed me from Barcelona," I explain. "It looks so pretty. Have you ever been?"

"No…but I've always wanted to. It's a travel photographer's dream." Charlie's forehead creases the slightest bit.

I wonder if he had the opportunity to go, but turned it down because of work. It wouldn't surprise me in the least.

"Which friend is this?" Charlie asks.

"She's the one who found my therapist for me. She's so supportive, and—"

Charlie's phone dings, and he looks down at the screen. "Oh, man," he sighs.

"What's wrong?"

"Sorry to interrupt you. It's my buddy Rob—the travel journalist. He just messaged me and said his publisher wants to see my photography before they extend a formal offer. But I haven't updated my portfolio in forever."

"When do they need it?"

"As soon as possible." Charlie exhales. "I have an album of more recent shots, but I'm not sure which ones to choose. Want to help me take a look? I could use your artistic expertise."

"Of course," I say, eager to see Charlie's work.

He hands me his phone, and my heart skips a beat the moment I lay eyes on the first photograph. It's of a sunlit cobblestone path leading to a sparkling turquoise ocean. I can practically smell the salty sea air. And the photos that follow are just as beautiful. Snow-capped mountains against gray sky. Rain puddles on the street reflecting wispy clouds overhead. A row of little houses painted in dreamy pastels.

Every now and then, there's a portrait. A photograph of an old woman in a headscarf looking out into the distance. A child playing with seashells on the beach. A man holding a lit cigarette, smoke coiled in the air like a snake.

And then, I see a familiar face.

A woman I know well—or thought I did.

My heart lurches. My hands are shaking.

There's nothing indecent about the picture. She's just sitting in the grass and smiling.

But the sultry way she's looking at the camera tells me she's no stranger to the man behind the lens. And judging by the looks of her, the photograph was taken relatively recently.

I gasp.

"Jenna, what's wrong?"

My mind is racing. Trying to put the pieces of this puzzle together. Praying they don't fit.

There has to be some other explanation.

"Jenna?" my boyfriend says again when I drop his phone onto my tangled bedsheets.

I look up at his beautiful, loving face. His eyes are laced with worry, waiting for me to answer him.

But my heart is racing. And my mouth is dry. By the time I finally say something, my voice comes out thin and shaky.

"Charlie…how do you know Vanessa?"

twenty-three

I can't believe it. Only a moment ago, I was looking at a picture of Vanessa on *my* phone.

Now here she is again, on Charlie's screen. The only difference is, her hair's shorter in this picture than I've ever seen her wear it—so he must have photographed her before I met either of them. But when? And why?

My mind's still spinning as the blood drains from my boyfriend's face. The rosiness I know him for is gone and, for a moment, he just blinks at me. "*You…*know Vanessa?"

I nod, trying to temper my mounting anxiety, but no such luck. "I met her in art class. Her aunt is my teacher." *How do you know her, Charlie?* I want to ask again, but the words get stuck in my throat.

"Oh," he says, sounding hopeful. "So you and Vanessa are just acquaintances, then?"

I shake my head. "I haven't known her long, but we've already become close friends. She's the one who encouraged me to go to therapy, and found Esther for me."

"Hmm." He purses his lips, and I try to make sense of the change in his expression, which seems more concerned now than thoughtful. "And you said her aunt is your art teacher? I thought Marie worked at a bank."

"She retired," I explain before my brain can process the significance of what Charlie just said.

When I do, my stomach churns. "Wait—you know Marie, too?"

He frowns.

At this point, the odds that Charlie and Vanessa are only casual acquaintances are not in my favor. They must have dated in the past. Maybe it was years ago.

But if it was years ago, why does Charlie look like he's about to break my heart?

"Jenna," he says, taking my hand. "Vanessa and I were engaged."

My jaw drops. "*What?*"

I'm floored. Vanessa was engaged to my soulmate? How is that possible? She just left Nico at the altar. She never mentioned another broken engagement. "When did this happen?"

The color comes back to Charlie's cheeks, but it's not the happy flush I know and love. His eyes shy away from my gaze, embarrassed. "We were supposed to get married four months ago. But it didn't work out."

I pull my hand from his. "No," I say flatly. "That's impossible."

This can't be happening.

I replay every single conversation I've had with Vanessa in my head, searching for answers—but I come up empty.

"She told me she was engaged to a guy named Nico," I say, a small part of me hoping this could all still be some big mistake we'll laugh about later.

My boyfriend sighs. "I'm Charles *Nicolas* Sutton. My mom chose my middle name in memory of her dad, Nicolas St. Pierre, who passed away before I was born. He was Haitian—"

"Like Vanessa," I say, tears welling in my eyes. I remember Charlie telling me he was a quarter Black on his mother's side, but he never mentioned his grandparent was from Haiti. The fact that he and Vanessa share this special connection stings my heart in the most unbearable way.

He nods. "My whole life, I went by Nico. It's what my mom called me as a baby, and it stuck. But after things ended with Vanessa, I knew I needed to make some big changes. Start fresh. I didn't want to be Nico anymore. Nico was uninspired, unhappy—and down on his luck. So I decided to go by my first name instead."

My vision is blurry.

Charlie is Nico.

I think back to the last time Vanessa mentioned him. We were at the wine bar, and she was upset because she'd gotten several missed calls from him. Sam and I were convinced he wanted her back.

What if we were right?

Earlier, when I asked if he'd been to Barcelona, Charlie frowned. I thought maybe he'd missed an opportunity to travel there because of work. But now I know the truth. If Vanessa hadn't left him at the altar, he'd be there with her at this very moment—on their honeymoon. Is that where he'd rather be? In Europe with Vanessa, instead of here with me?

I feel like I'm going to be sick. I'm terrified he's still in love with her, but I don't have it in me to ask him.

"She told me you've been calling her a lot," is all I manage to say.

Charlie runs a hand over his face. "I have—but it's not what you think. I've been calling to tell her I stayed in Chicago. She thought I was moving back to New York, and I didn't want her to be surprised, in case we ran into each other."

"I didn't even know you'd lived in New York," I say, completely bewildered.

Last night, I would have told you that I knew Charlie inside and out. Now I feel like I'm in bed with a stranger.

He sighs. "In the past nine years that I've worked for Sutton's, my dad has sent me to six different cities. New York was one of them. I lived in Manhattan for a year. I met Vanessa my first week there, and we became friends, then…"

He flushes, and I spare him the discomfort of finishing the sentence. "One thing led to another," I say, nodding.

"A year later, my dad announced he was moving me to Chicago," Charlie goes on. "And when I broke the news to Vanessa, she proposed."

"*She* proposed?" I repeat, surprised. "I never knew that."

"I was completely caught off guard. We were in a relationship, yes, but we hadn't had a single conversation about marriage. I didn't know how to respond. She was my best friend, and I did love her, but…" He looks at me with wistful eyes. "She wasn't the love I always dreamed of, Jenna."

I take a ragged breath.

"But how long was I supposed to wait for you? It would be crazy to spend the rest of my life searching for someone I'd only ever met in my dreams, wouldn't it?" He shrugs, looking defeated. "So, I said yes. And we moved to Chicago together."

"And planned your wedding, and your future together," I say, wiping my eyes.

"I was going through life on autopilot. Why else would I plan to marry someone I wasn't head over heels in love with?"

It's a rhetorical question, of course, but an answer comes to mind right away. Charlie told me, not too long ago, that he "aims to please." Granted, we were talking about his skills in bed—but it's obvious the sentiment applies to more than just his sex life.

Charlie Sutton is a people-pleaser. He doesn't want to disappoint me. He certainly doesn't want to disappoint his dad. Is it possible he's so conflict-avoidant that he would walk down the aisle with the wrong person, rather than risk breaking their heart?

"Vanessa did me a huge favor when she ran out of that church," he goes on as my thoughts continue to spiral. "Even though I was stunned at the time, there's no doubt in my mind that she made the right decision."

His words do nothing to alleviate the uneasy feeling in my gut. Right now, though, I'm more worried about his former fiancée's feelings than my own.

"But…what about Vanessa? What if she's having doubts?" The sadness in her eyes whenever she mentions him is unmistakable.

Charlie shakes his head. "What do you mean?"

"I'm…" My voice cracks, and I have to pause to collect myself.

"What?" he asks, his eyes troubled.

"I'm afraid she's still in love with you," I tell him over the sound of my hammering heart.

"She's not, Jenna. Trust me. She loved me as a friend. Maybe she still does. But she was never in love with me. That's why she called off the wedding."

"But she left you to find the love of her life, right? Well, it's been four months, and she hasn't been on a single date. What if she hasn't moved on?"

"I don't know," he replies. "That seems unlikely." But he'd looked so sure before, and now that certainty is gone.

"If she does regret her decision," I begin, "what kind of friend would that make me?"

A man-stealing vixen, like so many women assume I am when they look at me. But this time they'd be right.

"Even in the short time I've known Vanessa, she's been the most loyal friend I've ever had. She introduced me to her culture, her friends, and her family. She took care of me when I was depressed. She found me a therapist, and even drove me to my first session. Charlie, she waited an hour and a half in her car, just to make sure I was okay afterward…"

His brows knit together.

"I don't know what to do," I continue, through tears.

"We're going to figure this out. I promise." He kisses the top of my head, but the sweetness of his gesture only makes me sadder.

When I turn to him, I see the resolve in his eyes. His gaze is steady, and devoted, and reminds me of the way he looked at me last night, when we made love.

How did we get from there to here? I thought Charlie was my storybook happy ending. But now…

He's Nico. My faithful friend's ex-fiancé.

My lip quivers. "It's so hard for me to wrap my head around the fact that, if Vanessa hadn't decided to call off the wedding, you'd be her husband right now. You were going to *marry* her, Charlie…"

He runs a hand over his head. "Look, I'm not proud that it took being left at the altar for me to realize how complacent I was being in my life. But I guess it was the wake-up call I needed. Because the next morning, I picked up my camera again, Jenna—and it was the happiest I'd felt in ages. And I was so high off that feeling that, when Vanessa texted me from her sister's to ask about picking up her things from our apartment, I told her she could keep the place. I was going to stay in a hotel for a few weeks while I wrapped things up at Sutton's, and then I was going to quit. I thought I'd move back to New York, and find work as a photographer—"

I blink back more tears. "But you couldn't do it. You couldn't disappoint your dad."

My boyfriend looks down at his lap, ashamed. When his eyes come back to mine, they're pleading. "The timing wasn't right. Just think—if I'd gone back to Manhattan, we never would have met. But I have no more excuses. I'm going to leave Sutton's, Jenna. I promise."

I heave a sigh. "Are you sure? Or will you just continue settling?"

As soon as I say the words, fear hits me like a punch to the gut. It's definitely a pattern in his life. So, how can I be sure Charlie truly wants *me*?

He already looks so sad, it devastates me to ask him—but I have to. "What if I'm not the girl of your dreams, Charlie? What if you're just settling for some green-eyed blonde who looks like her?"

I sob, heartbroken. Charlie reaches out to hold me, and I want so badly to let him comfort me, but I'm spiraling.

This is what you get for letting your guard down.

This is what you get for believing in love.

This is what you get for believing you're worthy.

I know these are only thoughts—not truths. I've worked on being mindful of my triggers with Esther. But being aware of my negative thoughts doesn't make them disappear. All I can do is choose whether I want to give in to them, or fight. To sink or swim.

A familiar wave of grief threatens to pull me under. But when I stay limp in Charlie's arms, not returning his embrace, he pulls me onto his lap and lifts my face so I'm looking at him.

"Jenna, trust me—you are not a rebound. This is not me settling. There's no one on this earth I'd rather be with. I love you," he says, his eyes glistening.

"Or maybe you love the idea of me," I say, suddenly questioning everything.

"No," he says with more conviction than I've heard in his voice before. "I love your grit, and how hard you worked to make it where you are today. I love your resilience, and how you found a way to love again after the most devastating loss. I love your passion and devotion to art—and your talent completely blows me away. I love your dry sense of humor. The way your eyes smile when you talk about your sister, because you're so excited to finally be close to her. I love the adorable way you scrunch your nose when you giggle, and how you sigh, sometimes, in your sleep."

He wipes my tears with the sleeve of his sweatshirt, just like he did the first time we met.

"I love everything about you. We're meant to be together, Jenna. Nothing has changed since last night. Nothing."

I shake my head. "*Everything* has changed, Charlie. You're Nico! And you know what upsets me most? You never once mentioned you were engaged. Even after I told you all about Hunter. Why?"

His jaw tightens. "I was going to tell you, I promise. I just needed to work up the nerve.

The truth is, I was afraid you'd see me differently."

My forehead crinkles. "Why would I do that?"

Charlie turns bright red. "Because—it's fucking embarrassing, Jenna. I mean, I was left at the altar. It's not exactly a glowing endorsement."

The pain in his eyes kills me. I take his hand and thread my fingers through his.

"I'm so sorry," I say. "I didn't think about it that way."

"Look, I want you to understand," he continues. "Even though I look like this now, I'm still the same lanky, acne-ridden kid on the inside. The kid who couldn't get girls to give him the time of day. Confidence does not come naturally to me."

I bite my lip. "Really? But in bed, you're so…assertive."

He gives a wry laugh. "Yeah, well, that wasn't intuitive either. When my first girlfriend, Amanda, broke up with me, she told me I'd never once given her an orgasm. Apparently, she'd faked it every single time. I was so upset. So you know what I did? I went online and read every article about female pleasure I could find. For weeks, I researched techniques, like I was studying for an exam. And when I found the courage to start dating again, I saw to it that my girlfriends were always more than satisfied."

I can't help but giggle through my tears. "That's very noble."

Charlie circles his arms around my waist. "Jenna, I know you think I'm perfect, but I'm far from it. I've always known that. Now you do, too. The only things that come effortlessly to me are photography—and being with you."

I heave a sigh.

"Everything else, I have to work at. Standing up to my dad, and not settling for a career I hate, are at the top of that list. But I'm willing to do the work. I want to be the best version of myself for you. For us."

"I want to believe you," I say. "I do. But I'm not sure I will until I see it happen. You planned to make major life changes after Vanessa called off the wedding, too. But you didn't."

Charlie nods. "You're right. I shouldn't expect you to believe I'll change when I've done nothing to prove it to you. So I will."

My eyes well up again. "And in the meantime…"

Concern washes over my boyfriend's face.

"I think we should take some space," I say, sniffling. "I need to have a heart-to-heart with Vanessa when she gets home from her trip on Saturday. Now that I know you're her ex, spending time with you behind her back feels like a betrayal."

The dejected look on Charlie's face makes my heart ache.

"I don't want to break up," I tell him, "but I need time to think. This is a lot to process."

Even if Vanessa somehow happens to be okay with me and Charlie dating…what if talking to her confirms my fears about him? Maybe she ended things because she got tired of hearing him swear he'd change. Maybe she decided he never will. And what if she's right?

Charlie's eyes narrow, like he's reading the ambivalence in my gaze.

But he nods, regardless. "I understand."

"You do?"

"Some time apart will be good for me, too," he says with a sigh. "Because if I'm going to prove that I can be the man you deserve…I have a hell of a lot of work to do."

twenty-four

H*e's Nico.*

It's the first thought in my head when I wake up in the morning—even three days later.

I must have really pissed someone off in a past life for karma to come back and bite me like this.

I thought Charlie Sutton was the one. I was sure the stars were aligning for me. Now I have no idea if we're meant to be together. It certainly felt like it.

I want, so badly, to believe that fate tied me to Charlie long before we ever met. I can't ignore the magnetic pull I feel toward him. It can't just be a coincidence that I ran into him by the elevator that night. I've been running my entire adult life— Runaway Jenna, always moving from one place to the next— but maybe I wasn't running away. Maybe this whole time, I've been running toward something. Toward Charlie.

And now the universe goes and pulls a stunt like this. Right when I get to the point in my life where I'm done settling, I meet a man who settles for everything. Who almost married the first real female friend I've had in years.

It feels like a cruel joke.

And, god, do I miss him. I know I asked for space, but every day I hope to see a note under my door—a photo to let me know he's thinking of me. But there's been nothing. He's playing by the rules I set, again, like a true gentleman. Or maybe he's taking the path of least resistance, which I hate to say, wouldn't be unlike him.

Or, worse still, maybe he's having second thoughts about me.

Needless to say, I'm a wreck. Luckily I've been keeping myself busy working on the portrait of Nadine's mother. She's beautiful. Like a raven-haired Grace Kelly. And she has the same sparkle in her eye that her daughter has. It's fun to paint someone so vibrant and full of life.

It's comforting to know that, no matter what happens from here on out, I will always have joy and passion at my fingertips, with a blank canvas and a fresh palette.

But I want Charlie too, dammit.

I want him more than anything. I want him to figure out a way to extract himself from his miserable job without tearing apart his family. I want him to know how good it feels to shake off what doesn't feel authentic, and pursue what brings you joy. I want him to be by my side when I travel outside the country for the first time. I want to see art with him, and make art with him, and make love to him, over and over for the rest of my life.

But what if he doesn't change? What then?

That's as far as I let myself go when I'm spiraling. Well, it's as far as Esther recommends I go, and this time I'm following her advice to the letter. My tender heart can't afford not to.

Yup, therapy's been a lot of fun this week. Poor Esther. She's abandoned her chair a few times to sit with me on the couch. But I'm so grateful to have her to lean on. I should probably reimburse her for all the tissues and tea I've consumed while crying to her about Charlie's alter ego.

I'm trying not to think about him now, as I'm on my way to Tati Marie's painting class, but it feels impossible. Vanessa won't be there today, thankfully. She and her sister, Denise, rebooked their flight home from Barcelona so they could stop in Miami to see their parents. But they'll be back tomorrow, and Vanessa and I have plans to meet. I told her I'd come over with a bottle of wine, and we could catch up.

She has no idea just how much catching up we have to do.

"Jenna, dear?"

"Oh! Hi, Marie," I say with a start.

When I walked into the classroom, she'd been busy talking to another student, so I went straight to my easel and started painting. I have no idea how long she's been standing next to me, because I was stuck in my head, worrying about breaking her niece's heart.

"You're jumpy," she says with an eyebrow raised. "Everything okay?"

"Oh my gosh, yes!" I say with my fake, bright smile. "Of course. Totally."

It's not like I've been having crazy hot sex with your niece's former fiancé, or anything. And I'm definitely not madly in love with him, if that's what you're wondering.

Marie frowns. "Have you thought about whether you'd like to contribute one of your paintings to my friend's art show? I need to give her an answer soon."

I sigh. "I'm so sorry, Marie. I thought I had a piece picked out, but…now I'm not so sure." I can't possibly show Marie Charlie's portrait, now. I'm sure she'll recognize him.

"You need an unbiased eye," she says. "Let me help you. What are you doing after class? I can come over."

I nearly drop my paintbrush. "Oh! Um, you mean…today?"

She raises her eyebrow again and nods. I bet she thinks I'm hungover, or hopped up on caffeine, or both. I guess that's better than her knowing the truth. The thing is, I'd love her opinion on the other pieces in my collection.

I guess I could tell her I need a minute to set up, then run into my studio and cover Charlie's painting with a sheet—just like I did before he came over. He didn't suspect a thing.

My heart stings thinking about him.

"Of course," I finally say. "Thanks. I could use your help."

"Very good," Marie answers. Before she turns away, she places a tender hand on my shoulder, and it's all I can do not to burst into tears.

I thought I was done bottling up my feelings like this. I guess all I can do right now is channel my emotions onto this canvas. We're working on still lifes today, which is not ideal. But I have to say, by the end of class, the bowl of fruit I painted does look a little sad.

Tati Marie follows me back to my place in her car, and it isn't until we're in the elevator that it dawns on me there's a chance we might run into Charlie.

My palms start sweating. How did I not think of this before? I should have sent a message to warn him. It's too late now, because I'm not getting cell reception in the elevator. But even if Charlie's standing there when the doors open, he'd have the wherewithal to pretend he doesn't know me, right?

"Do you have fresh ginger?" Marie says as we're approaching the twentieth floor.

Again, her words startle me, and I nearly jump out of my skin. "Um…ginger? I don't think so. Why?"

Marie squints at me. "I think you're coming down with something. I want to make you tea."

The doors open, and my eyes go wide, fully prepared to see the man I love standing in front of me and Tati Marie.

But no one's there.

I heave a sigh of relief and smile at my art teacher. "Oh, I'm fine, thank you. It's just my period. I get mind-numbing cramps."

She nods, seeming satisfied with my answer.

I lead her down the hallway, toward my apartment. But as I'm about to put the key in the lock, I hear a creak.

I know that creak.

It's Charlie's door.

I spin around. "Oh my god, Tati Marie!" I squeal, hoping I'm loud enough to keep Charlie from leaving his apartment.

Marie's brow furrows, but she remains even-keeled. "What's the matter, Jenna?"

Luckily, my boyfriend's door stops mid-creak, then closes

again. He must have heard me—thank god.

"I'm so sorry, Marie. I just saw, um, a giant bee. But don't worry, it's gone now." It's a terrible lie, considering we're in the windowless hallway of a concrete skyscraper. But improv isn't my forte—I'm no Dex Oliver.

When we're in my apartment, I pour her a glass of wine and invite her to sit at the kitchen island while I set up my collection. I debate taking Charlie's painting out of my studio and hiding it in my bedroom, but my place is open concept, and I'm afraid Marie will ask me what I'm doing. Then I consider stuffing the portrait into the small closet in the corner of the room, but it's already full of art supplies, and I'm afraid it'll get ruined by a rogue can of paint thinner, or something. I'd be devastated.

So I move the painting away from the others and cover it with a sheet again. But when I walk out of the room to get Tati Marie, she's busy at my kitchen counter—mixing a whiskey drink, judging by the bottle of Jim Beam I forgot all about—with freshly squeezed lime juice and honey.

"I'm sorry, Marie. I would have offered you whiskey if I remembered I had some."

"This isn't for me," she says, handing me the glass. "It's for you. Tati Marie's special remedy. I usually take it for a cold, but Vanessa says it works for cramps as well."

"That's so thoughtful," I say, fighting tears as I remember the similar way her niece took care of me. "Thank you."

I take a sip, enjoying the warmth of the whiskey as it goes down. Within seconds, I feel calmer. "It's working already," I tell Marie, who smiles.

When I take her into my art studio, she takes her time studying each one of my paintings. Her eyes are smiling, but she's quiet. She walks back and forth, looking and nodding. Finally, she stops in front of Hunter's portrait.

"Was he your boyfriend?"

"A long time ago, yes," I say before taking another sip of my drink. A month ago, the question would have sent me into a tailspin. I'm so grateful I can think about Hunter now, without feeling guilty.

Marie steps back and eyes the portrait again, tilting her head from side to side, and observing it from different angles. After about a minute of this, she turns to me. "Your work is mesmerizing, dear. You could pick any one of these paintings for the show and stun the crowd."

I grin, imagining art lovers admiring my work, as I've admired the work of so many others. It would be a dream come true.

"This piece," she says, going back to Hunter's, "evokes a stronger emotion for me than the rest. I see love here, Jenna."

I nod. "There was love."

"But not passion," Marie says.

I shake my head. "No, not back then. I didn't know what passion felt like until recently." I'm not sure why I say the words out loud. Maybe it's the whiskey.

"So why not paint him? The man who taught you what passion is," she asks. "Imagine how powerful it would be."

I drain my glass and put it down. "The thing is, Marie…I did paint him. But more than that, I fell in love with him. And for the briefest moment, I had everything I've ever wished for. And then…I got the rug pulled out from under me again."

I start bawling, and Marie takes me in her arms.

"So you're not sick," she says, rubbing my back. "It's heartache you're suffering from. When did you break up?"

"We didn't." I step back and look into Marie's eyes, which may as well be Vanessa's, they're so similar. A pang of guilt cuts through me. "It's more complicated than that. He has this history of settling in life, and I'm worried he's settling for me."

Her forehead crinkles as she listens.

"And not only that," I go on. "If we stay together, our relationship might hurt someone else. A friend I care deeply about. Because I just found out the man I'm in love with is her ex."

Marie only nods. She doesn't suspect I'm talking about her niece—but if I don't stop now, she will.

Maybe it wouldn't be the worst thing. She knows Vanessa better than I do. What if she can say something to put me at ease? Confirm that Vanessa only ever loved Charlie as a friend, like he said? I'd feel a lot more comfortable telling her the truth if that were the case.

"And your friend…she still loves him?" Marie asks.

"I don't know," I admit. "The thing is…" I look down at my feet, and my words are nearly a whisper. "She left him at the altar."

My art teacher gasps. "Jenna? What are you saying?"

Her reaction stuns me. She's usually so cool and calm. I open my mouth to answer her, but all I can do is cry.

Now she knows. I see it in her eyes. There's nothing left to hide, so I cross the room and uncover my boyfriend's portrait.

I take a deep breath and wipe my cheeks. "He introduced

himself to me by his first name," I begin.

Marie's eyes are fixed on the painting, not on me, but I continue.

"And when I told Vanessa I was dating a guy named Charlie, she didn't suspect a thing. I mean, it is a common name. And I had no idea he used to go by Nico."

Marie doesn't respond, but only studies the face of the man her niece almost married.

"I'm going to tell Vanessa tomorrow," I continue. "But I'm terrified. I have no idea how she'll react."

I wish Marie would say something. Every second that passes in silence makes me more and more anxious.

Finally, I hit my limit. "Do you hate me?"

She turns to me and rests her hand on my shoulder, like she did in class earlier. "Of course not, Jenna. I know you didn't mean for this to happen."

I sniffle. "Thank you for saying that."

"I was only being quiet because this piece took my breath away," she explains. "It's your finest work."

"I think so, too," I admit. "But I don't know if I feel comfortable showing it now…under the circumstances."

Marie nods. "I understand. Like I said, all of your paintings are impressive. I'll tell my friend at the gallery to expect one portrait from your collection, and you can take some time to decide which one. To me, the choice is clear."

"Thank you," I say, my heart heavy. "I'm just worried about upsetting Vanessa. I'm scared she hasn't moved on. She says she doesn't regret calling off the wedding, but she hasn't started dating yet. Has she?"

For a moment, I allow myself to be hopeful. Maybe Vanessa's tight-lipped about her love life with friends, but shares more with her family.

Unfortunately, the frown on Marie's face tells me otherwise. "Vanessa's been secretive these days. Well, I call it secretive—she says she's busy with work, but I'm not so sure. I wish I had an answer for you."

"It's okay," I tell her. "Thanks, anyway."

She looks back at Charlie's portrait. "But there is one thing I can say, Jenna."

I turn to her, my forehead creased.

Marie gives me a sympathetic smile. "I never once saw him look at Vanessa this way."

My hands are trembling as I stand outside Vanessa's door at precisely 6:59 p.m., praying that I can manage to calm my nerves in the next sixty seconds or less.

I'm not sure what I'm most anxious about. Telling my friend that my boyfriend, Charlie, also happens to be her ex, Nico? Asking her if she's still in love with him? Hearing her explain why she didn't want to marry him?

I'd honestly rather have a root canal than have this conversation. And I *really* hate going to the dentist.

I close my eyes and rehearse what I'm going to say for probably the hundredth time today.

Vanessa…I just found out that Charlie is Charles Nicolas Sutton.

I had no idea—I swear.

The last thing I'd ever want to do is hurt you.

But I'm in love with him.

Do you love him, too?

What do we do? Where do we go from here?

I look at my phone. It's seven o'clock.

I knock.

My heart thumps as I hear Vanessa's footsteps getting closer. It takes a Herculean effort to unclench my jaw and unfurrow my brow.

I plan to throw my arms around her as soon as I see her. She'll be bright-eyed and smiling, and totally unsuspecting. I'll squeeze her tight and, for a moment, at least, I'll get to enjoy the normalcy between us.

But when Vanessa opens the door, I freeze.

She looks…I don't know, bewildered? Flustered maybe?

"Hey," I say, my brows knitting back together. "Is everything okay?"

She sighs. "Sorry—I just got some news that came as a bit of a shock."

A pang of worry hits my gut. "It's not about Tati Marie, is it?"

Vanessa shakes her head. "No, it's not, thank goodness." She gestures for me to hand her the bottle of wine I'm carrying. "Here, come in."

I follow Vanessa, relieved. Marie's been more of a maternal figure to me than any other woman I've known. She's encouraged my friendship with her niece. She's supported me as an artist, and given me the amazing opportunity to show my work. And last night, she even took care of me—making me her special "remedy" when she thought I was coming down with something, and comforting me when she found out I was lovesick.

Wait a minute.

Is it possible Marie told Vanessa that Charlie is Nico? Is that why my friend's so out of sorts?

She doesn't look back at me once as she leads me through her living room. She doesn't say a word. Not, "It's so good to see you!" or "Can't wait to catch up!" or "Hey! I heard you're sleeping with my ex! How's that going?"

As we get closer to her kitchen, I start to feel like I'm walking the plank.

Take a deep breath, I remind myself, my stomach churning. Vanessa's shock could have been triggered by any number of things. Unemployment rates. Climate change. Endangered species. This probably has nothing to do with me and Charlie.

Except…he's standing in her kitchen.

When I see him at her island, I gasp. He knew I was planning to talk to Vanessa today. So why is he here? And why does he look so uncomfortable? There are beads of sweat on his forehead.

He's also heartbreakingly handsome. Did he get more gorgeous in the four days since I've seen him? When his eyes travel from Vanessa to me, his gaze softens, and that same magnetic pull draws me to him. I want to run into his arms, but I can't. What if I never will again?

"I told Vanessa," he says.

"Oh." I turn to look at my friend.

She clears her throat. "He said you were planning to tell me today. And that you didn't feel comfortable seeing him again until after we talked. I appreciate that."

I nod, shying away from her gaze. Without that signature grin on her face, Vanessa intimidates me. I feel so small, all of a sudden. There she is, tall, and lithe. She's the perfect height for Charlie.

They look good together.

They've been together. Slept together. Laughed together. Planned a wedding together. She's known him much longer than I have. I have no right to be jealous, but I am.

I also feel guilty for robbing my friend of her beautiful smile.

My eyes fill with tears. "I'm so sorry, Vanessa."

"You didn't mean for this to happen," she replies, sounding like Tati Marie. She's still unsmiling, but her tone is gracious, which makes my heart hurt even worse.

"How are you feeling about all this?" I ask her, trying to ignore my racing pulse.

"I only found out ten minutes ago. Nico just got here." She faces him again. "Sorry—I mean, Charlie."

He turns crimson. "You can still call me Nico, if you want. It's fine."

Vanessa sighs. "I think we need to open this bottle of wine."

"Agreed," her ex says.

"Please," I beg.

Vanessa uncorks the bottle and pours out three glasses. She sits in the middle of the island, and Charlie and I pick chairs on opposite ends, as far away from each other as possible.

You'd think we were an estranged couple at a mediation. I've felt his gaze on me since I arrived, but I'm so anxious about upsetting Vanessa that I don't even want to make eye contact with him.

I finish half my wine in one large, noisy gulp. When I put my glass down, Charlie and Vanessa are looking at me. "I'm sorry,"

I say. "This is *incredibly* awkward."

Out of the corner of my eye, I catch Charlie attempting to suppress a smile.

"I know," Vanessa replies. "I'm still trying to wrap my head around everything. I mean, what are the odds?"

"Slim to none," I say before draining my glass. The way Charlie's looking at me with adoring eyes is almost impossible to ignore.

Vanessa pours me more wine, then takes a sip of her own. "To say that I'm stunned is an understatement. But, for the record…I'm not upset."

"You're not?" I ask, my eyes wide.

"This is partly my fault," she replies, looking down at her glass. "I let you believe I wasn't over him."

I squint at her. "I don't understand."

My friend exhales deeply. "I haven't been honest with you. Or anyone, really—until recently."

I shake my head. From across the island, Charlie appears to be just as confused as I am.

"Honest about what?" I ask.

She takes a deep breath. "I've been seeing someone."

"Oh," I say. I allow myself to full-on look at Charlie this time, and he's breathing a sigh of relief. I turn back to Vanessa. "Why didn't you tell me?"

I've shared practically every detail of my life with her—because I've felt so comfortable in her presence, from the first day we met. I thought she felt the same way. I'm disappointed, honestly.

"It has nothing to do with you, or our friendship," she replies, as though reading my mind. "This was about me…feeling guilty."

"Why?" Charlie asks, tilting his head.

She turns to answer him. "I never should have proposed to you. I did it because I panicked. I'm thirty-two years old, and I want a family. When you told me you were moving to Chicago, I was terrified of starting over again. I was afraid I wouldn't find someone as thoughtful and kind as you—"

"So, you settled," Charlie says.

"It's awful, but it's true. You deserve so much better than that. And the fact that I ran out on you, in front of your family and friends…I don't know if I'll ever forgive myself." Tears fall down her cheeks.

"It sucked," Charlie admits. "But you did us both a favor, V. You're not the only one who was settling."

Vanessa's face lights up for the first time since I got here. "Really?"

"When you proposed, *I* panicked," Charlie explains. "I didn't want to hurt you. Because I did love you…but as a friend."

Vanessa lets out a breathy laugh as she wipes her cheeks. "I've never been so happy to hear someone say they were never in love with me."

Charlie wipes his brow. "That makes two of us."

Well, I guess I don't have a reason to feel so jealous anymore. The knots in my stomach ease a bit, but I'm still eager to move on from thoughts of Vanessa and Charlie together. "So, tell us about this guy you're dating," I ask my friend.

"He's a social worker, too. We met about a month after I

called off the wedding, and I wasn't ready to date yet. But he sat next to me at a continuing education seminar, and when we started talking, there was obvious chemistry. We had lunch together that day, during a short break mid-training, and it was the best date I'd ever had—even though you could hardly call it that. I felt like I'd known him forever."

I know the feeling, I think, sneaking a peek at Charlie. He's eyeing me too, the hint of a smile on his lips. And even though his former fiancée is talking about the best date of her life with another man, there's no indication on my boyfriend's face that he's hurt or offended.

"He asked me for my number, and the next night we went to dinner. Before I knew it, I'd seen him every single day that week. But for me to jump into a new relationship so quickly seemed like another rash decision—and I told him that. I went back and forth a lot. But he was incredibly patient with me. Eventually I couldn't fight the fact that I had feelings for him.

"I didn't trust myself, though. I wanted to make sure that what I felt was real. That I wasn't just rushing into a relationship because I wanted to get married and have kids. That's why I didn't tell you when I started dating him, Jenna. Or anyone else, for that matter. I only told my sister a few weeks ago, because—" Vanessa looks down at her lap.

"What?" I ask.

She winces. "I wanted to know if she'd be okay with me taking my boyfriend to Europe, instead of her. I felt awful even suggesting it—"

"Knowing Denise, I'm sure she was happy for you," Charlie says.

Vanessa nods. "She was so relieved to hear I was dating again. She said our whole family was worried I wasn't over you. So I shared the news with my parents, too. My boyfriend's mom and dad also live in Miami, so we decided to spend a few days there after our trip to Europe. We met each other's families, and it went really well." She pauses, and her smile fades.

Charlie raises his eyebrows when she looks at him. "What's up?"

"This isn't too weird for you, is it?" she asks. "I mean, here I am talking about taking another man on the trip that was supposed to be our honeymoon. And introducing him to my parents, and—"

I'm glad she asked, because I was wondering the same thing.

But my boyfriend shakes his head. "Honestly, V—it doesn't bother me. That trip was a gift from your parents, first of all. But more importantly, if you have the opportunity to experience Europe with someone you love, you should take it." His eyes dart to me for a split second, and my pulse quickens, thinking of all the times I've fantasized about traveling to Italy with him. Then he turns back to Vanessa. "I'm really happy for you."

She sighs, relieved. "Okay, good."

"And I know how close you are with your family. It's great to hear your boyfriend got along well with your parents, too."

It's a perfect answer. But what else would I expect from Charlie? *Is this man too good to be true?*

As soon as the thought occurs, I push it out of my mind. It's probably some deep-rooted defense mechanism from the years I spent believing I didn't deserve love. But those days are over now.

"Thanks," Vanessa says, nodding. "I only wish Tati Marie had been there, but she'll meet him soon enough. When I called earlier today to tell her about him, she was over the moon."

My heart swells. Marie must have been worried about how this potential love triangle would shake out.

"I planned to tell you tonight, Jenna. I wanted you to meet him, too," Vanessa says to me, her gaze sincere. "Which is why he's coming over. He should be here any minute."

She looks between me and Charlie before she continues. "Is that okay? Obviously, I didn't anticipate the three of us would be having this conversation tonight. Or ever, really."

I glance up at Charlie, who shrugs. "Well…I'd like to meet him," he says, an earnest look on his face.

I nod. "Yes, of course. Me too."

Vanessa exhales. "Good. It'll make things less awkward—don't you think?"

"It couldn't hurt," I say. Across the island from me, my boyfriend looks as happy as I've ever seen him. And why shouldn't he be? He and his ex cleared the air. Neither of them have residual feelings for each other. His girlfriend doesn't have to worry about breaking her friend's heart anymore.

But Charlie's pattern of not wanting to disappoint people, at the expense of his own happiness, worries me even more now. He accepted Vanessa's proposal because he didn't want to upset her. How do I know he wouldn't do the same with me?

A knock at the door startles me. Vanessa's boyfriend is here. I guess I don't have time to agonize over this now.

"That's him," she says, her face lighting up for the second time tonight. "I'm going to chat with him in the hallway first, and fill him in on what he's missed so far. It might take him a few minutes to process this, too."

The moment Vanessa leaves the kitchen, Charlie's on his feet, moving to sit next to me. Grinning, he threads his fingers through mine. "I told you this would all work out."

My forehead crinkles. "What about, um…the other stuff we talked about?"

"My job?" he asks.

I nod.

His smile dims the slightest bit. "I'm working on it."

It's not exactly convincing.

"How've you been the past few days? I really miss you. I haven't reached out at all, because you said you needed space—but I just want you to know I've been thinking about you." He sighs. "A hell of a lot."

"I miss you too." It's all I have time to say before Vanessa walks back into the kitchen, followed by her boyfriend.

He's a few inches taller than Charlie—maybe 6'4"—and quite handsome. He looks like he could be mixed, too. His dark hair is buzzed short, and he has hazel eyes that pop against his light brown skin, even behind the pair of glasses he's wearing.

He beams at us. A bright, kind smile that reminds me a little of Vanessa's.

No—that's not it.

His smile is familiar, but it's unique. And when his gaze lands on mine, my forehead creases.

"Wait a minute…I know you," I tell him.

Recognition lights his eyes. "You went to Beachwood Middle

School."

"I did," I reply—but I still can't place him.

"I'm Asher," he says. "Asher Abadie."

twenty-six

If I remember correctly, Asher Abadie's dad was in the military, and was stationed near Beachwood for a couple of years. I don't think I spoke to Asher once while we were in school together. He seemed nice, but he was shy, and mostly kept to himself. I always wondered if he had a crush on Sunny, though. He sat behind her in science class, and his gaze never drifted far from her, even though all he could see from that vantage point was her pretty hair.

"I'm Jenna Andersen," I remind him.

"I know," he says, exchanging a smile with Vanessa.

"On our trip, Asher mentioned he lived in Beachwood briefly, and we realized that you were in school together," she tells me. "That's why I invited him over tonight. I thought it would be a fun surprise."

"Small world," Charlie says to no one in particular.

"Tell me about it," Asher replies, and the two men chuckle.

"Good to see you again, Jenna," he continues, reaching for my hand first, then my boyfriend's. "And you must be Charlie?"

"Formerly known as Nico, yes," he says with a sheepish grin. "Is it too soon to laugh about this?"

"I think you need a symbol. Like Prince," Vanessa teases. Asher chuckles again.

"Guess it's not too soon," I answer Charlie.

"Why don't we sit in the living room?" Vanessa goes on to suggest. "I'll open another bottle of red."

Charlie looks to me for guidance. "Sure," I reply. "Sounds good."

He takes my hand and leads me to the living room, then sits at the very end of Vanessa's couch. When I'm seated next to him, he puts his arm around my shoulder, and I can't help but melt into him. My mind may be full of doubt, but my body knows what it wants. I guess that's not the worst thing. This double date is strange enough as it is without me advertising my inner turmoil. I lean into Charlie and delight in the warmth of his body against mine—for now, at least.

"So, Asher, what have you been up to since middle school?" I ask when he and Vanessa are settled at the other end of the couch, and the four of us are sipping merlot.

He chuckles. "Well, I made a few more moves around the country with my family, until I graduated high school. Then I studied psychology at Northwestern, and got my master's in social work at The University of Chicago. I've lived here ever since. I run an agency that offers mental health services to military families."

"That's incredible," Charlie says. "Sounds like a rewarding career."

Asher nods. "I'm very lucky to be doing work I'm passionate about."

My pulse picks up speed, triggered by the mention of job satisfaction, and I wonder if Charlie feels the same way. But his heartrate remains steady where I'm leaning on him. At the same time, his arm travels from my shoulders to my waist, and he pulls me even closer—like he can sense my apprehension and wants to comfort me.

"You remember Sunny, right?" I ask Asher, changing the subject for the sake of my nerves. "She went to Northwestern, too."

He turns to Vanessa, who's wearing an amused grin. "Yeah," he says. "Sunny and I dated for a while in college."

My jaw drops. "No way! I had no idea. Sunny and I didn't keep in touch back then. We became closer recently."

Vanessa looks up at her boyfriend. "Ash told me all about Sunny over a pitcher of sangria in Barcelona. She did a number on him. Broke his heart."

Asher laughs. "It wasn't *that* bad."

"He was going to propose," Vanessa mock-whispers to me.

"Seriously?" I ask Asher, who's smiling wide, and doesn't seem at all rattled by the topic of conversation.

"I wasn't going to propose. Well…not imminently, anyway."

"You bought her a ring," Vanessa teases.

"A *promise* ring," he clarifies, laughing. "I was going to give it to her after graduation, but she broke up with me about a month beforehand. On our one-year anniversary."

"He cried for weeks afterward," Vanessa says with an exaggerated pout.

Asher shakes his head. "It was a week—tops," he tells me and Charlie.

I wince. "Ouch. I'm sorry. But don't take it personally. She just never stopped loving Dex."

Asher chuckles. "Yeah, I wasn't the least bit surprised when I heard about their wedding in the news. I remember her crushing on him so hard during middle school. I'm happy for them, though. It all worked out for the best, right?" He turns to meet Vanessa's gaze, and I can practically see the sparks fly between them.

"Looks like it," I say, grinning at my friend and her new beau.

The four of us spend the next hour sipping wine and chatting. Laughing. It's more fun than you'd ever imagine hanging out with a pair of exes—and their new significant others—could be.

Asher and Charlie take an instant liking to each other. Turns out they're both really into baseball. I find myself wishing that I were as knowledgeable about the sport as Christy, because once the men start talking about stats, they may as well be speaking a foreign language. Like my boyfriend, Asher played Little League growing up. Now, he's coaching a T-ball team for his agency's youngest clients. It's the sweetest thing, seeing his eyes light up when he talks about it.

"Asher's amazing," I tell Vanessa when we're in the kitchen later, putting together a charcuterie board. "And you guys seem so happy together."

Vanessa shakes her head, a dreamy smile on her face. "You don't know the half of it. I've never felt this way before. We have so much in common, from music, to food—to our profession, obviously. We never run out of things to talk about. And he can't wait to start a family, just like me. To be honest with you…"

"Yeah?"

"I could always tell that Charlie wasn't eager to have kids. So, if that's something you're worried about—don't be," she says.

I nod, feeling relieved. "He did tell me that he's never dreamed of being a father. But it's good to hear it from you, too."

Especially since it's so hard to tell what Charlie wants, when he's so busy pleasing others. And, as happy as Vanessa seems with Asher, now that I'm alone with her, I want to be sure she isn't upset with me.

"So you're really okay with me dating The Artist Formerly Known As Nico?" I ask. "It isn't weird for you?"

She laughs. "The way I see it, we can choose to let it be awkward, or we can choose not to. He and I were friends, more than anything else. It's a lot like the relationship you had with Dex. And you and Sunny are totally cool, now, right?"

"Yeah," I say without hesitation. "I was never in love with Dex, and everything worked out the way it was meant to."

Vanessa smiles. "Exactly. And honestly? I can see you and Charlie being really happy together."

"You can?" I ask, my heart fluttering.

"He's such a great guy," Vanessa tells me. "Kind. Thoughtful. Creative. Whip-smart. We just didn't have the right chemistry. If you two have it—"

My cheeks warm.

"I don't see what could go wrong," she continues.

I want to ask her opinion about Charlie's people-pleasing,

and his tendency to settle for everything, but I hear footsteps coming our way. *Dammit.*

"Need any help?" Charlie asks, with Asher entering the kitchen right behind him.

"You can grab the charcuterie board," Vanessa tells Charlie. "Want to get us some plates, Ash?"

"My pleasure," he says, winking at her.

The four of us head back to the living room, where we stay until close to eleven, polishing off our second bottle of wine and devouring every last piece of charcuterie. Before we call it a night, we promise to get together again soon.

When we're alone in front of Vanessa's building, Charlie turns to me. "How'd you get here?"

"Cab," I say. "I figured I'd be drinking a fair amount of wine tonight. I was so nervous to tell Vanessa about us."

"That's why I talked to her first," he says, looking down at his shoes. "I hope you don't mind. I wanted to unburden you of some of your stress. Plus, I don't have the richest history of being proactive, and…I want to fix that."

A hopeful smile forms on my lips. Maybe he *can* change. "I don't mind at all," I say. "I appreciate it."

He nods. "I'm parked up the street. I can drive us home—I didn't drink much."

"Thanks," I reply, tempted to abandon my reservations and go all in with Charlie Sutton. I mean, here's this wonderful man who wholeheartedly believes we're a fairytale: two artists who were destined to be together. Who had given up on love, then found each other in an unexpected twist of fate. It's so beautiful, and romantic—and instead of embracing the man I've always wanted, I'm asking him for space.

Suddenly he's not the one I'm doubting. It's *me*.

Am I sabotaging this relationship?

Am I expecting too much from him?

Against all odds, Vanessa's happy that Charlie and I are dating. But I'm hardly able to appreciate it, because I'm so stuck in my head.

"What's wrong?" Charlie asks when we're in his Range Rover. He was about to back out of the spot, but puts the car back in park when he sees the look on my face.

"I'm afraid I'm going to lose you," I say, my eyes welling with tears.

He takes my hand. "Lose me? Jenna, all I want is to be with you. I'd be kissing the hell out of you right now if you hadn't asked me for space."

"That's what I'm worried about. I feel like I'm giving you an ultimatum: leave your job at Sutton's, or we can't be together. But Sutton's isn't just a job—it's your family. Not to mention, it's financial security. And I'm asking you to give it up to be a starving artist with me?"

"You're not asking me to do anything I don't already want to do," he says. "Trust me. And I don't think we'll be starving. We both have plenty of marketable skills to fall back on, if need be."

"But I'm asking you to quit on *my* timeline—and maybe that's unreasonable." I heave a sigh, my lip quivering. "The thing is, though, Charlie, you've been working for your dad for nine years—not nine months. And nine years is a long time to be miserable, especially when—"

My breath hitches.

"When what?" Charlie asks, his eyebrows drawing together.

My lip quivers. "When you never know what's around the corner."

Now I understand where this sense of urgency is coming from. I know all too well how short life can be. How quickly circumstances can change without warning.

"Hunter had his whole life ahead of him," I explain. "He was so young. And he was healthy—until he wasn't. I felt so guilty after his death that I didn't think I deserved happiness. Now, I finally believe I do. No one knows how much time they'll get, Charlie. But I want to make the most of mine. To live life to the fullest. And I want you to do that with me."

He holds me as I cry. "That's what I want, too. I'm going to prove it to you, I promise."

With his heart beating so calmly against mine, it's impossible not to believe him. Relief floods me, and I smile, feeling the happiest I have all night.

Until a clap of thunder booms from my boyfriend's pocket.

What ironically perfect timing.

Charlie ignores the hailstorm of texts from his dad at first. But they keep coming at lightning speed. Finally he lets go of me and reaches for his phone.

"I'm sorry," he tells me. "Just a second."

He lets out a lengthy exhale, reads the messages, then silences his cell. After pocketing it again, he pinches the bridge of his nose. "I, um—I have to go back to Denver. I'm leaving first thing tomorrow morning."

My heart sinks. "Oh."

"But don't worry. I'll be back in time for the art show."

"The art show's in two weeks," I say, stunned. "You'll be gone that long?"

"Most likely," he says, frowning. "Fuck. I have so much on my plate at work already. I don't know how I'll get anything done, now that I have to travel again."

My gut clenches.

"What about those new hires your dad was looking to make? Any progress there?" I ask, even though I'm sure I already know the answer.

He frowns, looking defeated. "Not yet."

My sadness ebbs, replaced by a wave of frustration. "Let me ask you *this*, Charlie—how long has your dad been telling you he's planning to hire additional staff?"

My boyfriend's gaze shifts to his lap. "I don't know." After several seconds, he blows out a resigned breath. "A while."

"And have you confronted him about what's taking so long?"

He clenches his jaw. "Jenna, you have to keep in mind—he's not only my dad. He's my boss. That would be unprofessional."

My eyes widen. "It isn't unprofessional, Charlie. It's called advocating for yourself. Your dad walks all over you, but you'd rather be quietly miserable than speak up and disappoint him. Is that how you want to live your life?"

His face reddens as he looks at me, stunned. "Jenna, I don't want to argue with you."

I cross my arms. "Of course you don't. Because you're so

afraid of disappointing people that you were willing to marry the wrong person—"

"That's not fair." He pinches the bridge of his nose again, just like he does every time he gets a text from his father. An attempt to stifle his emotions, I'm guessing.

"No, *you're* the one who isn't being fair, Charlie. You're not giving yourself a fighting chance at happiness, because you're so concerned about pleasing others. Well, I know what it's like to have a father who doesn't support your dreams. But I stopped caring about his approval a long time ago. Wanna know why? Because approval isn't love." I take a deep breath. "You can't love someone if you refuse to see them for who they are."

Charlie purses his lips. "We've talked about this before. I'm his only son—it's complicated."

"But your dad isn't the only person you're afraid of disappointing. He's at the top of the list, sure—but where does the list end? I mean, your first girlfriend wasn't satisfied in bed, so you read every sex guide on the internet to make sure you never disappointed a woman again?" I bite my lip. "And yes, I'm being a total hypocrite, because I enjoy your skills *tremendously*. But why put that pressure on yourself, Charlie?"

He can't look me in the eye. All I hear is his shallow breath as I continue.

"From the moment we met, I've been wondering if you're too good to be true. Now I know why…it's because you're a people-pleaser. Your need to meet other people's expectations is dictating your life," I tell him. "If all you're worried about is making other people happy, how will you ever figure out what *you* really want? Or how you really feel? You're so damn agreeable—I mean, you just told the woman you were about to marry *four months ago* that you're thrilled she has a new boyfriend. Is that even true?"

"Of course it's true! Why would you think otherwise?"

"Because you always say exactly what I want to hear—"

"And that's a bad thing?" he asks, dragging a palm down his face. "Jesus, Jenna! I don't know what you want from me."

I throw my hands up. "I want you to be yourself! I don't need perfection from you—I need you to be real. I'm working hard in therapy so I can live a life that's true to who I am, and I won't go backward. If I'm with a man who settles because he's afraid to be himself, then I'm settling, too. Don't keep putting everyone's needs ahead of your own, Charlie. Choose yourself first. *Then* choose me. It's the only way we'll be happy together."

He grips the steering wheel with white-knuckled hands and rests his forehead between them. "God, I hate this."

I put my palm on his knee. "I know you do…but I'm not sorry for confronting you. Conflict happens in healthy relationships. If we're going to get through this, to our happy ending, then you have to be willing to handle it."

After a beat, he finally looks at me again.

"Okay," he says, nodding, a wistful look in his eyes. Then he takes my hand and kisses it, his beautiful long lashes fluttering closed.

Every time he touches me, it's all I can do not to close the gap between us. Taking space is as torturous for me as it is for him. I hope he knows how badly I want him to rise to this challenge.

To fight for our happily-ever-after. I have no doubt he's capable. I'm just terrified that *he* doesn't believe in himself enough to try.

His gaze is on mine again, and he must see the worry all over my face. "Look, I know this isn't easy for you, either, Jenna. Just try not to give up on me, okay?"

I heave a sigh, my eyes stinging. "Okay." It's all I can say without bursting into tears.

"Good," Charlie says, nodding again. But the air hangs heavy between us, and we drive the whole way home in silence.

twenty-seven

Seven days later, Christy's back in town to visit me. I was in tears on the phone while filling her in on the whole Charlie/Nico debacle, and she booked a flight without me even having to ask. She'll be staying through the art show next weekend, since she has plenty of unused vacation days. She and Kyle never traveled anywhere—not unlike our mom and dad.

To say I'm relieved my sister's here is the understatement of the year.

I've been a nervous wreck counting the seconds until I see Charlie at the art show. That is, if he's still even planning to come. I have no idea what he's thinking. He's a thousand miles away, and we haven't talked since he drove me home from Vanessa's and hugged me outside the door of my apartment, while I tried not to cry.

I haven't even gotten the chance to tell him that I finally made the decision I've been agonizing over for weeks: I'll be showing his portrait at the gallery next Saturday. It's my grand gesture. My way of telling him that I believe in our love story. That we *are* meant-to-be. That Charlie Sutton and I were tied together, somehow, before we even met. And that our run-in at the elevator was destiny.

"What do you think?" My sister walks into the living room wearing a little black dress that barely covers her, um, assets. "Too short?" she asks, scrunching her nose.

I squint at her. "Is that mine?"

She sighs. "Well, we're going out tonight, and I want to look good. Your clothes are sexier."

I laugh. "They're also made for a petite woman, which you are not. You look amazing, though."

"You really think so?" She smooths the fabric over her stomach.

"I know so," I insist.

But Christy doesn't look satisfied.

"What's wrong?" I ask her. "When we went out for drinks the last time you were in town, you were so carefree and confident. You attracted guys like a magnet."

She plops down next to me on the couch, pulling down the hem of my tiny dress. "I've put on another few pounds since then."

My forehead creases. "I thought you said you were happy to gain some weight after you stopped marathon training."

"Well, I was excited about the first five pounds, because I thought the curves looked good on me. But the second five pounds…" She shakes her head. "I'm not so sure anymore. I was in the best shape of my life when Kyle and I were together—"

"Because of all those long runs you hated," I remind her.

"I know. But when I was running, I could eat whatever I

wanted without a care. That doesn't seem to be the case anymore," she goes on, frowning.

"Honestly, Christy…I used to worry about you when you ran that much. You were all skin and bones. I think you look incredible now."

Her eyes fill with tears. "Well, I don't feel incredible. That's why I wanted to borrow your dress. Because it's stretchy, and all the clothes I brought with me are too tight. I think it's partially because I'm bloated from my period, but still…I feel disgusting."

"Oh, Christy," I say, rubbing her knee. "I always feel disgusting when I'm on my period. Don't worry, okay? We're going back to my closet, and we're going to find a dress that fits you perfectly."

She leans back on the couch and heaves a sigh. "Okay. But can it be something at least a little sexy? Because—"

My sister looks away from me, embarrassed.

"Because what?"

Her lip quivers. "I'm sorry, I don't know why I'm dumping all my issues on you tonight. I'm supposed to be here to support you, not the other way around."

"Are you kidding? We're sisters," I tell her, taking her hand in mine. "We support each other."

And I have to say, with all the times I've leaned on Christy, it feels great to be the supportive sister for once.

"True," she says with a hint of a smile.

"Great," I confirm with a nod. "So, lay it on me."

"Well…we're hanging out with Sam and Vanessa tonight, and I've never met them, so I looked them up on Facebook. They're both *gorgeous*," Christy continues with a pout. "And so unique-looking. Then there's you—my bombshell big sister—and I just feel so plain, in comparison."

My heart aches knowing Christy still feels as insecure about her looks as she did when we were growing up. I wish she could see what I see. So, I grab her hand and lead her to the mirror in my foyer.

"You are a classic beauty, Christy Andersen," I begin. "And I'm not only saying that as your sister. I'm speaking as an artist who did your portrait, so consider this my professional opinion."

She half-smiles at my reflection.

"Your features are very symmetrical, for one thing," I go on, "and we all know that symmetry is aesthetically pleasing. I loved painting your almond-shaped eyes, and your pert little nose—and don't get me started on this cupid's bow."

I expect her to laugh, but her shoulders slump. "All I see are small eyes, a small nose, and thin lips. Boring, boring, boring."

I put my hands on my waist. "Then you need to get your vision checked. There is nothing boring about you, Christy. Do you know how many women out there—including your own sister—wish they had auburn hair like yours? Not to mention that smattering of freckles on your peachy skin?" Smiling, I pinch her cheek.

Finally, she giggles. "The freckles are kinda cute."

"They're beautiful. *You* are beautiful, Christy. Now, let's go get glammed up and have some fun."

One hour, and one movie-worthy makeover montage later, Christy and I are walking into the bar to meet Vanessa and Sam. From the moment we step inside, my sister is already turning heads. She's wearing a strappy red dress I bought months ago, but forgot to have hemmed. It fits her perfectly, and she looks hot as fire in matching red lipstick and the bold cat eye I gave her with my liquid liner.

Vanessa and Sam are at a high-top table with a pitcher of margaritas when we walk in.

"You must be Christy," Vanessa says with her beaming smile as she wraps her arms around my sister.

Sam takes her turn hugging Christy, then squeals. "I was not expecting Jenna Andersen's little sister to be a ginger! What a pleasant surprise!"

We all look at her, confused.

"My best friend growing up had the most beautiful red hair," Sam explains. "She was the sweetest, funniest person I'd ever met. But her family moved abroad when we were in sixth grade, and we lost touch. I was devastated for all of middle school. To this day, whenever I see a redhead, my heart skips a beat. You're so rare and magical. Like unicorns."

"Why, thank you," Christy says as she flips her long, wavy hair. The smile on her face is unmistakable, and I'm grateful to Sam for boosting my sister's confidence.

"I hope you like margaritas," Vanessa says as we all sit at the table. "Because tonight…we're celebrating."

"What's the occasion?" I ask as she pours drinks for me and Christy.

"My assistant director came back from maternity leave this week, and she's taken so much work off my plate," she says with a huge grin. "I finally feel like I can breathe."

"Cheers to that," Sam toasts as we all clink glasses.

But Vanessa's announcement makes me think of Charlie and his work woes, and even as I'm smiling for my friend, my heart sinks. I try my best to shake off the feeling, so no one notices.

"So, what's your story?" Sam asks, turning to my sister.

Christy takes a sip of her margarita. "Well…I'm a literary agent, and I *love* my job."

Vanessa's eyes light up. "What kind of books do you rep?"

"Book club fiction is my jam," my sister answers, eager to talk about her work. "I love the commercial appeal of the stories, mixed with the literary writing style."

"Do you represent any romance writers? That's my favorite genre," Vanessa says with the rosy glow of a woman in love.

Christy shakes her head. "I only started feeling drawn to romance novels again recently. I just broke up with my boyfriend of eight years, and he was the polar opposite of romantic, so love stories were a little triggering for me."

Sam nods as she sets down her glass after taking a sip. "Well, good for you for calling it quits. Life's too short to settle for anything that doesn't knock your socks off, that's what I say."

Ugh. Now we're talking about not settling? My heart plummets even further.

My sister takes another sip of her margarita before she responds. "Kyle definitely didn't knock my socks off. He wouldn't even have sex with me if it wasn't a Friday night between the hours of nine and eleven-thirty."

Sam is mid-gulp again, and chokes on her drink. "You can't be serious," she says after clearing her throat. "What happened at midnight? Did his dick turn into a pumpkin?"

Christy laughs, then rolls her eyes. "Kyle had a very rigid sleep schedule. He had to get eight hours a night, no matter what. And Saturday was the only morning he could sleep in. But he insisted on being up at eight for his morning run."

Sam grimaces. "I bet he was *terrible* in bed. No one that uptight could possibly be a good lay."

Vanessa and I exchange the type of amused grin that Sam usually elicits with her unfiltered comments, but my sister just shrugs, unfazed. "Well, I don't have anyone to compare him to. But I guess I did do all the work. He would always just lie there."

Sam brings her palm to her forehead. "You poor, sweet, girl. Do you need me to help you find a man? I've become incredibly skilled at detecting bad lovers before they make it to my bed. It's my superpower. I guess it comes with experience," she goes on with a proud grin.

Christy laughs. "Tonight is girls' night, and I want to get to know you and Vanessa, so no, thank you. But…maybe after the holidays?"

I tilt my head. "What's happening after the holidays? Are you coming back to visit?"

Christy beams. "Not to visit…to live."

My jaw drops. "Oh my gosh! Really? You're moving here?"

She nods. "I talked to my boss, and she said I could keep my job and work remotely. I might have to fly to New York every now and then, but it's official—I'm moving to Chicago in January."

I jump out of my seat and throw my arms around my sister.

"I can't believe it! I'm so excited, Christy! We're going to have the best time living in the same city."

"I've already started looking at apartments online, and there's a beautiful building not far from you, with several two-bedrooms available," she tells me. "We can be neighbors!"

Neighbors. My mind flits to Charlie again, and I have to swallow back tears.

"And I can finally go to my first Starlings game next spring!" my sister exclaims. Christy became a diehard fan of Chicago's MLB team when they came back from a string of humiliating defeats to win the World Series two years ago.

I'm about to suggest that my equally baseball-obsessed boyfriend and I could accompany her to a game or two—but what if he and I aren't together next season?

"Sounds like we have another cause for celebration," Vanessa says, topping off everyone's drinks. "To Christy moving here—and joining our crew."

"To Christy!" Sam and I say as we all clink glasses again. And I do my best not to think about Charlie.

"Thank you. I'm so excited for this next chapter to begin," my sister replies.

Once we've taken sips, I catch Sam looking at me out of the corner of my eye.

"What?" I ask, a little on edge, because I never know what to expect from her.

She winces, but there's mischief in her eyes. "I'm sorry, but… can we just take a moment to talk about how weird it is that Charlie is Nico? Vanessa told me right before you got here."

So much for not thinking about my boyfriend.

"And let me just say, I did *not* see that coming," Sam goes on before taking a gulp of her margarita. "Quite the plot twist."

Blood rushes to my face. I can't even look at Vanessa, but she reaches across the table for my hand. "Jenna and I agreed not to let it be weird, right?" When my gaze meets hers, she winks at me.

I heave a sigh. "So nothing's changed since you've had more time to think about things? You're sure you're still okay with it?"

"I promise," she says, squeezing my fingers before she lets go. "I'm so happy with Ash, he's all I can think about, anyway."

"Okay, good." I glance briefly from Vanessa to Sam. "Because I don't want to be that girl no one trusts around their boyfriends."

"I don't think of you that way—I promise," Sam tells me, looking as serious as I've ever seen her. "I know we got off to a rocky start because I worried you were a threat to Sunny. But you put that fear to rest pretty quickly. And the more I get to know you, the more I like you. You're a good egg, Jenna Andersen."

A good egg. It's what Charlie's cousin Maya called me, after we took her yoga class on the beach. It was such a perfect day with him. And, that night, we slept together for the first time. I miss him so much, my chest aches. Then my lip quivers.

"Jenna? What's wrong?" Christy asks, her hand on my shoulder.

I burst into tears.

My sister and friends gaze at me with concern, their foreheads crinkled.

"I don't know if Charlie and I are going to work out," I admit, wiping tears from my eyes.

Christy, already up-to-date on my boyfriend troubles, rubs my arm as I continue. "He's a chronic people-pleaser—and he's terrified of conflict—and I'm not sure I can trust him with my heart. I mean, he would have married you, Vanessa, if you hadn't been brave enough to call off the wedding. All because he didn't want to upset you. So, how will I ever know if he's being genuine with me? And he's been miserable working for his dad for the last nine years, but hasn't worked up the courage to stand up to him."

Vanessa nods knowingly.

"I'm not sure he'll ever change," I continue. "I told him I needed space after the whole Nico Reveal, and we argued after we left your place on Saturday. Now, he's in Denver for work, and I have no idea what's going through his head."

Sam, Christy, and I all look to Vanessa for guidance.

"You and Charlie argued?" she asks, stunned. "And he actually agreed to give you space?"

I nod.

Vanessa raises her eyebrows, looking impressed. "That surprises me, to tell you the truth. We never fought once the entire time we were together. And if I was ever annoyed with him over something small, he wouldn't rest until he'd smoothed things over. He couldn't stand me being upset with him. It may not seem like much, but he's making progress, Jenna. He's passionate enough about your relationship to argue over it. And I bet it's killing him to give you space, but he's doing it anyway. That just goes to show how much he cares about you."

I sniffle. "You really think so?"

Vanessa nods. "I saw the way he looked at you last week, at my apartment. I never once caught him looking at me like that. If there's anyone he'll change for, it's you."

I wipe my cheeks again. "Thank you. That means a lot."

Vanessa's words are nice to hear, but they're only her opinion, of course. I won't have the answers I'm looking for until I see Charlie again. And even then, there's no guarantee he'll be able to stamp out my uncertainty.

So, back at my apartment later that night, while Christy's showering, I take my journal of wishes out of my nightstand. And for the first time in twelve years, I add a sketch.

It's of Charlie. *Only* Charlie.

He's in the Tuscan countryside. He's got his camera strapped around his neck.

And he's happy.

It's the morning of the art show. Charlie's portrait is out of my studio now, already on display at the gallery. Christy dropped it off yesterday, while I was wrapping up one of my final design projects with a client. It was probably for the best that I didn't deliver the piece myself, since I can't even glance at it without getting misty-eyed.

Everywhere I look, I see reminders of Charlie. Even now, as I'm sitting next to Christy at my kitchen island, finishing the omelet she just whipped up for me. Who knew that eggs could be so triggering? All I can think about is the expertly prepared breakfast my boyfriend made me the morning after we first slept together—and now there are tears in my coffee.

My sister tilts her head, her eyes full of sympathy. "Are you afraid he's not going to show up at the gallery?"

I nod, a sob escaping my chest. Christy puts an arm around me as I answer her question between sniffles. "I'm already nervous enough for tonight as it is. What if my painting isn't well-received? What if the only people who can appreciate it are the people who know me? Maybe strangers won't be moved by a portrait of Charlie, and the loving way he looks at me. And what if he never looks at me like that again?"

"Take a deep breath," my sister says, her tone calm and even. "First of all, your work is extraordinary—anyone can see that. And second of all…I believe what Vanessa said at the bar last weekend. Charlie's fighting for you, Jenna. He's given you space for two whole weeks, when it's probably everything he can do not to call you. I think we're going to walk into the art gallery tonight, and he'll already be there, waiting for you, with flowers and a heartfelt speech—"

I sigh. "I think we watched one too many rom-coms this week, and you've lost touch with reality."

Christy's shoulders slump. "Maybe. But…I want to believe in soulmates. I want to think that love can be written in the stars."

When she arrived last weekend, I showed her the sketches in my journal, and told her about Charlie's dreams. She wouldn't even consider the possibility that it's a coincidence.

"I mean, we never got to see that kind of love with Mom and Dad. And the cosmic connection between you and Charlie? It's just so beautiful, and romantic…"

Now my sister's cheeks are streaked with tears.

My eyes go wide. "Oh no…I broke you! I never should've subjected you to all those sappy movies."

Christy shakes her head and sits up straight, regaining her composure. "No, I'm fine. It's just that, we Andersen sisters deserve our own epic romances, don't you think? And we're going to get them, dammit! First you, then me."

"Yes, boss." I giggle. "You definitely deserve a more exciting love story than Kyle."

Christy laughs, but then the amused look in her eyes fades, replaced by alarm. She gasps.

"What?" I ask, concerned.

"Oh my gosh…is Kyle like *Dad?*" She grimaces. "Stern, unwavering, unadventurous…"

"Dull as dishwater?" I volunteer.

My sister's palm meets her forehead. "Ugh. Talk about daddy issues."

"Well, I'm pretty sure I have mommy issues," I tell her. "Every time Tati Marie gives me one of her big, warm, hugs, I feel like I'm going to cry. Mom never hugs us like that."

"Do you ever wonder how we were even conceived?" Christy crinkles her nose.

"By the two least affectionate people on the planet? Um, yeah. But I don't think Mom was always like that."

"What do you mean?" My sister turns toward me, intrigued.

"I used to go snooping around in her closet sometimes," I confess. "She was always so closed off, I felt like I barely knew her. So I would search for clues. One time, I found these old photographs from when she was younger. Late teens, or early twenties, maybe. She was with this guy—her boyfriend, I'm assuming. He had his arm around her, and she looked happier than I've ever seen her."

"He must be the one who got away. Poor Mom," Christy says with a deep sigh. "Oh! Speaking of which…this is the time I typically call her."

"You call Mom? Like, every week?"

Christy nods. "I call her every Saturday, and I call you every Sunday. That's my routine."

I guess I shouldn't be surprised. My sister's always been good about checking in regularly. She's the glue that keeps the Andersens together. I think she still holds out hope for the kind of close-knit family I gave up on.

My forehead creases. "What do you even talk to her about?"

I get a wry smile in return. "Literally nothing. She tells me about the weather in Beachwood…I tell her about the weather in Manhattan… Sometimes she'll tell me about a recipe she found that turned out well. That's about it. And she's never mentioned any old boyfriends she used to be happy with."

"Do you talk to Dad?"

Christy smirks. "Of course not. He's always at the country club. And why would he want to talk to me, anyway? I'm pretty sure he felt relieved of his obligation to parent me once I got into an Ivy League."

"What a jerk," I say, rolling my eyes. "So…does Mom know you're moving to Chicago?"

My sister shakes her head. "Mom doesn't even know I broke up with Kyle."

"She has no idea I'm painting again either. You know…that was the only time I ever really saw her smile? When I was little, and she watched me paint."

"She always said you had natural talent," Christy remembers.

I'm getting teary again. "I wish we had the type of mom who

cared about what was going on in our lives."

My sister frowns. "I think she cares."

But her questioning tone tells me she's trying to convince herself as much as she's trying to convince me.

"Let's call her together," she goes on to suggest.

I wince. "Wouldn't you rather just watch another romantic comedy and ignore reality a little longer?"

"We can do that after. You should tell her you're painting again, it'll make her happy."

"Are you gonna be honest with her about your life, too?" I challenge my sister.

Christy shrugs. "What've we got to lose? I mean…look at how close you and I have gotten," she says, her reluctance turning to resolve. "Maybe we could get closer to Mom, too, if we put in some effort. She's been married to an asshole for thirty years, after all. We should probably cut her some slack."

"Alright, let's do it," I say, trying my best not to give in to the flurry of nerves in my stomach.

Christy grabs her phone, and we head over to my couch. After she dials, she puts the call on speaker.

My mom picks up on the first ring. "Hi, honey," she says, sounding tired, but pleased.

"Hey, Mom. Guess who I'm with?"

"Hi, Mom," I chime in.

"Jenna! Oh my gosh, honey, are you in New York?"

"No, Christy's here," I say.

"I have some news, Mom," my sister begins, wasting no time. "I broke up with Kyle. And I'm moving to Chicago in a few months. My boss is letting me work remotely—so I thought a change of scenery would be good for me. And being close to Jenna, of course," she goes on, smiling at me.

"Oh…I'm sorry to hear about your breakup," our mom says, her tone gentle. But she goes quiet after that. "Well, I'm happy my two girls will be together," she finally adds.

"You should come visit after I move here," Christy suggests. "We can have a girls' weekend, just the three of us."

Mom lets out a small chuckle. "That sounds lovely…but you know I've never traveled by myself before."

"There's a first time for everything," I tell her.

"I don't know… Your father wouldn't last a day without me. He can't even scramble an egg."

Christy's eyes roll back in her head, and she takes a deep breath.

"That sounds like his problem," I tell our mom.

"Just think about it—you don't have to decide now," Christy adds in a more diplomatic tone.

"Alright," Mom says, but I'm sure it's only so we'll move on.

Then Christy turns to me and gives an encouraging nod, indicating it's my turn to share.

I bite my lip in response. "Um, Mom…I also have some news. I started painting again, recently. I thought you might like to know."

I can hear her take a stunned breath. "Jenna, that's wonderful, honey. You were always so talented. Oh, that just makes my day."

Christy and I exchange surprised smiles. This is as excited as I've heard our mom in a long time.

"Thanks, I appreciate it. So…how are you doing?" I ask,

shrugging at my sister, because making conversation with our mom doesn't come naturally.

Mom heaves a sigh. "Well…I don't know, girls. Your father and I…"

"Oh my gosh, are you getting a divorce?" Christy squeals, her face lighting up.

I elbow her, stifling a laugh, and whisper, "Tone it down," but she's still beaming.

"No, no—nothing like that," my mom says, and Christy deflates. "It's more like…a rough patch."

Christy puts the phone on mute and turns to me. "When did they ever have a smooth patch?"

I snort.

But then, I see an opportunity. My mom is obviously unhappy—and has been for as long as I remember. I wanted to talk to her about therapy in person, but why wait if she's going through an especially tough time right now?

When my sister unmutes the phone, I say, "You know, Mom…I started therapy recently, and it's been so helpful. Maybe you could talk to someone, too. About Dad…and your rough patch."

Christy gives my shoulder a supportive squeeze, and we look at each other's anxious faces, waiting for our mom to answer.

"Oh, I don't think your father would appreciate me telling a stranger about our marriage troubles," she says.

"Whether *you* go to therapy or not isn't his decision to make, Mom," I tell her. "He doesn't even have to know. Don't you handle all the insurance paperwork, anyway?"

Dad's always treated Mom like she's his secretary—delegating administrative tasks to her because his time is too valuable, apparently.

"That's true," she says after a beat. Christy and I exchange excited glances again.

"So, you would consider it?" my sister asks.

Mom heaves a sigh. "Oh, I don't know. How would I even find someone?"

"I'll find someone for you," I jump in. Just like Vanessa found Esther for me. Now I can pay it forward, to help my own mother. "I'll ask my therapist if she has any recommendations. Even if she doesn't personally know anyone near Beachwood, I'm sure she can point me in the right direction."

"Well…"

"I'll send you the referrals as soon as I get them!" I blurt out, before she can come up with an excuse.

"Okay, Mom, we'll talk to you soon!" Christy adds, then hangs up and raises her hand to high-five me. "Nailed it," she says when our palms meet.

I shrug. "I guess we'll see. That went a lot better than I thought it would, at least."

"Things are shifting, Jenna. The Andersen women are going to take the world by storm. And tonight's going to be great for you—I know it," she goes on, maybe noticing the apprehension on my face.

I can't help it. Every time I think about the art show, I think about Charlie and our uncertain future.

"Come on, let's go pick our outfits, so we don't have to worry about it later. Then we can spend the rest of the day watching movies again."

"Sounds good," I say forcing a smile. I may as well try to relax and enjoy the afternoon with my sister.

But as I pass the open door of my art studio and see the portraits of every important person in my life *except* Charlie, I have to fight like hell to ignore the sinking feeling in my heart.

I'm not gonna lie—when I walk into the art gallery, a sizeable part of me is convinced that the first face I'll see is Charlie's. And not just his portrait hanging on the wall. Charlie Sutton, in the flesh, his eyes lighting up when he meets my gaze. Relief written all over his face when I run into his arms and we share the same air again, finally.

I guess Christy got in my head. And the movies we binge-watched all week, that all end with a perfectly timed reunion under the most romantic of circumstances. Soulmates' eyes meeting across a crowded room. Confessions of love made in front of a misty-eyed audience. Thunderbolts, and passionate kisses in the pouring rain.

And music. Always music.

The gallery is an ideal setting for grand gestures. There's bossa nova playing over the speakers, and the lights are dimmed to showcase the artwork. There are votive candles and fresh flowers on high-top tables, where people are sipping champagne and indulging in little desserts served by cater waiters. The overall effect is pretty sexy. I can easily picture myself kissing Charlie in a dark corner, his hands around my waist, pulling me into the Jenna-sized space between his arms, where I belong.

But he's not here.

"It's still early," Christy says to me with an encouraging nod. "I'm sure he'll walk through the door any minute now."

"Of course he will," I say, my voice thin and unconvincing.

"Oh my gosh, Jenna, look!"

I turn, hoping to see Charlie, but, instead, my sister's pointing at the crowd standing around my portrait of him.

A jolt of excitement surges through me. I never imagined my piece would draw so much attention. And I had no idea it would be hanging in such a prime location. There are two walls opposite each other featuring works by local artists. My painting is on the wall at the back of the gallery, smack-dab in the middle. It's the best spot in the house, because it's where your gaze goes when you first enter the room.

Unless you're me…and you're fixated on how your latest, and potentially greatest, love story is going to tie up in the end. In that case, your eyes are darting all around, looking for your boyfriend amid abstract still lifes, and impressionist landscapes, and some interesting modern pieces—like the one hanging on the front wall, which appears to simply be a canvas covered in bubble wrap.

With a wistful smile, I think back to the morning Charlie and I spent at the Museum of Contemporary Art, coming up with hilarious interpretations of the more abstract works on display and laughing hysterically about them. I wonder what he'd make of this bubble wrap piece. I'm sure he'd say something witty, like, "It must be a commentary on *pop* culture."

My eyes tear up. This is pathetic—even bubble wrap makes me think of Charlie.

"Okay," Christy says, taking hold of my shoulders and turning me so I'm facing her. "You need a pep talk. I know it seems like tonight is about Charlie, but it's not. It's about *you*. This is your first art show ever. And if you want it to be the first of many, you need to focus. You're the only artist here who's drawn a crowd around their piece. That just goes to show how talented you are!"

I nod, taking in her words.

"There are people here who are impressed by your work, and they want to talk to you about it," she continues. "So put your game face on, okay? This is what artists do. Remember when Lola Piper went through that very public breakup while she was on tour, and still put on the best goddamn shows of her life? You need to channel that energy."

I take a deep breath. Christy's absolutely right. This is such a huge milestone for me, and I don't want to spend it crying over a guy—even if that guy is Charlie Sutton, who's had a hold on my heart since I met him. Maybe even before, if I let myself believe in cosmic connections.

But whatever ends up happening between us, I know I'll be okay. I have art, and I have friends, and I have Esther. And best of all, I have this newfound closeness with my sister, that I'll never take for granted.

I even have hope, for the first time since I was a kid, that Christy and I might be able to have a better relationship with our mom.

I'm going to be just fine.

"Okay, boss babe," I say to Christy. "I'm ready to do this. And I like this side of you, by the way. No wonder you're such an esteemed literary agent."

She smiles, and looks at me with that mischievous glint in her eyes that I love. "Well, tonight, I'm an *art* agent. Representing up-and-coming painter, Jenna Andersen. Look—I even have her business cards in my purse."

"Oh, good call. I didn't think to bring any, because they're for my design business, but I guess that's better than nothing, right? Where did you find them, in my desk?" I shake my head. "I wish I'd thought to make new ones."

"One step ahead of you, sis," Christy says, handing me her stack. "I figured you had a lot on your mind this week."

"Jenna Andersen, Painter," I read as the biggest smile blooms on my face. "Thank you so much," I say, then wrap my arms around my sister.

"Let's go," she says, taking my hand.

But we're intercepted by a tap on my shoulder. As I turn around, my heart picks up speed.

It isn't Charlie, though. It's Tati Marie.

My eyes light up, even though she's not the person I was expecting. "Marie, this is a dream come true. Thank you so much for making tonight possible."

"You made this possible, Jenna," she says. In typical Tati Marie fashion, her forehead is creased, but her tone is warm.

"This is my sister, Christy," I say, eager to introduce the two.

"I've heard many wonderful things about you, Marie," my sister chimes in.

"It's a pleasure to meet you," my art teacher replies. And when Marie gives her a big hug, Christy looks at me over her shoulder, as if to say, "You're right—her hugs are amazing."

I nod knowingly.

"Vanessa's on her way," Tati says when she separates from my sister. If I'm not mistaken, there's a gleam of excitement in her eyes. "She's coming with Asher."

"That's great," I say, only slightly triggered by the returning fear of Charlie not showing up for me.

I'm making progress.

Even an hour later, when Christy and I have talked to no less than fifteen art enthusiasts about my work, and my sister's brokered two new commissions for me, I'm not teary-eyed.

Maybe it's the high from the deals Christy just made on my behalf, but I'm excited. This is a new life for me. Gallery shows, and art collectors, and me in my smock, painting. I can't help but smile.

This is what I've wished for—for a very long time.

"You're killing it," my sister whispers in my ear.

"No, *you* are."

"We make a good team," she says, putting her arm around me.

After another forty-five minutes, we've talked to Vanessa and Asher, who came straight from a dinner date in Little Italy and are holding hands as they walk around the space, eyeing each other more than the artwork. They're obviously very much in love.

I'm happy for her.

And Sam is here with—let me see if I can get this straight—the lead guitarist of a Brooklyn-based indie rock band, whom she had a friends-with-benefits relationship with while she was studying at NYU, and she still sleeps with whenever he's in Chicago for a gig. He's leaving tomorrow morning, which might explain why they're off in a dark corner, groping each other.

I'm happy for Sam, too. She's not in any rush to settle down, and I respect that.

"He's gorgeous," a woman's voice says from beside me.

I assume she's talking about Sam's guitarist, who's undeniably attractive, but when I turn to face the woman, her eyes are on Charlie.

Charlie's portrait, that is.

"How much?" she asks, eyeing my painting.

"This one's not for sale," Christy says. I'm relieved we talked about this ahead of time, because we've gotten many inquiries—especially from older female art collectors.

"Too bad," this particular older female art collector says. At least she's not pushy, like some of the others.

"My client would be happy to paint a custom portrait for you, if you're interested," Christy goes on, handing the woman my new business card.

"Sign me up," she says. "I have the perfect subject. My high school beau, James Winston. I'm sure I have a picture of him somewhere. He looked just like a young Elvis Presley."

"He sounds very handsome," I say as Christy shifts gears back to business, closing the deal for me.

I've never seen her this self-assured, and it's a great look for her. She's in her element, relying on her sharp wit and intellect. That's her comfort zone. If she can just figure out how to maintain this level of confidence when it comes to men and dating, she'll have the world in the palm of her hand.

By the end of the night, she's on cloud nine—and I have a list of commissions and potential new clients a mile long. It's hard not to be thrilled about it.

I can't believe Charlie didn't show up, though.

The crowd is clearing out. Vanessa and Asher are continuing their date at a jazz club on the other side of town. And Sam and her guitarist are at her place, getting it on, I assume. The gallery will be closing soon.

"Maybe he mixed up the dates," Christy offers, reading my mind.

"No," I say, shaking my head. "He knew it was tonight. But… it's okay."

My sister looks devastated. She wanted to believe in this love story as much as I did.

"I thought Charlie and I were soulmates, too," I tell her. "I bought into the fairytale. But my story doesn't end with a man who can't stand up for himself. Who won't fight for his own happiness. If he isn't here tonight, then…he's not the right person for me, Christy."

She circles her arms around me. "You'll find the one you're meant to be with. And so will I. We'll go on double dates, and celebrate our engagements, and be in each other's weddings.

It'll be a new chapter for both of us, and it's going to be the best one yet."

"Yes, it is," I say with a heavy, but hopeful, heart. It's a relief to be able to feel both of those things at once.

For so long, I wouldn't let myself wish anymore. I wouldn't let myself believe in happy endings. But now I do. Even if this isn't my happy ending, I can hold out hope that mine is still coming.

And that means I've come a long way.

"I'm going to hit up the ladies' room before we leave," I tell Christy.

"I'll wait for you outside," she says.

I walk to the far side of the gallery, then down a long hallway to find the restroom. I don't really have to use it, so much as I wanted a moment to myself before going home for the night. There's so much on my mind. My excitement over the success of the show. My disappointment over Charlie.

I stand in front of the mirror, and I let myself feel sad. I let my eyes tear up. I let my heart ache. I let myself unravel a little bit, knowing I'll be okay. I remind myself, again, that I have art, and Esther, and my sister, and Vanessa and Sam. And maybe even my mom, eventually. And every time a wave of grief washes over me from the loss of Charlie, I'll remember how much I've gained.

I take one deep breath before I head back to my sister, then open the door to the hallway.

But as soon as I turn right, someone crashes into me.

"Oh my gosh, I'm sorry!"

It's an automatic reaction to the impact. But even as the words are coming out of my mouth—even before I step back so my eyes can meet his—I know in my soul, it's Charlie.

It's not the first time we've crashed into each other, after all.

This time he isn't gazing at me with stunned surprise, though. He looks exhausted. And disheveled. His hair is mussed up like I've never seen it before. He's in the sweatpants he sleeps in, and his t-shirt has a hole in it. I'm pretty sure there's a smudge of dirt on his cheek.

"I saw your sister standing outside—I recognized her from the portrait you painted," he says, breathlessly. "She just left. She said she had your spare keys and wanted to give us time to talk. I put her in a cab, I hope that's okay."

"Of course it is…thank you." I want to reach out for him, but he looks so serious. "Charlie, what's wrong?"

He drags a hand over his face. "Jenna, I just had the worst two weeks of my life." He pauses for several seconds, maybe trying to figure out where to begin. Whatever happened, I'm guessing it's a long story.

"See…when I left for Denver," he finally goes on, "I had a plan. I was going to interview candidates to replace me at Sutton's. I was going to find additional support staff, and when I quit my job, I was going to hand my dad a stack of resumes and tell him not to worry, because I took care of everything. And then I was going to fly back to Chicago and surprise you here tonight with a grand, romantic gesture. I was going to be here when you walked into the gallery, *not* looking like I got run over by a truck—which nearly happened by the way—"

I gasp.

"And everything was going to be *perfect*." He laughs, but his smile is more ironic than amused. "But the universe had other plans. And you know why?"

I shake my head.

"Because I learned *nothing* from our argument, that's why. You said you didn't need me to be perfect, and my first thought was that I needed to come up with the perfect exit plan to please my dad, and the perfect grand gesture to convince you I'm worthy of you. And I did. I had it all figured out—but then everything went to hell."

He pauses to catch his breath.

"The candidate I liked best to replace me ended up accepting an offer somewhere else an hour before I was going to give my dad her resume. I'd come so close to pulling off the perfect escape from Sutton's…and when my plan fell apart, I was beside myself."

My hopes are dashed. I think I see where this is going. There's no way Charlie would leave his dad in the lurch.

"I cried, Jenna," he admits. "That's when I realized how miserable I'd been, and I knew I had to quit. So, that's what I did."

"Wait—really?" I ask, unable to believe my ears.

He nods, but his expression is still somber. "Since I didn't have a vetted replacement to offer my dad, I told him I'd stay on a few more months to help find the right candidate and assist with the transition. As long as it didn't interfere with my job offer in Italy this summer."

"Oh my gosh," I say, my heart fluttering with excitement. "You're going?"

When he nods, a smile forms on my lips, but Charlie doesn't

notice because his eyes are squeezed shut. He pinches the bridge of his nose before telling me the rest of his story.

"My dad was livid that I was quitting—especially to pursue photography. And he went off on me. Normally I'd just sit there and take it…but I was so fucking tired. I hadn't slept the entire time I was in Denver, because I was doing the work of three people, while also conducting interviews—and missing the hell out of you, if I'm being honest. So I just broke. I gave my father a piece of my mind and, let me tell you, it was a long time coming."

He heaves a sigh and looks at me.

"Will you and your dad be okay? Or…do you even want to be?"

Charlie shrugs. "To tell you the truth…I think my father respects me more now than he ever did. He's still not my biggest fan at the moment. That's okay, though. I guess this is what it took for me to realize I'd rather have his respect than his approval."

My eyes fill with tears, I'm so happy for him. But he's on a roll, and I can't get a word in before he continues.

"But while I was arguing with my dad, I lost track of time, and I missed my flight to Chicago. And the only other flight that would get me here on time was booked. So I rented a car."

"You drove here from Denver?" I ask, incredulous. "How many hours is that?"

"Fourteen. Which would have been fine, if there hadn't been a torrential downpour in Denver that slowed traffic to a screeching halt. Then, I got a flat tire in the middle of Nebraska—"

My eyes go wide. "Oh no…"

"Yeah, it wasn't ideal. I'd only changed a tire once before in my life. But I had my phone and access to YouTube, so that helped. I hit a few snags, and even ripped my shirt, but eventually I did it. And I was just about to get in my car when I saw a semi coming at me at full speed. I moved out of the way as fast as I could, and I must have dropped my phone, because the next thing I knew, it was smashed to pieces right where the truck had driven over it."

"Oh, Charlie," I sigh. I feel so awful for him, I want to throw my arms around his neck and kiss him all over his dirt-smudged face.

"I'm so sorry I missed the show, Jenna. But at least the night's not a total wash," he says, his expression softening. "I still have a surprise for you—if you want it."

My eyes light up. "Of course I want it."

Charlie smiles for the first time tonight, then reaches for my hand. We walk down the hall together, back to the artwork on display. The gallery's mostly empty now, except for a few stragglers and the staff members, who are busy chatting with patrons as they leave. It's the perfect setting for a romantic surprise. The dim lights, the flowers and candles, the music playing over the speakers.

Charlie stops when we get to the center of the room. "Stay right there," he says, his eyes glimmering.

I watch as he continues toward the wall opposite my painting. To the odd modern art piece I noticed before. The canvas covered in bubble wrap.

It's Charlie's surprise for me.

I shake my head, laughing at myself. I can't believe I thought it was modern art.

Charlie tugs at the wrapping to unveil what's underneath, and I bite my lip in anticipation.

But nothing happens. The bubble wrap won't budge.

"Wow. They did a pretty thorough job covering this up," he tells me. "I'd asked them to use a sheet—the way you'd hidden the portrait of me in your studio—but I guess they didn't have one."

Charlie tries again, with more force this time. He's unsuccessful.

"So much for a dramatic reveal," he jokes.

"Let me help you with that." Odette—Tati Marie's friend, and the owner of the gallery—rushes over with a pair of scissors and begins cutting into the plastic covering. "Marie told me you wanted it hidden under a sheet, but this was the best I could come up with."

My heart swells over the fact that Vanessa's aunt helped Charlie set up my surprise.

"I appreciate you letting me add a piece to the show," my boyfriend tells Odette. "And I'm so sorry I was late. Thank you for keeping this wrapped until I got here."

"It's no problem at all," she says. "Most people thought it was a commentary on pop culture. I even got some offers on it, which I was sorry to turn down."

I stifle a laugh, feeling vindicated.

A minute later, Odette is still cutting off strips of bubble wrap with a very determined look on her face. Charlie offers to help, but she promises she's nearly got it.

He chuckles in my direction. "This surprise isn't quite going as planned."

I giggle. "Seems pretty on brand for you today."

"I shouldn't have used so much tape," Odette reflects, still hard at work. "I'm sorry, Charlie—the sheet would have made your surprise much more dramatic."

"It's fine," he says, smiling at me.

My heart swells. I'm thrilled he's taking this all in stride.

"There we go," Odette says with a satisfied sigh.

The plastic covering drops to the floor slowly, and rather anticlimactically. When I look up, Odette's still standing in front of the piece, so I have no clue what it is yet.

"Thanks again," Charlie tells her.

And when she turns to walk away—

I'm looking at myself.

It's one of the pictures Charlie took of me at Olive Park, during our mini photoshoot. He showed me some of the photographs afterward, but never this one.

It's cropped the same way I paint my portraits—with the focus on my eyes. And the way I'm looking at him…

"It's the exact same way I'm looking at you," he says, nodding toward his portrait, behind me. I look back and forth between my painting and his photograph, both smack dab in the center of opposite walls. Jenna and Charlie, gazing into each other's eyes from across the room—lovestruck.

My lip quivers. "This is the most romantic thing anyone's ever done for me."

"Jenna, this is our love story. You're the woman of my dreams. And I'm the man of your…doodles."

I giggle and wipe a tear from my cheek.

"And I would love for you to come to Italy with me this

summer," he says. "So we can make all your drawings come true."

My hand flies to my heart.

"I would love that, too," I say, right before I start sobbing.

Charlie walks to meet me in the center of the room. But as soon as he takes me in his arms, the fluorescent overhead lights turn on.

"So much for mood lighting," Charlie says, squinting as his eyes struggle to adjust.

"Sorry, kiddos!" Odette yells from the front of the gallery, over the bossa nova still playing in the background. "You're welcome to stay, but we need the overheads on to clean up."

"We'll be out of your hair in a minute," Charlie says with a grin, then turns back to me.

I heave a sigh, smiling ear-to-ear. All I can think about is how much I want to kiss him, and run my hands through that adorably mussed-up hair.

"I'll try to make this quick, while we still have mood music," he goes on with a chuckle. "Jenna, when I realized I was going to miss your show, my instinct was to beat myself up for disappointing you. And that's what I did—for hours, driving through Nebraska. Even after I'd just stood up to my father. You know what they say about old habits..."

He purses his lips.

"But somewhere just outside of Omaha, I forgave myself. And that's progress. Because normally I'd ruminate over something like this until I had the chance to fix it. The need to please is so ingrained in me, Jenna—I can tell you right now, I'm not going to change overnight. But I'm working on it. Two weeks ago, I never would have shown up here looking this way."

He glances down at the hole in his shirt and pulls at it.

"*This* is me trying," he goes on. "This is my grand gesture. It's not what I originally planned. And it's not perfect. But it's me."

If this were a romantic comedy, the music would swell, and the camera would orbit around me and Charlie Sutton as we locked lips, undisturbed, until the credits rolled.

Instead, the bossa nova cuts out, and someone starts vacuuming up front.

But that doesn't stop me from kissing him.

And afterward, when his loving gaze meets mine, I say, "It's better than perfect, Charlie. It's all I ever wished for."

ONE YEAR LATER

I wake up early, even though I have a long day ahead of me and could use the extra sleep. But I'm too excited—and nervous. I've been dreaming of this moment my entire life, and it's finally here. Our friends and family from out of town are on their way. All of the planning is behind me, and the only thing left for me to do is put on my dress and show up.

Charlie's sleeping soundly. But I may just have to wake him, because there's only one thing that can help me relax right now, and I'm sure he won't be too upset if I ask for it.

I snuggle up to him, reach my hand under the covers, and into his boxers. A smile forms on his lips, even though his eyes are still closed.

"Last night wasn't enough for you?" he jokes, a sexy, sleepy rasp in his voice.

"I need another fix to get me through until tonight," I tell him, grinning when his gaze meets mine.

Charlie shifts on top of me. "You nervous?"

I heave a sigh. "I just want it to be perfect, you know?"

"No, I don't know…because *perfect* is no longer in my vocabulary," he teases. Then he peels off my tank top and kisses my breasts. "Unless we're talking about these…"

"Mmm," I moan as his tongue flicks my nipple.

He pulls off my underwear next.

"Or maybe we're talking about this," he says, tracing circles between my thighs with his fingers before he slowly slides one inside me. "Because *this* is definitely perfect."

I arch my back, my entire body pulsing with need. "I honestly don't know what we were talking about anymore, Charlie."

"Well, then…I guess my work here is done." He props himself on his elbow and licks his finger, savoring the way I taste.

"Not so fast," I say, pressing my hands against his chest, then straddling him when he's flat on his back. I take my turn planting kisses on his chest, then work my way down his abs and slide off his boxers.

There was a time when people-pleasing Charlie was so focused on pleasuring me that he'd rarely let me reciprocate. Those days are over. Now I get to work on him with my mouth and tongue for as long as I want—which is typically as long as it takes for me to drive him so wild with desire that he pins me down and has his way with me.

It's exactly what he's doing right now, and it's certainly helping me clear my head. Instead of worrying about how the day will unfold, all I can think about is how incredible it feels to have sex with someone who knows and loves me so completely.

I try my best to delay the orgasm Charlie's orchestrating with his deep thrusts, intent on enjoying our mind-blowing chemistry as long as I can. But a girl only has so much willpower. When I can't hold back anymore, my soulmate reads my cues and unravels with me, making my climax that much more explosive.

Afterward, I lie on top of him, panting, and blissful—enjoying the feel of his heart beating against mine.

"Did that hit the spot?" he asks.

I giggle. "It hit *all* the right spots. But now I need a shower," I say, fanning my sweaty face.

"Same," he replies. "I guess I'll go back to my place. If we shower together, I can't promise I'll keep my hands off you, and I know Christy's coming over soon."

I nod. "Fair enough. But, for the record, I can't wait for you to officially move in."

"It'll be like an endless summer," he says with a smile, recalling our trip to Italy for his first official gig as a travel photographer.

It was magical. Three months of falling deeper and deeper in love with Charlie in one of the most romantic places in the world. We ate decadent meals, and had incredible sex. I painted breathtaking landscapes, while Charlie took stunning photographs. I'd never seen him happier. And when I snapped a picture of him in the Italian countryside with a camera strapped around his neck, I realized that my latest wish had come true.

Even amid those dreamy days and nights, though, my favorite part of our trip was falling asleep in my boyfriend's arms and waking up next to him every morning. Charlie felt the same. So when we got back to Chicago, he found a subletter, who'll be moving into his place next month.

Not much will change, since he's practically living with me already. But I guess we'll be taking more showers together, since Charlie Sutton can't keep his hands off me. Oh, well.

"Until then, enjoy the extra space in your closet," he says, putting his boxers back on. "Soon it'll be full of perfectly tailored suits that I don't plan to wear very often."

"I don't mind. You don't have to wear a thing—I prefer you naked, anyway."

"Oh, I know where your priorities are, Jenna Andersen," he teases as he puts on the rest of his clothes.

"I love you," I say, while he's grabbing his keys from my dresser.

He walks to my side of the bed and leans down to give me a kiss. "I love you more."

I just shake my head, smiling at him.

"I'll see you later," he tells me. "And don't be nervous. I'll be by your side the entire night."

I chuckle. "You'd better be."

He winks at me, then leaves for his apartment.

When I open the door for Christy, she's got a huge grin on her face, and an even larger cup of takeout coffee.

"Late night?" I ask as she strolls into my place and makes a beeline for the couch.

She takes a seat, then looks at me, biting her lip. "I know this is your big day, Jenna, and I don't want to make this about me…"

I plop down next to her, my eyes wide with excitement.

"What happened?"

I've never seen my sister like this before. She has the glow of a woman in love. I wonder if she met someone she had an instant connection with—the way I felt, when I ran into Charlie.

"Well," she begins, her freckled cheeks flushing. "Sam and I went to the bar at the Sofitel hotel last night, and we met a group of guys who were in town for their friend's bachelor party. And the best man, who was *extremely* attractive, told me he had a thing for redheads, and long story short…"

"Yes?" I ask as my sister lets out a dreamy sigh.

"I had the most amazing one-night stand," she tells me, flipping her wavy hair.

Oh.

So, she's not in love. But this is good, too. When she moved to Chicago back in January, Christy decided she wanted to play the field for a bit. After eight years with Kyle—the first and only guy she'd ever slept with—she needed to know what else was out there. But dating in the Windy City is challenging in the dead of winter, when Chicagoans rarely leave their homes unless they have to. So my sister's journey to find good sex got off to a slow start. She had more luck meeting men in the spring, but the first guy she brought home finished so fast, she wound up driving him home at nine, then spending the night in *my* bed, crying.

Her next few experiences happened over the summer, while I was in Italy with Charlie. That's when Sam took Christy under her wing and they became close friends. My sister had a lot of fun, and added some notches to her bedpost—though she described the trysts as "good, but not earth-shattering." I could relate, since the earth never shattered for me either, before I slept with Charlie.

"I think part of the reason last night was so great is because I feel more comfortable, now that I've been with a handful of guys. But this man was *talented*." She blushes again. "It was amazing."

"I'm so happy for you," I say, smiling. "But if it was so good, why not see him again? Does it have to be a one-night stand?"

She shrugs. "He lives in Austin. Plus, we have absolutely nothing in common, outside of enjoying each other's bodies. He's a tech guy, and he doesn't read for pleasure. You know how hard that was for me, with Kyle. On the nights we weren't having sex—which were aplenty—I would've loved to just read next to each other in bed, and talk about our books. Maybe it's silly, but reading is my life. It's my job *and* my passion, and I want to share that with the man I end up with. But Kyle took no interest in my work at all. If I ever tried to read him something beautiful from one of the manuscripts I was reviewing, he'd roll over and start snoring before I'd even finished the first paragraph."

"I know how important that connection is for you. And I get it. It's like me and Charlie—we can talk about art for hours. I love that."

"Speaking of Charlie…I bet he's so excited for tonight."

"He's been counting down the days," I say with a smile.

"And how are you feeling?" she asks, her hand on my knee.

I sigh. "Excited. Nervous. I keep worrying about my dress."

Christy's brow wrinkles. "Your dress is gorgeous. What's there to worry about?"

"You don't think it's too much? Maybe I should've gone with something a little less dramatic."

She scoffs. "It's *your* day. You're supposed to look like a movie star."

I laugh. "It's my art show—not my wedding."

"It's your first *solo* art show," she reminds me. "This is a big deal."

"I know it is," I admit, my heart fluttering. "That's why my palms are so sweaty. I just wish Mom were coming. She's been doing so well since she started therapy and meds—I really thought she'd come for the weekend."

"You should have asked her again," my sister scolds me.

"I asked her *three* times," I insist. "She just doesn't want to leave Dad—and it's not like he'd ever consider coming. Art shows aren't the type of accomplishment he'll brag about to his colleagues."

Christy grits her teeth at the mention of our father, then takes my hand. "Well, it's going to be an incredible night, I guarantee it. There are plenty of people coming to support you. And this time you don't have to waste a second worrying about Charlie's intentions. I know he did the hard work to get here…but I don't think he would've quit Sutton's and become a photographer if you hadn't pushed him. I see how grateful he is, every time he looks at you. That man loves you with his entire heart and soul."

"Trust me, I know," I say, my eyes glistening. "And to think—I almost gave up on finding him."

Christy and I arrive at the gallery an hour before the show. Tati Marie and Odette, who've basically become my surrogate aunts over this past year, are putting the finishing touches on a floral arrangement by the front door.

Marie greets me with a hug first. "What an exciting night for you, Jenna, dear. You've worked so hard this year, and look at how far you've come."

It's true. Since I wrapped up my design work, I've been devoted to painting. And I've earned enough money from commissions to believe this can be a sustainable career.

"Thank you, Marie. Taking your class was one of the best decisions I've ever made."

She wipes a tear from her eye.

"Yowza," Odette exclaims before giving me a kiss on the cheek. "You're a knockout."

When she steps away, I look down at my dress again—midi-length and metallic gold, featuring a dramatic plunging neckline and flared skirt. With my red lips and blonde hair, I feel like Marilyn Monroe.

"It's not too much? I don't normally question my style choices, but I don't want to take attention away from my art." I glance at Christy, who looks incredibly chic in her black sheath and a tailored jacket. "Maybe I should borrow your blazer."

My sister shakes her head. "First of all, you look stunning. Second of all, I need the blazer. I'm in 'art agent' mode, remember? That's why I'm here—to get you sales," she teases.

"Honey, your paintings are as stunning as you are," Odette tells me, "so keep shining bright, and stop worrying." She winks at me. "Besides, you already have guests."

I look toward the opposite end of the room and spot a tall man in a baseball cap, dark jeans, and a gray long-sleeved shirt. He's facing away from me, and I'm guessing he didn't hear us walk in over the merengue music coming from the loudspeakers. Or maybe he's just distracted by the adorable baby he's wearing in a carrier.

"Dex Oliver," I say as Christy and I walk toward him.

When he turns around, eight-month-old Stella squeals and claps her hands. She must just be a happy baby, because there's no way she'd remember me. I met her once, about four months ago, when Charlie and I drove up to Beachwood for Sunny and Dex's belated housewarming party. The Dexters have been living in their newly constructed dream home since before Stella was born, but decided to wait to celebrate, so their friends and family could meet her.

"Hi, little doll," I say, grabbing one of her teeny, tiny feet.

"We came early so we can get Stella down for bed at a reasonable time. I hope you don't mind," Dex tells me.

"Of course not. I still can't believe you guys drove all this way."

"We wouldn't miss it." When Dex leans down to hug me, Stella giggles into my hair.

He wraps an arm around my sister next. "Hey, Christy. Good to see you."

"This is the most beautiful child I've ever laid eyes on," my sister gushes.

Dex half-smiles, then kisses his daughter's head. "She gets it from her mother."

"Speaking of Sunny," I begin to say, but just then, I follow the sound of high heels clacking, and turn to see her walking over to us from the bathroom.

She looks more beautiful every time I see her. And it's not like she's changed much physically—it's just the happiness she radiates. She's married to the love of her life. They have a gorgeous baby girl. And she's published two romance novels, which are flying off the shelves of every bookstore.

"I had spit-up on my dress…I think it's all gone now," she says, eyeing her shoulder before hugging me and Christy. "It's so great to see you both. And congratulations, Jenna. Your paintings are breathtaking."

"Thank you so much. That means the world to me."

"Sunny can't decide which ones she wants for our house," Dex says, smiling at his wife.

"These Italian landscapes are just so beautiful," she tells me. "We're trying to narrow it down to three, but it's tough."

"Three?" I say in disbelief. "Wow. You guys are too kind."

"And *you're* too talented," Sunny quips back.

"Speaking of talent," Christy chimes in, "if you ever need a literary agent, Sunny—"

"You'll be the first one I call, trust me," she promises. "Your reputation precedes you—you're the best in the business."

Smiling, my sister shrugs one shoulder, as if to say, "She's not wrong."

"But right now, self-publishing is working well for me," Sunny goes on. "I want to work on my own schedule, especially with Stella being so little."

"That's fair," Christy says, reaching for the baby's hand. "I mean, who wouldn't want to spend all day with this cutie pie."

Stella grins, right on cue.

"How about you, Dex? Are you still traveling a lot for work?" I ask.

He shakes his head. "I'm taking some time off from speaking engagements, so I can be home with my girls. It's been nice living in our own little bubble—just the three of us."

"We're making the most of it while we have him all to ourselves." Sunny trades a smile with Dex that makes my cheeks warm. "But he's got big plans for the Dramatic Hearts Academy."

"I've heard wonderful things about the program," Christy says, which comes as no surprise. Dex's wildly successful initiative to use the dramatic arts as a tool to help kids with anxiety has gotten great press coverage over the past year. "Are you hoping to expand?"

He nods. "We're in schools across the country now, which is a dream come true for me. But eventually, I'd like to develop an offshoot of the program for adults. I'm still working out the details, but it'll be called the Dramatic Hearts Club."

"That's amazing," Christy and I say, almost in unison.

Not to be outshone by her superstar dad, baby Stella starts wildly kicking her feet to the upbeat music playing over the speakers. We all laugh and smile, which excites her even more. Then Dex takes her little hands and starts dancing to the music himself—and I'm glad there are no paparazzi here, because it's literally the cutest thing I've ever witnessed. Seeing Dex as a dad warms my heart.

"I think my ovaries just exploded," Christy says in my ear as Dex twirls Sunny, and the happy family of three dances together.

"Aww, I can't wait to be Auntie Jenna. I'm going to spoil your kids like crazy—you know that, right?"

"You'll be the cool aunt they run to with questions about life, and love, and art," my sister says, grinning.

"It'll be my best job yet," I reply, and Christy squeezes my arm, her eyes glistening.

"So, where's Charlie?" Sunny asks, when the Dexters are done dancing.

"He should be here any minute," I say. "His parents are coming, too, which surprises me. Things are still a little tense between Charlie and his father. When we went to Denver for his mom's birthday in May, his dad scowled the entire time."

"Sounds familiar," Christy mutters under her breath.

"But Charlie still managed to enjoy himself," I go on. "I'm so impressed with how he's learned to let things roll off his back. He rarely lets his dad get under his skin anymore."

When the gallery door opens, letting in the bustling sounds of the city, my heart skips a beat, expecting to see Charlie. But it's his parents who've just come in—without him. And his dad is wearing a frown, as always.

"Speak of the devil," I sigh. "I'm going to go say hello."

"Let's decide on landscapes before someone else snags them all," Sunny tells Dex as Christy and I walk to greet the Suttons together.

"Hi, Simone," I say, enveloping Charlie's mom in a hug.

"So happy to see you, sweetheart," she says, beaming.

We get along well—which isn't surprising since my boyfriend's kind, thoughtful nature so clearly comes from her.

His father, on the other hand, gives me a stern nod. "Jenna," is all he says.

I take a page from his playbook, wiping the smile off my face. "William."

"Where's Charlie?" Christy asks on my behalf.

"He had a quick errand to run," his mom says. "Don't worry, he'll be here shortly."

My sister and I trade sideways glances.

"I'm going to look at your pieces," William Sutton barks, then walks away.

I turn to Simone, who's grinning. "He is so impressed by you, Jenna. I think he might be your biggest fan."

My eyes go wide. She can't possibly be talking about her husband, who's never once cracked a smile in my presence. "*William* is my biggest fan?"

"Oh, yes. I know he has a funny way of showing it, but William's never worn his heart on his sleeve. If he shows up, though, that means he cares. Otherwise, he'd be back in Denver, working. And he's here for Charlie, too. William's proud of both of you."

"Does your son know that?"

Simone nods. "I made them sit down and talk earlier this afternoon. It was mostly William grunting, and me translating for him, but I think we're all on the same page now."

"That's such wonderful news." It makes me even more excited for Charlie to get here. But even after Mrs. Sutton joins her husband, and others begin to arrive, their son's still nowhere in sight.

In the meantime, Christy and I greet the newlyweds, Vanessa and Asher. They eloped a month ago, on a trip to Hawaii—much to the dismay of their families, who were hoping for a big celebration. But Vanessa had no interest in planning another wedding. And since she and Asher are both eager to start a family, they decided not to wait.

Now the happy couple are talking to Sunny and Dex and, from the looks of it, there's no bad blood between them. It's the first time Asher and Sunny have seen each other since she broke his heart in college—but it's obvious from the smiles on everyone's faces that everything worked out the way it was supposed to.

"I have to say, I'm feeling a little left out," someone says behind me and Christy.

"Sammy!" my sister squeals, wrapping her arms around her favorite wingwoman. "Left out? Why?"

Sam hugs me, then nods toward our friends. "Because you guys have all slept with each other. I mean…Sunny's slept with Asher and Dex, and Vanessa's slept with Asher and Charlie. And Jenna, you've slept with Dex and—where is your hot boyfriend, anyway?"

I shrug. "Running an errand, apparently?"

"Well, if I find out the six of you have some sort of wild sex party after the show tonight, and I'm not invited—I'm going to be very upset," Sam pouts.

Christy giggles as I bring my palm to my face, smiling. "We

will not be having an orgy, Sam. Don't worry."

Sam shakes her head. "Never say never! Because, this one time, I—"

"Auntie Sam!" Sunny says, coming up to us with Stella at the exact right time to spare us the details of Sam's story.

"How's my baby girl?" Sam says, taking Sunny's daughter from her. "You want to walk around? Come on."

Sunny watches them walk away with a grin on her face—then her brow crinkles. "I'd better follow them. You never know what's going to come out of Sam's mouth, and I don't think she has a lot of experience conversing with babies."

"That's probably a good call, considering she was about to tell us about the time she had an orgy," I agree.

Sunny nods and rushes after Sam and Stella.

When we're alone again, Christy glances at her watch.

"What time is it?"

"Seven," she says.

I heave a sigh. "Charlie's late. I can't imagine what kind of errand he's running."

"He's not late yet," my sister insists. "He has another twenty-seven seconds."

I give a wry laugh. "What are the odds that—"

And that's the precise moment Charlie walks through the gallery door.

With my mom.

"Oh my gosh!" My hands fly to my mouth, and I look at Christy. "Did you know about this?"

She shakes her head, looking equally stunned. "I had no idea."

My eyes fill with tears as Christy and I run over to them. "Mom," we both say, throwing our arms around her.

Ingrid Andersen looks amazing. She's always been beautiful, but the sadness in her eyes that weighed on her so heavily seems to have lifted.

"I can't believe you're here," I tell her. "I'm so happy."

"You have your boyfriend to thank. He was relentless," she says, winking at him. "But I'm so grateful. Now that I have my first solo trip under my belt, the world is my oyster."

I wipe a tear from my cheek. "Thank you so much," I say, pulling Charlie close while Christy talks to our mom. "How did you convince her?"

He smiles, looking dashing as ever in one of the tailored suits that will soon be hanging in my closet. "I just told her how important it was for you to have her here. Eventually, she came around. But her flight was delayed—"

I laugh. "Of course."

"I'm lucky I didn't get a speeding ticket, the way I was driving from the airport to make it here on time," he says, wiping his brow.

I kiss him like there aren't dozens of people walking into the gallery to see my artwork.

When we part, I look over at my mom, whose wide eyes are scanning the room—from my collection of portraits hanging on the far wall, to my landscapes displayed opposite them.

"Oh, Jenna," she says. "I am so, so proud of you."

"Thanks, Mom," I reply, my heart fluttering.

Then the spark of wonder in her eyes turns into something fiery. "I'm so angry at myself for not standing up to your father sooner. I never should have allowed him to keep you from painting."

Christy tilts her head. "*Sooner?* What do you mean? Did you actually stand up to Dad?"

Mom sighs. "Well…"

Christy nods. "It's about time you gave Dad a piece of your mind. Way to go, Mom."

Ingrid Andersen grins, a mischievous glint in her eyes that reminds me of Christy. "I did better than that. I kicked that brute to the curb. We're getting a divorce."

My sister jumps up and down, then wraps her arms around our mother, who's crying tears of joy. It makes sense that the sadness she's carried around for years has lifted.

"That's wonderful, Mom," I say, taking my turn to hug her.

But while I'm thrilled my mother just rid herself of a lot of dead weight, I'm surprised I feel so numb about the man she's leaving. Christy despises him, and for good reason. And I could easily say the same, but I must have stopped caring at some point. He severed our connection a long time ago—if we ever had one to begin with. I mean, he's never supported my dreams. He isn't here for one of the most significant nights of my life. I guess Simone Sutton made a good point about her husband. William won't be winning a Father of the Year award anytime soon, but at least he cares enough to show up.

"And the best part is," Mom goes on with a victorious smile, "he's so helpless without me, he had to move in with your grandmother."

Christy cackles. "Well, it's her fault for raising a numbskull who can't even do his own laundry."

"Maybe I'll move here, so I can be close to you girls," my mom muses. "There's nothing tying me to Beachwood anymore. Wouldn't it be fun? Christy, we could even go looking for love together. Two single gals, out on the town, searching for *the one*. What do you say?"

"Yes, Mom, please!" I exclaim. "That sounds great, doesn't it, Christy?"

My sister tilts her head, considering my mom's offer. "It sounds like a cute premise for a romance novel. I'd read it."

"Then, it's settled," my mom says, her green eyes sparkling.

"Perfect!" Christy exclaims. "Well, I'd better get to work. I mean, these paintings could sell themselves—but that takes all the fun out of it for me."

"I'll come, too," Mom says, following her.

I turn to Charlie. "I don't think this night could get any better."

He kisses the top of my head, then puts his arm around my waist. "Let's go meet your adoring fans," he says, leading me into the crowd.

The show goes off without a hitch. Sunny and Dex settle on *four* Italian landscapes, and the happy family of three manages to leave the gallery before anyone recognizes them.

Vanessa and Asher also pick a painting for their new home. Then they leave, but not before Tati Marie scolds them again for getting married in secret. She says she'll only forgive them when they give her a grandniece or nephew. Vanessa's response: "Why do you think we're rushing home? We're working on it!"

And Christy does what Christy does best, expanding my list

of clients—with our mom working as her assistant. I can't help but smile thinking about the adventures that are in store for us Andersen women in the Windy City. Well, the Andersen women, plus Sam. When the show's all but over, she takes my mom and sister out for celebratory drinks.

But when Charlie and I are about to leave the gallery and head home, an all-too-familiar face appears in the doorway.

"We're closing in five," Odette says, before she looks into the man's ocean-blue eyes and her jaw drops.

"I'll only be a minute," Grady Brooks tells her.

I look up at Charlie, stunned.

"What are you doing here?" I ask when he walks up to us.

He runs a casual hand through his jet-black hair. "My art dealer says you're the next big thing. Thought I'd come by and take a look."

"Well, you're a little late," Charlie says with a sympathetic grin.

The movie star's eyes narrow at my boyfriend before he turns back to me. "You look well, Jenna," he says, his gaze nowhere near my face.

"I don't believe we've met," Charlie interjects without a hint of irony in his tone. "I'm Charlie Sutton. Jenna's fiancé."

Fiancé?

Charlie extends his hand, which Grady shakes while sporting an unmistakable scowl.

"Fiancé, huh? Congrats. Where's the ring?" he says, eyeing my finger.

My boyfriend doesn't miss a beat. "At home, on her nightstand.

We just got engaged, but we wanted the focus to be on her artwork tonight, not on us. We'll celebrate tomorrow, right babe?"

"Right," I say, playing along. I have to say, Charlie's acting is superb—and it's having the desired effect. Grady looks insanely jealous. I guess his twisted mind is still hung up on the fact that his "charm" never worked on me.

"Well, I don't want to overstay my welcome, so I'll just have my art dealer reach out. Good to see you, Jenna," he says, ignoring Charlie.

But Charlie will not be ignored. "It's too bad you didn't come earlier. Dex Oliver was here. What a stand-up guy. Finest actor of our generation, I'd say. Wouldn't you agree, um—I'm sorry, I didn't catch your name."

"It's Grady," I say, holding my breath so I don't burst into laughter.

Grady rolls his eyes, and I'm pretty sure I hear him mutter, "Jackass," as he walks away.

"That was a fun surprise," Charlie says, looking pleased.

We're still laughing about the encounter when we walk through the door of my apartment.

"You're definitely a better actor than he is," I say. "You really had him going with the whole engagement bit. The details about my ring being at home, on the nightstand, were a nice touch."

"I was pretty convincing, wasn't I," my boyfriend says with a glimmer in his eye that I'm not sure I've seen before.

He takes me in his arms and we kiss...

But now I can't help wondering if Charlie's performance was so authentic because he *wasn't* acting. Could there actually be a ring on my nightstand?

"Hold that thought," I tell him. "I'm going to freshen up. I'll be right back."

As soon as I turn away from him, I feel silly for even bothering to check. Charlie and I haven't talked about getting married yet. We know we're in this for the long haul—and maybe because we're happy being a family of two, we don't feel the need to rush down the aisle.

But if I'm in no hurry to marry Charlie Sutton, why is my heart racing as I step into my bedroom and turn on the light? Why do I hope to see something shiny glinting under my bedside lamp?

And why am I so disappointed when I don't find it?

I'm about to turn back around, when I realize something's out of place.

My journal—my sketchbook of wishes—isn't in my drawer, where it usually is. It's on my nightstand, and it's open to the last page. With sweaty palms, I pick it up.

There's a new sketch in it, that I didn't draw. They're just stick figures—but I know exactly who they are, and what they're doing.

It's Jenna, holding a notebook. And behind her is Charlie, on one knee. With a ring in his hand.

"I lied to Grady," he says when I spin around. "The ring was in my jacket pocket all evening—not on your nightstand."

I laugh, and at the very same time, tears start streaming down my face.

"I wanted to propose to you a year ago, Jenna," he confesses. "After your first art show. But I knew I still had a lot to prove.

I'm the man I am today because of you. I'm the happiest I've ever been because of you. And I want to spend the rest of my life making you as happy as you make me."

Charlie looks down at the ring before he continues, and all I can think is, *How did I ever get this lucky?*

"I told your mom last week," he goes on. "I wanted to keep it a secret until she got here, but this was the only way I could convince her to get on a plane by herself. I was afraid she'd give away the surprise when we arrived at the gallery, but I have to say, she has a great poker face. You never would've guessed she'd just been in your apartment, sitting right here on your bed, while I drew that masterpiece."

I clutch the notebook to my chest, sobbing and smiling.

"My parents know, too," he continues. "I'm sure your mom's told Christy by now. We're all going to celebrate tomorrow. Well, I don't want to assume...I haven't even asked you my question yet."

"Ask me," I say, wiping my face and taking a shaky breath.

Charlie's lip quivers. "Jenna Elizabeth Andersen...will you marry me?"

I've watched hundreds of movies where the happy couple gets engaged in the final scene. But none of them prepared me for what I'd feel in this moment. It's like my life flashes before my eyes, and every emotion I've ever had along with it. Every heartbreak and hurdle that led me to Charlie. My happily ever after.

I'm crying so hard I can barely speak. Thankfully, I only need to say one word.

"Yes," I tell my fiancé in between heaving sobs.

Charlie takes the journal out of my hands and puts the ring on my finger, his eyes shining. Then he stands up and pulls me into his arms as I ugly cry. After he kisses my forehead, he wipes my cheeks with his sleeve. It's his signature gesture, after all.

"I'll be fine," I say with a tearful laugh.

"Are you sure about that?" he teases.

"Yes," I tell him. "I've just always been a sucker for a happy ending."

THANK YOU!

As an independent author, your support means the world to me. If you enjoyed *If My Wishes Came True*, please consider leaving a review on Goodreads or your preferred bookseller's site. Not only does your thoughtful feedback make my day, it helps put my books in more readers' hands.

Want more Jenna and Charlie?

If you're anything like me, you're not ready to part ways with this pair of soulmates. Scan the QR Code below for a Bonus Epilogue, and find out what happens when the newly-engaged couple take a whirlwind trip back to Italy.

ACKNOWLEDGMENTS

Jenna and Charlie's romance would not exist if it weren't for my parents' inspiring love story. They grew up worlds apart and met while my dad was traveling for work. My mom won't shy away from telling you it was love at first sight. She says that, after their first date, her heart skipped a beat, and she knew right away she would marry my father. She even called her own mother and told her as much.

Believe it or not, my mom was right. My parents lived on different continents and scarcely saw each other, but that didn't stop them from getting engaged within two months, and married within three. Now you know why I believe that some love stories are written in the stars. Could a meet-cute like this be pure luck or coincidence? Sure. But I prefer to think it's fate.

It certainly felt that way when I went out with friends one Halloween weekend, looking forward to a girls' night after a string of bad dates made me swear off guys entirely, and the most handsome man I'd ever seen asked if he could take me to dinner. I forgot all about my vow and said yes. Several weeks later, I was lunching at the Walnut Room at Macy's in Chicago, which is known for a special holiday tradition. While you're dining, fairy princesses visit your table, ask you to make a wish, then sprinkle you with fairy dust. I didn't have to think twice about what I wanted that year—to marry the man I'd only just met. And while I'll admit, the fairy dust *did* look a lot like store-bought glitter, my wish still came true.

Maybe magic exists when we choose to believe in it. When we take a moment to bask in the warmth of sunrays on our skin, or savor an iced latte from our favorite coffee shop. When our summer anthem starts playing on the car radio the minute we hit the road. Or when we meet someone we click with right away. I'm grateful to say I know this feeling well, and not only in the context of romantic love. To my book coach and editor, Emily Colin; to my beta readers, Parissa Andideh, Emily Giger, Sarah Imberman, and Abigail Stapler; to my event coordinators (and cheer squad), Jenn Bush, Gaby Choi, Puja Kapadia, and Jane Kenyon—I am beyond happy our paths crossed. Thank you for your unwavering enthusiasm and support, and for being the most amazing friends.

To my readers, I'm infinitely thankful for you, too. You're helping me make my dreams come true. My goal is to return the favor by writing stories that feel real, relatable and, ultimately, uplifting. I hope the magic of Jenna's story inspires you.

Finally, to my kiddos, whom I adore with my entire heart and soul—may all your wishes come true.

ABOUT THE AUTHOR

Nathalie Theodore is the IPPY award-winning, Amazon bestselling author of *If the Stars Align*, *If My Wishes Came True*, and *If We Play Fair*, the first three novels in her Dramatic Hearts Club series. A lawyer-turned-therapist and novelist, she writes love stories that dive deep into the psychology of her characters, using her background in mental health to create beautifully flawed, true-to-life protagonists. In addition to writing, she enjoys spending time with her family in their hometown of Chicago. More often than not, you'll find her at a coffee shop, a bookstore, or a baseball game.

CONNECT ONLINE

NathalieTheodore.com
Facebook @DramaticHeartsClub
Instagram @NathalieTheodoreWrites
Substack @NathalieTheodoreWrites

ALSO BY
NATHALIE THEODORE

THE DRAMATIC HEARTS CLUB SERIES

If the Stars Align
A standalone friends-to-lovers romance that spans a decade

(Sunny & Dex)

If My Wishes Came True
A standalone love-at-first-sight romance with a plot twist

(Jenna & Charlie)

If We Play Fair
A standalone enemies-to-lovers fake-dating baseball romance

(Christy & Holden)

SCAN THE QR CODE TO READ MORE